CHECKMATE

Susan —
Thank you for biting the bullet.

Marc Applewhite
July 23, 2015

CHECKMATE

As always, this is for Heather

Mavis Applewater

ALSO WRITTEN BY Mavis Applewater AND
AVAILABLE FROM Wednesday Afternoon Press:

Everlasting
Tempus Fugit
That Thursday Afternoon
Home For The Holidays
Whispering Pines
Checkmate
The Price I Paid

www.wedapress.com

CHECKMATE

Wednesday Afternoon Press

Mavis Applewater

Mavis Applewater

CHECKMATE

NOTE: If you purchased this book without a cover, you should be aware that it is stolen property. It was reported as "unsold and destroyed" to the publisher, and neither the author nor the publisher has received any payment for this "stripped book."

This is a work of fiction. All characters, locales and events are either products of the author's imagination or are used fictitiously.

Checkmate

Copyright © 2014 by Mavis Applewater

All rights reserved. No part of this book may be reproduced in any manner whatsoever without written permission from the publisher, save for brief quotations used in critical articles or reviews.

Orginal Cover design by Ann Phillips

Cover design by Lindsey Palmer

A Blue Feather Book
Published by Wednesday Afternoon Press
Boston, MA. 02148

www.wedapress.com

ISBN: -13: 978-1505489798
ISBN: - 10: 1505489792

First Edition, July 2014
Second Edition December 2014

Mavis Applewater

Printed in the United States of America and in the United Kingdom

ACKNOWLEDGMENTS

When creating a work such as this, none of it happens because of only one person. Having said that I would like to thank the following people: my publisher Emily Reed, who stuck it out after my real life kept getting in the way. I need to thank Mary Phillips my beta reader for calling me on the carpet more than once. Thank you to the best editor Nann Dunne; how that woman keeps her sanity is an amazing mystery. She didn't even threaten to set me on fire this time. I need to thank my mother-in-law, Lillian, who loved The Brass Ring so much she thought a sequel was in order. I also need to thank my brother-in-law Shane whose knowledge of prison life was invaluable. Before you ask, no he wasn't an inmate. Thank you to my dear friend Val Brown who gave money to a very worthy cause to become a character in Checkmate. Speaking of names, for a very long time this book was simply known as Brass Ring Two; thank you so much Sandy Thornton for giving it a proper name. Thank you to the women who led the way in my so-called life, Nana, Grammy, Ann Marie and Sunny. I need to thank my Mom for everything she continues to do. Most of all, I need to thank my wonderful wife Heather who, for some unknown reason, puts up with this crazy writer.

PROLOGUE

It made perfect sense once all the pieces were snapped into place. Not that it mattered now. CC understood all too clearly that in the very near future she would be dead. If not dead, teetering very close to the edge of death. Hell of a time to find out she'd been right all along. She found it hard to be smug. Self-satisfaction failed to mesh with the act of digging her own grave.

She trembled ever so slightly each time the shovel crunched against the earth. She paused for a moment to brush the sweat from her brow.

"Keep digging." Her companion stressed the point by aiming the 9mm at CC's body.

"Maybe I'm not in a hurry." CC couldn't resist taunting her captor.

Her impertinence was answered by a loud click of the gun's hammer being cocked. The click echoed through the dark woods. "Haste does make waste," CC quipped in a valiant effort to mask the fear coursing through her body.

Boldly she gripped the handle of the shovel before thrusting it into the dirt. "Although," she slowly began toying with the dirt. "I must say shooting me down like a dog and ditching my body in the woods lacks a certain finesse. I kind of expected more out of you."

"You have only yourself to blame, Detective," was the answer, followed by a cruel chuckle. "If you hadn't been such a know-it-all pain in the ass, your ending would have been far more creative. In fact, you would have enjoyed a little more time on this earth. But you just had to figure everything out and shoot your big mouth off. Personally, I prefer a more inventive approach to these matters. But in times of need, a good old-fashioned shoot 'em and ditch 'em always works. If it makes you feel better, I promise to be more creative when I take care of your little friend."

"Don't!" CC jerked the shovel up.

"Don't what?" The barrel of the gun gleamed in the moonlight.

The taunting laughter did nothing to abate the anger that was choking CC. Being mocked only spurred on her ire.

"Need I remind you, Detective?" The taunting voice cut through CC's soul. "At this very moment, you are in the middle of fucking nowhere. You're digging a ditch that in all likelihood will become your final resting place. You are in no position to be making idle threats. Face facts. You're a bit late to make good on any of your promises."

The harsh reality of the words was like a sharp blow. CC's shoulders slumped. She was defeated. *'Not the way I thought I'd go out.'* She lowered the shovel and stared at the tiny mound of dirt. It wasn't her own demise that troubled her. No, what truly broke her heart was that she had failed Jamie. Now the love of her life was left vulnerable to a psycho. She would have broken down and cried if not for the knowledge that she would give the twisted freak some sort of sick thrill.

Her lips curled into a defiant sneer. "I have never met

anyone so perfectly suited for their profession."

"Thank you."

"It wasn't a compliment."

"I know."

CC wasn't certain, but she could have sworn she heard a hint of sympathy. She wondered if perhaps all was not lost. She decided to give it one last shot.

"I guess I just don't understand how someone so intelligent becomes a murderer." CC struggled to make her words sound sincere.

"Killer," came the stern response. "Or assassin if you prefer. Why should my intelligence surprise you? After all, Simon Fisher was a smart boy."

"Not smart enough." After all these years, just the mention of his name set CC on edge. "Lucky is more like it. That slimy little creep should have been locked up long before I ever heard his name." Her little tirade was greeted by a wry chuckle. CC was encouraged by the response. "Unlike you, that shit-for-brains made a long list of mistakes."

"Now, now, Detective. Give yourself some credit. You alone got him. Hell, you got him to confess. You were the one who locked him away, making the world safe and sound for dykey little blondes."

"Until you came along," CC said.

"Circumstances beyond your control. If he wasn't a stinking rich little bugger none of this would have happened, and we'd never be having this conversation. Sadly for you and yours, I'm a consummate professional. Which is why it truly is a pity Fisher is just as rich as he is crazy. I mean since my services come at such a high price tag."

"Worth every penny, I'm sure." CC prayed that she sounded sincere. She felt she had the opening she so desperately needed. Then maybe, just maybe, Deputy Dumb Ass might pull her head out of her butt. If that happened, there might just be a happy ending after all. CC took a calming breath before playing her last card. "You know if it wasn't for that one mistake."

"What mistake?"

That slight hint of panic in her captor's voice gave her a glimmer of hope. The sight of the gun wavering made her heart beat just a little faster. She didn't allow herself to feel happy, not just yet. At that moment, she just prayed her ploy would work.

She heard a snicker. "Oh, I get it. A stalling tactic? Kind of lame coming from you." The cruel laughter that followed shredded her hopes. Dread didn't even come close to what she was feeling.

Then the laughter stopped. "You know what, Detective?" the voice said in a cooing tone. "You deserve to have your say. After all, no one, and I mean no one, has ever gotten this close to me. Put your little shovel down for a moment, and tell me how you solved the great mystery. Must be a hollow victory knowing that the final proof that you were right will be proven by your death. Still, as I said, you've outdone all the others. Tell me all about me. Just remember to keep your feet and grubby little hands inside that ditch or I will shoot you right between your baby blues."

"Fair enough." CC dropped the shovel to the ground. Her aching hands were the only part of her that felt any sense of relief.

"I really do want to know how you figured it out. Tell me, what was my mistake?"

"You don't know?" CC said. "Well, okay then. Your plan on the surface was brilliant. I'll give you that. You know how I got involved. The funeral and then the beach, but what sealed it for me were the bees and the keys."

CHECKMATE

CHAPTER ONE

Things had been set in motion long before CC found herself being held at gunpoint. On a chilly night in September, her wife had just come in from work. Jamie, a doctor, worked the late shift in the emergency room at Boylston General hospital. CC also worked the late shift, but as a homicide detective with the Boylston Village Hills Police Department.

Despite their demanding jobs, they led a quiet life. Most of the time. Sometimes life was anything but quiet. CC had no idea just how unsettled their lives were about to become. She returned from work, finished packing her travel bag, and set it by the front door.

"I hate that you have to go and do this," Jamie said when CC found her pacing around their bedroom.

"James," CC softly murmured the pet name she had given her wife almost two decades ago. "I know you hate this part of our lives. I'll be on the first flight back." She wrapped Jamie in a warm embrace.

Jamie pressed her body tightly against CC's. "I wish we could stay like this forever," she said with a heavy sigh. "How much time do we have before Stevie comes to take you to the airport?"

"Half hour." CC shrugged. "I'm meeting her over at her place. Whatcha' got in mind, Doc?" she added, trying to turn the mood into a playful moment. She wanted to leave Jamie with a sense of security. She shivered from the feel of Jamie's hands running up along her sides. "Emma," she said to Jamie who was tugging CC's shirt out of her jeans.

"She's sound asleep at Stevie's. I'm going over to their side of the house while Stevie is shuttling you to Logan."

Buying the old Victorian house and converting it into two separate homes had worked out well for the unusual family. Stevie, CC's younger sister, had built-in babysitters for her daughter, Emma, while CC and Jamie had privacy. Most importantly, the close-knit family could stay close without tripping over one another.

CC released a soft moan. Jamie had a way of completely distracting her. *After all these years, she still drives me insane*, she couldn't help thinking when she felt the feathery touch of Jamie's lips caress her shoulders. She was baffled as to how quickly her blouse and bra ended up on the floor.

"How did my clothes end up down there?"

"Shh." Jamie flicked her tongue against CC's nipple. "You're leaving town, and I need to make certain that you don't forget me."

"With any luck, I'll be gone less then twenty-four hours."

"An eternity." Jamie captured CC's nipple between her lips.

CC caught the look in Jamie's eyes. It was a mix of desire and impatience. She knew it would be foolish to argue. She laced her fingers through Jamie's hair and pressed her closer. CC struggled to stand, giving into the feel of Jamie capturing her erect nipple between her lips. Jamie suckled her harder.

It was so easy for CC to give in to Jamie's desires. From the first time to that moment, the passion between them only grew stronger.

CC whimpered in protest when Jamie's attention was drawn away from her breast. She was about to voice her objection when she felt Jamie's mouth delightfully move down her body. She released a throaty groan. Jamie blazed a trail down CC's taut body. In the back of her mind, she realized they didn't have that much time. When she felt the button on her jeans being released, she couldn't care less if she missed her flight.

CC balanced herself, while Jamie tugged her jeans down her thighs. She murmured softly when Jamie placed feathery kisses across her abdomen.

"Baby," she pleaded.

She parted her legs, allowing Jamie to lower her panties. She shivered when Jamie's warm breath caressed her bare thighs. Jamie parted her with her tongue. CC reached down and pressed Jamie closer. CC trembled from the feel of Jamie eagerly licking her wetness. She cried out when Jamie suckled her clit between her lips. CC tried to speak and beg for more. She just couldn't form the words. Instead she gave into the delightful feel of her wife suckling her engorged clit.

Jamie held her captive, wasting no time before plunging two fingers deep inside CC's warm wet center. She took her harder. CC fought to stay standing as her body quivered. Her knees began to buckle. Jamie feasted upon her harder. CC struggled to hold on. She cried out and gave in to the passion as she collapsed onto the bedroom floor. Her body shook while Jamie held her in a tender embrace.

CC began to caress Jamie's body, only to have her hands stilled. "We don't have time," Jamie said. "You need to wash up again."

"And whose fault is that, spoilsport?" CC managed to choke out the words from her raw throat. She struggled to her feet. "I left my bag over by the door, so you could repack it."

"I'm not going to repack your . . . " Jamie's objection faded. "Okay, I am. You know me all too well. You just don't know how to pack. I'll meet you at Stevie's." She gave CC a quick kiss.

"I love you," CC said with smile.

She took a quick shower and chose a new outfit that would be comfortable for the cross-country trek. She made her way downstairs, resetting the alarms along the way. She paused in the kitchen and noticed the chess set that was set up in the corner by the breakfast nook. For a moment, she studied the Disney characters that the chess set was composed of. She and her seven-year-old-niece, Emma, had an ongoing game.

She smiled at the move Emma had made. "Very clever."

They had bought the chess set at the Disney store, and Emma proved to be a quick study. Secretly, CC wanted the heroes characters, but since Emma chose them, she didn't want to appear childish in front of the second grader.

CC thought for a moment before moving Jafar, one of her bishops. She captured a Dalmatian, which was one of Emma's pawns. Then she made her way over to the other side of the house to meet up with her sister.

Deep in her heart she wanted to stay. She wasn't looking forward to this trip.

* * *

The flight to the opposite coast was not only uneventful, it bordered on tedious. The only high point was replaying the memory of Jamie kneeling before her. CC did love the way her wife gave her a proper send off, she just hated the reason for her departure. On paper, taking a trip to California every few years sounded like a dream come true. These trips were by no means a vacation. She flew to the opposite side of the country whenever Dr. Simon Fisher was being evaluated. The good doctor was incarcerated in a maximum-security, federal mental hospital for the criminally insane. Detective Caitlin Calloway was the reason why.

A few years back, little Simon was well on his way to becoming a full-fledged doctor when a little matter of his being a serial killer got in the way. His quarry was small, blonde, athletic types who reminded him of his high school sweetheart. He fell hard for these women, most of whom failed to notice him and, as luck would have it, turned out to be lesbians. It helped CC's efforts to put him away for what she hoped was forever when she managed to get Simon to confess to where he hid his high school sweetheart's body.

Dr. Amelia Richards, an FBI shrink who helped put him away, described Simon as a serial killer with only one victim. He was killing the love of his life over and over again. His girlfriend, Janie, had gone off to college and fallen in love with another woman. Unable to deal with the rejection, Simon killed her.

Fisher went on with his life, leaving a trail of bodies along the way. He only made one mistake. His mistake was choosing to complete his medical training in Boylston Village Hills, Massachusetts, a small town that was part of the city of Boston. There he crossed paths with Dr. Jamie Jameson who was a petite blonde with an athletic build and the love of Detective Caitlin Calloway's life. When Simon tried to kill her girlfriend, CC took it very personally. In the decade that followed, Jamie and CC married and Simon spent twenty-three hours a day wandering around a glass-enclosed cell. He would have had a little more freedom if he hadn't tried to escape on a number of occasions.

It pleased CC that Simon's arrogance hadn't waned. It kept

him locked up tighter than ever. She and Jamie feared the day some idiot would declare that Simon was no longer crazy and set him free. Granted, if that unlikely event ever happened, she had a backup plan. For now, she had to go before the board and explain that Simon Fisher was a whack job. He was always nuts, and no matter how many drugs or hours of therapy he endured, he would remain a psycho who should never be allowed to walk the streets. Alas, there were laws that needed to be complied with.

CC and a list of others who had helped lock up Simon would say their bit. The prison shrinks would say their bit, and of course, Simon's lawyer, who was usually new to his case, would say his bit.

Two things worked in CC's favor. Simon would never admit to killing anyone. He claimed that CC had framed him in an effort to steal his girlfriend. The doctors and lawyers would point out that Jamie was never his girlfriend. Dr. Jamie Jameson was now CC's wife. All nice and legal, thanks to the laws in Massachusetts. Simon's stoic demeanor would quickly unravel, and he'd start ranting like a complete lunatic. His lawyers would claim CC baited him. The panel would only hear Simon's insane ranting. Detective Brooks and CC would feel vindicated then grab dinner. She could set her watch by it.

CC went through the process of entering the secure facility for the mandatory hearing. Once inside, she took a moment to collect her thoughts. Seeing Fisher was never easy. The only good thing about looking into his beady little eyes every few years was the knowledge that he was locked up.

"Detective," an uneasy voice said from behind her.

A long time ago, Caitlin had learned there wasn't a polite way to greet someone who had lost their child to senseless violence.

Richard Jensen blamed her for not sending Simon to prison instead of getting the little psycho locked up in a federal loony bin. He wanted Simon to pay for his daughter's life with his own.

"I can't believe we have to go through this again." His words were quiet, yet CC could feel the pain behind them. She had to agree. She wanted Simon locked up somewhere dark and for someone to lose the key.

"I know." It was the only thing she could think of saying.

"My wife passed on coming this time. It takes too much out of her. Seeing that smug little bastard sitting there acting as if he's the victim."

"My wife feels the same." CC struggled with the words. "She stayed in Boston."

"Look, Detective Calloway. I know I've said things in the past. I understand you did the best you could to get him off the streets. I was angry. Hell, I'm still angry."

"Mr. Jensen, you have a right to be angry. At me for not getting enough evidence to lock him up. At him for doing this. At the cops here and in all those other cities for not stopping him sooner. Please trust me that if for some bizarre reason he gets out of here, he won't get away."

"Why didn't we see it? Why did I trust him with my daughter? Why didn't she trust us enough to tell us that Simon wasn't the nice boy we thought he was? Why didn't she tell us she was gay? We would have kept loving her."

"Tough stuff to deal with when you're so young." CC tried to comfort him.

"How did your parents deal with it?"

"They threw me out of the house. It was complicated."

"Shame on them," he said. "At least they know that you're alive. Shame on them." He turned away and entered the room where Simon's review was to be held.

CC wasn't surprised that he chose to sit alone in the back corner. Richard Jensen would more than likely spend the rest of his life searching for answers.

She tried to make herself comfortable in the hard plastic chairs that had been provided. Brooks took a seat next to her. He was a big man, his graying hair thinning despite his attempts to cover it up. She did notice he was looking much fitter than he had in the past.

"Always thought it was a shame they didn't send the little shit to Pelican Bay." Brooks snorted with disdain.

"You're looking well," CC said.

"Quit drinking and smoking." He smirked. "I even took up jogging."

"All of your bad habits at once." She was impressed. Brooks lived to chain-smoke. "Couldn't have been easy."

"Easier than I thought. After you caught the little snot bag, my life got a whole lot easier. Even seeing my kids on a regular basis."

"Good for you."

"Life's been so good, I've turned in my papers."

"No," CC whispered so she wouldn't disturb the proceedings. "Must be going around. My partner's doing the same."

"Max? You've been together a long time."

"I rode with him when I was a rookie and for a while after that, until he got his gold shield. Then when I got mine, he asked to partner with me. He's been by my side forever. I think our last case got to him."

"How's life treating you? Enjoying married life?"

"Can't complain." CC fought against the blush that crept up along her neck.

"I see Jamie passed on attending again," he said softly.

"It's too hard on her. The whole thing brings back too much pain. Besides, we have a new house that needs everything fixed. Apparently, despite my butch exterior, I suck with power tools."

"Another myth destroyed. There's Malcolm." He nodded towards Simon's father.

"I can't imagine how hard this is on him," CC noted.

"At least he isn't in denial like the old lady." Brooks jerked his thumb to the opposite side of the room where Simon's mother was seated.

CC groaned. "She's never going to see the light. Didn't you know we framed her baby boy? All those women who look exactly like his high school sweetheart turning up dead is just a coincidence. We must have planted Janie's body under the boathouse. No other explanation. Do we really need to be here?"

"They need you here." Brooks' tone was stern. "One look at you and Simon gets antsy. Then when you explain that you and Dr. Jameson are happily married, he'll show the board just how loony toons he truly is. God help us if he ever gets out. Still have that backup plan?"

"Florida and Texas. Three bodies not listed in the original plea agreement. They happen to fall in two states that will fry him before he gets a chance to lie his way out of it. Texas won the coin toss on who gets first crack at him. If he ever steps outside of this place, there will be a Ranger waiting on the steps."

CC hadn't hesitated to offer the information to the out-of-state authorities. Simon Fisher was off the streets. The burning question was for how long? The day he entered the mental facility, she ran his DNA profile. When she got three hits on cold cases, she called the locals and let them know.

She did feel bitter that she had been forced to settle. The Jensen family wasn't the only family of victims that were less than pleased that she had only managed to get Simon locked up in a hospital instead of prison. They all wanted vengeance.

"There's Janie's father," Brooks whispered.

"I saw him earlier," CC answered, mindful to keep her voice low. "Don't know how he holds it together. I know I shouldn't have, but I promised him there was no way Simon was going to walk. It's a promise I plan on keeping."

"I always liked your style, Calloway. Now blow Fisher a kiss and set him off so we can get dinner."

"Not that much longer," CC said with a snicker. "I'm next."

While waiting to be called, CC couldn't help noticing that Simon's father seemed relieved, while Simon's mother appeared to be annoyed. She smirked when she noticed that Simon was doing everything in his power not to look at her. His new lawyer was a tall blonde who didn't ask many questions but did keep up a soft murmuring to herself that CC couldn't help but notice.

When CC's turn came, the federal prosecutor had her recount the events that led up to Simon's arrest and confession. There really wasn't much to ask. Most of CC's testimony hinged on Simon's confession. How he talked as if Janie was still alive and then revealed where he had hidden her body. On the advice of his extremely stunned and angry counsel, Simon took a deal.

"I don't have any questions for Detective Calloway," the new lawyer said. "As I have previously stated, persons who knew Dr. Fisher in the outside world have no bearing on this hearing. We are here to determine whether or not his treatment has been successful. Detective Calloway's presence at these proceedings only serves one purpose and that is to agitate my client."

"Point taken, again," one of the board members said with a hint of boredom. He addressed the prosecutor "Mr. Burkhart?"

"I have only one last thing to ask Detective Calloway."

"Go on."

"Detective, are you married?"

"Yes." CC said.

"Objection."

CC squirmed uncomfortably in the witness chair. Each time she announced that she was involved with Jamie and later married her, the little snot went ballistic. Most of the attendees found it entertaining. There was the notable exception of Simon and the poor bastard who was representing him. All in all, it usually wrapped things up fairly quickly.

"Despite what Ms. Cockburn thinks, this question is pertinent," Burkhart said. "Dr. Fisher's stability is the central question. In the past, his response to Detective Calloway's personal life has given us a clearer view of Dr. Fisher's state of mind."

CHECKMATE

While the lawyers and the panel jockeyed back and forth, CC sat there not really paying attention. All she could think of was what an unfortunate last name Simon's lawyer had been stuck with. She was also pondering if she was working pro bono since this was the first time she had spoken during the hearing. While the other witnesses testified, she sat next to Simon scribbling on a notepad and humming *Hey, Diddle, Diddle*. CC wondered whether Malcolm finally locked Simon out of his trust fund, or had Ms. Cockburn simply drawn the short straw at the firm?

"I think Mr. Burkhart has a valid point," one of the members of the board said. CC recognized him from previous hearings. The guy always seemed to enjoy watching Simon go off the deep end. "Detective Calloway, you may answer the question."

"Yes."

"And who are you married to?"

"Dr. Jamie Jameson."

"Lying bitch!" Simon jumped from his chair and almost knocked the table and his attorney over.

Order was called for, but it was useless. Simon ranted on about how CC was a lying dyke who framed him in a futile effort to steal his girlfriend. It further bolstered the prosecutor's case when Simon kept confusing Jamie's name with Janie's. Poor Janie Jensen, whose only mistake had been being Simon's first girlfriend and subsequently his first victim. The hearing wrapped up fairly quickly after Simon had to be restrained and medicated.

"Well, he's off for a healthy dose of Haldol and a four-point restraint."

CC shrugged when she rejoined Brooks. "Lawyer doesn't look

too upset."

"Probably the best he could afford. I heard Malcolm cut off Simon's trust fund."

"Oh." CC nodded thoughtfully. "I thought she pissed off her boss and this was her punishment. Know a good seafood place?"

"I'm in the mood for steak."

After a relaxing dinner, CC kept her word and was on the first available flight back to Boston. She didn't get home until well after three in the morning. Still, leaving the drama behind her and crawling into bed with the love of her life was well worth the lack of sleep.

* * *

While CC was on the West Coast ruining Simon Fisher's day, her wife Jamie was back home. She stood in the yard pretending to rake. Normally, she enjoyed her time outside, pruning and planting. It reminded her of the times she spent with her mother and grandmother back in Maryland.

When CC, Jamie, and Stevie purchased the house, they had discussed hiring a landscaper. Thankfully Stevie shared Jamie's interest in getting out into the fresh air and trying to do a little manual labor. For Jamie it was perfect, spending time with her sister-in-law or alone, outside enjoying the day. Since she worked the late shift at the hospital, she had all day long to go out and get dirty.

That day, Jamie was far too occupied with what was happening on the other side of the country. They had good lives, except for the constant reminder of what happened when Simon entered the scene. The only good to come out of the whole fiasco was that she and CC were reunited. But she felt that would have happened without all the psycho drama and bloodshed.

"Hey there." Stevie's voice disrupted her troubling thoughts. The lanky brunette pointed to the patch of ground that Jamie had raked so hard she had begun to turn the soil. "I think you got that spot."

"Crap."

"It will be okay."

"I know." Jamie tried to sound confident. She just couldn't shake the feeling that one day it was all going to unravel. "Come join me? I know playing on your computer pays the bills, but it's too nice to be stuck inside."

"Maybe later." Stevie hesitated. "Can you do me a favor? I have a client meeting in the morning. Can you drop Emma off at school?"

"No problem," Jamie absently agreed, her mind still three thousand miles away. "Another client meeting? Been doing a lot more of those."

"No choice." Stevie grimaced. "The economy isn't very cooperative these days. If I lose another client, I don't know if I'll be able to keep up."

"Don't worry. We're ahead on the mortgage, thanks to your Uncle Mac. That was quite some envelope he slipped us after we got married."

"Uncle Mac is good that way." Stevie beamed. "Enough about money. You're right, it is far too nice to be hiding indoors."

Stevie dashed inside leaving Jamie alone with her thoughts. Jamie finally smiled when Stevie raced outside and grabbed a bag of mulch. "I was thinking we need a splash of color along the walkway,"

Stevie said.

"Look, it's Misty," Stevie whispered while tugging on her gardening gloves. She nodded toward the mail carrier who was making her way towards their house. "Morning!" she excitedly greeted the woman.

Jamie rolled her eyes wondering what Stevie liked best about their new home, the size, the yard, or the sexy mail lady? Jamie offered her good morning before stepping away. She preferred not to watch Stevie act all goofy around Misty. Jamie couldn't understand it. Normally, her sister-in-law was confident and easygoing with everyone she met. Around Misty for some reason, Stevie got positively silly.

"Why don't you just ask her out?" Jamie said after Misty had made her way to the next house.

"And if she says no? We'd never get our mail."

"Good point."

"What is this?"

"A card." Jamie noted the obvious as she began to clean up and put away her gardening tools. It was getting late. She needed to start getting ready for work. She grunted when Stevie thrust the card at her. Jamie's eyes widened when she looked at it. "Who sent it?"

"No return address." Stevie scrunched up her face. "No signature."

"A Father's Day card," Jamie said. "Definitely the wrong house."

CHAPTER 2

The following morning began a tad too early for CC's tastes. The sounds of giggling disrupted her sleep, and she tried to hide under her pillow. The hysterical giggling continued. "Argh!" She reached for her lover. She needed Jamie to make the annoying giggling stop before CC was forced to shoot something.

"Coffee?" She slapped the empty mattress. Still nowhere near a conscious state, she kept slapping the spot where Jamie should be sleeping. After several moments of grasping at empty air, it finally occurred to her that Jamie was not nestled beside her. When CC had arrived home a few short hours ago, Jamie was fast asleep. She had snuggled up against her wife and listened to the sweet murmuring sounds she made as she slept. Now in the stark light of day she wearily lifted her head.

"No Jamie." She smacked her lips. Her eyes finally blinked open.

"Aunty Caitlin?" her niece, Emma, screeched from downstairs.

A loud "Sssh," quickly followed Emma's piercing shrill. "Yeah, that'll work." Defeated, CC climbed out of bed, scowled, and descended the staircase.

"Coffee," she said, unaware of the angry glare Jamie was sporting.

"Auntie Caitlin!" Emma squealed and jumped off of her chair. The impish seven-year-old darted across the kitchen and attached herself to CC's leg before Jamie could intervene.

"Peanut?" CC tried to sound joyous.

"Don't," Jamie said before CC could reach down and scoop Emma up in her arms. "You're not awake yet."

Somewhere in the back of her mind, CC recalled being half-asleep and injuring her back while picking up Emma. The injury hadn't been serious, damaging her pride more than her back.

"Coffee?" she repeated hopefully. In her foggy mind, it seemed like a reasonable request.

"Counter," Jamie said and sighed.

CC moved directly towards the coffeemaker perched on the counter. She was unaware that Emma remained attached to her leg. The youngster failed to loosen her grasp as CC poured her coffee. She paused for a moment to inhale the delectable aroma, took her first sip, and felt the world righting itself. A second sip encouraged her to look down at the child clinging to her.

"Peanut?" She was suddenly curious as to why a small child was latched onto her. "Why?" She directed the question towards her wife.

"I love these morning chats," Jamie said wryly. CC simply sipped her coffee. "Stevie had a meeting with a client."

"Feed me," Emma sweetly pleaded.

"Want some coffee?"

"Yes!"

"No," Jamie said sternly. Somewhere in the midst of her fog, CC knew Jamie was right and that for some reason it was bad to offer a seven-year-old a cup of coffee.

"Cereal?" CC slowly lifted Emma up and placed her back in her chair.

"Yes!" Emma once again said gleefully.

"No," Jamie said.

"What?" CC frowned. "We have boxes of the crap."

"And according to your sister, that's just what it is."

"Cocoa Krispies, please?" Emma was not above begging. "Fruit Loops?"

"Uh, no." CC was forced to decline. "There's way too much sugar in those."

"Which is why Stevie doesn't want Emma eating cereal here," Jamie explained.

"Can't blame her for that." CC had to agree. Nothing but high-octane sugar-laden junk lurked in the cupboard.

"Hey." Jamie defended her actions. "I buy the kind that I like, since you don't eat the stuff. Besides, they're full of vitamins and calcium. It says so right on the box." She held up a box of one of her favorite breakfast treats.

"And apparently they're also magically delicious." CC groaned. "Where is it you went to med school?"

"Cook for your niece. I need to take my shower."

"I can handle it." CC watched Jamie stomp off. "So, fruit?"

"I don't like fruit."

"Eggs?"

"I don't like eggs."

"Oatmeal?"

"I don't like oatmeal."

"You liked it last week."

Emma sat there with her little arms folded across her chest. "Man, you are so much like your mother. Fine, how about French toast?" She was quickly running out of options.

"Yes, please."

"Cool." CC blew out a breath in relief.

"With caramelized bananas and a dusting of confectionary sugar," Emma said with authority.

"Someone's been watching the Food Network with Auntie Jamie." CC began to prepare a simple version of French toast.

"You're getting basic toast dipped in egg batter, Wolfgang."

"Boring." Emma sighed dramatically. "And I like Cat Cora."

"Something else you got from Aunt Jamie."

"Can't wait until she's a teenager," Jamie said and chuckled upon entering the kitchen. "Want me to take over?"

"No thanks, James." CC smiled. "The coffee's kicking in. Sorry I wasn't swift on the uptake."

"Auntie Caitlin won't caramelize bananas for us," Emma said and scowled.

"Ogre." Jamie snickered.

"She shouldn't be able to pronounce half those things much less request them for breakfast." CC placed a simple breakfast in front of the little critic.

"I'm not the o ne who lets her watch Court TV," Jamie said.

"It's not called that anymore. And I only let her watch because I was on it. She wanted to know what I did."

"Yes, letting a seven-year-old know what you do at your job is brilliant."

CC looked over at her wife and tried to figure out just what she had done to tick her off? The tension was rolling off Jamie's body. Then it hit her. Jamie wasn't mad at her. She was upset by where CC had been. The trip was an ugly reminder that, someday, Simon could be free.

"It went okay."

"So you said when you called." Jamie's response was gruff. "Sorry." She shook her head. "It's not you, it's—"

"I know."

CC set down her coffee mug and wrapped her arms around the woman she loved. She rested her head against Jamie's. She released a terse sigh when she felt Jamie's tension easing. CC had learned a long time ago sometimes the best thing to do was say nothing. She held her wife, enjoying the feel of her body pressed against her own. If they had been alone, things might have progressed further. Yet, with Emma sitting at the kitchen table, just holding Jamie was more than enough.

"Need me to stay home?" she asked when Jamie stepped out of her embrace. She was filled with a sense of relief when Jamie smiled up at her.

"No, I got my new kids starting today, but thank you."

"Ah, new doctors." CC nodded. "Well, scaring the bejesus out of the residents always puts a spring in your step." CC was joking, but she understood the added tension this day caused. Simon had been one of Jamie's students. At first she handled him the same way she handled all of her residents during their rotation. When it became clear that Simon had what everyone assumed was a crush on her, she made it clear that she wasn't interested. That's when the stalking began, and bodies started showing up. The hardest part of everything that had happened all those years ago was the tragic events had reunited Jamie and CC and would always be remembered.

"Maybe you should stay home."

"You need me to?"

"No," Jamie answered with a soft smile. "You just look beat."

"Nah. I'm okay. It's not like I'm going to do anything at work. I swear ever since Max decided to put in his paperwork, my work is limited to counting paper clips and watching him read about boats."

"Boats?"

"Yeah, he's decided that since he's moving to Florida, he needs a boat. Started out as a small motorboat, and now he's looking at yachts."

"I know you're bored," Jamie carefully began to say. "But I'm not about to complain that you're out of harm's way for the next few months."

"Peace and quiet. You'd think I'd enjoy it." CC kissed Jamie on her cheek and turned. She was horrified when she spied her precious niece. "What is she wearing?" She wasn't at all pleased to hear her wife snickering behind her.

"It's my new baseball cap," Emma boasted while sucking down her breakfast.

"It's an Orioles hat."

"Auntie Jamie gave it to me. Do you like it?"

"Uh, sure." CC was unable to believe what she was seeing. "James? It's an Orioles hat."

"I know."

"But this is Boston."

"And the Orioles are my hometown team."

"I know. But, seriously, the other kids will pick on her."

"Oh, please. They don't even pick on little Jorge, who wears a Yankees hat."

"That's just wrong."

"Caitlin. Emma, likes her hat. I know you're a die-hard Red Sox fan. If your season tickets hadn't clued me in, your collection of fifty some odd T-shirts would have tipped me off. I on the other hand was raised in Maryland."

"We aren't even married in Maryland."

"Not yet. Emma, do you like your new hat?"

"Yes! It has orange and black."

"Fine." CC reluctantly caved in. "Change is good, I guess."

Jamie rolled her eyes.

"What? I'm agreeing." CC stole another cup of coffee. She knew Jamie didn't believe her. CC was already formulating a plan to get rid of the hat.

"Oh, before I forget, this came yesterday." Jamie handed her a Ziploc bag with a greeting card sealed inside. "Probably nothing, but I thought you'd like to see it."

"Happy Father's Day." CC stared at it feeling completely confused. "Trying to tell me something?"

"It came for Stevie yesterday. No return address and no signature," Jamie said. "Just the card."

"I'll have one of the lab guys take a look." CC was still trying to understand the meaning behind the card. "Just in case any of our new neighbors aren't as friendly as they pretend to be."

"That's what I'm afraid of."

"Emma, I took one of your Dalmatians," CC said. She knew she shouldn't boast. She was trying to teach Emma the importance of the game and how to be a gracious winner or loser. Plus she understood that learning the basic strategy of a chess match could be very beneficial for her niece's learning skills. The days of allowing Emma to win had passed not long after she grasped the concept of chess. CC hoped that by understanding the game, Emma would be more prepared in life.

"I know." Emma cleared her plate from the table. "Check."

"Huh?"

"Check."

Her almost bored tone irked CC just a little.

"I'm ready." The imp shouldered her backpack.

CC flinched with pain when she stubbed her toe while trying to race over to the chessboard. She stared at the board, dumbfounded by what she was looking at. "Good move," she finally managed to say. "Poison Pawn. I walked right into it."

"You let her?" Jamie asked.

"No, don't need to anymore. The kid is almost outplaying me."

"She's seven. How old was Stevie when she started to outplay you?"

"She isn't outplaying me." CC struggled to keep her voice low. "Stevie started outplaying me when she was about fifteen."

"You taught me the move," Emma said, alerting them that she could hear them. "I don't want to be late. Sandy Holliston promised she was bringing something wicked cool for show-and-tell."

"Great. She's sassy and smarter than we are." Jamie cringed. "Again, can't wait till she's a teenager."

* * *

While CC was doing her best to wrap up breakfast and infuse more coffee into her weary body, Deputy Val Brown strode into a Connecticut police station dragging a sorry excuse for a human being behind her.

"Deputy Val Brown, US Marshal," she announced and flashed her badge. "I believe you lost something." She shoved Tommy Bigalow forward. "Turned up down in DC."

"Heard you caught him," the desk sergeant said and

chuckled. "Bigalow, you pain in the ass. Next time we'll let them keep you."

"No, thanks." Brown handed the sergeant the paperwork. "We have enough criminals in the capital."

"Most of them were elected."

"No kidding." Val snickered as she handed over Tommy along with his paperwork. "He's all yours. I just need to check in with the local field office."

"Hey, I'm hungry," Bigalow whined.

"Shut up." Val smacked him on the back of the head. "Tommy, my boy, when you stop stealing little old ladies' pension checks, you can dictate when you eat. In the meantime, pipe down, you little pissant."

After having placed Tommy safely behind bars for at least another six months, she hoped, Val made her way over to the local US Marshal's field office to drop off the last of the paperwork. She was looking forward to heading back to DC. More importantly, she was looking forward to a little downtime, alone in her cabin in Virginia. Just her, the peace and quiet, maybe a nice bottle of wine, and if she got lonely, she knew a bar where she could find companionship.

She shed the standard-issue black blazer, revealing her well-toned body. Mentally, she was counting down the time it would take to get back to DC. If she did it right, the trip would take less than ten hours. Checking out, another half an hour tops, and she'd be on the road.

She handed over the paperwork ready to beat feet out of the stuffy office when it happened. An agent was complaining about someone at the Boston field office not listening to a request for a

BOLO. She tried not to pay attention. She had plans. Plans that, for the first time in her life, meant she could just kick back and chill. Then she heard them mention the fugitive was a child molester. She became slightly interested, yet still cautioned herself not to get involved. Related to a cop. Okay, slightly more interested. Then she heard the name Caitlin Calloway, and before she could stop herself, she opened her mouth and did the one thing that always led to trouble. She volunteered.

Chapter 3

CC made a couple of quick stops downtown, including a visit to one of her favorite forensic geeks, Dr. Corey McDowell. She gave Corey the odd greeting card after explaining that it had nothing to do with a case. She threw in a bribe of chocolate frosted cupcakes. That and a promise not to tell his wife he wasn't sticking to his diet. Her bribes made him agree to run a few tests on the Father's Day card. Once she completed her errands, she made her way over to the station.

Once she entered the station, she was eager to start her day.

"Another shooting last night," she said to her partner, hoping for some kind of reaction.

"Gangbanger." He gave a grunt without bothering to look up from the brochure he was reading. "Leave it to the task force."

"Yeah, just like all the others." CC plopped down in her chair.

"Not my fault," Max said, still enthralled with his brochure.

"The only ones killing each other these days are gangs. That isn't our turf."

"Nothing seems to be our turf lately," she said with disdain.

It was wearing on her. CC was accustomed to being active. Max's new lack of ambition was taking its toll on her. She got it. He was getting short. A permanent vacation was looming on the horizon. It didn't make sense to get hurt now.

On the other hand, she was still on the job. But he was the senior officer. If he said they didn't move, they didn't move. For the first time in her life, Caitlin Calloway understood that remaining idle was far more exhausting than busting her ass was. She looked over at Max, who at that moment, was happily flipping through brochures, ads, leaflets, and what-not for new boats.

She glanced at the stack of files to her right. "What about—"

"Domestic, murder-suicide. Once the forensics were in, we closed it. You did the paperwork on it before you left. You should be happy. For the most part, there is peace and harmony looming over our fair city. Enjoy the serenity."

"I'll give you serenity," she muttered under her breath.

"Don't." Max barely peered over the boating magazine he was reading. "Keep this up, and you'll jinx us. Next thing you know, we'll get caught up in something convoluted and dangerous."

CC grunted. It wasn't helping her cause that most of the homicides in the Boston area were gang related or domestic. Just her luck that murder was on the rise, and the majority of them were turned over to the gang task force.

Her gaze returned to the stack of files. It was paperwork. For the first time since she began her career, it was completed paperwork. The fact should have made her happy. It didn't. She rolled her shoulders, prepared for another day of nothing.

"Jamie gave Emma an Orioles hat."

"So?" Max shrugged.

"She has a perfectly good Sox hat." CC tried to defend her discomfort. "Not one of those pink ones either. Bought it for her myself."

"She can have more than one hat." Max furrowed his brow. "Leave the kid alone."

"It's just," CC tried to settle down. "Never mind. Go back to finding the perfect fishing boat." Out of the corner of her eye, she caught a glimpse of a curvy blonde. "Mulligan." She greeted the smiling woman.

"Calloway." Leigh Mulligan nodded in return. "I hope I'm not interrupting."

"Hah!" CC couldn't resist barking out. Max had the bad manners to chuckle. "What brings you up here, Detective?"

"I have this case." Mulligan started to offer a file to CC. "I could use a second opinion. If you have a moment, I'd appreciate a little help."

"Beats the hell out of sitting here watching my arse grow," CC quipped before tossing a pencil at Max.

"Missing persons isn't our territory," Max said. "But if you're that bored, give Mulligan a hand. Share some of those superior detective skills I taught you."

"You taught me?" She snapped open the file. "The only thing you taught me is where to find the best donuts. Eighteen-year-old nanny, missing for nine days."

"Au pair from the UK," Mulligan said. "Annie Fraser. Employer claims she just up and quit."

"You don't believe them?"

"No, I think she's dead."

"Go on."

"Here's the time line. Annie Fraser got up, fed the two Stern children, boys, just before seven. She had them dressed and out the door just after eight. Took them to preschool. Went to the library. Picked up the kids just after one in the afternoon. Walked them to the park. Walked them home, gave them a snack, and had them down for a nap around three. Then, according to the lady of the house, Mrs. Natalie Stern, she quit and walked out. That was on the twenty-seventh. She hasn't been seen or heard from since. None of it makes any sense," Mulligan said. "This kid talked to her parents at least three times a week. Then all of a sudden nothing."

"How does she usually get in touch with them?"

"Skype."

"Simple, easy, and free." CC mulled over the information.

Skype was a great way to communicate. All the girl needed to chat with her parents was a computer and an Internet connection.

"Did she use the family computer or her own?"

"Her parents said she had a laptop," Mulligan said. "They bought it for her before she left home so she could keep in touch with them. She also had a cell and a prepaid international calling card. But she mostly used Skype."

"Where is the laptop?"

"I have no idea," Mulligan said. "The family who hired her won't let me check her room. The wife claims that Annie quit and she could care less where the little whore is."

"Would that be a direct quote?" Max asked suddenly interested.

"Yes."

"I can see why you're concerned," CC said. "Let me run this by the boss. If he's okay with it, I'd like to check things out with you."

"Thanks."

She got up from her chair and cast a glance at Max, "Interested?"

"I'm busy." He waved her off.

"Yeah, watching the clock ticking away must be exhausting." CC charged over to Captain Rousseau's office.

There was almost a spring in her step. She couldn't believe how excited she was to finally have something to do. She had to remind herself that the case could turn into nothing. A teenager away from her family for the first time in a new city. Young Annie could have simply developed a case of wanderlust. But something about her employer's reaction didn't feel right. The most likely scenario was that the man of the house had crossed the line and the wife sent the girl packing. No need to bother with formalities when your marriage is at stake. Just kick the kid to the curb and be done with it.

CC's own mother had done the same when she was all of fifteen. She didn't hesitate throwing the teenager out on the streets when she discovered that she was gay. Then again it might have had more to do with CC's constant accusations regarding her stepfather's depraved behavior.

Fortunately, Caitlin wasn't a typical teenager. Unknown to her mother and stepfather, she already had two jobs and had rented a room. She had prepared herself for the day her so-called parents would exile her from her kid sister's life.

"So what do you think?" she eagerly asked her commanding officer.

"I think it's worth a look," he said. "And a little fresh air wouldn't kill you."

"No kidding."

"Yeah, about that." He sounded hesitant. "Let me know how you like working with Mulligan."

"Yeah?"

"Just a thought. Max is leaving an open spot. As you may suspect, cutbacks are coming. He did me a real favor by turning in his papers."

"Which would mean that there really isn't an opening."

"Yeah, there is," he mumbled. "Andy."

"Damn."

"Not a word," he said. "He's had his chances. How many different ways can you tell a guy to sober up or get out?"

"True enough." CC couldn't help agreeing. Andy had long passed being a functioning alcoholic. A drunk with a gun wasn't a good combination. "Does that mean I'll be riding with Frank?"

"I haven't decided." He surprised CC with a smile. "You're a very popular gal these days. Everyone wants Max's chair."

"Normally, I'm only popular during baseball season, thanks to my season tickets. What's making me the hot chick all of a sudden?"

"You're kidding right? You have the highest closure rate in the city." He shook his head. "Hell you've banged up two serial killers. That Fisher idiot, and let's not forget back when you were uniform you were the one who collared Jeffrey Charles West."

"Geez." She flinched. "That sick fuck. That was dumb luck,

and you know it."

"I hate when you act all humble. It usually means that you're going to hit me up for something big or do something incredibly stupid."

"Maybe I'll do a little of both just to annoy you."

"Out! Try to do something useful."

"Yes, sir."

"Mulligan! Let's roll!" she shouted across the squad room.

"Where to first?"

"The employment agency. It's getting late. I'd like a quick chat with them before they close for the night. Then we should swing over and have a chat with the Sterns."

"I take it you're driving?"

"You catch on quick."

Chapter 4

Val made good time getting to Boston. The tip about Beaumont's whereabouts sounded too good to be true. The caller wished to remain anonymous. Nothing new about that. Most people didn't want criminals to know that they were the ones who ratted them out. If the tip wasn't bogus, Beaumont would have arrived at 7:00 p.m. at the Peter Pan bus terminal located at South Station, Boston. By the time the tipster had called in, it was too late to catch the bus at one of its stops. They were going to try to catch the bus on its route. It all seemed a little iffy by the time Val entered the conversation. The best hope seemed to be to catch the runner when he got off the bus in Boston.

If the information was good, this would be a very quick and hopefully satisfying trip for Val. Which might calm her boss down. He was less than pleased when she phoned and tried to explain why she was putting her personal time on hold. If it weren't for the words "child molester," he probably would have told her to stay out of it.

Once she had the okay, she tried calling the Boston field office. After speaking to Deputy Finn of the Marshal Service, Val was less than happy. She got the distinct impression the man was doing nothing more than blowing smoke up her butt. Upon arriving in Boston, her suspicions were confirmed. Nothing had been done. No be-on-the-look-out alert, better known as a BOLO, was issued, the local cops hadn't been notified, and not one person thought it prudent to swing by the bus terminal to check out the story. Finn's attitude irked her. She knew his type. "I'm a man and I've been doing this longer so don't tell me how to do my job." She hated guys like Finn. No matter how wrong or pigheaded they acted, she had to work with them and deal with the fallout.

After trying to discuss the matter with Finn face-to-face, she was no longer upset. She was pissed off beyond belief. It was all she could do to keep from whipping out her stun gun and expressing her displeasure. She resisted the urge and politely excused herself from Finn's office. She took a calming breath and reached for her cell phone.

"Tanner, it's Val. Who do we know in Boston?" She listened to Tanner's suggestion. "No I'm not looking to get laid," she growled. "I need to step on some toes. I've got to get around an arrogant bureaucratic dipstick. Got a name?" She couldn't help pumping her fist when Tanner supplied her with an all-too-familiar name. "Yeah, that'll wake up the locals. No, I've got his number, back from when we did that little job together in Bogotá. Thanks, Tanner." Val punched in the number. After jumping through several hoops, she reached her caller.

"Val? How the hell are you?"

"I'm fine, sir. Just hit a little problem in Boston," she said. "I hate to bother you."

"Knock off that 'sir' crap," he scolded her playfully. "Just tell me what you need."

"Just looking for a little interagency cooperation."

* * *

CC was humming as she navigated the streets of Boston. It felt good to be outside and doing something. She prayed that the girl would be found safe and sound. If it weren't for the nagging feeling that something was amiss, she would have sent Mulligan on her way. The employment agency had little to offer. Mrs. Stern failed to contact them to inform them that Annie was no longer in their employment. Which in itself sent up a red flag. If Annie had just up and quit as the Sterns claimed, why wouldn't they report her actions to her employer?

CC parked in front of the oversized monstrosity that was the residence of Natalie and J.M. Charles Stern. She quickly surmised that the Sterns were Village Hills people, the type that felt a need to distinguish which part of the city they lived in. CC couldn't stomach snarky posers who lived to prove that they were better than everyone else.

"This should be interesting," she muttered as they approached the front door.

"You again?" Mrs. Stern seemed surprised. "Now what?"

"Good afternoon, Mrs. Stern." CC took the lead. Her tone was pleasant, masking her disdain.

Mrs. Stern was thin with signs of going to the gym on a semi-regular basis. Her fashionable yet still age-appropriate clothing matched her neatly coifed hair. Something about this woman immediately irked CC. It was the way she spoke, her lips never quite parting. It was very Wellesley or Vassar, very Village Hills. The cold, polite tone of someone who was quite certain they were better than you and most people walking the planet. Basically she was a snob. CC hated boorish people who assumed that the world truly did revolve around them.

"I'm Detective Calloway, and I believe you've already met Detective Mulligan."

Mrs. Stern simply grunted in response. Not a guttural grunt, just an annoying throat clearing that informed the officers that they were wasting her precious time.

"I know you're a busy woman," CC said. "Ms. Fraser's parents have been a nuisance. Detective Mulligan tried to explain that a girl that age is capable of anything."

"That is what I have been trying to tell you people." It hadn't escaped CC the way Mrs. Stern stressed the words *you people*. It was a primitive maneuver to once again inform CC and Leigh that they were wasting her time. "The girl was a whore, spreading her legs for anyone."

The unexpected harsh words were another tip-off that something was most definitely amiss in the Stern household. Mrs. Stern stood there, her thin arms folded tightly against her chest. CC studied her for a moment, mentally sizing up the woman. After Mrs. Stern released a dismissive sigh, CC went into action. She took a step back so she wasn't towering over the tiny woman. She clutched her chest as if she were in shock.

"My goodness." CC shook her head while Leigh gaped at her. "I'm sorry, but having that element around your family must have been extremely trying. Still, you know how some parents are. The Frasers won't believe what is blatantly obvious. If it's not too much trouble, could we have a look around Annie's room? There might be a clue as to where she ran off to."

"No." Once again her tone was polite, yet CC could detect an underlying bitterness.

"Mrs. Stern—" Leigh said.

"I said no."

CC took a calming breath while casting a reassuring glance at the formidable Mrs. Stern. She had quickly deduced the only way to get anything out of this woman was to bow down before her. She needed to let Mrs. Stern think she had the upper hand. It was a classic chess move, just like the one Emma had cornered her with earlier that morning.

"Detective. Mulligan," she said to Leigh, "Mrs. Stern has been through enough. She trusted that girl to look after her children. My apologies, Mrs. Stern. She isn't married. Divorced," she said in a hushed tone. To further forge their solidarity, she waved her wedding band in Mrs. Stern's direction.

Mrs. Stern released a deep sympathetic sigh as if to say that she understood. Leigh's jaw dropped as she watched the exchange.

"I am sorry to bother you with all these petty details," CC said. "When Annie left, how did she do it?"

"I beg your pardon?"

"Did she call a cab, walk, or perhaps a friend came and picked her up?" CC relished the fact that Mrs. Stern finally seemed off balance.

"She just left." Mrs. Stern hesitated. "Like I told this one." She wagged a finger at Leigh. "Up and quit and walked out the door. Probably to the trolley stop at the bottom of the hill."

"Mrs. Stern." CC's voice oozed with sweetness and light. "We won't disturb you any further. Although I can't promise that we won't return. I wish that I could, but as I've said before, the girl's parents just won't listen to reason."

"If you must."

Mrs. Stern thrust a dismissive wave and closed the front door. The detectives silently shuffled back to the car.

"I don't miss the old Crown Vics," CC said as she stood before the sleek black SUV. "These are more comfortable and fit in a little better. Okay, time for our next move."

"Can I just ask what that was all about?" Leigh seemed more curious than angry.

"That lady isn't going to let us in," CC said. "I know her type. She's right, and the rest of the world should shut up and listen to her. The kids are probably pampered little snots."

"From what I've seen of the Stern boys, yes they are," Mulligan said. "We're not going to find out anything if we don't get a peek in the girl's room."

"We need a nosy neighbor."

"A nosy neighbor?"

"Everyone has one or is one." CC scanned the pristine tree lined neighborhood.

"Across the street," Leigh said. "Every time I've been here, I noticed a nice older lady out in her garden, watching me. Nothing overt, but how much pruning does a bush need? There she is." Leigh waved to the silver-haired woman who appeared to be attending to her rose bushes.

CC smiled when the woman returned the wave. "Nosy and friendly. I love it. The icing on the cake would be if she hates Mrs. Stern." They made their way across the street.

"Good morning," Leigh said sweetly. "I just love what you've done with your yard. I'm Detective Mulligan and this is Detective Calloway."

The woman flashed a perfect smile. She stripped off her gardening gloves and offered her hand. CC was impressed by the woman's firm handshake. Maybe she did spend all day in the garden.

"Thelma Himple. Just like Cagney and Lacey. Oops, sorry. You must get that a lot."

"Yes," CC said and smiled. "But we never get tired of it. Just wish some of our cases were as exciting as theirs. It is far too nice a day to spend it back at the station doing paperwork."

"I miss the distinction of having four seasons," the neighbor said, "but I have to admit having summer so late in the year is nice. Confuses the bejesus out of my crocuses, though."

"Having the same problem at my place," CC said. "Loving the weather, but it's a new house and the garden is shabby in comparison to yours." CC rambled, fully aware that Mulligan was carefully watching her. "I hate to bother you, Dr. Himple . . ." CC abruptly cut herself off when she noticed the older woman's eyebrows lift, apparently questioning how CC knew of her occupation. "My apologies. I noticed your name on the mailbox. Occupational hazard. We notice things."

Dr. Himple nodded. CC instantly liked this woman who seemed completely at ease with herself and the world in general. So unlike her neighbor.

"Speaking of noticing things..." the doctor began to say hesitantly. "The police seem to have taken an interest in my neighbors. Tell me there's something scandalously exciting happening."

"Wish we could." CC smiled, wishing she could share their suspicions with the kindly older woman. "We just had a few questions about the Stern's au pair."

"Annie?"

"She hasn't called home in over two weeks, and her parents are very concerned."

"Oh, dear."

"Have you seen or heard anything that might help us track her down?"

"You think she ran off?" She gasped. "Not that one. If anything I'd be looking at..." Her voice trailed off as she seemed to realize what she was about to say.

"What is it, Doctor?" Mulligan asked. "Her parents are terribly worried."

"I don't know anything certain." Dr. Himple hesitated. "It's just that, well, Natalie wasn't very nice to the girl. If you ask me, I think she was jealous. Then again, when wasn't she jealous? You'd think that husband of hers was Warren Beatty. "

"When was the last time you saw Annie?"

"A couple of weeks ago," she confidently answered. "Annie may have been very young, but let me tell you, she was quite reliable. Those two boys were more than a little difficult to handle. Annie is a good kid. Very polite and the patience of a saint."

"Do you think Annie might have had enough and thrown in the towel?" CC asked.

"No." The response was adamant.

"Even with Mrs. Stern's snotty behavior?"

"She wouldn't. Annie was humbled by her parent's scraping the money together so she could make this trip. She couldn't let them down."

CC and Leigh thanked the good doctor for her time before deciding to pay Mr. J.M. Charles Stern a visit at his office. CC tensed slightly as she made her way through the mid-afternoon traffic. Navigating the streets of the financial district was difficult enough; adding the lateness of the hour turned it into a horrible experience.

"I liked the way you handled yourself," Leigh said. "It's true what they say about you."

"What do they say?"

"That you could sell snow to an Eskimo."

"Hah!" CC barked, thoroughly amused by the comment. "Right. That lady was easy. I'm guessing by all the time she's spending in the garden that she's retired and probably not by choice. Doctors hang on forever. They talk about retiring, but they're addicted to their work. Dr. Himple seems to have a lot of time on her hands. I'm willing to bet she's a widow. Also sticking her with a lot of free time. She just needs someone to talk to."

"I doubt that the Sterns make for good company." "There didn't seem to be anyone else on the block around her age. Too many minivans, which means middle-aged or twenty-something soccer moms. Something I seriously doubt that Dr. Himple has a great deal in common with."

"You're thinking no kids?" Leigh seemed to be intrigued by CC's assessment.

"The house is too small. By the looks of it, she's lived there for a long time. Annie was probably very bright and well spoken. I think she and Dr. Himple enjoyed chatting."

"Yeah, the Sterns don't strike me as the type to do a coffee chat with the staff."

"From the vibes I get from Mrs. Stern, I have a feeling that most of the world doesn't meet her exacting standards."

"How did you know that I'm divorced?"

"Lucky guess." CC said. "Very few cops get through with only getting hitched once."

"You let those ladies think that you're married to a man. Why?"

"They assumed. Although I think the doctor wouldn't have batted an eye, Mrs. Stern would have tried to act overly cool with it. I wouldn't have gotten as much out of her as I did. She places her family above all else. She also thinks they are above anyone and everything. I made you out as a lost divorcee and me a happily married woman. Next time I'll let slip that I'm married to a doctor. That should narrow the gap just a wee bit."

"So, if you're the happily married one and I'm the hapless blonde floozy, does that make me Cagney and you Lacey?"

"No." CC chuckled.

"Why? Because Sharon Gless was so much hotter than Tyne Daly?"

"See, you do catch on quick." CC finally found a place to park. "Now, we need to get moving."

"And just what is your game plan?"

"Ever play chess?"

"Yes, with my dad. Why?"

"Familiar with the term 'removal of the guard'?"

"Kind of. You want to remove Mrs. Stern's protection so..."

"So she's vulnerable. And when you're vulnerable, you make mistakes."

"What about a squeeze? You know building up pressure until

she can't keep up with our moves?"

"If we try that, she'll have her defenses up. Or worse, her lawyer on our butts," CC said, impressed by Mulligan's knowledge of chess. "If we can catch her off balance, we've got a shot at finding out something other than the fact that Annie is missing."

* * *

The office was typical of financial firms that littered the district. CC often wondered what these folks really did all day long. They always seemed busy, yet given the way the economy was circling the bowl, what did they do for forty-some-odd hours a week? A good-looking man directed them toward J.M. Charles Stern's office.

"Snaps, will be with you in a moment," he informed them.

"Snaps?" CC couldn't resist.

"College, nickname. He had a thing for wearing suspenders." He chuckled. "Well, until . . ."

"He met his wife?" CC finished for him.

"Yeah," his smile dimed. "Oh, here he is." He quickly blurted out.

"Mr. Stern, I'm Detective Calloway and this is Detective Mulligan," CC offered her greeting as his college pal darted out of the office.

J.M. Charles Stern was thin, a bit on the wiry side. He and his wife were a picture-perfect suburban couple. Hair properly coifed, nannies for the children, and a gal who came in twice a week to clean. Like his wife, he spoke proper English clouded by a hint of disdain.

"I have met Detective Mulligan previously." Since he failed to offer his hand, CC refrained from doing so. "Any luck? I'm quite surprised that Annie hasn't been in touch. She appeared to be far more responsible."

"Appearances can be deceiving." CC tried to gauge just how much this man knew about what was and wasn't happening in his happy home. "When was the last time you saw or spoke to her?"

"The morning she quit."

"Did she seem distracted?"

"Not at all." He shook his head as if trying to understand the situation. "Everything was normal. Annie said she was taking the boys to the park. I was more than a little surprised when I returned home that evening and my wife informed me that she tendered her notice."

"Well she didn't," CC said. "She didn't give the standard two weeks. Annie walked out."

"Yes." He cleared his throat. "So unlike her. And not come by and get her last check or belongings. It doesn't make any sense. Then again, my wife…" His words trailed off, and a look of confusion clouded his face.

"Mr. Stern, we hate to take up your time," CC quickly began to say when he seemed to be losing his train of thought. She suspected that if he started thinking about his wife's version of events, chances were he would quickly clam up. "Would you mind if we took a look at Annie's belongings? It might give us some hint as to where she's staying. Maybe there's a friend or schoolmate we haven't spoken to yet that might know something."

"Of course. Just let me…"

CC was on her cell phone before he could finish what he was saying. She knew he was about to call his wife to clear things with her. Mr. Stern contacting his controlling wife was the last thing she wanted.

"I just need you to confirm that with the ADA." She thrust the phone at him. His eyes bugged out. "Just need to keep things on the up and up. Annie might try to blame you or us for invading her privacy. Teenagers can be unpredictable. No one wants a lawsuit when all any of us are trying to do is put her parents' worries to rest."

He seemed baffled by her actions and threats but conceded and gave his verbal consent. CC had just gotten exactly what they needed. Max loved it when she pulled a fast one on some hapless idiot. She was going to miss the way he'd shake his head and call her slick.

"Thanks." CC smiled graciously after she concluded her call. "Trifling details can be tedious. I guess I don't have to tell you that." She nodded towards his overly organized desk.

"Oh, I understand," he said, although CC could detect a lingering sound of confusion in his voice.

"We'll let you get back to business." They tried to appear casual as they made their departure as quickly as possible.

"That was interesting," Leigh said while CC drove with urgency. "Let me see if I can follow your reasoning. Mr. J.M. Charles Stern just gave his consent allowing us to search his home. Something the formidable Mrs. Stern is against. He has no idea at how pissed off his wife is going to be. But since you had him give his consent to our ever friendly ADA I'm assuming it was Collins he has no recourse."

"I just wish I could have called in the techs," CC said. "His wife is going to be pissed."

"I know it's wrong to feel good about this." Leigh gave a snort. "But knowing that we're going to disrupt Natalie Stern's day pleases me."

"Yeah, me, too."

"More importantly, I'm hoping we discover something that will help us find Annie," Leigh said. "You are good. Everyone we've talked to, you've somehow reminded them this is about Annie."

Upon arriving at the Stern residence, they learned the lady of the house had dropped her faux politeness and opted for a more hostile approach to her guests.

"I told you before that you can't invade my privacy," Natalie Stern bellowed in the most unpleasant manner.

"I understand how upsetting this is," CC said soothingly. "Perhaps you should contact your husband? He gave permission. In the meantime, we just need to see Annie's room. We'll be out of your way as quickly as possible. Again, perhaps you should call your husband. I swear if we didn't keep track of them, they'd forget to eat."

"Really?" Mrs. Stern sounded suspicious. "And just what does your husband do?" Once again her condescending tone was painfully obvious.

"I married a doctor." CC brushed past the annoying woman.

"Really? Then why—"

"Oh, my pension might come in handy," CC offered in a conspiratorial whisper. "Like I said, if we don't keep track of them, Lord knows what kind of trouble they can get into. I'm just thinking ahead and putting a little something aside."

"Smart girl."

"Now if you could just show us Annie's room? We can get out of your hair, and I can head home for the day. Plus if we clear out all of her things, you won't be troubled by any of this any longer."

Mrs. Stern reluctantly showed the detectives the way. Her hesitation only further confirmed CC's suspicions. When she saw the state of Annie's room, her heart dropped. Everything was in place except all the bedding had been torn off the bed and tossed onto the floor.

"What happened to this girl?" Leigh voiced CC's fears.

Chapter 5

They took all of Annie's things back to the station. Wayne needed to go through the laptop and cell phone. Leigh personally wanted to go through the phone log.

"Pretty girl." CC stared at the picture of Annie Fraser and her family. She had found the family portrait resting on top of the girl's nightstand.

CC couldn't shake the sick feeling in the pit of her stomach. The way the girl's bed had been trashed didn't fit. Who keeps their room immaculate then tosses their sheets around?

"Who walks off their job in a foreign country and leaves behind everything including their passport?"

"No one."

CC felt her stomach churn as she gazed at the image of Annie laughing happily, surrounded by her parents and her two older brothers. It was the same with all cops. When the victims are so very young, full of life and promise, the loss seems immeasurable.

"I used to do that," CC said.

"What's that?" Leigh glanced at the picture.

"Look at the jacket and belt Annie is wearing. I'm willing to bet they belong to one of her brothers. When I was a kid, my older brother couldn't keep me out of his closet."

"I only have sisters," Leigh said with a smile. "But all my friends used to raid their brothers' closets. Nice belt. Armani? I would have swiped it. So, do you still ransack your brother's closet?"

"He died." CC tried to shrug it off. She liked Mulligan; she just didn't feel a need to divulge the convoluted details of her troubled childhood. "You can tell that's Armani from this picture?"

"Oh yeah."

"Any luck with the cell?"

"Annie didn't lead an exciting life. She called the employment agency, the Sterns, BC a couple of times, the library, and with the aid of an international calling card, she called home. The calls back to Kensington were the most frequent. The husband seems clueless. He struck me as a gutless wonder since the first day."

"No kidding. I worry about people who let their girlfriends or wives change them. Mrs. Stern is the key to this case. Getting her to be more forthcoming is going to be a challenge."

Max flopped down in his chair. "Can't get a woman to talk to you? Must be losing your touch, Calloway."

"Bored suburban housewife. You want to take a shot at her?" CC challenged him in hopes that he might actually get out of his chair for something other than another cup of coffee.

"Good looking?"

"Eh, one of those skinny, tight-lipped, 'I went to Wellesley' types."

"I hate those broads," Max said. "The only time they talk to a guy like me is when they're working a fund-raiser for their kid's school or trying to beat a ticket."

"Shirley know you try to chat up other women?"

"You know, that's who could hold their own with that type."

Max wagged his finger at her. "My wife can outsmart those tight asses anytime, anywhere."

"Did Shirley ever try to change you?" CC studied him closely. "How you dress or act?"

"Don't all women?" He laughed. "Nah, not really. But after we were married, she started buying my clothes and giving me the 'is that what you're wearing' shtick."

"Good Lord. Are you telling me this is the improved version?" CC gasped with mock horror, fully aware that Leigh was watching their banter very carefully. "Fair enough. I get it from Jamie now and then. She's much more fashion savvy than I'll ever be. I do miss having cartoon characters on my underwear."

"We're cops. What do we know," Max said. "Well, except Mulligan. She cleans up nice."

"Thanks, I think. So Jamie is the fem."

"No." CC laughed. "Everyone thinks so, but she's much more athletic and handier with power tools than I'll ever be. Mulligan, did you see that picture sitting on Stern's desk of him and his wife?" She had begun to study the picture of Annie and her family again.

"Yeah, the same belt."

"You're certain?"

"It's Armani. Not much chance of mistaking it."

"I hate that designers put their names all over things." CC grimaced but was silently impressed by Mulligan's observations. "I mean what's up with charging six hundred dollars for a bag that isn't practical and promotes the company that made it? I blame Gloria Vanderbilt. She started that whole designer jeans crap. Personally, I'll take a well-worn pair of Levis any day. I still can't see how you can tell it's an Armani."

"Trust me."

"So, what have you got?" Max asked. "I can see those wheels turning. You're onto something."

"I got a missing kid, who dutifully called home and seemed devoted to her job and studies. Who for some reason just up and left her job not taking any cash, her laptop, cell phone, or her passport. The only person who seems to think she did this voluntarily is the wife who claims that the girl is nothing but a whore. This is the same person who was the last person to see Annie alive. I've got a room that is as neat as a pin except the bed, which has been trashed. I've got a wife who has a jealous streak when it comes to her husband. What I got is an itch to look at the wife's GPS records and no grounds for a warrant to do so."

"Annie didn't drive much," Leigh added. "Mr. Stern said she was nervous that she would end up driving on the wrong side of the road. She mostly walked or took the subway. Mrs. Stern was most displeased that she subjected the children to such an unhealthy environment."

"Another exact quote?" Max asked.

"Oh yeah."

"She's a snotty bitch," Max said. "Why the GPS on the family car?"

"You know why," CC replied.

"Help Mulligan out."

"Because she had to get rid of the body," CC said. "Two-car

garage with an entrance off the kitchen. Easy stuff to move a small girl like that without anyone, even the nosy neighbor, catching on."

"Other than the bed, I didn't see any overt signs of foul play." Mulligan sounded almost disappointed.

"There isn't always a blood trail when you kill someone." CC sighed heavily. "We need to know Mrs. Stern's movements on the day that Annie disappeared."

"Why are you so certain that the wife offed her?" Max asked. "Maybe she and the husband had a thing going, and he's got her stashed somewhere. Or he made a play, she turns him down, he freaks thinking Mrs. Snooty Pants is going to find out and he kills the girl."

"Then why was the wife the last to see Annie?" CC said. "Plus I don't think this guy takes a leak without clearing it with his wife. Just to be on the safe side, Wayne is looking at Annie's laptop to confirm that she really was the good kid everyone thinks she is."

"Almost everyone," Mulligan added. "Mrs. Stern's attitude has made me hinky from day one. She didn't even pretend to be concerned about Annie's whereabouts. Which tells me she knows exactly where she is."

"What kind of car does the wife drive?" Max began his ritual shifting in his chair, making it squeak. CC often wondered if he did that just to annoy her.

"One of those Mercedes SUVs."

"What is the point of that?" Max scoffed. "Get a minivan or get a luxury car."

"Mulligan, what would you like to do?" CC asked. "It is your case after all."

CHECKMATE

"Easy to forget with this one. She's like a steamroller." Max aimed his thumb at CC.

Leigh smiled. "She's made a lot of headway."

"No, I've just come up with more guesses," CC said. "And that's all they are. Without any proof, not much you can do. Except lean on the wife. No way the husband is going to give you permission for anything else. I'm thinking Mrs. Stern has already ripped him a new orifice by now. Whatever you're going to do, I'd do it quickly before the Feds get involved."

"Any ideas you have, I'd be grateful," Mulligan said. "I don't think I can keep the Feds from taking over. I've got a missing kid from another country. Her parents are going crazy. Not that I can blame them. I can talk to the neighbor again. Maybe she saw something that day and didn't think it was important."

"You can try, but I'm thinking she told us everything and enjoyed doing it. We got nothing," CC said. "I can't take another lecture from our esteemed attorney general on what does and does not qualify as probable cause."

"Seriously? Coakley scolded you?"

"Scolded, spanked, and—" Max added.

"Hey." CC cut him off. "The deal is we need to find out what happened, without blowing the case. We've all been through this far too many times to count."

The three of them sat there stony faced, seemingly awaiting divine intervention. Mulligan's face skewed as she took another look at Annie's cell phone.

"Maybe we don't need to look at Mrs. Stern's GPS," she said

quietly. "Maybe we could just look at Annie's."

"Excuse me?"

"Almost every cell has a GPS," Leigh said. "And Annie didn't like to drive. Still she had a routine to follow that involved the family. If we follow where the nanny was, perhaps we can find some of Mrs. Stern's stomping grounds."

"Good call. Let's go see Wayne."

Leigh seemed pleased by the compliment. She held the cell tightly as they made their way over to Wayne's lab. Fortunately, the Crime Scene Unit was just down the street.

"Why are you so fascinated by Annie's belt?"

"I'm not." CC shrugged. "It's just that I noticed the suit jacket with her stuff. It was hanging in the closet. Why not take the belt? Then again maybe the brother took it back or she didn't take it with her. Or she did and I just didn't notice it."

"I doubt that there is very little that goes unnoticed by you, Calloway."

"Sucking up? I like it. Thinking about making a move?"

"It's no secret how screwed up the budget is," Leigh said. CC liked that Leigh was direct with her answers. "Do you know Krassowski?"

"That dick?"

"My partner."

"Oops."

"No oops. He is a dick and a whole list of other things my mother would never approve of my saying," Mulligan said. "Word is there might be a spot opening in homicide. It's a move I wouldn't object to making. Besides who wouldn't want to ride with the woman who bagged Jeffrey Charles West?"

"Why is everyone talking about him today? Look, Max turned him over to the Feds," CC said. "He was the one who ran the sick bastard's prints."

"Rumor has it that was because you asked him to."

"Hey, he was a gold shield. Me, I was still a lowly foot soldier."

"What tipped you off?"

"With West?" CC rolled her shoulders. "It was outside the Garden. A Celts game had just let out. We lost, so the crowd was surly. West looked like everyone else. Stocky guy with a hoodie. Thing was, he had his hand attached to his jewels and he was muttering. I brought him in on a PC and followed a hunch."

"What was he muttering about?"

"It's a wonderful life." CC laughed. "That's all the guy did was quote lines from the movie."

"*It's a Wonderful Life*? With Jimmy Stewart?"

"Yeah. West wouldn't shut up, but he never said anything, like his name or why he was wandering around Boston with his hand on his nuts. All he did was quote lines from the movie. I've heard that he did the same thing during his trial. Had a kid a few years before that and named her Zuzu Petals. The guy was seriously fucked up."

"Zuzu Petals West?"

"A line from the movie, I think. Like I said, the guy was seriously screwed up. When we busted him we found his manifesto. It was a bunch of papers with all of Jimmy Stewart's lines from the movie. It was tucked into a copy of Catcher In The Rye."

"I heard Florida couldn't wait to fry him."

"Can't argue with his sentence," CC said. "He was one sick bastard. Wayne, tell me you have good news." She greeted the tech who had a way of making her life easier.

"Calloway." Wayne, the shy tech, returned her greeting. "I see you brought your friend back. I haven't had a long look at the laptop yet."

"But you've had a look. Look at this, too, while you're at it." She nudged Mulligan to hand over the cell phone. "We need to know where's it's been. Everywhere it's been."

Wayne peered over his glasses and gave her a weary look. "You don't ask for much."

"Still waiting for world peace. What did you get from the laptop?"

"I'm not done."

"But you've looked." Her tone grew terser.

"Annie Fraser's life was more boring than mine."

"Not possible."

"She kept in touch with friends and family back home," he said while fiddling with the cell phone. "She was taking a class at Boston College. One of the nighttime extension courses. Child psychology. She was doing well. Made a couple of friends at class. That's it."

"We need the friends' names, addresses, and I mean real addresses. Don't be giving me, 'I can find Johnny at I'm-a-big-stud-muffin dot com.'"

"I'll send it over." He plugged something into the cell phone. "How was California?"

"Same."

"As long as he stays locked up." Wayne grunted. "I'll get this together and e-mail you the results."

"Send it to Mulligan. It's her case."

"Really?"

"Yes, at this point in time, Annie Fraser is a missing person."

Wayne shook his head. "No one leaves behind all of their gadgets."

* * *

After trading information with Leigh and Wayne, CC made her way back to her desk. She glanced at her watch and noted she had a few hours to kill. Max was busy on the computer, looking at bigger and better sailboats.

"Do you even know how to drive one of those things?" She taunted him as she plopped down in her chair.

"It's sail. You sail a boat. I'll learn. Come next April, I've got nothing but time on my hands."

"Uh-huh, whatever you say, Popeye." CC clenched her jaw. She hated that Max was leaving. He had trained her, took her under his wing, and when she was promoted to detective, he was the first to ask to partner with her. Not having him to turn to was going to be strange.

"You better get a damn big one. After a week of listening to you nonstop, Shirley's going to need something big to transport your body."

He ignored her jab. She busied herself with making notes on the Fraser case. "What am I doing?" she muttered under her breath. "It's not my case."

"Can't help yourself."

"Aren't you going to miss it, Max?"

"Nope," he answered finally looking up. "There was a time when I would have but not now. I'm done. I'd say it's your turn to shine, but you already do."

"God, you're not getting all sappy on me are you?"

"Not a chance, Calloway. I'm just saying—"

"Calloway!" Leigh Mulligan's frantic voice cut off whatever Max was trying to say. "I think we've got a break. Nosy neighbor just called in a disturbance at the Stern residence."

"Max?"

"Go." His voice was soft, yet CC detected a sadness in his eyes.

She offered a nod and grabbed her jacket. Before she could catch her bearings, she was following behind Mulligan who seemed determined to set a new land-speed record. CC didn't argue about Mulligan taking the lead. She silently reminded herself that it was Leigh's case. She had to admit Mulligan looked cool, confident, and in control. Leigh navigated the streets, her face perfectly masking any excitement she may have felt and her eyes carefully hidden behind her designer sunglasses. CC's wife and sister would know the designer, but to her, they just looked expensive.

"Wayne found a couple of inconsistencies on Annie's phone," Mulligan said. "I sent a team to Albemarle Park. Based on the towers her phone hit, the park is in the middle of things. Plus the day she disappeared she was at the park with the kids. The local parks department locks it up at dusk. They think it will keep the local teens from hanging out at night. As much as I hate to say it—"

"The woods that run along the back are a great place to dump a body," CC said when Leigh's stoic veneer slipped. "I know the park, played a couple of softball games there. It's hard when it gets to this point. I'd love to find this kid alive and well. We've both been here before. We can hope."

"It would be nice." Mulligan brought her SUV to a screeching halt, blocking the Stern's driveway. "After you. I think we've already established that Mrs. Stern doesn't like me."

A high-pitched wail cut through the air. "Then again, I think we have probable cause," CC blurted as the duo raced towards the house. Without bothering to knock and with their guns drawn, they huddled in the doorway. CC thanked their good fortune when she saw that the front door was ajar.

"Police!" she announced as they burst into the home. "Whoa!" It was the only thing the seasoned policewoman could think to say.

The scene they discovered was the last thing either expected to find. They held their guns steady aimed directly at Mrs. Stern. Mr. Stern was on his back on the floor in the foyer, his face beet red, his body trembling with pain. Above him stood his loving wife, holding a recently fired taser gun. She had hit her target perfectly and seemed to be preparing to send another jolt to Mr. Stern's groin. The poor man couldn't speak.

"Drop it!" CC's body tensed when she spied the maniacal look in the soccer mom's eyes. "Now!"

Mrs. Stern growled. The thirty-second delay kicked in and sent another painful jolt to her husband's manhood. CC shuddered when he released a painful wail.

"I said drop it, lady! Or I'll have DSS here in two minutes to take your kids!" It was the only threat CC could think of, but it seemed to work. Natalie Stern's head spun around.

"You can't!" she screamed, waving the taser around.

"Really?" CC became aware that Mulligan was already on her cell requesting backup and an ambulance.

"You're tasering your husband's nuts," CC said, wondering why this woman couldn't grasp the gravity of the situation.

Chapter 6

Jamie's sullen mood had lifted by the time she arrived at work. She loved her job at Boylston General. Working in the ER with the constant rhythm made her feel alive. One thing clouded her mood. It was time to take on a new team of residents. Boylston, like most hospitals in the Boston area, was first and foremost a teaching hospital.

Jamie used to love teaching, watching a bunch of clumsy know-it-all youngsters turn into some of the best caregivers she had ever seen. A decade ago everything changed. Simon Fisher came along. He murdered one of his classmates and began stalking Jamie. She no longer felt at ease around her students. She wanted to teach them the value of doing no harm and how to fight the good fight even when the pencil pushers for insurance companies tried to tie their hands. She wanted to give these kids a chance to make the world a better place. She just couldn't allow herself to get close to them.

Over the passing years, she constantly questioned why she had never seen the darkness in Simon. If he hadn't tried to kill her, she would have gone on thinking he was a nice, sweet young man. Her wife and her boss kept reminding her that it wasn't her fault. Whackos rarely wear a label announcing their defects. Simon had been killing young women for years with almost no one suspecting that he was deranged.

She took a calming breath before entering her boss's office. She loved working with Jack. Although lately his attention seemed to be divided. After almost thirty years of marriage, his wife decided she was tired of being ignored. Jack assumed that his move to a one-bedroom condo along Revere beach was temporary.

"Ready for your new students?"

"Of course." She relaxed into a chair and sipped her coffee. "The best and the brightest just like always."

"Doesn't make them good doctors," he shrewdly noted with a yawn.

"That's why they need us."

"Hmm."

Jamie couldn't help but notice how tired Jack looked. Despite his insistence that the separation was temporary, she could tell it was taking its toll on him.

"How are things going?" she finally asked.

"Paperwork is dragging me down. Nothing new there."

"Not what I was asking about."

"Oh, you mean the separation? Ah, it won't be much longer. In the meantime, I'm enjoying my bachelor digs. I always wanted to live at the beach, but Joyce didn't like the school system. Newton was a much better choice for the kids and us."

"Now that the boys are grown, maybe you could think about moving somewhere closer to the water," Jamie suggested. "Once you and Joyce patch things up."

Jamie felt a twinge of guilt by making the suggestion. She had run into Joyce a couple weeks ago and got the distinct impression the separation was anything but temporary. Joyce was tired of waiting. Tired of taking second place in Jack's life. They had worked hard, built a home, and raised two wonderful sons. Joyce wanted to enjoy their life together. Jack didn't want to ease back at work or change the status quo.

"I don't know," Jack casually answered, confirming Joyce's accusations that the man was comfortable with his life as it was. "The house is paid for. No sense pulling up stakes when I just got everything right."

"Change can be good."

"You sound like my wife."

"Wouldn't want her for a boss." She laughed it off. "I've got one of those to answer to myself. Okay, let's go over the list of new residents."

Jamie and Jack went over the files on the new residents before tackling a stack of paperwork from various insurance companies. Jamie loved working in emergency medicine. The paperwork, on the other hand, sucked the life out of her.

"I know what the rules say, but we saved the guy's life." Jamie felt a familiar frustration. "Sometimes I think insurance companies would be just as happy if the patient died rather than run a simple test."

"Preaching to the choir," Jack said with a groan. "It might be nice if all these suits didn't get involved and just let us practice medicine. Speaking of which, if we're done I'm due upstairs for the weekly ball busting about the budget."

"Are they considering cuts?"

"Not yet." Jack sighed heavily. "Don't worry."

"The economy has everyone worried."

"I know. That's one of the reasons the ER is so busy. Nothing has been mentioned about scaling back. So you can tell the nurses and everyone else that for the moment we're good."

"Thanks."

"Jamie, I'm going to do everything I can to keep our team together."

Jamie said her goodbyes, gathered her notes, and went off to meet her new class of students. The eager group of freshly scrubbed faces was gathered around the nurses' station. Jamie allowed herself a small smile before she prepared to start playing the role of "Mean old Dr. Jameson." Secretly, she hated having to put the fear of God in them from the get-go

"Rule one, don't get in the nurse's way," Jamie said, snickering at the stunned looks on their faces. "Blocking the nurses' station isn't helping them do their job. Over here, people, we have rounds."

Again Jamie silently laughed at the stunned expressions. Every time she began a rotation, she couldn't help wondering if she was equally clueless when she first began her medical career.

"We seem to be short." She noted the absence of at least one student.

"Just so we're clear, I don't care. I don't care if your girlfriend just dumped you. I don't care that you're tired. I don't care how much money mommy and daddy paid to get you here. I care about the patients. If you do your job right, you change someone's life. Make a mistake and people die. If you don't know something, for the love of whatever God you worship, ask." Jamie's eyes narrowed when she spied a late arrival trying to sneak into the back of the group. "Rounds begin at exactly seven-fifteen a.m. That means you are here and prepared at seven-fourteen. Am I clear Dr. Tierney?" The young woman hiding in the back seemed surprised that the formidable Dr. Jameson knew her name. She nervously shifted from one foot to another before making eye contact with Jamie.

"What? I was here." She made the mistake of trying to argue. "I was in the lounge."

"Here is here," Jamie said with a cold smile. "Dressed, fed, watered, and whatever else needs tending to before you get here. Not being here means you're absent. I know most of you think you're ready. You've finished school, and we call you doctor. You're not ready. Again, screw up and people die. I don't care about whatever excuse keeps you from being here on time. What I do care about is the health and welfare of our patients. You should also know that I hate repeating myself. Let's begin."

Jamie's head was throbbing by the time she finished rounds with the residents. It was always the same: too many of them were trying to earn a place of grace or show off. A couple showed promise, asking questions instead of trying to show Jamie how smart they were. She hated that she had to shame most of them into humility. But as she said when she first greeted them, make mistakes and people die.

* * *

Jamie watched her young charges carefully. Tierney and Alvarez were doing their best to keep their tempers in check. Raymond Windsor was one of the patients that proved some people just shouldn't leave their homes. Jamie had caught snippets of his triage where he insisted that the nurse give him a brand new pen and clipboard. He also insisted that she sanitize her hands every two seconds.

Germ phobia wasn't uncommon in this day and age. He insisted that the young doctors sanitize their stethoscopes three times, use a brand new blood pressure cuff, and change their rubber gloves every time they moved. After four agonizing hours, Mr. Windsor was still suffering from a common cold.

"Put the fear of God in them?" Stella, the charge nurse, grinned as she handed Jamie a cup of coffee.

"Thanks." Jamie wearily accepted the coffee. "'First do no harm' sounds simple doesn't it?"

"You would think." Stella snorted. "Don't worry, I'm certain they hate you by now."

"I did warm and fuzzy once. Didn't really work out."

"So long as they fear you and respect my people, they'll be okay," Stella said. "As for warm and fuzzy, it's highly overrated. CC get home all right?"

"Yes. And no, he didn't get out."

"Wasn't going to ask. If that weasel squirmed out of his trap, I doubt tall, dark, and deadly would let you out of her sight."

"Tall, dark, and what?" Jamie laughed. "Yeah, that sounds like my wife. Oh, here comes one of my kids."

"She was the quiet one."

"Don't let that fool you. She was studying everything."

"Really?"

"Is it true that the nurses have a pool going on who's going to wash out first?"

"Now, Dr. Jameson, would I allow such a thing?"

"Uh-huh. Put twenty on Tierney for me."

"You got it."

"Dr. Alvarez, can I help you?"

"I don't mean to interrupt," the petite young brunette said. "I just had a question about the schedule."

"Yes?" Jamie's response was cool and controlled.

"I have a daughter, and I know that doesn't matter, but—"

"It does matter." Jamie was pleased that her time wasn't being wasted with a ridiculous request. One year she had a new resident request starting his rotation a little late so he could go skiing in Aspen with his girlfriend. He was shocked when Jamie denied his request. "Let's go to my office and see what we can work out."

Before they reached her office, each of the residents sought her out. Most of them wanted to stroke her ego, which for Jamie was a huge mistake. A couple had legitimate comments or questions, and Jamie took extra time with them.

"Was I ever that young?" She dropped a stack of files on Jack's desk.

"I don't know. I got you fully formed."

"I've got one kid who hasn't been on time for anything," Jamie began to rant. "She thinks that if she is on hospital property that qualifies. How in the hell did this kid get to this level in life without being able to tell time? Oh, and there is another one who compliments everything I say. He does it again, and I'm setting him on fire. They reach this point and think they've made it. And the world should kiss their ass because they're a doctor. Oh, don't give me that look."

"Same look I give you every year." Jack laughed. "The names change, but the kids are all the same on the first day. Don't forget they're scared. Has anyone thrown up yet?"

"Did I miss a pool? Oh, man, if these poor kids only knew that we bet on them screwing up..."

"It's all in good fun. Besides, I was the first in my class to upchuck."

"And now look at you, three steps below God at this fine hospital."

"Four steps, and will you let me know how Murphy does?"

"Hasn't thrown up, yet." Jamie's pager vibrated, alerting her that she was needed back in the ER. "Time to get back to it. I'll catch up with you later."

When she had left the treatment area to go to Jack's office, all was quiet in the ER, nothing more than the usual bumps and bruises. Now it was a flurry of activity. She wasn't surprised to see the new residents standing around looking very frightened and confused.

"Morgan, Hennessey, and Jacqui," she said and beckoned her colleagues. "Take two and put them to work." She pointed towards the youngsters. "Tierney, Alvarez, and Murphy," she called out just as the ambulance bay doors burst open. "You three are with me." She snapped on a pair of rubber gloves. "Talk to me," she said to the EMT in a softer tone.

"Thirty-three-year-old, adult male, vitals are good."

"And you're smirking because?" Jamie asked as they wheeled the man, who on paper should be the picture of health, towards a treatment room. "What seems to be wrong with Mister...?"

"Stern." The EMT kept smirking. "Electrical shock to his

genitals."

"Excuse me?"

"His wife tasered his nuts," a feminine voice from behind them informed her.

"Whoa." She winced along with everyone else in the room. "On three," she told her residents, who fumbled slightly before successfully loading the weeping man onto a new gurney. Jamie checked his vitals while glancing over at the blonde who had been following them. The woman politely held up a badge. Jamie simply nodded and set about instructing her students on what to do. Young Dr. Murphy seemed to be the most uncomfortable. Jamie wasn't surprised, since he was the only man in the room.

"How many times was he..." She paused, searching for the correct words.

"Twice that we know of. Probably more."

"Any particular reason why Mrs. Stern chose this course of action?" Her question had nothing to do with the man's health; Jamie was simply curious. Still, she knew everyone in the room couldn't wait to hear the answer as to why a man's wife would try to fry his vital parts.

"She thought he was having an affair with the nanny."

"That would do it," Jamie said wryly before returning her attention to her students. Mr. Stern howled in pain throughout the entire event. "Do you know how many volts he got zapped with, Detective..."

"Mulligan. We're guessing it was the standard fifty thousand volts. The taser, along with Mrs. Stern, are downtown with Detective

Calloway."

"CC?" Stella asked and grinned when Mulligan nodded. "She must be loving this."

"Would you like me to contact my partner to confirm how many volts?"

"Not necessary. I can find Detective Calloway if I need her. Thank you, Detective Mulligan. If you don't mind, we have to help Mr. Stern. I'll come get you."

"CC has a new partner?" Stella questioned as they continued their work.

"News to me." Jamie sighed while her patient pleaded for his momma.

Jamie and her team did what little they could to alleviate Mr. Stern's pain before arranging to admit him. Once she felt confident enough to leave the fledgling doctors alone, she sought out Detective Mulligan. It wasn't hard to find the attractive woman, who was easily chatting with the nurses.

"Detective?" Jamie was curious about the woman who was suddenly working with her wife.

"Any news?"

"Not much to tell you." Jamie kept her tone even. "Mr. Stern suffered from a severe electrical shock."

"No kidding. Got to see it firsthand."

"Poor bastard." Jamie cringed. "We're admitting him. He's heavily sedated at the moment. He didn't say anything useful during his treatment. Mostly he just wailed, cried, and generally begged for mercy."

"Hey, I don't have the same equipment, and I felt for the guy."

"Me, too," Jamie couldn't help but agree. "Then again, you mess with your kid's nanny…"

"We don't think he did," Mulligan said. "We think the wife is a bit off. Right now, your wife sorry, I recognized you from the picture on Calloway's desk, she's questioning Mrs. Stern."

"I bet she's enjoying that." Jamie gave a laugh. "Are you all right?" She noticed a slight bruising on Mulligan's jaw.

"His wife punched me," Leigh grumbled. "One of your people already checked it out. Not that I needed it."

"You needed it for the arrest report." Jamie smiled. "I'm familiar with the need for paperwork."

"Being married to CC, you must be well versed in police procedures."

She was pleased that Mulligan had acknowledged her relationship with CC. It was a small thing, but it gave her comfort that this woman understood that CC was spoken for. She trusted CC; it was just nice to have all the cards on the table. In their early days, CC and Jamie had more than their fair share of misunderstandings.

"Are you new to homicide?" she asked.

"No," Mulligan said with a charming smile. "I'm with missing persons. This case turned into a kind of a crossover."

"I get it." Jamie nodded. "Can't talk about an ongoing investigation."

"An ER doc married to a cop. It must get interesting at

times."

"To say the least. I need to get back to it." Jamie offered her hand, pleased when Mulligan returned the gesture with a firm handshake. "It takes a long time to find a bed for a new patient. Why don't you keep Mr. Stern company?"

"Thank you, Dr. Jameson. I'll have a uniform stay with him. I need to go." Mulligan's voice turned grim as she checked her cell phone.

Jamie turned to resume her duties when she heard her name being paged. "Ah, that would be my wife calling to tell me know she's working late."

Chapter 7

CC had spent the better part of an hour with Mrs. Natalie Stern listening to her grouse about being held captive and calling her husband the most unflattering names. Then she expanded her vocabulary to some very nasty words regarding teenage girls.

"Again, Mrs. Stern, I advise you that you do have the right to remain silent." CC prayed that the nasty woman would heed her advice.

"Why are you keeping me here?" Mrs. Stern screeched. "I need to be with my children."

"Your in-laws are with the boys," CC said. "And you're here because you've broken the law."

"Please."

CC cringed at the way the woman tried to dismiss her. "Again, possession of a taser gun is illegal."

"I need to protect myself."

"Shooting your husband with a taser gun is considered assault, not self-defense."

"Bastard deserved it."

"Shooting him twice and refusing to stop is, again, assault and then there is resisting arrest and assaulting a police officer. You struck my partner when she tried to put the handcuffs on you."

"You people broke into my home and put me in handcuffs like I'm some sort of criminal. The nerve of you people!"

"We entered your residence because you were tasering your

husband." CC was stunned by the woman's insolence. "You could have killed him."

"Serves him right, the lying, cheating, son of a bitch."

"Who do you think he was having an affair with?"

"That British slut," she bellowed, as if it was obvious.

"Where is she?"

CC leaned forward when Mrs. Stern parted her lips. She was going to say it. CC could feel it in her bones. Then just as suddenly, Natalie Stern said, "I'd like to speak to my attorney" and turned mute.

"Okay." CC shrugged. "Have it your way. There will be an officer by to take you to booking. I hope you enjoy waiting for your attorney while sitting in a jail cell. Oh and I hope you know a good lawyer. Somehow I don't think your tax guy is going to be up for this."

Natalie Stern didn't even flinch. She still possessed the same annoyed look of boredom she had displayed since CC placed her in the back of a squad car. Unable to resist the urge to irk the woman, CC made a production out of snapping shut the folder in front of her and storming out of the room. She unclipped her cell phone from her belt and dialed the familiar number.

"Dr. Jameson, please." She rolled her shoulders in an effort to relieve the tension that had been building. "Hey, honey, I'm going to be late. Oh you did, did you?" She laughed when Jamie explained how she already met Mr. Stern. "I've got another call. I'll see you when I get in tonight. Love you."

"Love you, too. Stay safe," Jamie said and ended the call.

"Calloway," CC said to her other caller. She patiently listened as Mulligan explained the situation. "I'll be there as soon as I can." CC disconnected the call. She wanted to burst back into the interrogation room and throttle Natalie Stern. Instead, she entered the room adjacent to the one Mrs. Stern now occupied.

"Dennis, stop the tape. She asked for a lawyer," she told the tech who had been watching and taping the interview.

"Enjoying the show?" she asked Max, who was lurking in the corner.

"She didn't even blink." Max grunted. "The only thing she's done since you left is yawn."

"What can I say? She's a douche bag," CC said with a snarl. "Mulligan's on her way to the park. They found a body in the woods. I'm going there. Would you mind printing and booking Mrs. Stern?"

"I'll enjoy it."

"Are you interested now?"

"Now we have a body. That makes it homicide. Want me to sit on the Queen Mother while she waits for her lawyer? Or shall I just shove her into the disgusting, most crowded cell we have available? You know, the one where we park the working girls and junkies."

"It's like you read my mind."

Chapter 8

CC felt her stomach churn when she approached Mulligan, who was standing over the body. The woman was smaller than CC thought she would be. CC fought to keep her mind on the clinical.

"Female, late teens, early twenties," Marissa Vergas, the medical examiner, explained. "You taking over, Calloway?"

"We're sharing with missing persons."

"You know how to share?"

"Time of death?" CC ignored the jab. Marissa was an excellent medical examiner and a sore loser. A dozen or so years ago, they had dated. It had been brief. CC had moved on and mistakenly assumed that Marissa had done the same.

"The decomp has progressed, but the cold snap we've had the last couple of weeks makes it hard to pin down. I'd say at least a week. I'll know more when we get her back to the lab."

"We'll be in touch."

"What? You don't want to know cause of death?"

"I figured that expensive designer belt wrapped around her throat might have something to do with it." CC couldn't resist pushing the ME's buttons. She turned to Mulligan. "Armani?"

"Yes."

"Mrs. Stern lawyered up," CC said as they walked around the small mound of dirt that had become Annie Fuller's final resting place. "Max is booking her on the assault and weapons charges. Sticking her in a cell while she waits for her suit. Don't know who she'll call. I doubt a lady like that has a criminal defense mouthpiece on speed dial." She wasn't certain if Leigh had heard her. The detective just stood there staring down at poor Annie's body. "You okay?"

"No," Mulligan answered grimly. "I knew it. I knew it the first time I talked to Natalie Stern. Hell, I even knew why. I could just feel it."

"Now, we need to use that, so she doesn't get away it."

"Wish I could just beat the snot out of her. I've already called for the warrant. Should be ready before we get to the Stern's residence."

"You're way ahead of me." CC nodded with approval. "You go, and I'll meet you back at the station. I want to stop off at the hospital. I've got a couple of questions for Mr. Stern. Marissa, is there any way you can put a rush on this?" She hated asking the surly doctor for favors but the stakes were high.

"Strangled teenage girl dumped in a shallow grave? Calloway, you didn't even need to ask. Swing by the lab before you head back to the station."

"Thanks. Mulligan, if Mrs. Stern's mouthpiece shows up, why don't you start without me?"

"She hates me," Mulligan said. "Unless taking a swing at someone is the way she shows her endearment."

"Could be," CC tried to joke, feeling concerned by Mulligan's lack of confidence. "Look, you know what to do. If you're worried that she's going to get the best of you, take Max into the box. We don't have a lot of time. She'll be arraigned on the assault charges first thing in the morning."

"I'm not letting her walk."

"Good."

Chapter 9

Val was upset by the way things had turned out. "I should be on vacation," she muttered as she circled the quiet neighborhood. She had planned on checking out the house hours ago. For some reason, the GPS in her government issued sedan decided to take her on a tour of the entire state of Massachusetts.

She slowed the car and peered through the darkness as she caught a glimpse of a light. She calmed her breathing and studied the scene as best she could. She could see clearly through a window. A woman and a young girl sat watching television. The scene was peaceful.

"Let's hope it stays that way." She caught sight of a curtain move two doors down. "Good neighbors to boot." She smiled, assuming someone had noticed her car. She put the car in gear and went on her way.

* * *

CC grinned when she spied Jamie leaning against the nurses' station with her back to her. She crept up behind her, signaling for Stella not to give her away. She nuzzled Jamie's neck and purred when she felt her wife shivering against her touch. Things might have evolved in a different direction if they weren't in the middle of the hospital emergency room.

"Exciting night?" CC playfully whispered in Jamie's ear.

"Could be. But my wife is working late," Jamie teased turning to find her wife smiling down at her.

"Sorry about that."

"No, you're not." Jamie reached over and squeezed her arm.

"I haven't seen you this happy for a while."

"How are your new recruits? Give them the 'do your job or people die' speech, yet?"

"Am I that predictable?"

"You, predictable? Never. You can tell me all about the new goofballs tonight. In the meantime, I need to see a man about his nuts."

"Ah, Mr. Stern." Jamie nodded. "He's in bay three, crying like a baby. There's a uniform sitting outside. How crazy is his wife?"

"Just enough to be dangerous," CC said. "If you're sleeping when I get in, should I wake you?"

"You better." Jamie gave CC's backside a quick pat.

Bolstered with a sudden sense of urgency, CC quickly maneuvered her way around the treatment areas until she found Charles Stern. She paused for a moment to have a word with the officer who was standing guard.

"Door open, ears open," she told the bored looking patrolman.

"Anything you say, Detective."

"Thank you, Rodney." She blew into the treatment room. J.M. Charles Stern was curled up and still whimpering. CC couldn't fault the man.

"Which was more painful, the way your wife behaved or having your nuts toasted?"

"Get out of here," he said and groaned.

"I know it's been a long day." CC couldn't help feeling smug.

"I just need to take care of a couple of things first. J.M. Charles Stern, you have the right to remain silent; you have the right to an attorney,"

"What!" he screeched, sounding like a little girl. "I'm the one who was assaulted."

"And you refuse to press charges. Good thing here in the Commonwealth we can do it for you. Domestic violence is a very serious issue."

"Then why are you reading me my rights? I thought you only did that to people that you're planning on arresting?"

"We do." CC kept up her cheerful demeanor. "This has nothing to do with your assault. Personally, I couldn't give a damn if you were banging the nanny. She was over eighteen."

"I wasn't."

"Don't care." CC shrugged. "Unless that's why you killed her."

"I . . . what? She's dead?"

"Not to worry. Juries can be sympathetic. You got caught in a trap. Your wife obviously suspected something. The girl wouldn't take no for an answer. These things happen. A moment of rage. Now where was I? Oh yeah, you have the right to remain silent."

"What in the hell are you talking about? Annie's dead?"

"Come on, you knew that didn't you?"

"No! I had no idea. I had nothing to do with this. I swear I never touched the girl."

"You keep practicing that." CC felt the pieces slipping into place. It was no small wonder Natalie Stern ruled her household with an iron fist; Mr. Stern's spine seemed to be made of Jell-O. "Remember you have a right to an attorney. If you cannot afford one, one will be appointed for you. Do you understand your rights?"

"Yes, I understand. But I didn't do anything."

"Of course you didn't. Sorry, you've had a long day. Now, your wife is in jail, your boys are with your parents and your vital parts are on ice. All because a long time ago you dated someone else."

"What?"

"College wasn't it? I'm assuming it was before you were married."

"How did you know? Look that was nothing." He tried to defend himself. "Natalie and I hadn't been seeing each other for that long. I went to a concert with another girl. Aerosmith. I knew Natalie wouldn't have enjoyed it. That's it. That doesn't mean I had an affair with Annie. She's a child."

"Was," CC harshly corrected him. "So, an innocent trip to see Aerosmith, over a decade ago. That's why your wife doesn't trust you? Seriously, you couldn't have been that surprised she snapped. Women can be so mistrusting. When I first started dating my wife, an old flame of mine kissed me. I was surprised. It wasn't planned or welcome. But who should walk by at that very moment, but my girlfriend."

"What happened? After she caught you?"

"I explained what happened, and she forgave and forgot," CC calmly explained. "That's what normal people do. They don't hold a grudge. They don't hold it over your head for the rest of your life.

They don't shoot you with a taser gun. And they most certainly don't kill the nanny. Before you get sucked in and start defending your loving wife, ask yourself something. Is this the person you want raising your sons?"

The stunned look on his face spoke volumes. CC had what she needed from the man. He gave her a tidbit of information that could prove useful. Most importantly, CC had managed to plant a seed of doubt. She had seen it time and time again. The spouse commits a heinous crime, and for some reason, their other half not only stands by them but begins to believe whatever lie the lawyers spin for the press and the jury. CC was hoping to nudge a wedge between the happy suburbanites. If Natalie Stern was forced to stand alone, there was a very good chance she'd crack.

CC made a quick trip to the morgue and crime labs. She gathered what she needed and headed back to the station. She ducked into the observation room and offered Dennis a cup of coffee while he watched the scene.

"How is she doing?"

"Mulligan?"

"Yeah." CC watched in an effort to gauge what was going on. By the way Max was leaning back, she felt confident that Leigh was on top of things.

"She's got her spinning her wheels," Dennis said and took a sip of his coffee. "Helps that the lawyers seem dazed and confused. The older one is her estate attorney. The kid is the criminal lawyer. The old guy called him in after he realized how deep of a pile his client stepped in."

"Geez, is that kid old enough to shave?"

Dennis shrugged. "He had his card. I doubt he passed the bar all that long ago."

"That could be a problem." CC grimaced. "Let's hope he's smart and not out to prove how good he is."

"So far he's just sitting there looking like he's going to piss himself. Mulligan said she found what you need in the husband's closet. She said to tell you it's in the box." CC noticed the standard cardboard box resting on the table. "She's been showing Mrs. Stern pictures."

"Annie's family?"

"No." Dennis chuckled. "Magazine pictures. Your vic had a crush on Shemar Moore, you know… the actor. Nothing stalkerish. Just the usual teenage girl stuff."

"Really?"

"Listen."

"Take a look, Mrs. Stern." Leigh slid a copy of People magazine over to the confused woman. "That was Annie's dream man. Can't say that I blame her. Shemar Moore is seriously hot."

"I got to agree with Mulligan on that one," CC said.

"Really?"

"I feel very secure in my sexuality, but even I have to admit that is one good-looking guy. Don't you think so?"

"Guys don't notice things like that."

"Maybe." CC returned her attention to the interrogation.

"Now look at him and look at your husband." Leigh slid another photo across the table. This one was of the Stern family.

"This guy is tall, dark, buff, and very handsome. No offense, but your husband is a scrawny, dweeby guy. Not even close to Annie's ideal man. Why in the world would you think she'd even look at him twice?"

"Good," CC said. "Time for me to make an appearance."

CC swooped into the interrogation room filled with confidence. She kept a large envelope close to her chest.

"Mind if I join in?" She pushed Max aside so she could sit next to Leigh. "Mrs. Stern, so nice to see you again. I hope you're enjoying our accommodations."

"You piece of..." Natalie Stern snarled. "You had me locked up in that disgusting cell. The people, and I use the term loosely, were disgusting. I plan on filing charges."

"Yeah, me, too." CC yawned. "Nice pictures. So tell me which is harder, being locked up with your fellow citizens or having an attractive teenager flaunting her bits and pieces around your husband?"

"The girl was a slut."

Both CC and Leigh looked over at the lawyers. The older one seemed concerned. The younger one seemed confused. CC couldn't help thinking that a halfway decent lawyer would have called an end to the Q and A long before CC arrived.

"You can't blame her," CC said when the lawyers failed to object. "She was a kid. Interesting how you keep referring to Annie in the past tense."

The youngster finally spoke, "That doesn't mean anything."

CC felt a jolt of adrenaline when his voice cracked. "Sure it does. So, what was it? The way she threw herself at good old Snaps or-"

"How did you...?" Natalie's face turned beet red.

"Hey, I get it. You trained him. Forgave him. And here he goes again, sneaking off to an Aerosmith concert with some British chippy. Worse, messing around in your house. The house you picked out. You did, didn't you? Found the right neighborhood. The perfect house to raise your children, and this girl comes in and takes what's yours. So tell me, where did you find it?"

"What?"

"Her bed was trashed." CC opened the envelope without revealing the contents. "Under the bed? Beneath the mattress? Between the sheets? Kind of ironic, since if it wasn't for you, he'd still be wearing those silly suspenders. Yeah, if it wasn't for you, good old Snaps would be trolling rock concerts with some phi beta fuck 'em whore. So where did you find the belt?"

"What belt?" The youngster tried to intervene, seemingly unaware of the wild look in his client's eyes. "I think this interview is—"

"The nightstand!" Natalie bellowed. "The whore left it out in plain sight. Flaunting their dirty little affair in my face. I showed her."

"Yes you did." CC grimly slammed the evidence bag containing the belt that had been wrapped around Annie Fraser's neck. The same belt that had choked the life out of the vibrant young woman. "This belt? This is what you used to choke the life out of her? I bet she denied the affair when you found you in her room."

"Lying bitch."

"She stood there in your home, lying to you." CC shook her

head. "You had the belt. Proof that she was screwing your husband. I bet you bought this belt for him, didn't you?"

"Of course. I can't let him shop on his own. She told me I had no right to be in her room. Her room? Then she called me insane for accusing her of sleeping with my husband. I had the proof."

"Yes, here it is." CC tapped the bag. "You had to protect your family. Claim what is yours. What woman wouldn't?"

"I wouldn't," Leigh said.

"You." Mrs. Stern brushed her off. "What do you know? A divorced civil servant."

"Tell us about it," CC said. Mulligan slid a legal pad of paper and a pen across the table.

"That's enough," the older lawyer finally said. "Natalie, we need to take a moment."

"No." Mrs. Stern shook her head. "That girl was ruining everything. My sons listened to her more than to me. What does that tell you?" Filled with self-assurance, she snatched up the pen.

"Natalie." Once again, the lawyer was unable to stop his client. Natalie Stern muttered bitterly while furiously scribbling down her thoughts.

"Seems your client is ignoring your advice, counselor." CC couldn't help rubbing salt in the wound.

"For now," he said.

"Annie Fraser was a British citizen," Leigh forewarned the suits. "They aren't happy. Neither am I. Annie was nineteen. She had her whole life in front of her until she had the misfortune of meeting your client." While making her point, Leigh slid a sheet of paper over to CC. Max nodded while CC smiled at the waiver. Natalie Stern had been advised of her rights, and she had even signed the papers to prove it.

"For the love of God, Natalie, stop writing."

"What kind of deal are you offering?" The younger lawyer watched in horror as his client shoved her signed statement into CC's hands.

"None." CC sounded bored while she read the statement. "Why would we? She's confessed in writing and on audio and videotape. She'll be arraigned in the morning." CC checked her watch. Her eyes bulged as she noted how much time had passed. "Make that in a couple of hours. Relax, boys, she'll hire someone new. All you have to do is enter a not guilty plea. Just one more thing." She nodded to Leigh.

Leigh removed another evidence bag from the cardboard box. She tossed the belt onto the table.

"What?" Natalie sputtered.

"That's your husband's belt," Leigh said triumphantly. "We executed a search warrant and found it in his closet. That" she stressed while pointing to the other belt. "is Annie's belt."

"No. I know what I saw. This is some kind of cop trick. I won't be fooled."

"Look at the pictures again," Leigh said. "The one of Annie with her family back in England. She's wearing the belt. You murdered the girl because she had the misfortune to share your sense of fashion. She never touched your sorry excuse of a husband."

"You did," CC said. "Shot him in the nuts with a taser gun.

Which is illegal on so many levels. The saddest part of all of this is a young girl is dead because you were too lazy or stupid to look in your husband's closet. Do you need a moment with your counsel before we kick you back to your cell?"

Natalie Stern sputtered and howled about being framed. CC, Max, and Leigh ignored her. They packed up the evidence and made a hasty retreat.

"I feel like I need a shower," Leigh said once they made it safely into the hallway.

"Calloway!" Justine Harper, a young ADA, emerged from the audio room. "How much do I love you?"

"Feeling chipper this morning, are you?"

"I watched the whole thing. Damn, you got her good."

"Yeah." CC handed over the signed statement. "Mulligan did the work. This was her case. I just wish we had found the girl alive."

"We all do," Justine said. "But I'm not going to feel bad about having a slam dunk in my pocket."

"Don't get ahead of yourself." CC rolled her eyes. "You know by the time she hires a smarter, more expensive suit, the circus will really get started. He'll argue probable cause, all of a sudden Natalie's idyllic childhood will be traumatic because Daddy raised his voice once or missed a dance recital. Or my all-time favorite, she'll claim she should have been on meds and the fairies told her to do bad, bad things. If by some miracle, her confession and the interview tapes get booted, we've got nothing and she walks."

"Just get me your statements, ASAP."

"Thanks for reminding us," Max grumbled. "Us being new in town and all. Come on, ladies, I'll buy the coffee."

* * *

Val knew she had ruffled more than a few feathers. She didn't care, and she wasn't in the mood to stroke bruised egos. She dove right in. With a team together, she would start a plan. She figured that Beaumont had limited funds available and would be looking to stay with friends or family. But she couldn't really find anything that would indicate he had anyone in the area who gave a damn about him. She'd keep digging to see if she could shake something loose.

In the meantime, she put together the teams, one to watch the Calloway sisters and another canvassing the local shelters and rooming houses. On the run and just out of prison, this guy was probably on a budget. The bus ticket would only set him back thirty bucks or so. Still, Val was betting that the little money Beaumont earned from his crappy roofing job didn't leave much for shelter or food.

Where the hell was this guy? Why the hell would he go anywhere near his well-armed and extremely angry stepdaughter? Or did he just run to safer ground and was she wasting precious time?

Chapter 10

Jamie had a short meeting with Jack before he left for the day. Then she met with the other doctors who would be assigned interns and residents. She knew who she wanted to keep for herself. Alvarez topped the list. She had to give her a day shift instead, so the young doctor could work out her babysitting issues. Jamie was impressed. Not only that as a single mother she had put herself through med school, the young woman was showing signs that one day she would be a great doctor. Jamie hated handing her brightest student over to another doctor.

"Sucks being the boss." Jamie posted the list and listened to the usual grumbling and complaining from her students. No matter how fair she tried to be, someone was always unhappy.

"Nights? For real?" Tierney groused.

"We could switch you to the butt crack of dawn," Jamie said. She smirked at the look of horror in Dr. Tierney's dark brown eyes. "Nights means you work with me."

"Cool." The young woman quickly backpedaled.

"Yeah, cool." Jamie didn't have the heart to tell Tierney she had put her on the late shift because she doubted her ability to make an early call.

Alvarez took a moment away from the others to thank Jamie for her schedule. "I wish I was on your team but—"

"I get it." Jamie smiled. "I wanted to keep you, but you have little Lola to worry about. This is tough enough without the added responsibility you're carrying. If you have any questions or needs, my door is always open."

Jamie went back to work, unable to avoid hearing the comments from her new students. Half of them felt slighted that they hadn't made her team. The other half were relieved, since she had the reputation of being a hard ass. Those that did make her team were either elated or frightened. She chose the best and the worst to work with her. The best since they deserved it and the worst because she wanted to keep an eye on them. She instructed the students to meet with their respective team leader as soon as possible. Then she reminded them to check the schedule each day since changes were always happening.

Jamie loved emergency medicine, but she hated the paperwork and useless nonsense that went along with being in a supervisory position. There were times she wished she could go back to being a basic ER doctor. But that wasn't what Boylston General had hired her to be. Then again, with the threat of budget cuts looming on the horizon, she could end up being just another doctor.

She kept the team together for the rest of the night. The young doctors tried to keep up. Jamie chuckled when she heard one of them complaining how busy it was. Stella just glared at the youngster.

"This? This is slow," Stella told the whining student.

"She isn't kidding. Now move," Jamie added for good measure.

"Coffee?" Stella suggested once the frightened student darted off.

"I'll meet you in the break room, right after I check to make sure none of them has killed anyone yet."

When Jamie made the rounds, all was well with the exception of Tierney who was nowhere to be found. Jamie muttered under her breath before heading into the break room to join Stella.

She had to stop herself from shouting when she found Tierney sitting with Stella, enjoying a cup of coffee and a snack.

"Hey," Tierney said as if she hadn't a care in the world.

"Isn't there something you could be doing besides eating cookies?"

"Uh-huh, just leaving." Her head bobbed up and down as she slowly stood.

"And, Tierney, rethink the earrings." Jamie noted the large hoops. "If you have a junkie on the table, they'll rip those right out and not in a nice way."

"Good to know."

Jamie furrowed her brow as she took a seat and Tierney remained in the room. "Yes?"

"Is it true that your cold tude is just an act?"

"You're direct. I'll give you that. Hate to disappoint you, but this isn't an act. I am a bitch."

"Right. That's why Alvarez is on a shift that works around her daughter's day care schedule."

"Look," Jamie said slowly, "I used to try the soft 'let's be friends' approach. But I had a problem with one of residents. And now I find it best to keep my distance."

"What happened?"

Jamie wasn't put off by the girl's directness. "He killed another resident, along with at least eight other women. By the time the police figured it out, he tried to kill me," Jamie said in a matter-of-fact tone. "So, no, I don't do warm and fuzzy."

"Damn."

"Could you get your ass back on the floor?" Jamie tried to sound gruff. She failed. Despite this girl's obvious lack of dedication, there was something endearing about her. Much to her surprise, Dr. Tierney actually complied with her request with very little stalling.

"That one sees right through you," Stella said with a grin.

"Hey, I'm still a hard-ass."

"Right."

The night wore on with the usual mishaps, paperwork, and issues that only Jamie seemed to be capable of dealing with. After Mr. Stern and his police escort had been moved to a room upstairs, Jamie set about finishing up neglected administrative duties. Her wife was working late, and both of them were probably in for the long haul tomorrow.

Finally, around four in the morning, she was on her way home. When she pulled up to the Victorian home that had been converted into a duplex, she felt at peace. When the three were first shown the house, it was in desperate need of love and hard work, and they fell in love with it. This was home. The only thing missing was Caitlin's Subaru in the parking space next to her own.

Jamie shouldered her work bag and headed into the house. She paused and checked to reassure herself that everything was all right. Another little gift from her time with Simon Fisher; she was overly cautious. Nothing seemed amiss, so she disabled the very high-tech alarm system. One of the many great things about being married to a cop her wife knew the best security people in the Boston area. She reset the alarm and put her work bag aside. She wasn't troubled that CC had to work late. Given their professions, when one or the other had to work late it could easily mean well into the next day or even the day after that.

She stripped and showered and donned more comfortable clothing. In the kitchen, she put on the tea kettle. A quiet house after a long day called for one of two things: a long hot bubble bath or a nice hot cup of tea. If the night was rocky enough, both were needed. The kettle whistled, and she set about brewing her tea. The knock on the door that connected Stevie's side of the house to theirs wasn't a surprise.

Stevie had probably been waiting up for either her or Caitlin to get home and, when she heard the tea kettle, decided to visit. How good it felt to have family so close. Her own family was back in Maryland, which wasn't that far. Yet, there were times when it felt like a million miles separated them. Having Stevie and their niece, Emma, just a door away felt comforting.

"Morning," her sister-in-law said.

"Come on in. Can I get you a cup?"

"No thanks. Just waiting up for you crazy kids."

They settled on the sofa. Jamie flipped on the television out of habit. She selected the local news station and turned the volume down so she could chat with Stevie.

"How did the meeting go?"

"Good." Stevie handed Jamie an expensive-looking 4g phone. "I got a new client and some free stuff to share. I'll transfer from your old one. It will take a moment." She explained connecting the phones to her laptop with a cable. "Once this is in place, your new account will be activated."

"Cool." Jamie studied the new gadget before retrieving her old cell for Stevie. "This is nice. I can shoot movies in HD, go online, and probably bake a pie. I love it."

"I have one for Caitlin as well." Stevie finished transferring Jamie's information. "You can go online and download about a gazillion different apps. You know just in case you have a sudden need to know the weather in Istanbul."

"Thank you."

"Don't thank me. Thank my new client." Stevie handed the shiny new phone back to Jamie. "I was getting worried after losing three clients this year. One went belly up, another decided to cut back and do their own website, and Marcus Styles died. Not a big surprise. Everything that man ate was deep fried. This is the first year I've not only failed to gain new clients, I've lost some. Of course it happened right after we bought this place. Don't get me wrong, I love this house and the neighborhood."

"I know." Jamie reluctantly set aside her new toy. "Your condo was paid off, and now we have a mortgage and a bad economy. Like I said yesterday, we're ahead. Don't worry. If the hospital starts cutting back, I know I can find work. And it seems CC feels certain that if the department starts making cuts she's going to be okay. Speaking of which..." Jamie's attention was drawn to the television. "I think this is why she's working late." She turned up the volume.

The overly perky newscaster said, "Natalie Stern, mother of two from Boylston Village Hills, will be arraigned this morning facing charges of assault and possibly murder."

"She tasered her husband right in the jewels," Jamie said. "Poor guy won't have any feeling in his tackle box anytime soon."

"Work!" Stevie gasped as CC entered the house.

CHECKMATE

"Whatever happened to doctor-patient confidentially?" CC teased her wife. She gave Jamie a quick kiss, shuffled into the kitchen, and studied the chessboard.

Jamie laughed. "I respect it. But if you think anyone who was working the ER tonight didn't go home and tell someone about poor Mr. Stern getting his nuts toasted, you're sadly mistaken. So, did she kill the nanny?"

"Yes," CC called out. "She's going to be arraigned in a couple of hours."

She finally made her move. "That'll teach you," she said, gloating, before she remembered she was playing with a child. "Tell Emma it's her move," she told Stevie when she returned to the living room. "Nice phone."

"I have a new client."

"Great news, sis."

"And she got free stuff." Jamie was already playing with the new gizmo.

"It's huge," CC noted.

"I have one for you."

"Oh, my old phone is fine," CC said while Jamie snickered.

Jamie understood that her wife feared new gadgets because she was more than a little technologically challenged.

"Your phone barely holds a charge anymore. Give Stevie your old phone, and let her explain what this new one can do."

"I just need to download the information from your SIM

card," Stevie tried to explain while CC reluctantly handed over her old cell phone.

"The what?"

"It's a tiny chip inside your phone," Stevie said. "It holds all of your information in your old phone. The new one is different. Same theory but different."

"But what about my numbers? I don't know any of them."

"That is why I'm downloading all of your information," Stevie patiently explained. "This new phone is a smart phone. You can listen to music, surf the web, send email, take pictures and videos, check the weather—"

"Can I make phone calls?" CC grumbled, shedding her coat.

"Yes." Stevie impressed Jamie by the way she stayed calm. "I'll go over everything with you."

"Just show me how to answer the phone and dial out. Oh, and I need to know how to shut the ringer off, for when I'm in court."

"Caitlin," Jamie said, "say thank you."

"Thank you, Stevie."

"It's okay, James, I've known my dear sister all of my life. Her limits when it comes to the technological advances of the twenty-first century aren't a revelation. If I hadn't insisted, she'd still be trying to use a beta max and dealing with basic cable. Not to worry. I'll show her how everything works, so she won't bug you to do it later."

"You are such a good sister in-law."

"I am."

"I don't need to do a bunch of stuff," CC tried to argue.

"Probably not," Stevie said. "But when you see everyone else doing it, you'll get all cranky."

"I can't even send a text."

"Now you can." Stevie pulled CC down onto the sofa and showed her how to slide the images around. "In fact you can send a voice text by tapping the little microphone. Or just use the keypad and type. That way you won't end up cursing at the autocorrect." CC's eyes widen with delight. "See you'll love this new phone."

"I hate the way they keep changing things," CC said.

"No, you don't." Stevie laughed. "You hate that Emma is better at these things then you are. She's a kid. Which means she's going to surpass all of us. She already texts twice as fast as I do."

"She's too young to be using a cell phone." CC gave a huff.

"I agree, sis." Stevie showed another feature to CC, well aware that her sister's attention was already drifting. "Emma has a very basic phone that allows her very limited calling. I only caved in so she could get in touch with one of us in case of emergency."

"Okay, I'll try the new phone."

Jamie couldn't help laughing as Stevie painstakingly took CC through the basic steps to operating her new phone. She listened so she could work her own phone and help CC when she got stuck.

"I don't see why you would need a phone to film a video," CC said. "But thank you. I hate to cut things short, ladies. I need to take a quick shower before I head downtown for the arraignment."

"I need to get back and check on Emma. Enjoy the phones."

Stevie excused herself.

Jamie followed CC upstairs to the master bathroom. "Long day?"

"Yes." CC yawned and, much to Jamie's delight, stripped off her clothing. "It felt good."

"You're not the type that's happy with being idle."

"Sitting around doing nothing while the crime rate was going up didn't feel right." CC stretched out her tired limbs.

"Hmm." Jamie sighed. "Nice stretching."

"Pervert," CC teased giving Jamie one last peek before she stepped into the shower. "I think once the paperwork and court appearance are out of the way, I'll duck back here and try to catch a nap."

"Mulligan seemed nice," Jamie said absently, her mind far too busy watching CC lather her entire body. She was pleased that CC took extra care to rub soap over her firm full breasts.

"The boss is thinking of teaming us up together after Max clocks out," CC said. "He's worried about pairing two women together."

"The more things change," Jamie grumbled.

"There's going to be a spot open. With Max retiring and Andy not able to clean up his act, our department is going to be safe from any cuts."

"Think there will be cuts?"

"Don't you? I'm lucky. Seniority wise, I'm smack dab in the middle, so I won't get hit." CC rinsed off, and the sight of the soap sliding down her body nearly made Jamie swoon. "The

Boss said my closure rate is so high there have been a lot of requests to ride with me."

"I keep telling you that you're the best." Jamie wrapped CC up in towel. "And not just at catching the bad guys," she added before stealing a lingering kiss.

"I wish we could play hooky today." CC sounded wistful.

"The weekend will be here soon enough," Jamie added before she stole another kiss.

Chapter 11

Stevie took a deep breath when she stepped out into the crisp autumn air. The year was passing too quickly. They had just planted the asters to bring a little color to the yard, and now it was time to get back to raking up the leaves. Jamie was busy getting ready for an early meeting at the hospital, and Caitlin was wrapped up with her new case.

Stevie decided that she'd enjoy the fresh air. The fact that it was right about the time for Misty to deliver the mail was a happy coincidence. She tugged on her work gloves and began her work, keeping a careful eye out for the lovely mail carrier. She shivered slightly, unable to shake the feeling that she was being watched.

"Cop car." She spotted the sleek black SUV slowly circle by.

"That seems to be the general consensus." Misty startled her.

"Folks have been noticing it for about a week now. Freda and Ethel, the older couple down the block, called it in. The cops said they'd check it out."

"Really?" Stevie made a mental note to talk to her older sister about it. "Wait, those nice old ladies are a couple?"

"Oh, yeah. They got married a few years ago when the laws changed. For the longest time, I didn't realize it either. Turns out they've been together for almost sixty years."

"I'm loving this new neighborhood more and more." Stevie stole a glimpse of Misty's well-toned biceps. Silently, she cursed the change in weather that forced the attractive woman to stop wearing shorts on her route.

"You're a nice addition," Misty said shyly.

CHECKMATE

Before Stevie could think of something to say in response, Jamie rushed out from her side of the house. "Stevie? I'm running late. Would you mind calling the plumber?"

"No problem." Stevie cringed as Misty handed her a bundle of mail and went on her way. Jamie shouted her thanks before taking off.

"Great. Missed my chance to chat up the hot mail lady, and now I have to wait around all day for a plumber. This day sucks."

* * *

On that late September morning, Malcolm Fisher was in his favorite place in the world. Swinging his nine iron on a lush field of green. He was having the best game of his life.

"Not getting too much sun are you?" his caddy, Josh, asked.

"What?" Malcolm coughed.

"You're red all over."

Malcolm looked down at his arms before scowling. "Damn, never even felt it. Go in the bag and grab my EpiPen will you?"

"You got stung?"

"Must have. Wonder when the little bastard nailed me?" he grumbled as Josh handed him the EpiPen. "I just need to find a place to..."

"No one is around," Josh said. "Want me to do it?"

"Fine." Malcolm felt humiliated as he lowered his checkered pants slightly. "Just make it quick. I'm really not in the mood to have someone wander by and catch me with my pants down."

"Not to worry." Josh flipped off the cap from the yellow device and placed the plunger against Malcolm's thigh. Then he pushed and the medicine entered Malcolm's body.

Malcolm's face turned crimson. He fell and began convulsing. Before the ambulance could arrive, Malcolm Fisher was dead.

Detective Brooks attended the funeral. The two men shared an uneasy relationship. Brooks had spent years pursuing Simon. Malcolm hadn't thought much of the detective in the early days. After Simon's arrest in Boston, Malcolm finally accepted that Brooks wasn't a misguided idiot. It was Brooks who made the call to Boston.

Chapter 12

The day his father died, Simon had been summoned from his cell. No one told him why he was being escorted to a private conference room. He was shackled to the table and left alone. Simon tried to look timid as he sat in the sterile room.

"Dr. Richards and Dr. Watkins. I'm honored. What brings you around? Writing another book, Dr. Richards?"

Amelia Richards didn't even flinch. After spending quality time with Dr. Fisher, she had made it clear that she was ready to do whatever needed to be done in order to keep this man incarcerated for the rest of his natural life.

"I have some bad news for you, Simon," she said. "Your father passed away this afternoon."

"Dear God, no." Simon buried his face in his hands and appeared to be sobbing. "When is the funeral?"

"Day after tomorrow."

"I assume my lawyer will work out the details." He sniffed. "My poor mother must be beside herself."

"Simon." Dr. Watkins cut in. "You won't be attending. The chaplain will meet with you if you would like some counseling or perhaps a chance to pray."

"What?" Simon slammed his fist against the flimsy table he was shackled to. His tears magically vanished. "This isn't right. My father died. I should be there to comfort my mother. I have the right to say goodbye to him."

"No, you don't," Dr. Richards said. "You lost that right when you murdered nine innocent women."

"No one is innocent."

"Do you want to talk about it?" she asked. "How this makes you feel?"

"How do you think I feel?" he shouted. "My father is dead, and I can't even say goodbye. All because of some vengeful, delusional dyke. I want my lawyer. I am going to my father's funeral."

"We'll contact your attorney," Dr. Richards said. "But, just so we are clear, because of your attempts at escape you won't be allowed to attend. It's time for you to accept that actions have consequences. In fact, it's past time. We can discuss this in more detail if you'd like to set up a time to meet."

"We'll see." He waved her off. "At least, my father died doing what he loved. Nothing meant more to him than a good day out on the golf course."

"I'm sorry for your loss," Dr. Richards said. Simon was escorted back to his cell.

"He's a piece of work," Watson said with a grunt. "No way a judge lets him out. Of course it helps that his lawyer doesn't really seem interested in helping him. The day of his last hearing, I swear she was chanting *Three Blind Mice* under her breath. Some of them are nuttier than their clients."

"Harvey, didn't you hear what he said?"

"About no one being innocent?" He shuddered. "Yeah, that little bastard gives me the creeps."

"Not that." Dr. Richards fought to calm herself. "He said at least his father died happy on the golf course."

CHECKMATE

"We never said—"

"No we never said, and he didn't ask how or where his father died. How did he know?"

Chapter 13

CC had the day off and was busy with Emma, carving pumpkins. She loved days like this. Just time alone with her niece. It reminded her of when Stevie was little and she taught her baby sister how to carve a pumpkin. It also reminded her of when she was just a little younger than Emma. Sitting around the kitchen table, her mother busy cooking, her father and brother each taking turns to help her carve the perfect pumpkin. Life was simple, and her family was truly happy. That was before her brother, Donny, succumbed to the pressure of being bullied. Before her father and mother began to fight. Before her father chose to work long, exhausting hours rather than come home. Before her father, overwrought from stress, fell asleep at the wheel of the family Buick.

"That is a very scary pumpkin, peanut," she said. She frowned slightly at the Orioles cap Emma still insisted on wearing. Her cell phone rang before she could conjure up something clever to say that might encourage Emma to start wearing her Red Sox cap again. "Saved by the bell. Calloway," she greeted her caller without checking the number. She was just relieved that she managed to answer the phone. Normally, with the new phone the call went to voice mail before she could swipe the answer button properly.

"It's Brooks."

"Hey, hold on. Emma, put the knife down for a moment. I need to take this call. No, carving until I'm back . Got it, peanut?"

"Yes." Emma pouted, but she did as CC told her.

"Brooks?" CC's stomach churned as she ducked into the living room. She fumbled with the phone, still trying to get comfortable with the new gadget. "What's going on?"

"Relax," he said. "Simon isn't on the lam or anything."

"Shit, you scared me."

"Language!" Emma scolded her from the kitchen.

"Sorry, I'll put a dollar in the jar."

"What?"

"My niece busted me for cussing," CC sheepishly said. "What's up?"

"Malcolm Fisher died."

"When?"

"The other day. Some kind of allergic reaction while he was playing golf."

"He's allergic to golf?"

"You're a pain in the ass."

"That'll cost you a dollar," CC quipped. "So, what happened?"

"Bee sting or something like that. I don't know. Just thought you'd want to know. I went to the service, although I doubt his widow was pleased to see me."

"You framed her baby boy. Didn't you know that?"

"That woman will never face reality."

"Speaking of her baby boy," CC said. "They didn't let him out for the funeral, did they?"

"No," Brooks answered firmly. "Lawyer kicked up a fuss, but Simon's an escape risk. Can't blame anyone but himself."

"Never stopped him before."

"True enough. I just wanted you to know in case you wanted to send flowers or something."

"Mrs. Fisher hates me more than she does you," she said. "Malcolm told me once that he's involved with the National MS Society. I'll make a donation in his name."

"Auntie Caitlin?"

"I've got to go. Thanks for letting me know."

CC didn't know what to feel. She and Malcolm Fisher had formed an uneasy alliance. She respected the man's character. Most parents never accept their children's shortcomings. Mr. Fisher accepted not only what his son had done but what he was capable of doing. CC knew that it broke his heart, but he was determined to keep his son locked up. CC had learned in the passing years that there was nothing anyone could have done to stop Simon. He was a classic sociopath, and there was no rhyme or reason for it.

She retook her seat at the kitchen table and smiled, pleased that Emma had kept her word and wasn't playing with the knife. She put her phone down on the table and set about clearing away pumpkin guts. When she glanced over, she noticed Emma fiddling with her new cell phone.

She was more than a little curious as to what Emma was doing with her phone. She peered over and her jaw dropped. There sat Emma, easily guiding her way through a forest, fighting a dragon, and entering a castle.

"Those graphics are amazing." CC was unable to understand how realistic the game seemed that Emma had somehow managed to make appear on her phone. "How are you doing that?" She was completely astonished at how adept Emma was at what seemed like a very complicated game.

"This game is easy." Emma shrugged as if it were no big deal. She finished the game and handed CC her phone. "You can play chess on it, too. Did you have video games when you were little, Auntie Caitlin?"

"Have you ever heard of Pong?"

The blank stare she received was all the answer she needed. "Okay, let's get back to making the best jack-o-lantern ever."

By the time they finished, CC was convinced they had indeed made the best jack-o-lantern ever. She knew it was too early, and they would need to carve another set of pumpkins next month.

After chasing around a crazy suburbanite that thought killing her nanny was a dandy idea, a calm day spent with Emma was just what CC needed. Emma was innocent, sweet, and plotting on convincing her mother that they should get a dog. Emma was doing her very best to enlist her aunt into helping her.

"I don't know, Emma. A puppy is a big responsibility."

"I can do it, Auntie Caitlin."

"I'll talk to her but no promises." CC instantly regretted caving in. During Stevie's childhood, CC was the one who raised her. Their mother just let the youngster take over. CC felt a need to protect her sister. Sadly, the person Stevie needed the most protection from was her father, something their mother refused to believe. Now all these years later, after refusing to allow Stevie to get a puppy, she was in collusion with her niece. She would wait until later to talk to Stevie when she was rested and Emma was off to spend the weekend with her father, Brad.

* * *

Later in the afternoon, CC was sitting on the sofa watching television with Emma while Jamie was upstairs in her office working. She couldn't stop thinking about the phone call from Brooks. It was a shock to hear that someone she had just seen a short time ago had died. Normally, if they did, it was related to work, not her life.

"I'll be right back," she said to Emma who was wrapped up in the exploits of The Wizards of Waverly Place. "I just need to talk to Auntie Jamie for a moment."

"Okay." Emma shrugged. CC knew the little imp was still working on her plot to get a puppy. In many ways, Emma really did remind her of Stevie. If that was true, they were in for a fun ride over the next couple of years.

CC smiled when she peeked into Jamie's home office, which was right across the hall from her own. She loved watching Jamie. The doctor was wrapped up with some project on her computer, seemingly unaware that her wife was watching her. Or so CC thought.

"Are you just going to stand there?" Jamie asked, peering over her glasses.

"I'm admiring the view."

"Behave, we have the rug rat downstairs," Jamie said playfully.

"I just had a medical question." CC regretted her words when Jamie tore off her glasses and looked over at her with fright. "About someone else," she said quickly. "What can you tell me about allergies?"

"What kind? Are we talking mold spores, seasonal, pollen, or something more serious?"

"More serious. Like something that can kill you."

"Anaphylaxis," Jamie said in a careful tone. "Better known as anaphylactic shock. It's quite common. People can be allergic to a great many things that can kill them. Peanuts, medications, spider bites, and a whole list of other things."

"Like bee stings?"

"Bee venom is a very common allergy," Jamie said in a direct tone. "Without immediate treatment for anything from hives to difficulty breathing and swallowing, a person can die from being unable to breathe or from a heart attack. Usually, if a person gets treated right away with antihistamines and epinephrine, they should be fine. Most people with an allergy that severe carry an EpiPen."

"What's that?"

"It's about so big." Jamie demonstrated with her hands. "It has a plunger so a person can jab it into their thigh to shoot epinephrine into their system. Stops the venom from spreading, restores their breathing, and slows their heart rate. Someone die?"

"Malcolm Fisher went out to play eighteen holes and met up with a bee that didn't like him."

"That's a shame. He seemed nice," Jamie said in a sincere tone.

"I always felt bad for him. Not his fault his son is a psycho."

"I know."

"Anything else?"

"Thought you should know Emma is plotting to get a puppy," CC said. "She's wants our help."

"Good luck with that."

"I said 'our' help, Blondie."

"Again, good luck."

"If you think she's not going to drag you into this, you are sadly mistaken."

"I'm staying out of it."

"Yeah, right."

* * *

"No." Stevie was unmovable.

"But—"

"But nothing, sis. Maybe down the road, not now. Emma isn't responsible enough for a pet. Or have you forgotten about Goldie the fish?"

"There could have been something wrong with that fish."

"Or Emma overfed the poor little thing. A puppy is a lot more work than a fish."

"We have a big backyard now," CC said.

"Hey, you wouldn't let me have a puppy at her age, and for good reason." Stevie stood her ground. "I'm not saying never, just not now."

"You wouldn't let her have a puppy?" Jamie said.

"No. I had her practice with a stuffed animal. You know,

getting up in the morning to walk it, then again at night, and making sure it was fed."

"Which I eventually lost interest in," Stevie said. "After a solid week of getting up at the butt crack of dawn, the idea lost some of its appeal."

"I have no doubt," Jamie said. "What I was surprised by was that it was Caitlin who made that decision. When Stevie was Emma's age, you wouldn't have been that much older."

"Don't go there," CC said and groaned. "Mom was Mom, and Stevie's father was... well, you know."

"A big pedophile who was waiting to get you out of the way so he could try to put the moves on me and my friends," Stevie tersely explained. "No puppy. Is that clear?"

"Yes."

"What if we got one?" Jamie shyly offered.

"No trying an end run here, ladies. You forget the two of you work the late shift. Not to mention, given the nature of your careers, you don't punch out at an exact time. I'm the one who works from home. Ergo, I'm the one who'll be cleaning up puppy poop. No thank you. In a couple of years, Emma will be able to take on the responsibility. In the meantime, I'm getting her a stuffed dog, so she can practice."

"Okay." CC conceded defeat.

"If you want to help, stick around, sis. In a couple of years, you can explain lots of things to her like her period, sex, and how even though Mommy and Daddy are both big homos, she wasn't a planned pregnancy."

"Hell, no." CC flatly refused. "You're the mom. I was the one who told you not to go out drinking with boys. As for the puberty stuff, talk to my wife, the doctor."

"I'll take puberty," Jamie eagerly volunteered. "No way I'm explaining how you and Brad got dumped by your partners and ended up getting loaded and making a baby. I would skip over the part where Daddy was dressed up like Cher."

"She already knows her father is a drag queen." Stevie waved it off. "Thanks for watching her. I know it isn't what you had planned for your day off."

"No worries," Jamie quickly said. "We love spending time with Emma. And I for one think we'll have the best jack-o-lantern in the neighborhood. I hope we get a lot of trick-or-treaters. There weren't that many kids back in the old neighborhood. Too many young professionals and retirees in that condo complex."

"I know," Stevie said. "This place was a great find. Big house with separate sides, huge yard, and a good school."

"And the neighbors didn't even flinch when three Subarus, complete with rainbow flags and HRC stickers, pulled up in the driveway." CC couldn't resist snickering.

"Way to announce ourselves," Stevie said, chuckling. "Then again there are at least four other houses on the block that are sporting the same declarations. Speaking of which, did you know that Freda and Ethel Birkenstock are married? To each other?"

"Damn," CC groused.

"Told you." Jamie laughed. "You owe me a foot rub, my darling."

"How did you know?"

"The way they bicker. Only old married couples bicker like that. Just think, honey, someday that'll be us."

Stevie quickly changed the subject. "How is the case going? I thought I saw something on the news this morning."

"Oh, the psycho, suburban, murdering mom as the media likes to call her," CC said. "She's mounting her defense. Good thing, since Max has decided that was more than enough work for the year. The boss is still talking about bringing Mulligan into the department."

"Think she'll make a good partner?" Jamie asked.

"Yeah. The other news is I found out why everyone was talking about that West idiot a few weeks ago. Seems one of those news shows, or what passes for news these days, is doing a story on him. They want to interview me."

"You're going to be on TV?" Jamie felt proud.

"No, I passed."

"Oh, come on, sis," Stevie said. "It might be fun. You snagged one of the most prolific serial killers in history."

"No, I didn't. And he wasn't all that. Granted, he was a twisted freak, but in comparison to Dahmer, Gacy, and let's not forget Bundy, Jeffery Charles West was kind of lame. I mean to get busted acting like a dufus after a basketball game. What a moron. I did agree to talk to the reporter, but that's as far as I go. I have no desire to be on television. My life is interesting enough."

"Whatever, I need to get going," Stevie said. "Have a good night, ladies."

"I thought she'd never leave," Jamie murmured.

"Why, Dr. Jameson, whatever do you have planned?"

"Ssh." Jamie hushed her with a mischievous grin. "Come here." She playfully beckoned, curling her fingers into the belt loops of CC's faded jeans. She pulled her closer, reached up, and laced her fingers through CC's long dark hair. Her heart beat a little faster. It amazed her that after all these years the feeling remained the same. A simple look or glance could make her quiver like a schoolgirl. She nuzzled CC's neck, drinking in her scent. Each time she felt her lover's touch or drank in her distinctive aroma, she felt as if she was coming home. She clasped CC's hips, needing to feel more of her body touching her. The rough feel of denim frustrated her. Jamie's hand slid up CC's body. She had come to the conclusion that they were overdressed for the occasion.

"You're all sweaty," CC murmured. "But it smells good blended with the air of fresh-cut grass."

"I love having a yard." Jamie sighed happily while focusing on the task of ridding CC of her clothing. "Enough talk. I need a shower and someone to wash my back. Interested?" Jamie laughed as she watched CC's naked body racing up the staircase. "I'll take that as a yes." She giggled and raced after her.

She was delighted to find CC in the bedroom clad only in a pair of Scooby Doo boxer shorts. "My God, you're so sexy." Jamie shed the last of her clothing. "Just one thing would make this moment perfect."

"Anything."

"Drop the cartoon shorts." Jamie's pulse quickened as she watched CC slip her thumbs in the waistband of her boxers.

"You don't like?" CC taunted her. "I can't help but notice that you keep buying what you call real underwear."

"I like you in nothing." Jamie struggled to catch her breath as she watched the shorts slip lower. She released a soft growl when CC halted her movements. "I said nothing, woman." Her eyes narrowed when she caught the cocky smirk her wife was sporting. "Are you planning on teasing me?" She had meant to sound assertive; instead, her query squeaked out. The throaty chuckle CC released only served to fan the flames. Oh, yeah, she's in a feisty mood. Jamie secretly relished the thought, knowing that the payback was going to make for an exciting evening. "Paybacks, my love," she said, loving the way CC's eyes darkened with desire.

"Promises, promises." Jamie stepped closer, her desire growing with each step. She licked her lips, pleased when she noticed that CC seemed to be struggling to control her breathing. Jamie stopped just a breath away from CC's trembling body. She loved the differences in their height. Being so much shorter than her wife when they stood toe-to-toe, she was greeted with the wondrous view of CC's breasts.

"Fine, have it your way. I don't really need you to take off your shorts to ravish you." Jamie was pleased when she caught a look of surprise in her lover's eyes. "You'd think after all these years" she taunted her wife by raking her blunt nails up along CC's exposed thigh "you'd know better."

"I do," CC hotly whispered in Jamie's ear.

"Hmm," Jamie murmured. Her hand glided higher while her lips gently grazed the valley between CC's breasts. "Keep it up, and I'll have you on your knees begging for mercy," Jamie whispered against CC's flesh. She slipped her hand up along CC's thigh. She relished the feel of CC's body quivering from her touch.

She smiled when CC gasped as Jamie's fingers slipped beneath the leg of the cotton boxers. Her fingers drifted higher until she was greeted with her lover's overflowing desire. It was her turn to gasp. "Just what have you been thinking about?" she choked out before parting her wife.

"You," CC whimpered.

"Right answer." Jamie nudged CC's thighs farther apart. "God, you're so wet." She moaned with delight. She gazed up, and her pulse quickened when she was captured by the dark desire smoldering in CC's crystal blue eyes. They were locked in a fiery gaze. Jamie ran her fingers along CC's wetness. She watched as her wife fought to control her breathing. She licked her lips, slowly stroking and teasing, loving the feel of CC's clit hardening against her touch.

She continued to explore, pressing a single digit against CC's center. She slipped inside of her before quickly retreating. She smiled when CC released a frustrated growl.

"I told you I was going to tease you." She slid her thigh between CC's legs. She pressed her thigh against CC's wetness, rubbing eagerly against her. CC clung to her, encouraging her to ride against her. Once again, Jamie slowed her movements.

"Not fair."

"You have only yourself to blame."

"I'm dying here." CC cupped Jamie's full breasts. "It's been forever."

"Yesterday." Jamie groaned, relishing the feel of her nipples hardening against CC's knowing touch. "We made love yesterday." Her eager partner was far too busy pinching and teasing Jamie's nipples to listen. "Then again, that was so long ago." Jamie gave into the feel of CC's lips gently grazing the nape of her neck.

Jamie returned her attention to teasing her lover's clit while CC's kisses drifted lower. Jamie arched her back, pressing her erect nipple against CC's lips. She twined her fingers through CC's long dark hair. She used her other hand to stroke her lover urgently.

She had enough teasing. She guided CC backward and pushed her down on the bed.

"God, I want you." She hovered over CC's prone body. Quickly, she lowered the boxer shorts down CC's long legs. Then she slowly kissed her way back up along the newly exposed flesh. She licked the inside of her wife's quivering thighs. She cupped CC's firm backside and drew her closer.

The musky aroma of CC's passion invaded her senses. She parted her lover with her tongue before she began to feast on her overflowing wetness. She murmured with delight, savoring the taste of her wife's passion, while CC pressed her body tightly against Jamie's. She became lost in their passion. CC's pleas for release made her heart beat just a little faster.

Unable to resist her own body's aching for release, Jamie suckled CC harder, plunging deep inside of her until she felt her body shudder. One of the many pleasures in her life was listening to the sounds and watching her loving wife in the throes of ecstasy. She held CC as she melted against her.

"I love watching you," she confessed, completely in awe.

"I love you, Jamie," CC choked out before promising to ravish Jamie just as soon as she caught her breath. She also promised that if the phone rang she would shoot it.

Chapter 14

Stevie arrived home much earlier than she had planned. The night hadn't been what she had hoped for. She wasn't disappointed or surprised by the lack of excitement. A long time ago, she had realized that she had outgrown the bar scene. She needed a little more in her life than just being Emma's mother. She loved her daughter dearly and her career was fulfilling. She appreciated that she was granted the opportunity to make a living by doing something she truly enjoyed. Still she had other needs. The touch of another woman topped the list. She had given up on finding the one. At least for the time being.

Tonight she had been seeking a simple physical connection. Her daughter was away for the night. Her loving sister and her wife were otherwise engaged. It was the perfect chance to get out and find a little fun. From the moment she stepped into the overcrowded nightclub, she knew she was wasting her time. The room was packed with women she viewed as kids. The few that she felt were more age appropriate did nothing to spark her interest.

She sat on the sofa and kicked off her shoes while she tried to decide whether or not just to call it a night or try to get some work done.

"Maybe I should check on Caitlin and Jamie." She pondered the idea for a brief moment, but quickly realized the couple were probably enjoying a little alone time. "Yeah, they might not be up for company." She chuckled at the idea.

She climbed the stairs and showered. Once she tossed on a pair of ratty old boxers and a Red Sox T-shirt, she returned downstairs and made herself a cup of tea with a dash of honey. The house was too quiet. As she nestled on the living room sofa, she reminded herself that Emma would be home tomorrow. She had looked forward to having a little adult time; now in the calmness of the evening, all she wanted was for her baby to be home.

"Enjoy the quiet." She closed her eyes, ready to embrace the calmness.

Just as her body relaxed, a sharp knock at the front door disrupted her solitude. Frightened by the late-night visitor, Stevie raced to the door. She peered through the peephole while trying to calm the rapid beating of her heart. She hated peepholes. Everyone looked like a clown posing in front of a circus mirror.

"Okay, it's a woman," she muttered, not feeling any safer. "I think." She took another look. "Who is it?"

"Deputy Brown, US Marshal," the dark, distorted figure said in a stern voice. Before Stevie could ask, a badge displaying a circled silver star was displayed for her benefit. Stevie was cautious as she opened the door just a bit. She took a closer inspection of the badge. It seemed legit, and it would explain the strange car circling the neighborhood.

"Sorry." She didn't open the door any farther.

"Sorry to disturb you at this hour, ma'am."

"No worries," Stevie mumbled, taking a good look at her guest for the first time. Deputy Brown stood about five seven and was clad in a dark blazer, crisp white blouse, and firmly pressed black slacks. The standard issue attire did nothing to conceal the marshal's firm body. *Now why wasn't she hanging around the club tonight?* Stevie silently pondered.

"Are you Stevie Calloway?" the marshal asked in a curious tone.

"Yes."

"I'm here about Albert Beaumont."

"My father?" Stevie groaned with disgust. "Last I heard, the sick son of a bitch was rotting away in a Connecticut prison."

"He was moved to a halfway house."

"Isn't that just dandy."

"He's missing. It's probably nothing, but he failed to check in the other night."

"Great," Stevie said with a snarl. "Look, if you think he's here, you've wasted your time." She stepped aside, allowing Deputy Brown to enter her home. She admired the commanding gait the deputy possessed. "I haven't seen my father since my sister and I were forced to take out a restraining order against him and dear old Mom." Stevie took advantage of the deputy's back being turned to sneak a peek at her well-defined backside. At that moment, Stevie realized just how badly she needed to get laid.

"I saw that in his file." The deputy turned around to face Stevie. "Your sister was granted custody when you were sixteen?"

"My father is a pedophile, and my mother is an idiot. It wasn't a tough call."

"And your sister is a cop."

"That helped. Now if there's nothing else?"

"Just..."

Stevie was surprised by the hesitation and uncertainty in the marshal's voice. "You have a child? A daughter?"

"You're very thorough. Yes. Emma."

"Is she here?"

CHECKMATE

Stevie was unnerved by the way Brown's voice wavered ever so slightly. "No, she's spending time with her father." As nice as Deputy Brown was to look at, her reason for being there was more than a little unsettling. "Why?"

"Sorry," the deputy said softly, sounding slightly remorseful. "It's just that your father's type is young girls in your daughter's age range. It wouldn't be unheard of—"

"I doubt my, for lack of a better term, my 'father' even knows I have a daughter," Stevie said. "I cut off all contact with my parents a long time ago."

"I figured, but fugitives don't tend to be very smart."

"Good thing for you."

"Yes, it is." The marshal smiled for the first time. "Most of them head for one of three things, family, a home cooked meal, or sex. You'd think they'd just run as far and as fast as they can, but they usually don't. Mr. Beaumont was in a halfway house. He was close to being a free man, then he just ran. Doesn't make sense. Then again a lot of these guys lack common sense. Your sister lives next door?"

"Yes, but I'd come back in the morning." Stevie smirked at the way Brown's body stiffened. "Look, we're not hiding that sick son of bitch. She's spending some quality time with her wife. She'll be at her station tomorrow night. If I were you, that's when I'd go to see her. Now, if you don't mind?" She showed her visitor to the door.

* * *

CC was happily nestled in Jamie's arms, caressing the supple curves of her body. The sounds of the *William Tell Overture* disrupted her ministrations.

"What the…"

"It's Stevie." Jamie groaned with disgust. "That's the ring tone I programmed for her."

"You've got to be kidding me," CC groused, torn between making love to her wife and answering the phone.

"Better answer it." Jamie nudged CC off her overheated body.

"I like it better when you tell me to get my gun and shoot the phone." She grumbled snatching up the phone. "This better be good," CC barked into the phone. She listened, unable to believe what she was hearing. "Okay, I'm on my way over."

"What is it?"

"It's not good." CC crawled out of bed and tossed on the first articles of clothing she could lay her hands on. "I need to get downstairs."

"Baby, what's going on?"

"Stevie's father escaped."

Chapter 15

Deputy Brown stood on the stoop wondering why she was nervous. Perhaps it was anytime she had heard Caitlin Calloway's name mentioned, she sounded too good to be true. Based on some of the stories she had heard, she almost expected Wonder Woman to open the door. Val had also entertained a few ideas of how she'd engage in interagency cooperation. Pity, Brooks failed to mention that Calloway was a happily married woman.

Val knew in her heart that neither Beaumont's daughter nor stepdaughter had a clue as to his whereabouts. But there was a professional courtesy that she needed to extend. Not as up close and personal as she had originally planned. Still she was more than a little concerned that Beaumont might want to seek revenge. If Caitlin Calloway was half as direct as her kid sister, Val's work would be done not long after she knocked on the door.

I'd like to give her a heads up about Beaumont. Just hope she doesn't ask why I didn't do it sooner. She loudly rapped the brass door knocker. She tilted her head slightly when she detected a soft whirring sound just above her, but she didn't look up. She had deduced that she was on camera. Calloway was a cop, and given the events of her past, a little extra home security was to be expected.

Val reached inside her dark blazer, extracted her badge, and held it up for the benefit of the camera before she was requested to do so.

"Stubborn."

She jumped, slightly angry that she hadn't heard the occupant of the house stepping out onto her porch. It wasn't the smug tone in Stevie Calloway's voice that disturbed her. Val just wasn't accustomed to having someone get the drop on her.

"Just wanted to introduce myself," she gruffly explained when the door she was standing in front of opened.

"And now you have," another voice said.

"Somehow I'd thought you'd be taller," she said as she took in the infamous Caitlin Calloway. "From the way Brooks goes on about you. I thought you could walk on water. Deputy Val Brown, US Marshal." Val really enjoyed announcing herself. She missed the navy, but opening with a flash of her badge and announcing her job was cool. Another part of her thought she was a little dorky for getting such a kick out of it.

"Fugitive Task Force?" CC asked, taking a good look at the marshal's badge.

"Yes."

"You know Brooks, from San Diego?"

"Had a runner head out his way awhile back." She pocketed her credentials. "He and I became friends. He was always going on and on about this weasel named Fisher. Then a few years ago, he told me about the great CC Calloway who bagged him. I was in the area on another case, this popped up, and I decided to meet the legend."

"Uh-huh."

"Look," Val mumbled, knowing she was way out of her depth. "Consider it a professional courtesy. I seriously doubt that either you or your sister would harbor a criminal, much less one you hate so much. Shoot him, maybe, but not harbor. On the other hand, I looked at the file and I'm concerned that Beaumont might be wanting a little payback. After you took custody of your sister, there wasn't a cop up here or down in Rhode Island that wasn't watching this guy."

"Which is why he and dear old Mom beat feet to Connecticut," CC said dryly. "Where he got busted for trolling a playground. My sister told me that he bolted from a halfway house."

Val wasn't surprised that Stevie had called her sister to alert her to the situation. "Two weeks into his stay, he just stopped coming home," she said. "Not out of the ordinary. These buggers get a little taste of freedom and can't handle it. The only reason we're busting our hump on this bastard is because he's a level three sex offender. Add a personal connection to a cop."

"I get it." CC seemed to relax ever so slightly. "Stop by the precinct tomorrow after three. We can talk then. In the meantime, my niece is with her father who, believe it or not, is even more overprotective than I am."

"He is," Stevie confirmed with a smug grin that irked Val.

"If that's all, Deputy, I'll see you tomorrow, at the station."

Interesting was the only word Val could conjure up once she had returned to her black sedan. She had been honest with the stoic detective. She did just happen to be in the area and got caught up in the case. She didn't feel a need to explain that she was more interested in meeting the great Caitlin Calloway than she was in the case.

The deeper Val dug into the file, the more interested she became. It was a curious case. If she had to bet money on the reason why Beaumont bolted, she'd bet that either he found out about his granddaughter and decided to pay a visit or somehow Detective Calloway finally had dealt with him. If the situation resulted in the latter, Val certainly wouldn't lose any sleep over a dead pedophile.

If there was the slightest chance, however, that Emma

Calloway was in danger, she wanted to be there. Caitlin Calloway intrigued her almost as much as Stevie Calloway did. Now there was an interesting woman.

Why was a woman like that home alone on a night like tonight? Val shook her head, feeling the need to focus. She had a rabbit on the run. No matter how enticing the younger Calloway sister appeared to be, this was business. She started the car and set out to get to work. The Boston Police had their own Fugitive Task Force. One of the best in the country. They graciously allowed her to set up office as long as she allowed them to work the case with her. Capt. Mills had been assigned to watch over her. She was also working with the local marshals. Pity they didn't have one tenth of Mills's enthusiasm.

Val understood she was poaching in their backyard. The police weren't thrilled with her presence either. Feds and locals rarely got along. But she had a pedophile to track down, and her gut told her she'd find something here that would help in her quest.

She returned to the Fugitive Task Force office in downtown Boston and set about getting some work done.

"Tell me," she asked Mills, "what you know about Caitlin Calloway. She's with the three-three out of Boylston."

"I know CC," Mills gruffly answered. "She's a good cop. Damn good cop."

Val wasn't taken aback by her surly response. She had just asked about one of her own. In the world of law enforcement, what she had just done was the equivalent of questioning her sister's morals.

"Just asking."

"Look, I don't know what you think you're onto, but

Calloway is a good cop," Mills repeated. "Tell you what I do know about Calloway. She took a bullet to save her partner. And a few years back when she bagged that idiot Fisher, she had a shot. Didn't take it. Cause that's not who she is."

"She could have popped the weasel?"

"Hey, not like anyone in the room would have rolled on her. What would you do if you caught some psycho trying to kill your girlfriend?"

"I would have shot him and worried about my career later."

"She didn't. It wasn't her career she was worried about it was her soul. So, she played it by the book. Even got him to confess. Because she held it together, the Jensen family finally got to bury their little girl. Played the little shit like a fiddle. I heard his lawyers were there when she did it."

"She's smart." Val opened the file sitting in front of her. "And not going to do what I was afraid she would."

"Which is?"

"Waste Beaumont."

"Would you lose any sleep if she did?" Mills snorted with disgust.

"Not a wink," Val answered honestly. "But it's my job to find him. If I bring him back to Connecticut in a body bag, so be it. Anyone who hurts kids gets what they deserve. I'm not real particular what condition they're in when I bring them in. I need to track down his ex-wife. Looks like I'll be out of your hair soon."

"Promises, promises." Mills chuckled.

Val began to review the file. If Caitlin Calloway was half the cop she was on paper, the city was lucky to have her. Graduated from the academy near the top of her class. After completing her probation period, she did indeed take a bullet, two in fact. Somehow Calloway had managed to take down the shooter before he shot her partner, Max Sampson. Val was confused by the lack of information regarding the incident. She made a note to make a couple of calls. She could ask Mills, but she figured her earlier questions made her leery of her intentions. She kept looking at the file. Perhaps digging a little deeper would give her the answers she was seeking.

When CC was eight, her older brother Donald committed suicide. Young Caitlin found the body. A couple of months later, her father, Joseph Calloway, died in a car accident. Apparently, he fell asleep at the wheel of his Buick after pulling back-to-back double shifts at his job with GE. Thanks to the insurance company constantly questioning the circumstance, it was confirmed that he did indeed fall asleep while driving home from work.

"Poor kid," Val couldn't help saying. She kept reading. The next time Caitlin Calloway showed up in the system was a report she made to an Officer Francis Donnelly, accusing her new stepfather of trying to do things to her that were highly inappropriate.

Val felt a little more at ease after she finished reviewing the file. There were a couple of gaps in Calloway's history that had caught her eye.

She hoped that Beaumont had simply bolted, probably off to Mexico or Canada. She had already alerted her contacts North and South of the border. She just had to be sure that she wasn't hunting for a corpse. She'd meet with Calloway tomorrow, just as a formality. Her next stop was a visit to Beaumont's ex-wife.

"Mills?"

"Yup?" She grunted before turning to her.

"The file is a little vague about Calloway's on-duty injury. What's up with that?" She cringed when she felt the entire room tense up. Each member of the task force returned her question with an icy stare. "Okay. Did I do something wrong?" She didn't think the question was out of line. It wasn't even pertinent. Val was simply curious. She wanted to kick herself for that pesky overly inquisitive streak in her. "Come on, Mills. I'm not trying to start trouble. Just between us gals, I'm curious. A cop takes a bullet and it's just a blurb in her jacket?"

"Look," Mills said in a hushed tone and took a seat beside her. "It's kind of…"

"Hey, I was just curious." Last thing Val needed in her line of work was to piss off one of the leading Fugitive Task Forces in the country. "I don't need an answer."

"It was a routine traffic stop," Mills said quietly. "She was green. Just finished her probation. According to Sampson, the guy just starts shooting. Calloway was down. Max said they never saw it coming. He didn't have time to react. He's staring at this piece of shit aiming a gun at him, and Calloway got off a shot and took him down."

"She killed him?" she asked, thinking that was what had provoked the strange response. Then again if she had chances were that she wouldn't have been able to keep working the streets. Justified shooting or not a cop that wet behind the ears would have found themselves riding a desk for a really long time.

"Nope. The reason her jacket is a little light on the incident is because the guy was a CI."

"The punk was a confidential informant? So, when she pulled him over he panicked," she said. "Still doesn't explain the lack of info."

"A very special informant. Feds asked us to keep the whole thing under wraps. Calloway did as she was told. Sampson got his gold shield. Never even made the news."

"Great. They covered it up." Val grunted with disgust. "Well, she must love working with Feds. I'm screwed with her. What happened to the snitch?"

"Shot outside of a bar in Southie, never found the shooter." Mills shrugged as if it was no big deal.

"No shortage of suspects, I'm sure. You weren't kidding when you said Calloway took one for the team. She's never going to talk to me."

"To lock up her stepfather? She'll work with you," Mills said. "Told you before, Calloway's a good cop."

Val closed the file and thanked Mills. She didn't miss the way every cop in the room was looking at her. She wasn't bothered by the harshness in their eyes. She had pried into the life of one of their own. She was certain there were cops in that room who didn't like Calloway. CC Calloway may have been a good cop, but she was also a lesbian who was outdoing most of her male counterparts. Despite any prejudice they may have harbored, she was still a cop. Val, on the other hand, was a Fed. It took her a long time to realize that locals didn't like working with Feds, no matter how important the case. She packed up the rest of her stuff and headed back to her hotel.

After a long hot shower, she broke out her cell phone and laptop. She had to find Albert Beaumont. That was priority number one. She ran through the list of possible scenarios. If he was smart, he headed south: Mexico, Virginia, or Florida. Florida would be the best choice for someone Beaumont's age.

CHECKMATE

"He could blend in," she said aloud. "Retiree sick of the snow. He'd need a new identity. But he can find work. There are folks who will gladly pay a nice elderly man under the table to help him supplement his Social Security." She wished Ricky were there, if for no other reason than she felt a little silly verbalizing her theories to no one. Deciding she needed a little objective input, she picked up her cell and called him.

Val Brown and Ricky Samaria had been friends since their days at Annapolis. They had been through things that most people only read about in spy novels. When she left the Navy, Ricky, along with their close knit circle, followed. She joined the marshal service, and he went to Quantico.

"What's up, Brownie?" He used his pet name for her. "No good looking women in Boston?"

"Like you care," she said and laughed. It hadn't taken either very long back in Annapolis to realize the secret they shared. It was before "Don't Ask, Don't Tell." For some reason, neither she nor Ricky had been asked. At first they thought it had been an oversight. One they had been grateful for. If asked, they would have had to lie. Lying was a violation of the honor code. But no one asked.

Later they would realize they weren't asked because no one wanted them to answer. They, along with three other classmates, were being groomed for something bigger. In the end, the hypocrisy got to Val. Pushed into a corner by a bigoted redneck who happened to be a rear admiral, she outed herself.

The navy chose to ignore her admission. Odd, because ever since Don't Ask, Don't Tell was instituted, the military was flushing anyone and everyone who might be gay right out of the service. Still, Val Brown had always been much more than her file read. The government had no interest in allowing that information to be leaked out. The navy rested on semantics. Neither she nor her superior officer had used the exact words that would end her career. She was allowed to join the Shining Star program and retire. Now she was as out as she could be without losing her benefits.

"Ricky, I need you to look into some names for me."

"Don't you ever do your own work?"

"And yours most of the time," she teased him. "I don't know why the FBI puts up with your crap."

"Is this your way of sweet talking me? I thought you needed a favor."

"Fine, you big hunk of gorgeous manhood. Us lowly marshals don't have the same access to info you big bad FBI agents do. Give a helpless girl a break."

He laughed. "Who are you tracking?"

"Albert Beaumont. Took a hike from Gibbon Home, Bridgeport, Connecticut. He was doing ten to twenty for a level three."

"Child molester? Why didn't you say so? Okay, I've got his file. Arrests in Ohio, Maine, Indiana, and twice Connecticut, which should have gone down as a third strike. Got out for good behavior and reoffended less than two months later."

"I've got all that," Val said. "Most of those happened in the seventies. Nothing stuck except the one in Ohio. He did three years."

"Slap on the wrist. Then nothing until Massachusetts. Stepdaughter accused him of trying to get funny with her."

"Again, I'm on all that." Val tried to hurry him along. "I've had the team watching the usual spots: bus stations, train stations, the airport, and every no-tell motel in the area. I've got nothing. Don't tell me what I can find by going through the usual channels. I need your superior hacking skills. I need to get this guy. The stepdaughter who reported him is a cop now."

"Good for her," Ricky muttered. Val listened to him furiously typing. "Couple of domestic calls. Seems your cop took a baseball bat to the pervert when she was all of nine years old. She did it more than once. DSS investigated. Nothing happened. They bought the party line that the kid was upset because Albert was trying to take her father's place."

"Ricky, move into this century."

"The first cop, Francis Donnelly, took an interest," Ricky muttered. "By the time he tracked down Beaumont's history, the family had moved to Rhode Island."

"Yeah, I'm curious about that," Val said. "Not all of them moved. Caitlin Calloway was still enrolled at Beachmont High. Her mailing address remained the same. But from what I'm looking at, the Beaumonts sold the house. Except for school, She's off the grid for another three years. The next mailing address I can find is when she started college. She was living with her uncle, Michael Anthony Calloway."

"Bookie."

"Really?"

"Middle level, not big enough for us or the mob to give a damn about. And not small enough to fly under the radar." He quickly explained.

"One of my questions is where was this kid?" Val tried to sort it out. "She wasn't with the family and she wasn't living in the old house. I can't find a connection between her and the new owners. A family by the name of Nacster."

"You think there's another relative that might be hiding Beaumont?"

"Possibly. I'm also curious as to where a fifteen-year-old girl was living for all that time. Tell me about the bookie."

"Michael Calloway, better known as Mac C, holds court at the Lucky Seven in the West End," Ricky said. "Caitlin moved in with him and enrolled in Suffolk University. Graduated on time, not at the top of the class but not the bottom. Entered the academy, did well, not outstanding. Oh? She did us a favor back in eighty-nine."

"Yeah, I heard about that one."

"Arrested Jeffrey Charles West back when she was still a beat cop." He sounded impressed. "Nice collar. Simon Fisher was another piece of work. She has an above-average closure rate. Nothing odd in her jacket, except she did threaten a drag queen once."

"Beg pardon?"

"A Brad Quinn performs drag at Jacques Cabaret, on Broadway."

"Oh? Interesting. According to Caitlin's niece Emma's birth certificate, that's her daddy. Okay, I've got a couple of things that are bugging me. We have a possible sighting of Beaumont hopping on a bus heading north. If he knows about his granddaughter, I'm afraid he might try and get a little revenge," she said. "Then there is the ex-wife, Maria Beaumont. I'm coming up empty. All I got is she divorced Beaumont's sorry ass just after his first arrest in Connecticut. Then nada."

"Okay." Ricky's voice turned serious. Val listened to his

furious typing. "I got her."

"Where is she?"

"Waltham, Massachusetts."

"How far is that from here?"

"Right around the corner. About thirty miles or so. She's flying under the radar all right. Went back to the maiden name Gallagher. She's waiting tables off the books at a restaurant called The Watch Factory. Lucky for you, the IRS is looking at them or we wouldn't have found her. Before he bolted, did Beaumont make any friends?"

"No," Val said. "He kept to himself. Did his therapy. His advisor said Beaumont was typical. Said all the right things in group. Outside of group, he swore up and down he was framed. He told more than one of his neighbors that his bitch of a stepdaughter used her badge to set him up. Two weeks ago, he went off to work. Had a roofing job. Never checked back in. Like I said, I've got a maybe of him heading towards Boston. If he was smart, he would have headed south and disappeared."

"With an ex-wife, the daughter, stepdaughter, and granddaughter all living in the area…"

"You have to wonder if he's planning on paying a visit to one of them," Val said. "I'll pay a call on the ex-Mrs. Beaumont in the morning. Thanks for the help, Ricky."

He emailed her all the info he had collected. She needed sleep. Nothing new there. Flying by the seat of her pants was a constant in her life. The truth was, she enjoyed it. What she didn't enjoy was failure. The upside of her job was everyone she was seeking for the most part already had their day in court. It wasn't like in the movies. These people were criminals, no ifs, ands, or buts. On the rare occasion, her job allowed her to cross paths with someone like Stevie Calloway.

In the beginning, she had been looking forward to meeting Caitlin, the older Calloway sister. Brooks had built her up so much, Val was almost convinced that the detective was a figment of his imagination. Caitlin was okay. Not what she expected. Stevie, on the other hand, was a woman she wouldn't mind spending a little time with.

She couldn't help smirking while she thought of just how she might enjoy Stevie's company. She perused the file that summed up the young web designer's life. Born Stevie Joanna Beaumont to Albert and Maria Beaumont. Her older half-sister, Caitlin Calloway, was awarded custody of her when she was sixteen. A wall of blue showed up at the custody hearing with records proving that her loving father had a long history as a sex offender and her sister was a decorated police officer. A restraining order had been filed against both of her parents shortly thereafter.

Stevie legally changed her last name to Calloway when she turned eighteen. Graduated from UMass, Boston, with honors. Worked for Lotus, MIT, and Comtrel before opening her own web design business. Lived with a Katrina Wilson for four years. One child, Emma Liza Quinn. Shared ownership of her home with her sister and sister in-law. Paid her bills on time, no outstanding parking or speeding tickets. Stevie Calloway was a model citizen. And in Val's humble opinion completely hot. Val tried to shrug off her attraction; she had a job to do.

"I hope I find your sick-o father soon." Val leered at Stevie's RMV photo. "You, I'd like to get to know better." She yawned.

"Time for bed," she said out loud. Another bad habit she had begun over the past few years: spending so much time alone in hotel rooms, she started talking to herself. That and seeing how long it took to find some incarnation of *Law and Order* on television.

"I swear a woman never designed a hotel bathroom," she complained. "Really, I need to stop talking to myself. Maybe when this mess is cleaned up, I'll take that vacation I'm supposed to be on." She caught her reflection in the mirror. "Damn, I'm tired." She shook her head. She was still speaking out loud.

Chapter 16

Elizabeth Pryce was already awake before the old-fashioned alarm clock loudly clanged its bells. She gazed out the window. Cold and misty. She smiled. She loved everything about San Francisco; it possessed a charm she had failed to find anywhere else. Almost two decades ago, she and her college roommate had discovered the bay area when they took an impromptu road trip from Santa Barbara to San Francisco. It had been an awakening for both of them.

She fell in love with San Francisco almost as easily as she fell in love with her roommate, In college, she discovered freedom, books, and the first love of her life. Janie had opened her eyes to who she was and what she wanted out of life. Janie was everything to her. The day Janie told her that she loved her was probably the happiest day in her life.

Then just as suddenly Janie was gone. Not the usual way your first love walks out. Janie went home for the winter break. She promised Elizabeth before she left that she was going to break up with her boyfriend. The night before she was to return to campus, Janie called her. Simon was history, and they were about to begin their lives together. It would be the last time Elizabeth would hear Janie's voice. Janie never completed the two-hundred-sixteen-mile drive from San Diego to Santa Barbara. Elizabeth silently bore the pain of never knowing what had happened to her first love.

Then one day out of the blue the truth was revealed on the local news. There it was, all of her answers in one fell swoop. Janie's body had been found. Simon had murdered her on that fateful day. Elizabeth cried for three days and then she found peace. She knew what had happened, and she could finally say goodbye.

She no longer felt fractured. She embraced her city and her life and opened her heart. A bit late in the game to start looking for love.

CHECKMATE

She padded downstairs and set the kettle on to boil.

She opened the package that had arrived just the other day. She smiled. It was a promotional gift set. A collection of herbal teas and a small jar of honey. She looked at the card. *A gift for you.* Then it went on with the usual sales pitch.

Elizabeth would have tossed it in the trash if it hadn't been a collection of her favorite teas. The addition of fresh honey was something she simply couldn't resist. She finished the tea, enjoying it so much that she set aside the card. "I should buy some," she said, deciding that a second cup and a little more time lazing about was in order. She tried a different flavor, again adding honey.

"This is a perfect morning," she said with a sigh. A few sips into the second cup of tea, her perfect morning turned sour. She shifted uncomfortably and a sharp pain attacked her. She barely made it into the bathroom before all hell broke loose. Her plans to spend the day wandering around the city were cast aside after her third trip to empty her stomach.

Defeated, she crawled back into bed and curled up; the pain was pure agony. She tried to understand how she had become so violently ill so quickly. She prayed to the goddess for relief. The pain increased as her body kept purging throughout the day until she was too weak to call for help. She heard the house phone ringing, then her cell. In her weakened state, she was unable to call for help.

* * *

Concerned, Myra furiously knocked on Elizabeth's door. She had tried calling Elizabeth the previous day to confirm their plans for breakfast together but hadn't received an answer. When Elizabeth failed to meet her for breakfast, Myra tried not to panic. Just as she had done the previous day she called all of Elizabeth's numbers.

After her constant pounding on the door went unanswered, she called the landlord. Nothing in her forty-nine years had prepared Myra for what she found in Elizabeth's bedroom. Poor Elizabeth was curled up on the bed, her face forever twisted in agony. Myra released a shriek, and the landlord called 911.

One look at the scene, and the EMTs called for the police and the medical examiner. Dr. Logan Fergus pronounced Elizabeth Pryce dead. He was unable to determine the cause of death. All he knew for certain was she did not go gently.

Chapter 17

Val sat in a corner booth at The Watch Factory, sipping her coffee. She had finished her breakfast, and now she was focused on coffee and watching the waitress. She had hoped to pick up on snippets of conversation between Maria and her coworkers. The tired-looking woman seemed to keep to herself. She noticed the dull, defeated look in Maria's eyes the moment she sat down.

"Warm up?" Maria waved a fresh pot of coffee over Val's mug.

"Sure."

"Is there a reason you keep watching me?" Maria was just as blunt as her daughters.

Val sighed, reached in her pocket, and flashed her badge. "Heard from your husband?" She was tired and convinced this woman wanted nothing more in life than to be left alone.

"Not since they carted his sorry butt off to prison," Maria said with a grunt. "At least I hope you're talking about my ex. Might be real hard getting in touch with my first husband, unless you got a Ouija board."

"Not handy."

"So what happened? I thought Bert was locked up for good."

"Parole. Skipped out of the halfway house."

"Ain't justice grand?" Maria said ruefully. "So, you're gonna follow me around? Trust me, I don't want anything to do with that SOB. He did enough damage to my life. I got a good job here. I don't need trouble from him or you."

"I get it," Val said. "The thing is, I just can't take your word for it. There's a chance he was heading this way. The only people he knows up here are you and your daughters. I just want to find him and put him back in jail." She slid her card across the table.

"You've seen my girls? They okay? I mean are they—"

"They're fine." Val tossed money down on the table and shrugged. She knew it was cruel. If Maria was going to talk to her, she had to have some leverage.

She wasn't surprised to feel Maria's hand on her arm or the request for her to wait. "My shift is over at one. Is there any way we can—"

"I'm kind of busy." Val sounded bored. The pleading look in Maria's eyes gave her the upper hand. "Fine. I'll meet you across the street in the park."

Maria whispered a thank you, and Val grabbed her bag. After making her exit, she broke out her laptop and searched for a signal. She popped her Bluetooth in her ear and went to work. The life of a US Marshal might seem exciting in the movies; in reality, there were a lot of little details. Paperwork, legwork, and good old-fashioned work were involved. Tracking down someone who didn't want to be found went one of two ways: an early onset of stupidity and the guilty party was safely behind bars before the sun went down, or the guilty party was someone who possessed enough brain cells to fly under the radar. Albert "Bert" Beaumont was turning out to be smarter than Val had initially assumed.

By the time Maria joined her on the park bench, the only thing Val had to show for her efforts were a sore butt and a possible sighting at a fleabag motel on Route One. She was frustrated that no one was busting a sweat to find this guy. If it hadn't been for Mills and the leverage she pulled, Val would have been on her own on this one. Normally, that wouldn't bother her. But for a small city, Boston seemed to have a lot of hiding places.

When Maria arrived, she nervously took a seat next to Val, completely unaware that a federal agent had just been assigned to watch her morning, noon, and night.

"The girls, they're okay?" Maria timidly asked.

"As far as I could tell."

"Sorry. I don't have a right to ask, do I?"

"You tell me." Val's interest was limited to Albert. She was listening to Maria's sad tale simply because it might give her an idea as to where the weasel might be hiding. "I'm not here to judge you."

"Ever sit back and look at your life and wonder what the hell happened?" Maria asked. "I don't suppose you do." She gave Val a curious look. "I had a good life. A good husband. Joseph was the love of my life. He had a good job with GE. We had two beautiful children, and then it was all gone. Funny that when your world is about to collapse, you really don't see it coming. Donny, that was my boy, he was being picked on. We told him to ignore those boys, they'll get tired and leave him alone. That didn't work. They went from picking on him to out and out bullying him. Day after day he'd come home all beaten up. That was it for me. I went to the school. Twice. They claimed nothing was happening, except Donny's attitude had changed and his grades were in trouble. It was like they blamed him. It was early on a Monday morning when Caitlin found him. He hung himself. Nothing can prepare you for losing your child that way. After he died, everything changed. Joe ended up shutting down completely. He worked longer and harder hours. He fell asleep behind the wheel. No surprise since he had been working back-to-back doubles for weeks. Three months, that's how long it took for everything to happen. In three short months, I lost my son, my husband, and failed to see that my little girl was pretty much raising herself."

"Hard thing to live through," Val said.

"I never really pulled it together," Maria continued seemingly unaware that Val was even there. "About a year and a half later, I met Albert Beaumont. I called him Bert. Albert sounded too dorky. Caitlin seemed fine around him. Bert was like a Godsend. He treated me right, not like I was damaged goods. Most folks tiptoe around you after you lose a child. Lose your husband and your child, most people just stay away. Bert was great. A couple of months later he moved in, and we got married. In the beginning, when Caitlin started acting out, I thought she was just missing her father. I couldn't believe the things she said Bert tried to do to her. When she took a baseball bat to him, I was convinced that she needed help. Social services got involved when she went to the police. We all agreed that she was just angry about her dad. After Stevie was born, Caitlin doted on that girl. I let her. She watched her baby sister like a hawk. I had hoped that it would help, you know, that she'd start getting along with Bert. Things got worse. My husband knew just the right things to say, so no matter what, I'd believe him over my daughter. In the end, I lost both my girls, because I chose my man over my children." Maria grew silent. The look in her eyes was clear; she was beaten. She sat there seemingly unable to speak until finally she whispered, "I'm sorry."

Val sat there studying Maria. The woman seemed relieved to have finally told someone her story. It hadn't taken her long to realize that Maria was telling the truth. No way she'd accept responsibility then turn around and give good old Bert another chance.

"Miss Gallagher," she said slowly, "it couldn't have been easy."

"Don't offer me an out."

"I'm not. Like you said, you chose your man over your kids. That doesn't get you a pass. I just want to make sure he ends up where he belongs. You have my card. If you hear or see anything, call me."

"You're direct." A hint of a smile colored Maria's face. "My Joe was like that."

"So are your girls," Val said as she stood. "You want me to pass a message on to them?"

"No." This time Maria sounded defeated. "Like you said, I don't get a pass. But thanks."

During the short drive from Waltham to Boylston, Val tried to process everything she'd learned in the last twenty-four hours. It amounted to a whole package of nothing. Bert should have bolted, but instead he headed to Boston. She couldn't shake the sudden feeling he was there, lurking in the shadows.

"Who are you planning on visiting?" She couldn't help asking out loud as she pulled her sedan up to the curb by the police station.

Chapter 18

"That's the GPS tracking," Leigh said, handing CC the information. "Puts Mrs. Stern in the park the day Annie disappeared."

"During the kid's naptime," Max added. "Her suit is going to have a helluva time explaining that one."

"You didn't hear?" CC asked. "Mrs. Stern's new suit is none other than Gilmore Standorf."

"Well, that's just dandy," Leigh grumbled. "Has he ever lost?"

"A couple of times," Max said. "The last time was the People vs. Sasha. Calloway made him look like an idiot. Standorf didn't know whether he should spit or wind his watch."

"I remember that one," Leigh said and smirked. "A slam dunk as I recall."

"No such thing," CC said. "Which is why we need to check everything. Good old Snaps is still sitting on the fence regarding the assault charges."

"How can he stand by her? She tasered his nuts." Max shivered.

"Same as a woman in an abusive situation," CC said. "Right now, Mr. Stern is iffy at best. Then there is spousal privilege, and whatever other crap Standorf can scrape together to keep the evidence out. Our biggest edge is the statements Mrs. Stern made to Mulligan."

"Hard to explain," Leigh said. "Mrs. Stern claims the girl quit but didn't take anything with her, including her phone and her passport. GPS from the family SUV puts her in the park where we found the body. Standorf will go with hearsay. He'll also try to get her confession thrown out. We still have Annie's belongings being left in the house. No teenager leaves their cell phone behind."

"Standorf is shrewd." CC tapped her chin. "The DA needs everything we can get." The phone on her desk rang, breaking her train of thought. "Calloway."

"Calloway, it's Mills. We need to talk."

"What's going on?"

"It's kind of personal."

"What's up?" she asked, already sensing why Mills was calling.

"I-I heard something," she stammered. "It's about Albert Beaumont. I should have talked to you sooner."

"Yeah, I've heard he took a runner," CC said and grunted. "Had a US Marshal on my doorstep last night. I'll be honest with you, when Deputy Doodad showed up on my doorstep, I was ready to call Finn and rip into him. I can't figure why they think Beaumont would look me up. Last time I saw the guy, I called him a lying piece of dung and promised that he'd rot in jail."

"Word is he was spotted heading this way," Mills said. "Could be just on his way to Canada. Never know."

"Let's hope," CC responded quietly. "Thanks for giving me the heads-up."

"Hey, it's what we do. Again, sorry about not calling you sooner."

"I know how these things go."

"Truth is, it would have got lost if the out-of-towner hadn't pulled some mighty big strings."

"Brown?"

"Word is she has friends in high places. Good thing, because Finn wasn't listening to Connecticut. Still I should have given you a shout."

"Don't worry about it, Mills."

The call ended. Still troubled, CC returned her attention to Max and Mulligan. She tried to focus on the evidence. In the back of her mind, she kept asking one question. "Why in the world would Bert Beaumont come to Boston?"

"What is it?" Max wasn't one to waste time. He probably guessed something was bothering CC. Maybe it was the way she kept banging her desk drawers and cursing like a sailor that gave her away.

"Mills was giving me a heads-up about Albert Beaumont." Her mind was trying to process the information. "Seems he ducked out of his halfway house. Already had a visit from the Feds. He might be heading this way."

"Beaumont?" Max said. "Who in the hell let that bastard out of prison?"

"Don't care," CC muttered. "I just want to know why he's headed to Boston. The only people he knows here are me and Stevie."

"And your mother." A cool voice cut in.

"Ah, Deputy Dumb Ass," CC said with a snarl. "Any reason you chose to leave that part out of our little chat last night? You know, the part where he was in the area."

"Might be in the area."

"If his wife is here, that would explain it," CC reasoned.

"Ex-wife," Val said.

"Mom finally did something smart." CC tried to shrug it off. "Good luck with your search. If you find him, feel free to shoot him."

"Maybe we should discuss this somewhere else," Val suggested.

"We have work to do." CC didn't care if she sounded curt; she wanted this woman gone. "Some of us are interested in putting the bad guys away."

"Nice." Val grimaced. "I heard about your case. Suburban mom whacking the nanny. Sounds like you got her dead to rights."

"Never know," Max said, glaring at the marshal. "She's got an expensive mouthpiece."

"Murder rate is up around these parts," Val said.

"The economy is down," CC noted. "Most of what we get is gang related or domestic. Not much investigating involved. This case is different. Mrs. Stern is a pious pain in the ass."

"No lie," Leigh added.

"The one night she was in lockup, she managed to unite the skinheads and the sisters against her. Had to put her in protective custody."

"Sounds like a real piece of work."

"You could say that," CC said. "Now that you've played nice, are you ready to explain yourself? Why didn't you tell me Beaumont was in the Boston area?"

"Might be," Val repeated. "You know how these leads go. It might be a bunch of crap. I'll tell you what I know. I'd really prefer to do it in private."

"Fine. Do you like crappy coffee? Ours is the worst in the country."

"Actually, Paramus has the worst. Maybe we could get a breath of fresh air?"

"Dunkies?" Leigh and Max requested in unison.

"You want me to bring the both of you coffee? Break room's down the hall and to the left." CC charged out of the squad room with Val behind her.

"No offense," Val said, "but what the hell is it with this town and Dunkin Donuts? I swear there's one on every corner."

"Because there is. And before you ask, it isn't about the donuts."

"But the coffee sucks?"

"What? I'll ignore that, for the moment. Only because I have a list of questions for you."

"Such as?"

"Why didn't you tell me my beloved stepfather might be in the area? Why are you flying solo? Bit unusual for a marshal to be tracking a fugitive all alone." CC felt a steady pounding in her ears from her steadily rising blood pressure.

"I didn't tell you until I had to," Val said as she followed after CC. "No need upsetting you or your family. If I could bag Beaumont, then let you know, all the better. I haven't got him, just a feel that he's in the area. That's why I went to you alone."

"So you have a team in place?" CC stopped dead in her tracks. "You've been watching my family? Son of a bitch!"

"Mostly your sister." Val remained calm. "Wouldn't you? Come on, why else would he show up here, if not for his kid and hers?"

CC's stomach churned. It was too much. After all these years, her own personal bogeyman was back. She was furious that she and her family were being watched. "You should have come to me sooner."

"Come on, Calloway. You know what it's like. You have to get into their heads. It's a dark place. I'm doing what I have to do. The more I know, the easier it will be to catch him. There's no reason other than your family for him to come here."

"My mother."

"I don't think so." Val shook her head. "She saw the light after his arrest in Connecticut. Dumped him and ran. Chances are he doesn't even know she's here. Hell, I had trouble finding her."

"That's not comforting."

"Did you know?"

"I wasn't looking."

"Who does he know here besides you? You never left even after your family moved out of state."

"I didn't have a choice." CC fought the urge to throttle Val. "I was fifteen, and they kicked me out because I'm a big dyke."

"Where were you? I'm looking at a three-year gap."

"What difference does it make?" CC shouted only to receive a blank stare in return. "It isn't germane. The only contact I had with my family was my kid sister. Her safety was all I cared about. As for the rest, I got by."

"Someone had to be helping you. I know this is hard. I hate prying into another cop's life."

"Back then, it was considered striking out on your own." CC forced the words out. "Look, the last thing my loving mother said to me was, 'If that's the way you are, go live with your funny uncle.'"

"Jesus, you were fifteen."

"I never said we were the Waltons." CC was already weary of the conversation. "Like I said, I got by. With the exception of my sister, no one in the family knew where to find me. Eventually, I did end up living with my uncle. Just find Beaumont. My family has been through enough."

"I'll find him, and I promise to keep you in the loop. Just tell me, is there anyone who might have coerced him into coming up here? Like your uncle?"

"Mac?" CC scoffed. She knew what the good deputy was thinking. "Look, he was pissed when he found out what was going on. I told him to stand down. After all these years, why bother? Do me a favor. Mac C isn't a favorite with the boys in blue. Unless they need to place a bet. Most of them don't know he's my uncle. I'm a clean cop."

"I got you," Val said. "No one knows he's your uncle, and you'd like to keep it that way. I still need to talk to him."

"He's at the Lucky Seven. Usually hooked up to a tank of oxygen. Refuses to give up the smokes. Uncle Mac can barely walk across the street. I doubt he has the energy to set up a hit on a guy he hasn't seen in twenty-some-odd years."

"Thank you, and I will keep you in the loop."

"You better. Trust me, my bad side isn't where you want to be."

"I don't doubt that for a minute."

"He took a powder about a week ago?"

"Yes, why?"

"Could be nothing." CC hesitated, her heart thumping. With everything going on with the Stern case, she had forgotten about the strange greeting card. "I was in California for a night, and my sister got a weird greeting card in the mail."

"What did it say?"

"Happy Father's Day."

"Jesus." Val gaped at her. "Where is it? I need to have forensics look at it."

"They already are." CC unclipped her new cell phone. "Corey, it's Calloway." She listened to his grumbling for a moment before cutting him off. "Yeah, I know you're busy. Did you get a look at that card I dropped off?"

"Yes, and I came up with nothing. The only prints I can trace back to postal workers, your sister, and your wife. No DNA on the envelope either. Whoever sealed it used garden variety tap water."

"Hold on to it. There's a marshal by the name of Brown on her way to see you. Give it to her and tell her what you told me What about the DNA tests on those belts for the Fraser case?"

"You never let up," Corey grumbled. "Just got the results, two hits the victim and Natalie Stern. That should make the DA happy. So, do I get a cookie?"

"Your wife is going to kill me." CC almost laughed. "Help me wrap this one up and you get cheese cake."

"I love you."

"What?" Val asked once CC hung up.

"Dr. Corey McDowell has the card. No prints and no DNA. He'll hand it over to you and only you. Oh, and you might want to bring him a Twinkie or something."

"What?"

"There wasn't a case file on this. He's got a sweet tooth and a wife who has him restricted to rabbit food," CC said. "If you don't want him to bury you in red tape until the next ice age, bring the guy something he shouldn't be eating."

"How is it you get things done in this city? No wonder it took you eighty-two years to finally win another series."

"Hey!" CC was infuriated. Brown could question her skills all she wanted, but there was no need to bring her beloved Red Sox into it. "What are you, a Yankees fan?" Her jaw dropped when Brown smirked at the comment. "Oh, that's enough. First you're snarky about Dunkin Donuts, now you like the Yankees. I can't work with this."

* * *

Val did pay a visit to the Lucky Seven. It wasn't hard to find Mac Calloway. He was holding court in a back corner of the bar. As his niece predicted, he was indeed hooked up to an oxygen tank. Even at a distance, the man looked pale.

"A cop bar. Talk about hiding in plain sight." She shook her head, fully aware that everyone was watching her every move. "Mac C?" She showed her badge and kept her hands in plain view, alerting everyone in the room that her intentions were honorable.

"A Fed?" He stroked his bushy mustache. "To what do I owe the honor?" He motioned for her to take a seat. Her initial assessment of the bookie hadn't been far off. He was indeed frail, his probably once vibrant red hair now wisps of white strands. Yet there was a coldness in his dark blue eyes. This was not a man Val wanted to upset in any way, shape, or form. "Please sit," he repeated with a ghost of smile.

Val took a seat in the rickety wooden chair across from him. Unconsciously, she moved the chair slightly so she could view the entire barroom and not have her back to everyone.

"Smart." He nodded, not missing her action. "Not having your back exposed. Military?"

"Navy, retired."

"If you've come to place a bet, I should warn you that would be entrapment."

"I don't give a..." She almost laughed at his assumption. "I'm not here for a friendly discussion on tonight's game. I'm Val Brown, US Marshal. This is about a man who may have caused you some stress in the past."

"Not a short list."

"Albert Beaumont."

"Bert?" Mac truly seemed surprised. "If you're here to tell me that pissant isn't rotting away in a four by nine cell, I'm not going to be a happy man."

"You're not going to be a happy man."

"Don't tell me some bleeding-heart jackass put him in witness protection or some other bullshit?"

"No. Idiot took a runner."

"Here?" Mac looked as if he was about to fall out of his chair. "That would make him a new kind of stupid. Look, back in the day I didn't do anything because Cattie asked me not to. Kid is just like her old man, stubborn as all hell. I respect her."

"I just need to know if I'm looking for a corpse."

"I didn't hurt a hair on his chinny-chin-chin. But if I could-"

"Best you stop there," Val said. There was no way he was lying. The anger in his eyes was fresh. He hadn't known. Now he did, and that made Beaumont fair game.

"Blood on your hands isn't what your niece wants." Val shivered when she looked into his eyes. There wasn't a doubt in her mind that Mac already had blood on his hands. Since she was certain it wasn't Beaumont's, she decided to just let it be.

"I know, and keep quiet about Cattie. She's clean, no need tarnishing her badge. I love that kid and her sister. Those girls and little Emma are the only family I've got left." He paused to take a hit of oxygen. "You find him, before I do. But I have to tell you that sorry SOB wouldn't come anywhere near here. The only thing waiting for him in Boston is a target on his back. Much as I'd hate to break my word, I'm on my way out. Taking the trash out with me wouldn't bother me a bit."

"I believe you."

A sly smile crossed his lips before he took another hit of oxygen. His cell phone vibrated on the battered wooden table. Val took that as her cue to leave. She didn't say a word as he studied the text message. She understood guys like him. He wasn't a bad man. In fact at heart, he was a very good man. He just broke the law.

"You're a Yankees fan!" he shouted just as she stood.

She almost started to laugh, knowing that CC Calloway was determined to have the last word. She turned to him, confused by the twinkle in his bloodshot blue eyes. She was more than ready to counter with, "So, what," followed by a scathing remark regarding the Boston Bums. The words died on her lips, when she felt an ice storm assault her. The barroom was eerily quiet. Slowly she turned and realized where she was. In the back corner of a sports cop bar in Boston, and she had just been branded.

"Ah, crap." She looked down at a very amused man. Mac C might be on his last breath, but he was still a dangerous man. "Haven't been in a bar fight in a long time. This should be interesting."

"Do you mind if I take bets on how many teeth you'll lose?"

"Mac!" A heavy voice boomed, stirring up the crowd. "Why are you yanking my poor goddaughter's chain? Calm down, boys. This is my cousin Pete's niece." A bold figure emerged. Despite the man's advanced years, he was an imposing figure as he confidently made his way across the barroom. "Born and raised in Chelsea. Made her father proud and broke her mother's heart when she had Teddy's number nine tattooed on her arse."

Val blew out a heavy sigh of relief when the sturdy man

thumped her on the back. The crowd snickered and thankfully went back to their business. She had no idea who her savior was.

"Frankie, the kid's too sensitive." Mac laughed, breaking the tension "Told her not to bet the Colts over the Saints."

"She square with you?" Val's new hero played along.

"Oh, yeah." Mac waved it off. "Just giving her a good ribbing, boys," Mac said, ensuring there would be no more problems. "Why don't you let Uncle Frank walk you home?"

Val cringed, not missing the hard look dimming Mac's blue eyes. She understood that he wasn't merely making a suggestion. He was telling her that it was time to leave. Things could have turned very ugly if Frank hadn't intervened. She decided it was in her best interest to heed his advice.

"Yeah, thanks, Mac," she said. "Haven't had one like that pulled on me in a long time. You take care now." Frank led her safely out of the dimly lit barroom. "Uncle Frank?"

"Frank Donnelly, Boston PD, retired." He ignored her offer to shake his hand. "Got a call from Mills. Good thing I was in the area."

"How small is this city?" Val wondered if everyone in Boston was somehow related. "Hold on, Donnelly. I need to talk to you."

"About Beaumont," he said. "That's why Mills called me."

"Can we talk while we head over to the State crime lab? And thanks again for the save."

"Mac didn't mean—"

"Yes, he did. Not because he doesn't like me. He just wants his shot at Beaumont. Can't say that I blame him. Plus, I think the guy is just this side of crazy."

"My fault on that one." Frank's broad shoulders slumped. "Should have told him what was happening at the time. When he found out, that was it between us. Used to be good friends. He was right. Should have let him handle it his way. But I'm a cop..."

"I get it." Val readied her car keys. She did get it. It was the way Frank said that was *it* between us. She had a feeling that good old Frank and Mac were a lot closer than anyone knew. She couldn't help recalling the comment about CC going to live with her funny uncle. It made sense. Generational, these guys would never be open about who they were. Val felt a pang of sadness as she recalled her own isolation during her years of service. No matter what she did for her country, she was still at risk of losing her benefits if she was outed. It frosted her cookies that guys like Beaumont could roam free without a care in the world, but being gay still meant you were an outsider. A gentle nudge on her elbow disrupted her dreary thoughts.

"We can walk. It'll be quicker than fighting traffic and looking for parking," Frank said with another nudge before guiding her down the street. "It's about a block away from the three-three."

"Would you mind telling me about Beaumont?"

"Cattie was in trouble with her parents. Started whacking her stepfather with a baseball bat. Granted, she was always a firecracker, but that was a bit much. Sat her down and she told me that Beaumont tried to put his hand in her underwear. She was going through all the guilt trips and confusion that kids do when something like that happens. It broke my heart. I kept it together and followed the rules. And that slimy bastard had the social workers and everyone else convinced that Cattie was a liar."

"You believed her?"

"Yes. Back then, you couldn't just type a name into a computer and find out everything you need to know. I went looking. Hard to do, since he lied about where he was from. I kept an eye on Cattie. Told her to come to me if she was in trouble."

"That was it?" Val didn't believe it for a minute.

"It was different then."

"Yeah?" She knew there had to be more to the story.

"Took him for a ride down by the docks."

"Just to let him know you'd be watching." Val knew it was wrong, but at times, she almost wished cops could still pull stunts like that.

"And I did watch, and Cattie kept him in line." Frankie guided her along the narrow streets. "More so after Stevie was born. There were a couple of complaints over the years. A couple of Stevie's friends said stuff. Nothing we could prove. I'd stop by now and then just to let him know I was still watching. By the time I got my hands on his record, the family was in the wind. Later, when Cattie went after custody of Stevie, I showed up with a wall of blue and a stack of files. Maria didn't even put up a stink. Still can't believe how cold that woman was. I put the boys down in Rhode Island on watch. Thought we had Beaumont wrapped up. Now, he's back."

"Not for long, I hope." If this case had been a regular runner, she'd have had him by now, she was sure of it.

"Who are you seeing downtown?"

"Corey McDowell."

"We'll need to stop at the bakery on the corner."

"Are you serious?"

CHECKMATE

When they arrived, Dr. McDowell did hem and haw about a case number and federal-over-state jurisdiction. That was until Frank gave her a nudge and she forked over a bag of fudge-nut brownies guaranteed to melt in your mouth. She was stunned when he handed over the greeting card and a full report.

Chapter 19

Bert paced around the room wringing his hands. He couldn't believe he let himself get caught up in this mess. Everything was going good. All he had to do was show up at work and do his therapy. Okay, the job was crap. A man his age shouldn't be tarring roofs. The therapy was a joke. Say the right thing, and you're free. He knew nothing was going to change what he was. He just wanted to live his life. Sure, he hated his stepdaughter most of the time. The rest of the time, he could admit what he had tried to do to her. Those times were few and far between. He wasn't looking forward to starting over, registering as a sex offender, having his neighbors note his every move.

"Maybe that's what I need," he muttered to the empty hotel room. "I don't give in when I know they're watching. Having Caitlin watching and sending the cops after me kept me on the straight and narrow."

Silently, he wished he had experienced this revelation a couple weeks ago before that letter and cell phone showed up. The letter offered him a whole new life. A chance to start over again. New name, new place to live, with no one knowing what he had done. All he had to do was go back to Boston and let people know he was there. He had to be careful. Getting caught wasn't part of the plan. He hoped that wasn't part of the plan. The truth was, he didn't know the plan.

He got an envelope with a bus ticket to Boston and a key to a locker. In the locker were the first pieces to his new life. A little cash, a different prepaid cell phone, and a hotel room keycard. Not just any hotel, The Marriott Copley. After spending the better part of two decades in the segregated unit of Bridgeport prison, it was like a dream come true.

The plush hotel was nice. Very nice. He couldn't deny it. Still, there was something very wrong. The text messages he kept getting that told him to go for a stroll and don't hide from the security cameras didn't make sense. Why run, then show your face? It wouldn't be long before his stepdaughter got wind of this. Having a cop with a very big axe to grind chasing after him wasn't his idea of freedom.

The last text made him antsy. He was moving to a different motel, one out of the city but close enough that he could hop on the subway and run. It made sense to get away from all the cops and high-tech surveillance. The only thing he had to do was check out. Not a difficult task, since everything was paid for. He had to sign the name he had been given, Gilbert Osborne. The text said to take the subway to Boylston where he would have a hotel room waiting for him. Another new name and a new cell phone. He was to destroy and trash the present phone just as he had with the last one. He was happy to be leaving downtown Boston, although a little farther away than Boylston Hills would have pleased him. Still he had the niggling thought that something was very wrong.

"Grow a set," he told himself and grabbed the few belongings he possessed. He took one last look around the comfortable room. Just a little more time and he'd be free. New name, a place to live, and a little money. "Then why do I feel like it's all going to hell?"

Chapter 20

Val sat in the conference room, staring over the files and the greeting card. She tried to remain objective, but nothing this guy did followed the usual route. "Pussy, pie, or payback" was her usual game plan. Most runners go right for easy sex, a home-cooked meal, or vengeance. There were those who just ran as fast and as far as they could, but somewhere along the line, they stopped for pussy or pie. It was human nature after all. Payback was the only other option. The misguided urge to settle a score. It was the only thing that would explain why Beaumont came to Boston. As far as she could see, the one person Beaumont blamed for his sorry life was his stepdaughter.

"We've got your boyfriend!" Mills waved a disc around the conference room.

"What?" Val looked up from the meeting she was having with her team.

"Strangest thing. We got a tip. We also got him on camera," Mills said. "At the Copley."

"The Copley?" Deputy Mark Finn frowned. "Where is this prick getting the money?"

"He's staying there?" Val agreed with Finn's assessment.

"Don't know yet," Mills said, "but he's been on camera more than once around the mall that's connected to the Marriott. Here's a copy of the video."

Finn snatched it up and put it in the DVD player. Val was well aware that Finn felt like Val had stepped on his toes by coming into his city uninvited. Val refrained from reminding Finn that when she first arrived no one thought Beaumont would be stupid enough to come back to Boston.

Val had called Finn before coming up to Boston. She suggested he put a BOLO out on Beaumont and have someone watch South Station. Finn ignored her request. By the time Val arrived in the Hub, the only thing they had to work with was a video image of a man who might be Beaumont getting off a bus and accessing a locker at the station. It had taken time to get the image, since they were looking at the bus terminal not the train station. Mills had a hunch, and low and behold, there was someone who matched Beaumont's description wandering around the station.

Two things bothered her and Mills: The guy they spied on camera didn't take the bus as the tip suggested he would. He had also arrived three hours earlier than their informant had led them to believe. Val felt a gnawing in her gut.

Val was certain the man in the surveillance video was Beaumont. Finn didn't agree. The only reason Finn agreed to work with Val was because his boss told him to do so. Val couldn't care less if Finn wanted to take the lead or grab the glory. All she wanted was Beaumont locked up where he belonged. She was finally getting pissed off by Finn's condescending attitude. Mostly because Finn's arrogance had cost them valuable time.

"Damn, that's him." Val watched the tapes carefully. "Right out in the open. Doesn't make sense."

"He thinks we're not looking for him," Finn said. "There he is again."

"Geez, are you telling me this guy is staying at the Marriott? He's right around the corner. Why is he this close to home?" Val's brow furrowed. "Nothing this guy does makes any sense. Okay, Finn, take his photo to the Marriott and ask around. Keep me posted. The rest of you keep working your details. Watch the daughter and ex-wife. If Beaumont is planning on doing something stupid, I want us there. I'm going to drop in on Detective Calloway and update her. Then I'll meet up with you." She nodded to Finn who seemed less than pleased at being told what to do. "One thing, people. I know there's a connection to one of your own, but out of respect for Detective Calloway's reputation, let's try not to send Beaumont home in a body bag."

"What if he—"

"I didn't say he couldn't accidentally fall." Val secretly hoped that Beaumont would indeed have an accidental fall or bump his head. "He's a child molester. Any bumps he gets resisting is fine by me. All I'm saying is, unless he's going to shoot you, don't shoot him. Got it?"

"For the record, we don't cross the line," Finn said. "Never have. Never will."

"I didn't mean to imply that you would." Val didn't miss the way the rest of the team rolled their eyes at their boss's statement. "I'm just saying that with these types it's hard not to get worked up."

Finn fussed around, but he finally gathered the team and left. Val stayed behind to get organized. She needed a moment before she dropped in on Detective Calloway.

"Someone is helping this guy," she muttered.

"You knew that already." Mills gave a snort. "Come on, you sent word. We had him on tape at South Station. Think Finn will post a BOLO now?" she asked. "What do you think was in that locker at the depot?"

"Money, drugs, ID." Val shrugged. "Could be anything. My

question is, who left it? I've gone over Beaumont's pals from the pen. Like most of his kind, he was in segregation. Didn't really make any friends. None that could help him. He doesn't have any family, just the ex-wife and the daughter. There was something a buddy of mine came across. Something about his mother being in a nursing home back in Ohio. The unit there is checking into it. They can't find the old lady anywhere, so far. All he has here is the kid and the ex. I doubt either of them would want to see him again much less help him run."

"Doesn't fit."

"No, it doesn't." Val gathered up her gear. "Guys like this run. If they don't have any allies to turn to, they just run, far and fast. I find it hard to believe that this jackass ran to a city where he doesn't stand a snowball's chance in hell of walking away alive."

"I've heard that you and Calloway are a lot alike," Mills said. "Both of you fly on your instincts. What does that infamous gut of yours tell you?"

"We're being played."

Chapter 21

Jamie was out in the yard, enjoying the feel of the cool autumn air. She checked her watch. She wanted to get the yard at least partially raked before she had to get ready for her shift. She smiled when she realized she had a little more time to enjoy the outdoors. A nondescript Buick pulled up to the curb.

"Now, that's a cop car," she said to herself.

A slender woman wearing simple black pants, white cotton blouse, and a black blazer stepped out of the car. "And that would be a cop. Honey, it's for you!" she shouted, loud enough for her wife to hear through the open screen door.

"Dr. Jameson." Sunglasses hid the woman's eyes.

Stevie rounded the corner, and Jamie didn't miss the quick look of appreciation she gave the woman.

"Ah, Deputy Val. Back again?" Stevie said with a slight sneer.

"Good news this time?"

"I'm afraid not."

"Deputy Dumb Ass." CC's greeting was curt as she emerged from the house.

"Nice," Val shot back. "Any particular reason you're this snarky? Or is that part of your charm, Detective? Oh and thanks for almost getting me killed. Why'd you text your uncle and have him out me at a cop bar?"

"You don't seem any worse for wear. Serves you right. You knew Beaumont was here," CC growled. Jamie could see she was fighting to keep her anger in check. "It wasn't a gut feeling. You had him on tape at South Station."

"It was still a maybe."

"Even so, my sister and I should have been told sooner."

"How did you?"

"How did you think I knew?" She cut her off. "I don't know how tight you Feds are, but here we look after each other."

"You know what? You're right," Val said. "I sent out the warning and trusted it would be enough. It wasn't. I screwed up."

"When?" Stevie asked, surprising everyone. "When did you alert the police that he might be in area?"

"The day we got word that he had bolted and was on his way here." Val seemed to be thrown off kilter. Jamie suspected that she hadn't expected Stevie to be the one to push her against the wall.

"Hold on." CC cut in. "You sent out a BOLO on the first day? And just now, things are happening?"

"I met with some resistance," Val said. "But that's in the past. Things are in motion. I understand you're upset. Trust me, I want to find this guy."

"Then do it."

"Deputy," Jamie hesitantly began to say, "you must know how trying this is on my family. Just what is it your people are doing?"

"Everything possible, Dr. Jameson."

"Which is?" Jamie pressed not feeling encouraged by the stress clearly evident in the Deputy's voice.

"Why don't we step inside?" Deputy Brown suggested with a

careful glance over her shoulder.

Jamie felt uneasy when the woman hesitated before answering. She agreed with the suggestion and guided her wife and sister-in- law into their home.

"We've had a sighting in the city," Val said.

"Where?" CC asked.

"Copley Marriott. He checked out right before we got the tip."

"Beg pardon? That doesn't make any sense." CC sputtered.

"I know. We get most of these bozos because they think they can hide in a big city. As you know, Detective, that just leaves a paper trail. No one ever told them it's easier to hide in the middle of nowhere. Thing is, Beaumont isn't leaving a paper trail. One of the hinky things about this case is everything we got is because of anonymous tips. Something isn't right. Did he have any friends from when he lived around here?"

"My father never brought anyone over," Stevie said. "It was weird really. Then again, turns out he was weird."

"Bert didn't have any pals that I knew of," CC added. "Not like my father, who always had friends over to watch a game or barbeque. You know, guy things. Considering the past Bert was hiding, it makes sense now. Him hanging out at Copley Place doesn't. It's not like he's up to doing a little shopping at Neiman Marcus. Are you telling me Bert developed a sense of style while he was in prison?"

"I don't know what to tell you."

Jamie didn't miss the dejected look on the marshal's face as she made a hasty exit. The way the three of them silently stood

CHECKMATE

there was making Jamie nervous.

"Who gets to tell Emma that there's a chance she can't go trick-or-treating?" she asked when it appeared the standoff wasn't going to end.

* * *

While the Calloway clan was trying to decide the best way to inform young Emma her annual romp around the neighborhood dressed like whatever wonderful costume her father designed was out of the question, Bitsy Marsden was on the other side of the country preparing to go for a run.

She made it around the first lap, without breaking a sweat. As ran, she pondered why there was an issue with her she behavior? All she did was ask Mrs. Fisher if she was planning on selling her house. Bitsy thought she should get some compensation for having to live next door to the Fishers. She had tried to warn everyone that Simon was a major malfunction. She still shivered every time she thought about finding Bongo her dog dead after she turned Simon down for a date.

She knew all along it was him. Years later, when he was sent off to the booby hatch, she wasn't shocked. Why would Mrs. Fisher want to stick around? The only thing Bitsy did was politely mention the fact. With the real estate market being sluggish, she didn't want to miss the opportunity to make a bid on the Fisher property.

The bright spot for Bitsy that afternoon was an almost empty track. She was nearly alone, free to become lost in her thoughts. The only distraction was one other runner who possessed a poor sense of fashion. Bitsy found his all-black-vinyl running suit distasteful. "Very nineteen ninety." The stranger kept getting closer and closer.

Bitsy tried to maintain her pace, then she tried to outrun the stranger, who seemed to be gaining on her. With a large, empty track, they should have been able to give one another a wide berth. The dark, hooded figure closed in, challenging her. She was determined to win. She always won. Her lungs seized, and her body betrayed her. She conceded and moved to the right to allow the other runner to pass. She squeaked with surprise when she was pushed off the track. Fully prepared to spew a litany of curses at the other person's rude behavior, she choked on the words. Frantically, she felt her throat while trying to maintain her footing.

She was shocked to feel a warm stickiness greet her fingers. The reality of what had happened didn't fully hit her until she was lying on the ground gasping her last breath.

An hour later, the men's track coach found the half-naked woman lying in the brush beside the track with her throat slashed. Bitsy's senseless death sent a shockwave throughout the community. Outrage turned to relief when two young men were arrested in East Los Angeles when they tried to use Bitsy's credit card. The police failed to listen to the young men's frantic claim that they had found the credit card lying on the street.

* * *

The following evening, Professor Archibald Harden moved around the humble home the university had provided.

He was happy as he settled into his favorite chair by the fire. In his hands he held a very fine single malt scotch and one of his favorite books. At times he regretted trading Wisconsin for Texas. He had no choice. He couldn't stay in Austin after that nasty incident. Some young people could never be enlightened.

He shook away the unpleasant memory of the unhinged student who, after receiving a mediocre grade, tried to set fire to his office. He resolved to enjoy this perfect evening.

CHECKMATE

As he read, he felt slightly wearier than usual. He blamed the scotch; still he read on until he could no longer focus. Feeling light-headed and slightly confused, he closed his book. He hadn't thought he drank that much.

He fell back into his armchair and decided to give himself a moment before he attempted to navigate the staircase. Instead, he drifted off, dying peacefully in his sleep.

Harden's body was discovered after he failed to arrive for his morning tutorial.

The police who entered the professor's home were shocked to find him sitting in his chair, wearing no pants, his face painted with lipstick, blue eye shadow, and mascara. Most disturbing was the sight of his penis nestled in his right hand. Despite efforts by the police, word of his unusual demise spread throughout the small town. No one was eager to give his eulogy.

Chapter 22

Jamie was filled with apprehension when she arrived at the hospital. She needed to clear her head and focus on her job and not the strange events that seemed to be lurking around every corner.

She did have one detail to deal with. Deputy Brown had given her a copy of Bert's mug shot. Jamie swung by the security office. She smiled when Terrell greeted her. The kindly older man had been instrumental many years ago in helping catch Simon Fisher. Jamie never forgot it. Neither did the hospital, promoting him from parking lot attendant to higher up in security. The hospital overhauled the entire security system after everything that happened.

"Dr. Jameson," he said brightly.

"Terrell." She fought to keep her tone light. "How's your family?"

"Good and yours? How is that adorable niece of yours?"

"Growing like a weed. Maybe we should stop feeding her." The smile she was sporting vanished when she remembered that this wasn't a social call. "I have some business." She cringed slightly when she handed him the mug shot. "My wife's stepfather—"

"Let me handle things." He took the picture. "No need to explain. You just focus on making folks better."

"He's an escaped fugitive. A sex offender." She handed him Deputy Brown's business card. "I doubt he'll show up here, but if he does, call this woman. Please, if you see him, don't let him near any children." Jamie flinched when she saw Terrell shiver. "Sorry."

"No need." He patted her hand. "You just do your job and we'll do ours. I promise."

CHECKMATE

* * *

Jamie felt better after talking with Terrell. There was something reassuring about the man. Now she had to talk to Jack. It was bad enough that Jack was more than a little distracted with his marital problems and budget cuts looming over the emergency room.

"Hey, Jack," she said meekly when she stepped into his office.

"This can't be good if you're acting all shy." He shrewdly noted.

"It's probably nothing to worry about."

"Crap, what's wrong."

"As I said, probably nothing to worry about." She winced when his expression turned grim.

"Last time you said there was probably nothing to worry about, the nurses voted to strike."

She handed him a picture of Bert. "This is Albert 'Bert' Beaumont. There's a BOLO, a be-on-the-look-out, issued for him. He's a child molester who escaped from a halfway house in Connecticut. He might be in the area. I've already alerted security."

"My God, Jamie, you scared me," he said, relief showing on his face. "I thought you were going to quit or something. I'll alert the nurses. Wait. Why are you handing this out? Shouldn't the police be involved?"

"They are. So are the Feds. The thing is, he's CC's stepfather." She explained feeling sick.

"Oh."

Jamie didn't understand why, but for some reason she felt shame. She hadn't done anything wrong. She never even met the man. Still, admitting that you're related to someone like that made her feel like she needed a shower.

"I doubt he knows about me or where I work. We just want to be extra careful."

"Understood."

Jamie snapped into her business mode. "Okay, that's over with, so stop staring and let's get some paperwork done."

"What, no coffee?"

"You sound like my wife."

"And you sound like mine."

"How's that going?"

"Like you said, we have work to do." His reply was so quiet Jamie almost missed it. "Go get us some coffee."

"You're such a bully."

* * *

After Jamie finished up with Jack, she ducked into the break room and answered a call from her sister, Meegan.

"Love the new phone," Stella said when she entered the room. "What's wrong?"

"Apparently, my parents' squirrel problem is getting worse," Jamie said and snickered. "My sister's worried because our parents decided that the best way to deal with it is to let Dad shoot them. Meegan went over, and there was Dad trolling the backyard with a

CHECKMATE

shotgun."

"Not very humane."

"Not just that. Our parents' eyesight is waning. We're a little concerned about them playing with guns. I don't like guns to begin with, and the thought of Dad, with his cataracts, running around with a loaded shotgun, is unsettling. My poor stepmother. I wonder if she knew what she was getting into when she married him."

"You have guns," Stella said. "I mean I assume that you do."

"Two and they travel with CC. When she's home, they're locked up. She's always been very careful because of Emma. What's on the board today?"

"More folks afraid they have H1N1, an extreme case of flatulence, a broken leg, and Mrs. Bowers is back."

"Let's do the standard on the flu folks, and since I noticed that Tierney was late again, she can have the patient with gas." Jamie smirked. "Tell me our patient is an elderly obese man."

"Just so happens he is."

Jamie laughed. "Now maybe she'll show up on time. I like the kid, but she's not going to make it if she doesn't pull her head out of the clouds."

"The clouds? With that one, I'm willing to bet her head is firmly planted deep inside her lower anatomy." Stella scoffed.

* * *

Val's head was throbbing. A migraine was brewing. She wasn't certain who was to blame. It could be Albert Beaumont for being smarter than she had assumed. It could be the Calloway sisters for being a general pain in her ass. Then there was Finn who was a bastard who seemed to enjoy adding to her stress. He stood there looking at her as if she could magically pull Beaumont out of her butt.

"Go over it again." She demanded the time of playing nice had long since passed. While he glared at her, She silently vowed from this moment on it was time to kick ass. "Your team tracked him to the Marriott. He wasn't just hanging around. He had been staying there under the name Gilbert Osborne."

"We've been over this." He snarled.

"Let's do it again," Val said. "The room was booked and paid for with a prepaid Visa that has since been deactivated?"

"Yes." He grunted.

"CSU found a trashed cell phone which turned out to be a burner. Prepaid and bought in San Diego at the same Seven Eleven the prepaid credit card was purchased. Both were cash purchases, and any film we might have gotten has long since been dubbed over."

"CSU is trying to get the phone working, and they are using Cellebrite to access the call and texts history," Mills said.

Val should have been pleased that work was being done. That everything was in the works. She just couldn't shake the feeling that she was being used as a pawn in some sick game. If that was true, then any of her peers could be in on the game.

"Stop me when I get something wrong. Beaumont checked out and disappeared to parts unknown. We have no idea where this perv is hiding out or why he's here. Is that about it?"

"Yes, the subway is right there." Finn laid a map of the subway system out in front of Brown. "Copley station is on the Green

Line. From there you can go to North Station and pick up a commuter rail to the burbs like Framingham or Lowell. He could also hop on the Down-Easter and head up to Maine. Or he could have transferred to the Red Line, back to South Station. From there he could pick up Amtrak, heading anywhere in the country, or walk over to the Peter Pan bus terminal, again headed to anywhere in the country."

"How do you people navigate this?" All of the different routes, each color coded, boggled her mind. During her stint in the military, she had managed to navigate her way around jungles with nothing but verbal instructions and a knife. Finding her way around the city of Boston was a nightmare in comparison.

"It's easy." Finn had the bad manners to scoff at her. "Green downtown, Government Center, Copley, Park Street, all the way through Boylston, and to Newton if you are riding the D Line. Red will take you through Cambridge and all the way to Quincy. Blue will—"

"Stop!" Val shouted, stunning everyone in the office. She took a moment and tried to calm herself. "So, basically, he walked out of the hotel complex, and from what you're saying, he could be anywhere. Now my question is how does a kiddy fucker who's been locked up in segregation end up with an all-expenses-paid trip to Bean Town and a phone bought in California? According to the logs at Bridgeport, only his lawyer visited him. And the lawyer didn't really seem interested in his well-being. Who is bankrolling him? And why?"

She was slightly amused by the confused look Finn was sporting. The rest of the team seemed to be enjoying his distress as well.

She finally let him off the hook. "Never mind. How about the rest of you? Anything from the surveillance on the ex-wife or the Calloway sisters?"

"Nothing," Mills said. "He's been on the move for thirty hours now. Damn. Wish we had checked the video earlier. The tip came in too late."

"Yeah, I know." Val continued pacing. "Video at the Copley? isn't that how you got the Craigslist killer?"

"Exactly the same way, same hotel."

"That's right." Val furrowed her brow. "Everyone knows that. It's been all over the news, not just here but all over the country. It was on Dateline. Unless he's a complete idiot, which is entirely possible, Beaumont would know not to show his face at the Copley."

"Then why?"

"If I had the answer to that one, we'd have the bastard." Val ran her fingers through her hair. "Okay, I take it your subway has video surveillance?"

"Of course," Finn said.

"Mills, would you be available? I need you to come with me and help me get around the transit cops. Everyone else, get back to working your details."

"We don't call it the subway. Around here it's the T," Mills said. "Short for MBTA, Massachusetts Bay Transit Authority."

"I will never understand this city."

"Excuse me!" Finn barked. "And just what am I supposed to be doing while you're taking over?"

"You?" Val wanted to tell him to carry on being a useless jackass. "I need you to check out every hotel, motel, rooming house and watering hole in the city. This guy had to be heading somewhere. Let's hope it isn't somewhere in another state."

"You want me running traces?" He gasped.

"Got a problem with that?"

Val waited as everyone stared at Finn, who was glaring at her. Silently she dared him to say something, anything that would give her an excuse to have him thrown off the case. She egged him on with a cocky smirk that made him storm out of the room.

"Okay, now that the pissing contest is over," Val calmly said, knowing she had won, "get back to work and keep me updated on everything."

"That was incredibly risky," Mills said as they made their way towards the elevator.

"Had to be done. He wants the glory. I want the bad guy. Maybe now he'll be of some use. If not, at the very least he won't be in the way."

Chapter 23

When CC rolled into the station house, her mood was foul. She had just gotten off of the phone with Mills. The update wasn't what she had hoped for. Anything short of "We got him" was a major disappointment.

"Long night?" Max asked, his chair squeaking loudly. CC couldn't refrain from scowling at him.

"Not really. The dipstick my mother had the bad sense to marry is in the area."

"Not just a maybe?"

"Looks like he's been hanging around Copley Place."

"What?"

"Staying at the Marriott."

"Nah. How's a guy just out of the joint and on the run manage to hole up in a posh place like that?" Max argued.

"Don't know." She tried to keep her composure. "Right now, we need to deal with yet another pretrial hearing for the people vs. Stern. They're trying to get the confession tossed." She couldn't help smiling when Max barked with laughter. "Could happen," she said.

"You and Mulligan wrapped her up tighter than a virgin in a convent. I've got twenty that says the judge barely listens to her mouthpiece." Max scoffed at the idea.

"You're on."

* * *

Val felt like crap after poring for hours over grainy videotapes. The only thing she had to show for her efforts was a stiff neck and a possible glimpse of Beaumont heading towards the Boylston Hills stop on from what she understood to be the Green Line route. Which put him in the Calloway family's backyard.

Back at the office, she went through everything at least twenty times. Each time she came to the same conclusion: nothing made sense.

"Why would a man just out of prison run to the one place everyone wants him dead?" She couldn't help muttering out loud.

"Answer that and you'll find him." Mills took a seat at the table where Val was working. "Better still, why hide in places where you'll be seen?"

"It's a game. It's always a game with these jokers. Usually it's a lame game of tag. This time, I'm playing chess with someone who shouldn't have lasted long after his opening move. I have a better question for you. Why didn't Boston move faster? They got the call from Connecticut and just sat on the information."

"Finn got the call." Mills reluctantly mumbled.

"And?"

"And he hates Calloway."

"Enough to let a twisted fuck like Beaumont slip through his fingers?" Val sputtered thoroughly disgusted.

"I didn't think so, until this happened."

"What's his problem?"

"What do you think?"

"Taking things this far usually means something on the job o a woman." Val quickly surmised still not understanding why someone in Finn's position would let a slime ball like Beaumont slip through their fingers. "Since Calloway is one of those disgusting happily married types, I'm guessing that it was something that happened on the job."

"Wrong."

* * *

"Will you stop playing with that thing?" CC regretted letting Max use her phone.

"This thing is amazing. Look, this is the boat I want."

"Donald Trump doesn't have a ride that nice." CC snatched her phone back. "Perhaps you should lower your sights. Shirley must be ready to throttle you. How did you go online with this?" She waved the phone in his face.

"Here." He showed her once again how to use her phone to Google. "And this is how you send pictures or video. You can even do it while it's in the holder you wear on your belt. Or you can do a conference call, even a videoconference call, if you wanted to."

"Why would I want to?"

"You know, I'm the old fogey and I got this mastered."

"I just want to make phone calls."

"Seriously." Now Leigh grabbed the phone from CC. "This is an amazing phone. Mine isn't this nice. Half the reporters in there today are using something like this to stream a video to their producers. See you can send live video by doing this." CC's eyes glazed over as Leigh explained what appeared to be a simple task.

"The judge said no TV," CC said. "We're not even supposed

to have our phones in the courtroom."

"I'll be streaming," a sultry voice said.

"Laura Carson. Come to watch the circus?" CC greeted the former defense attorney who was now under the employ of a major television network. "Tell me the truth. Don't you miss the courtroom?"

"I spend almost every day in a courtroom. I just don't have to defend lying sociopaths anymore." Laura scoffed. "I still believe in the justice system. I just feel safer reporting the facts instead of creating excuses. Nice phone. Maybe you'll learn how to work it before the new model comes out. You do know that your ineptitude could cost you your butch card."

"According to my wife, I never had one. Are we going to be seeing more of you, Laura? I take it you're covering the Stern trial or, as you news people call it, the Whacko Soccer Mom trial. Where do you come up with these monikers?"

"My producer," Laura said and groaned. "Any chance you'll change your mind about doing an interview for my piece on West?"

"Nope."

"You have a call," Mulligan told CC.

"I didn't hear it."

"I reset you to vibrate since we have to be in the courtroom," Mulligan explained. "It's someone named Brooks."

"Cop from San Diego," Max explained.

"There's a case I wanted to pitch," Laura said, suddenly excited. "My producer shot it down. Not enough bodies and no trial.

It wasn't newsworthy."

CC liked Laura. In her day, the leggy blonde had been one hell of a lawyer. CC teased her about going Hollywood, but CC got it. Too many guilty clients walking the streets versus sitting in front of a camera wasn't a difficult choice for Laura.

"Brooks, what's going on?"

"Hate to bug you this early." He apologized.

"Middle of the day for me."

"I keep forgetting." He tried to joke, but CC could hear an odd note in his voice. "Look, I've got a bad feeling about something and need to talk to someone about it."

"I'm due in court in a few." She stepped away from the others so she could better hear Brooks. "You'll have to make this quick."

"It all started with the father, Malcolm Fisher."

"What do you mean?" Her mind was already trying to process why he had called her. "Was he into something?"

"No, not him. Elizabeth Pryce died about a week ago."

"Elizabeth Pryce?" CC searched her mind for the name. "Right, Janie Jensen's girlfriend. What happened?"

"The medical examiner has it listed as undetermined. I don't have all the details. It happened up in San Francisco. I couldn't get much, just it might be some kind of virus."

"Okay." CC pulled a notepad and pen out of her pocket and started to scribble. She had no idea what was going on. So far, Brooks wasn't telling her anything earth-shattering.

"A couple of days ago, Bitsy Marsden was murdered." Brooks' grave tone sent shivers down CC's spine.

"Marsden was Fisher's neighbor," CC said. She suddenly felt out of sorts. "The one who every time Fisher asked her out when they were teenagers, she turned him down. Then one of her pets would wind up mutilated."

"That's the girl." Brooks sounded far too excited. "Our Special Victims Unit is handling it. On the surface, it looks like a rape attempt. Her car turned up in a chop shop in East LA. A couple local youth were bagged trying to use her credit card."

"And?" CC wasn't connecting the dots. "One anaphylactic shock, one mysterious virus, and a random act of violence. I'm not seeing a connection."

"Don't you? They were all connected to Fisher."

"But not to each other." CC tried to reason as a dull pain formed in her temple. "Only one of them is listed as a crime. I'm not getting why you called."

"I guess I wasted your time. I just think we should be looking into this."

"I'm willing to peek if you think there's something worth looking at. I trust you. Hey, while I've got you on the phone, what can you tell me about a Fed named Val Brown? She's a US Marshal."

"Val?" CC noticed that his tone lightened." Brown's a good kid. Reminds me a little of you. Good instincts, smart, and generally plays by the rules. Retired from the navy, I think. Why?"

"She's here, working a case that's a little close to home."

"If I was looking for someone, she's who I would want on the case. She seems to have resources that we don't."

"Interesting." CC didn't know what to make of the information. She saw Judge Conrad's bailiff waving for them. "I've got to get my butt into court. We'll talk more about Fisher later. I've kind of got my hands full at the moment, but I promise to get back to you."

* * *

The pretrial motions went quickly. One look at the video, and the judge quashed the defense's motions. Despite her bet with Max, CC doubted that the defense would get the confession tossed. It probably didn't help their cause when Judge Conrad referred to her as an exemplary officer. Less than half an hour later, CC handed Max a crisp twenty dollar bill. She enjoyed getting him back in the game. She missed the banter, the friendly wagers, and generally annoying one another. When cops partner together, it's just like being married: there are days you can't live without one another and then there are days when you just want to shoot each other.

"What did Brooks say about Brown?" Max asked.

"Basically, I should trust her."

"You don't?"

"I guess I do. I just don't like the way this is going down. It isn't her. It's the situation. I thought I had seen the last of that bastard, and now here he is again. Or is he? I also don't like that she's been watching us. I really don't like the way she looks at my kid sister."

"You don't like anyone looking at Stevie."

"I practically raised her. Having some hotshot Fed ogling her like she's a piece of candy bugs me. Having her father running around scares the crap out of me. We don't want to let Emma go trick-or-treating."

"Hold on." Max held up his hand, halting her in her tracks. He had that worried look he got at times the fatherly look of concern that usually led him to try to take complete control of the situation. If anyone but Max acted that way, CC would throttle them. Coming from Max, it was like dealing with a parent.

"With Bert on the loose, it isn't safe."

"What isn't safe?" Mulligan asked as she approached them.

"The world in general," CC said with a grunt. "What was Krassowski doing here?"

"Oh, didn't I tell you?" Leigh sighed. "Since he's my partner, he's taking credit for the bust."

"He hasn't done any work on this case."

"Work?" Max said. "He hasn't done anything."

"I know." Leigh threw up her hands, obviously just as displeased as CC and Max. "When the first report was filed, he told me to forget about it because Annie probably got a taste of life in America and is off with some boy having a great time."

"Good thing you didn't listen."

"Now you understand why I'm looking to branch out."

"I can't say that I blame you."

All through the hearing CC kept thinking about Brooks' phone call. As much as she would love tacking more charges onto little Simon, she just didn't see a connection. "Max, what do you say we head back to the station and try to get some real police work done?"

"What about Halloween?"

"What about it?"

"Emma?"

"It's too dangerous. It's going to break her heart. She's got her costume all ready. Our new neighborhood seems much more into the holidays than our last. I'm dumping it on Stevie to tell her."

"Tell her what?" Leigh asked.

"With Beaumont on the loose, we've decided not to let my niece go out trick-or-treating. We thought about letting her dad, Brad, take her out, but Halloween is a big night for drag queens. Even if he could, I still don't feel like it would be safe. If Bert knows about Emma, he could know about Brad."

"How about I go with you?" Max said. "Between the two of us, we should be able to keep Stevie and Emma safe."

"I can join you," Leigh said.

"See, a police escort." Max beamed.

CC almost laughed at how eager Max seemed. "Thanks, guys. I'll run it by Stevie and see what she thinks. Now enough stalling. Let's get back to the station. Krassowski is heading this way, and I don't want to listen to him brag about how he solved our case."

Chapter 24

Jamie stood at the nurses' station reviewing charts, while listening to the latest gossip. Deep in her heart, she knew gossiping was wrong, but sometimes, she just couldn't resist. Stella and Evaline were in full swing. The main topic of conversation was, of course, which of the new residents were sleeping with each other.

"Nothing to add, Dr. Jameson?"

"I don't like gossip."

"Of course not. That's why you're always hanging around when our tongues start wagging."

"Coincidence."

"Of course," Stella said. "What is little Emma wearing for Halloween this year?"

"Uh..." Jamie hesitated, still not happy that Emma might miss the festivities this year. She also wasn't eager to reveal that Emma might not be able to go. The disclosure would require an explanation.

"CC thinks she's going as Wonder Woman."

"She thinks that every year."

"I know." Jamie laughed, completely understanding her wife's love for Wonder Woman. Yet she was clueless to what today's seven-year-old might find fun. "Emma's going as Belle from Beauty and the Beast. Her father's very excited." Jamie would be, as well, if Emma might actually get to wear her costume.

Jamie was completely unaware that Bert Beaumont was

wandering around the waiting room. He was there for one reason: he had received a text message telling him to do so. He tried to blend in. The sight of a young girl sitting off to the side playing with her Barbie doll made him nervous. He felt the stirrings beginning. He didn't want to stay, but the message said he had to. He was to stay there until someone noticed him. If anyone approached him, he was to say something to explain why he was there and make his exit quickly and quietly.

He took a seat in the moderately busy waiting room. The television was tuned to some inane talk show. He tried not to watch the little redheaded girl. He tried thinking about his new hotel. It was modest but not a flea trap. No room service, which meant he had to venture out. Even on the outskirts of a city, it was easy to get lost. Thoughts of ignoring his benefactor's instructions played in his mind. The girl's laughter distracted him and led his mind to a twisted place. *Busy hospital, it would be so easy.* He pushed down the urge. An amber alert was the last thing he needed. The last few text messages had promised that soon he'd be free. He could run far away and start over again. Maybe a new city and new name would give him the strength not to give in to the urges.

Unconsciously, he leaned a little so he could listen to the girl's chatter. *They always say something that helps you get close*, he silently reminded himself.

"What's your name?" he asked.

"Molly, come play over here!" A hostile voice broke in.

He gulped when he spied the angry-looking mother beckoning her child. Little Molly bounced over and took her place beside her.

"She reminds me of my niece," he said. Fear gripped his heart when he caught the disbelieving look in the young mother's eyes. Deciding he had been there long enough, he stood to leave.

"Sir?" A tall, older, dark-skinned man blocked his path. Bert's pulse quickened. The man was hospital security. "Can I ask who you're waiting for? Have you been to triage."

"Oh, not me." Bert fought to stay in control. "My niece, Mary. My brother and his wife are in with her now. Fell out of a tree," he added with a half-hearted smile. "I was looking for a place to smoke. Could you tell me where I might be able to grab a quick one?"

"The designated smoking area is located out the front entrance and up the walkway. You can't miss it. It's the glass enclosure with all the smoke pouring out of it."

"Thank you." Bert smiled and attempted to make his way around the man.

"Why don't I walk you over?"

"Huh?" Bert choked, unable to believe that his cover had been blown so quickly. He knew he was out of practice, but to get busted by a rent-a-cop in less than half an hour was ridiculous. "Thanks." He tried his best to look blasé. He figured he'd let this bozo walk him there, he'd even bum a smoke, and that would be the end of it. The Red Line stop was just a few feet away. He could be on the subway before anyone was the wiser. Much to Bert's relief, the man nodded and guided him towards the entrance.

"What was your niece's last name?" the security guard asked, stopping Bert in his tracks.

"What?"

"I'll have one of my men check on her condition." The man offered a toothy grin while holding up his two-way radio. "That way you'll know how much time you'll have."

"Shelley," Bert said before he could think better of it.

"Tom, this is Terrell. I have a four seven six. Could you check on a patient named Shelley, Mary Shelley? That's right, Mary Shelley." Terrell smiled. "I'll be with her uncle at the smoking area on the north side."

"You smoke?" Bert made an attempt at sounding casual.

"Cigars. Can't let the wife know."

"Tell me about it. If mine finds out I've been smoking, I'm in the doghouse."

Bert felt uncomfortable by how closely Terrell was walking alongside of him. He turned to head towards where he knew the smoking area was located. He had passed by it when he first arrived. He had mentally noted that it could be used as an excuse to make a hasty exit. Terrell seemed to be guiding him away from the smoking area. Bert knew he was in trouble. If he pointed out that they were heading in the wrong direction, his cover would be blown. If he kept following this seemingly innocent man, he more than likely would be walking into a trap.

His heart sank when he spied two state trooper cars pulling over to his left. Knowing he was in deep, he abruptly turned and sucker punched Terrell, sending the older man crashing to the ground. Bert huffed and puffed as he made a mad dash to the subway stop just across the street. His heart pounded as he darted out into oncoming traffic. He didn't stop or risk looking back; he just bolted into the station. Crashing into a woman with a stroller who was exiting, he took advantage of the open gate and raced inside and up the staircase.

Bert didn't stop to think about what he was doing. He let his fear-fueled adrenaline rush guide him. His lungs felt as if they would seize as he kept running. Not only were the police chasing him, but now the transit cops were hot on his trail for fare evasion. He just kept going, dodging in and out of the crowd, until he managed to slip down another stairwell and back outside. He just kept running, even though there was a small voice whispering for him to just stop and get off the merry-go-round. His life would be much less exciting if he simply let them take him back to Connecticut.

Instead of listening to the tiny voice of reason that was telling him he was being an idiot, he kept running all the way down Charles Street. Rush hour was in full swing. Bert simply slipped into the crowd and got lost. Once he had crossed Beacon Street, he knew the quickest way back would be to jump on the Green Line. He wasn't up for being caught on camera and running another marathon. Instead, he grabbed a tacky sweatshirt from a street vendor. The guy tried to barter with him. Bert didn't have time to waste, so he tossed the babbling man a twenty and slipped on the navy blue sweatshirt with the name of the city embroidered across the front.

Bert decided it was a good day to walk back to the hotel. The walk would take a good while, but he figured it was better than jail. While on his trek back, he received another text. He wanted to smash the phone against the sidewalk when he read the words. "Sit tight and wait for further instructions."

Bert felt sick. He knew not to try to contact his mysterious benefactor. The consequences for doing so had already been explained to him.

Chapter 25

Across the city, Val was on her way to Boylston General Hospital, cursing everyone and everything in sight. Mills had the unfortunate position of being trapped in the car with the irate deputy.

"Are you guys a bunch of cluster fucks or what?"

"Keep it up, and I'll shoot you," Mills said in a slow, direct tone. "I've called Calloway."

"What? No." Val careened the SUV around the narrow streets of the city.

"This turns into a one way," Mills told her. "Heading the opposite way." Val just growled under her breath.

She released a stream of curses when she tried to find a way out of the maze of streets that made the city of Boston a truly unique driving experience.

"You could have let me drive," Mills said. "I could have told you that GPS wasn't going to get you around this city."

"Why did you call her?"

"Satan shows up at her wife's job, and you don't think she's going to find out? I thought you were all for keeping CC in the loop." The statement was innocent, still Val didn't miss the hint of suspicion in the older woman's voice.

Val took a calming breath before answering. "I just don't want her to go off halfcocked. I'd rather know what happened before we talk to her. Ten to one, she's going to beat us there. She'll have little or no answers. If you were in her shoes, wouldn't you freak out? I'm not used to having a family member working this close."

"This piece of garbage isn't her family."

"I get that, but still there is a connection," Val said wearily. "Here we are. Finally." Her stress level was topping the charts. She had barely rolled to a stop before she jumped out. Silently, she prayed that a miracle had occurred and CC hadn't beaten her there. When she spied the taller woman pacing in front of the emergency room doors, her stomach churned. "This is not going to be fun."

* * *

To her credit, CC had not blown a gasket when Terrell explained the situation. She maintained her poise when she spoke to the State Troopers. Thankfully, Terrell did everything by the book, alerting the Feds the moment he spotted Beaumont. Then he kept a close eye on him, only approaching when he saw him trying to engage a little girl in conversation. That was something he couldn't risk. It broke CC's heart when he apologized for allowing Beaumont to escape.

"Terrell, this isn't your fault," she said. "You did everything by the book. The guy sucker punched you."

"What about the video?" Max demanded of the unfortunate State Trooper who was standing near him.

"We're waiting on the Feds."

"We're here," Val waved her badge hoping against hope it would calm Detective Sampson down. "Someone needs to bring us up to speed. Detective Calloway?"

"Terrell here can fill you in," CC said. "Then he's going inside to have his face looked at. No arguments, Terrell. My wife is already pissed that you haven't been looked at. I don't want to hear it when I get home."

"Okay, Terrell." Val blew out a terse breath. "Just tell me what happened."

She listened intently, gathering all the details, while Max made a fuss. She should have been relieved by Calloway's levelheaded attitude, but she didn't like the way the woman was clenching her jaw and pacing. Val felt the tempest brewing. She thanked the weary-looking man and sent him inside for treatment. By the way his face looked, she guessed his nose was broken.

"That's what happens when you trap a caged animal," she noted while carefully making her way over to Calloway. "I can't believe he used the name Mary Shelley. What an idiot."

"Which begs the question," Max bellowed, "of why can't you catch this rocket scientist?"

"My fault. I should have assumed he knew about Detective Calloway's personal life and had the hospital watched."

"He shouldn't have known," CC said angrily. "We kept it quiet for just this reason. My job is what it is. I don't want my wife's well-being put in jeopardy because of it."

"Is that why neither of you changed your names?"

"No, that was more personal. Moving on. I had asked Jamie to alert hospital security, just in case. Now tell me what you know and what you're planning to do about this situation." She spoke in a slow, direct manner that informed Val that she was expecting her to get moving and wrap this up.

* * *

Billy Ryan felt like hell. But he always felt that way. Lately, life seemed even more unbearable. He had known Bitsy since they were just kids. Attending her funeral had done a number on him. As soon as he shuffled in, the smell of lilies assaulted him. He wanted to gag. He didn't miss the accusing looks in people's eyes. They were always looking at him as if he was some sort of villain. So he dropped out of college! Big deal.

He hadn't exactly dropped out. He left before the university asked him to. His GPA had been circling the bowl for most of his academic career. Unable to keep his grades up to standard led to his frat asking him to leave. That and the trouble Simon Fisher had dragged him into. Accused of manufacturing GHB and being placed on academic probation, he had no option but to leave. It hadn't been his idea to cook up a date rape drug. In his convoluted mind, it was Simon's idea. Billy also had been Simon's alibi when his girlfriend disappeared. He still found it hard to believe that Simon dumped the body during their trip up to Tahoe. Granted, Billy had been wasted for most of the trip.

Hell, he had been wasted for most of his life. After Bitsy's funeral, he wanted to get in touch with a guy who could set him up. All he needed was a little cash, but the quaint area wasn't giving him any hope of finding someplace to hit. Then an angel appeared and offered him everything he desired and a place to crash. True, it was a grungy hotel in the city, but it came with treats.

Billy loved nothing more in life than doing speedballs, an injection of cocaine mixed with heroin. He couldn't wait to be alone and shoot up. His angel not only provided him with a stash of drugs, but was kind enough to provide a great big spoon and a pack of disposable lighters. All he needed to do was to cook up his concoction.

For the briefest of moments, he felt good. Just preparing the needle made him elated. He spread his toes, and his hand trembled as he placed the needle between them. With a smile on his face, he prepared for the euphoric feeling to encompass him.

He injected the drugs and the euphoria did indeed come. Then all too quickly, he felt a burning sensation. Not the normal burning that lit him up; this was an inferno. When he reached for his throat he was surprised to find it swollen.

He might have collapsed. He couldn't be sure. He was still in pain and pissed off that his high wasn't what he had been aching for. Again he mixed up another batch of drugs on the bent spoon and carefully lit a fire beneath it. He watched as it melted together.

"This time, it will bring me peace," he promised himself. He would repeat this plan two more times, unaware of how little time had passed since he first shot up. He had a slow, wretched death befitting his misspent life.

* * *

A short time after the maid found the body of the strange man in Room 313, the local police were called.

"Calloway, we're up. We got a body." Max slammed down the phone and grabbed his jacket from the back of his chair. They had just returned from the hospital, and neither was up for a case. Still, there was a part of CC that relished the distraction.

"Geez, you don't have to sound so happy about it."

"Come on, Calloway, let's log out a car and get this over with."

"Okay, Mr. Grumpy Pants," she said in a teasing voice.

"What about Halloween?" Max asked once they were *en route*.

"I need to find out what Stevie wants to do. None of this makes sense, Max. I feel like we're missing something. Something big. Tell me about the call."

"Dead guy over at the Edison. Looks like an overdose."

They pulled into the parking lot of the modest motel, waved their badges, and entered Room 313. CC flinched when she saw Marissa examining the body.

"Dr. Vergas, what do we have?" She tried to keep her voice professional. Marissa had been polite enough over the past couple of months. CC knew she was on edge, and lately almost anything could set her off.

"Looks like an overdose. Won't know for sure until I get him on the table and do a tox screen."

"We got a name, Roger?" she asked the patrol officer while she took a look around the room.

"William Wayne Ryan."

CC froze, and her heart stopped for a brief moment. Finally she looked over at the corpse. "Billy Ryan?" She almost gagged.

"What is it?" Max asked.

"Could be a coincidence," she said, her voice barely above a whisper. "I mean if it's the same guy. Billy Ryan was Fisher's alibi back when Janie Jensen disappeared. He was the reason why the cops never looked at Fisher back when everything started."

"No kidding? Well, let's have a look around and see what we can find. Maybe we can get a line on the dealer then turn this over to narcotics."

* * *

On the way back to the station, CC filled Max in on Brooks' phone call. She was irked when he failed to seem interested.

"It was an overdose."

"Yeah, still that makes four bodies all tied to Fisher."

"Four different causes of death, all explainable."

"I don't know," CC said. "I'm still calling Brooks."

"Wait until we get the tox screen back," Max told her. "In the meantime, why don't we swing by Government Center and visit Deputy Brown. I'm more worried about Beaumont than some junkie who didn't know when to stop shooting up."

"Good point. But I have a better idea." CC blew out the exhaustion catching up with her. "How about you head back to the station, and I go check on my wife? I just need to see her again, you know?"

"I get it."

* * *

Val was reviewing everything on the tape for the one hundredth time. Her head was throbbing, her back ached, and she felt like she had missed something. She followed a shadowy figure through the miles of tape. The only thing she knew for certain was Beaumont might have jumped on the subway, and if he did, he wasn't far from the Calloway sisters' backyard. That is if the grainy image she followed from Copley to Boylston Village Hills was in fact Beaumont. It looked like it could be him, and if so, then he was way too close for comfort.

She pored over a map of the area before requesting Mills' assistance. "Help me out here? This is the stop where I think he got off."

"Okay."

"What's that near? Are there any hotels?"

"A couple down this way." Mills pointed at the map. "There's a lot of shops and overpriced coffee joints along the main drag."

"And where is the hospital in relation to this?"

"Over this way, bit of a hike. Most people would drive or take the T."

"And how far is that from where the Calloway sisters live?"

"They're on the opposite end." Mills pointed out the route. "It's more of a suburban area. Walkable, but for the hospital, you'd have to travel by car or train."

"But you can walk it if you had to?"

"Why would you?"

"The police are chasing you," Val said. "I figure our guy bolted. He did his little run around the subway station and just hoofed it back to some motel. Or he hailed a cab."

"Already checked that out. No one picked up a fare matching our guy." Mills grimaced. "I can't figure this guy out. There's nothing here for him but a bunch of people gunning for him and he just keeps moving closer to trouble. Sound like any runner you've ever tracked?"

"No."

* * *

CC paced around the waiting room, her stomach tied up in knots. Even after Jamie emerged, she failed to feel a sense of ease. Before she had been called away, she only had a few moments with her wife. She needed to feel more of a connection. If she had her way, she'd grab Jamie and the rest of the family and run as far away as humanly possible.

"I'm fine," Jamie said.

"I don't like that he got that close to you."

"He doesn't even know I exist."

"If that was true, he wouldn't have been here."

"I'm safe," Jamie insisted, still not bringing any comfort to CC.

"Because of you, I'm safe." CC gave her a doubtful look. "You were the one who insisted I alert hospital security. Terrell was on it. If that guy hadn't hit him, they would have caught him. Thanks to you, the security is a lot better than it used to be. Because of you, Dietrich was sacked and a new system was put in place."

"That wasn't me, that was the hospital being embarrassed by hiring a serial killer." Bile rose in CC's throat. "You don't know him like I do. He can be very convincing. I told every adult I knew what he was trying to do, and he'd spin some tale and they believed him. Hell, half the time I'd believe him, and I knew he was lying."

"He's a sick man."

"Why is he here?" CC almost wailed. "The only thing that makes sense is he's out to hurt people I love. I can't let him do that."

"And he won't."

CC felt like a child again. Helpless against the man who made her life a living nightmare. Everything was going to hell, and despite Jamie's reassurances, she knew she had only herself to blame.

* * *

CHECKMATE

Val felt like an idiot. She had been pacing in front of the Calloway residence for a good twenty minutes, trying to calm her nerves. She needed to talk to CC. She hoped that the intuitive detective could help. She had stopped by the station and was frustrated to learn that CC decided to leave early. Not that she blamed her after having Beaumont strike so close to home. *Why didn't I have someone watching the hospital?* She silently berated herself. She knew the answer. She assumed that Beaumont didn't know about his stepdaughter's marriage.

"Are you going to be doing this all day?" Stevie Calloway's voice disrupted her pacing. Val stood there feeling extremely silly.

"Your sister isn't around, is she?"

Stevie laughed at the flustered deputy. "What did she do?"

"Nothing. I just wanted to compare some notes." Val couldn't understand why she was suddenly feeling nervous. "Her partner said she left early today."

"Come on. She said she gave it to you good. Something about Uncle Mac's bar. What did she do?"

"Almost got me killed," Val said. "I paid your uncle a visit, and next thing I know, there's a whole bunch of cops looking to hurt me over the Yankees."

"You're a Yankees fan?"

"Uh..." Val hesitated. Normally she'd shout her love for the Boys from the Bronx from the rooftops. Seeing the disappointed look in Stevie's dark brown eyes made her want to curse. "Maybe?" She was trying to act cool and aloof, but the sight of Stevie Calloway standing before her in a simple floral print dress was more than a little distracting. "The point is..."

"She got to you." Stevie stepped inside her home. "Come in." Val stood on the stoop for a moment, weighing her options. There really wasn't a valid reason for her visit, she just ended up there. "I said come in," Stevie repeated. "And wipe your feet."

"Yes, ma'am."

"Emma, this is Deputy Brown."

"Hello," the small child who was sulking at the dinner table mumbled without looking up.

"Emma."

"Sorry." Emma sighed dramatically. "Nice to meet you, Deputy Brown." She finally looked up from her homework.

"Better," Stevie said. "You'll have to forgive Emma. She's a little cranky today."

"Am not."

"Right. I'm sorry about Halloween."

"Why?"

"It's complicated."

"I hate when things are complicated."

"Me, too." Val couldn't help but agree with the impertinent child.

"Not helping." Stevie groaned.

"Well, I do."

"Can I at least—"

"No." Stevie quickly cut her daughter off. "Not until your

homework is done."

"Fine." Emma sighed again.

"Let me guess," Val said with a chuckle. "She wants to watch television?"

"No, play chess. Would you like a cup of coffee?"

Chapter 26

Val sat in the cozy breakfast nook and sipped her coffee while peering out at Emma who was dutifully doing her homework. Internally, she was searching for something to say. She had never been shy. Today she was completely flummoxed by her sudden inability to string together a simple sentence. The long list of women who faded in and of her life never saw her looking like a nervous, sweaty schoolgirl.

"Nice place," she finally managed to say.

"Thank you."

"Must be nice to be so close to your sister."

"Yes, it is."

"So, Emma plays chess?"

"Caitlin is teaching her." Stevie snickered, which only served to irritate Val. "Her father taught her when she was very young, and later she taught me when I was about Emma's age. And so on. Is that what you needed to talk about?"

"No."

Val could have kicked herself. She felt completely lame. All she wanted to do was catch the bad guy and go on her way. She turned to Stevie. One look in those soft brown eyes and she knew that catching the bad guy wasn't the only thing she wanted to do. She took a hard swallow, knowing that Stevie was waiting for her to say something.

"You heard about today?"

"Yes."

"I fucked up."

"Could you not do that," Stevie said quietly, yet sternly. "Jamie and I have a rule. No talking like a cop around the house. It isn't good for Emma. And quite frankly, I don't find foul language attractive. When Caitlin gets wrapped up in a case she forgets. It's eff this and eff that. She needs to be reminded that she isn't around the boys."

"Sorry." Val glanced quickly to ensure Emma hadn't heard her bad language. "It's like that, being a woman in law enforcement. You need to be one of the guys, and the talk gets randy to say the least."

"I understand," Stevie said politely. "After living with my sister for so long, I'm well acquainted with the way cops abuse the English language. I'm just asking that you not talk like a cop in my home."

"Sorry," Val apologized again. "I just... I'm not used to being on the short end. Guys like your father..."

"Please don't call him that," Stevie said in a hushed tone. "I hate him, and I don't want to have to explain things to Emma. Not yet anyway. I'm hoping a few more decades pass before I have to tell her that her grandparents are bad people."

"Can't say that I blame you." Val took another sip of her coffee. "I just wish I knew why he's here. It isn't because of your mother."

"How is she?"

Val cringed when she caught the distant tone in Stevie's voice. "All right, I guess. Remorseful, if that means anything."

"It should." Stevie seemed lost. "Did Caitlin tell you about the card I got just before all this started happening?"

"Yes, I picked it up at the crime lab." Val was relieved that the conversation turned to business. Discussing the criminal element was a subject she felt confident talking about. "Not much to go on. The card itself is very generic. Except it was sent three months late, and it was sent to a woman. Everything points to someone wanting us to know that he's here."

"Why? It doesn't make sense."

"I wish I knew," Val grumbled. "I guess it's time to track down your sister."

"She's home. Probably up in her office," Stevie said. "One of the good things about living in a great big house is each side has home offices and guest rooms. Emma has a bedroom on each side. Jamie and Caitlin have their own work space, which is good, because when either of them brings work home, it really isn't something I want to see. Much less have Emma stumble across. Let's go see my sister."

Val felt completely off kilter. While Stevie was talking, all Val could do was allow her mind to wander to some very salacious places. *I'm working!* She kept reminding herself. Ogling a runner's daughter was not allowed. Val wasn't blind, still she had never allowed herself to become this distracted before.

"What?"

Once again, Stevie's voice drew her back. She was about to say something when Stevie's hand came to rest on her thigh. She bit back a whimper from the warm feeling that was coursing through her body.

"Deputy?"

"Call me Val," she managed to say before forcing herself to stand.

Stevie moved to join her. "Emma, we're going next door. Finish your homework. No sneaking off to check out the chessboard. She got all cocky because she managed to get Caitlin in check." Stevie unlocked the door that joined the two homes. "Now she's on the ropes and kind of cranky about it. She's so much like my sister, it's a little scary at times."

"She's what, seven? And she got that far in a chess match with an adult? Is your sister letting her win?"

"No. It seems that Emma is a natural. Don't get me wrong, I'm proud of her. I'm just worried that she'll be running circles around me by the time she's a teenager. Caitlin! You have company!" She guided Val up the staircase. "Promise to play nice," she added with a wink to the deputy.

* * *

CC heard her sister call up to her and didn't pay much attention to it. She assumed it was Emma. She had three white storyboards set up. She flipped each of the boards around so Emma wouldn't see what she had been working on. She liked the boards. She could tape crime scene photos to them and make notes with erasable markers. They were the same as the white boards with aluminum frames they used back at the station. It meant breaking the rules and copying the official files, but if anyone noticed the transgression, they never said anything.

"Hey, peanut," she said, still assuming it was her niece.

"Hey there, cashew."

CC jumped, startled by Val's voice. She gritted her teet when she turned to find the deputy smirking at her.

"I thought Stevie was sending Emma up." She turned away from the cocky woman to flip her boards back over.

"Nice setup."

"Helps me think."

"Three different cases," Val wryly said, irking CC by taking a seat at her desk. "The nanny case, Beaumont, and what's that last one?"

"Something Brooks is interested in." CC glared at the woman who appeared to be making herself comfortable. "Malcolm Fisher died from anaphylaxis, more commonly known as anaphylactic shock. Basically, he was stung by a bee while golfing. Sadly he's allergic to bee stings. Elizabeth Pryce's death is still listed as undetermined. The San Francisco medical examiner is leaning towards a viral infection. Bitsy Marsden went jogging and had her throat slashed in what appears to be a rape attempt or a robbery. Cops already have two upstanding citizens in custody. Then we have Billy Ryan, junkie from the tender age of fifteen. He died from, surprise, a drug overdose. Malcolm and Bitsy died in San Diego, Elizabeth died in her home in San Francisco, and Billy died here."

"I don't get it."

"Neither do I." CC almost laughed. "Bee sting, stomach infection, random act of violence, and a drug overdose. Brooks thinks they're connected. More so, since I called him about Billy Ryan."

"What's the connection?"

"Simon Fisher."

"Ah, Brooks' favorite villain."

"Malcolm was Fisher's father." CC glared down at Val. "Elizabeth was the girl who the love of Simon's life dumped him for. Bitsy grew up next door to the Fishers. And Billy was Simon's frat brother, who was also his alibi at the time his girlfriend disappeared. Other than happenstance and crossing paths with Simon Fisher, these people have nothing in common. Much as I would love to pin more stuff on the weasel, I don't see a connection. It's just... I don't have time for this. Maybe after we lock up Bert." She turned back to the board that featured her elusive stepfather.

"Let's focus on that," Val said, moving out of CC's chair. "We finally got the information from the cell phone." She reached into her pocket and pulled out a notepad. "Damn subpoena took forever. Text messages only. The first ones instructed Beaumont to catch the train up here, empty a locker at the train station, and check into the Marriott under the name Gilbert Osborne." She grabbed a marker and wrote dates next to the messages. "Next, he received a message to take a walk around the mall. Another informed him to do the same. There was one reminding him to remember what would happen to him if he screwed up. Then another told him to check out of the hotel and trash the phone. Details to follow. His mistake was to throw the cell phone in the trash can in his room. I doubt that's what his friend had in mind. Here's the rub, the cell phone that sent these messages is the same number we got all of our anonymous tips from. We traced it to another burner phone purchased from a mini mart in Culver City, California. Cell towers put the calls coming in from LA, San Francisco, San Diego, Madison, Wisconsin, and right here in Boston. The number has since been disconnected. Here's my theory—"

CC cut her off. "Someone wants us looking for him. They've switched to a new burner phone. They're paying with prepaid credit cards and cash, so we can't trace anything. Why?"

"Don't know. Maybe this other case? It seems to be the only thing you're working on."

"The soccer mom who strangled her nanny? No way. As well educated as Natalie Stern is, she isn't as smart as she thinks she is. She has herself convinced that she didn't do anything wrong. I just love people like that."

"Me, too. It keeps me in business."

"Do you like what you do?"

"Yes, I do. I miss the navy, but this is exciting work," Val said. CC could feel the truth behind the words. "I get to catch the bad guys."

"I hear you." CC understood completely. "Answer me something. Why are you so keen to know about my high school years? It has nothing to do with the case."

CC felt uneasy when Val turned quiet. "When I came out," Val said slowly, "my loving parents told me never to come home again. I was already at Annapolis, so I didn't end up on my own. The navy was my family from that moment on. What happened to you could have just as easily been my fate."

"My parents told me to hit the bricks because they found out I had a crush on my gym teacher," CC said. "Or because I wasn't cutting my pervert of a stepfather any slack. I was already planning on running away. I just needed to find a way to take Stevie with me. I thought it was possible. What can I say? I was a kid. I found a place to live that didn't ask too many questions. I was already working a couple of jobs. When I said I was a sophomore, I was tall for my age and everyone assumed I was referring to college not high school. Right before I turned eighteen, a friend of my uncle's found out I was working the overnight shift at a self-serve gas station. They told Uncle Mac, and he was pissed. He took me in, made me quit my jobs and focus on my last year of high school. That's the whole sorry story. I understand why you wanted to know. What I don't like is being kept in the dark while you watch me and my family. I also don't like the way you're looking at my sister."

"I, um…"

"Save it. Let's forget motive for a moment. I'm referring to Bert's, not yours. Someone wants us chasing him. We want to catch him. Any ideas?"

"Just one." Val seemed nervous. "Someone wants him to keep playing peek-a-boo with us. We know that, so why not use it and set a trap?"

"Okay, but how?"

"Why is your niece upset about Halloween?"

"No way! You're not using my family as bait."

"Someone already is. The only hope we have is they don't know that we know."

"The only thing that means anything to me in this world is my family." CC tried to take a swing at Val. Before she knew what was happening, she was on her knees with her arm pinned behind her back.

"I told you to play nice!" Stevie's voice cut through the room.

***

Her head was throbbing as she broke up whatever was happening between Deputy Brown and her sister. Then she shuffled them to her place before sending Emma over to Caitlin's under the guise of allowing her to study the chessboard.

"Take your time, Emma," she called out. "Your Auntie Caitlin can be very crafty."

"Crafty?"

"A lot nicer than what I was thinking." Stevie said. "Okay, you two chuckleheads, does someone want to explain what is going on? Deputy Brown, is there a reason why you were beating up on my sister?"

"I wasn't."

"She wasn't." CC plopped down on the sofa. "I took a swing at her, that's all."

"I'm not used to seeing someone get the drop on you."

"Kind of a new experience, sis." CC sighed wearily. "I must be losing my touch."

"Or I'm good at what I do," Val said. "I spend a lot of time trying to arrest crackheads and other unsavory characters. I'm more than a little accustomed to folks trying to clean my clock. I didn't mean to hurt her."

"It didn't hurt."

Stevie covered her mouth in order to suppress a giggle. "Uh, why did you try to hit the nice deputy, Caitlin?"

"She's not nice."

"I can be."

Stevie looked at the two of them sitting there with their arms folded against their chest. Both women were doing everything they could to act and look tough. If the situation weren't so serious, Stevie would have been thoroughly amused. She watched the two of them stewing while trying to out-butch one another.

"Keep it up, and you're both getting a time out," Stevie sternly threatened. "Why did you try to hit Deputy Brown?"

"Because she suggested something ludicrous."

"It isn't," Val said. "I know it isn't something you're going to be comfortable with."

"Okay? What is your plan, Deputy?"

"Val," she said eagerly.

CC glared at her. "Don't do that."

"Val." Stevie fought against the urge to flick her sister. "You call it a case, but this is our family. Start at the beginning, and, Caitlin, I swear to God if you interrupt I'll smack you myself."

"Fine."

"I mean it."

"I said fine."

"Val, go on."

"I know this isn't easy for you," Val said. "Your... I mean Beaumont, is here for a reason. We don't know why, but it appears that someone is using him. Putting him in our sights just long enough to keep us chasing after him."

"Someone wants us to be looking for him? Why?"

"I have no idea. What I'm thinking is to be a tad more visible. Draw him out, and maybe after we get him locked up, we can find out who's funding his life as a stalker."

"Put my family in danger?" CC shouted and waved her arms

around like a lunatic. "Use them as bait? I don't think so!"

"Ssh, remember Emma." Stevie's heart was racing as she fully digested the situation. "Now I understand why Caitlin tried to smack you. I'm a little tempted to myself."

"I understand," Val said. "You mentioned earlier that Emma was upset about Halloween. Why?"

"Because, with everything going on, I feel it's too dangerous for her to go out. Caitlin's partner and another officer offered to escort her. I still don't feel comfortable with her going out, and Brad, her father, agrees."

"So you've talked about taking her out with an escort?"

"And decided against it," Stevie said.

"What if, in addition to the police, we add me and more marshals?"

"Again, I know this all part of your job." Stevie fought her anger. "Just another tactical mission. But for me, this is my daughter. The answer is no."

"I understand."

"Oh, now you understand?" CC said in a bitter tone.

"Caitlin, behave," Stevie warned her once again. "Val here is going to come up with another plan. In the meantime, go back next door and play chess with Emma."

"Stevie?"

"I swear, if you say I'm not the boss of you, I'm calling Jamie."

"Fine." CC huffed before getting up to leave. "Oh, and, you" she pointed to Val. "don't sit so close to my sister."

"Caitlin! Go play with your niece."

Stevie blew out a terse breath when her sister finally stomped out of the room. She glanced over at Val, who looked like she had just been to hell and back.

"Val, I appreciate that you're trying to do your job. There was a time when my sister had a normal childhood. I'm a little jealous of that. I only had her. My parents were distant. I never understood why, until the night when I had my one and only sleepover. I was about Emma's age, and some of the kids from my Brownie Troop were sleeping over. Everything was fun until Daddy tried to tuck us in."

"Jesus! Did he?"

"No, but he tried. Caitlin had taught me what to do if anyone, and she stressed 'anyone' tried to do something like that. She never said it might be my father."

"What happened?"

"I beat the crap out of him with Caitlin's baseball bat. Kind of broke up the party. I never really had a normal childhood after that. Not until I was a teenager and living with my sister. Our family is everything to us. Don't try and mess with that. My daughter is enjoying a happy, albeit unconventional, childhood. I will move heaven and earth to keep that intact. Having Bert back, knowing that he's so close to my child, scares the hell out of me. Now you're saying that someone put him up to it. You said my mother is in town. Could she be a part of this?"

"Doubtful. We've checked her out, and we're keeping a watch on her. She lives in Waltham."

"Makes sense." Stevie bristled slightly. "Caitlin's father and our brother are buried in the Waltham cemetery. The two people she loved most in this world."

"You don' know,"

"I do." Stevie felt the tears building. "After Donny and her first husband died, Caitlin said she changed. Before that, she was a regular mom. She baked cookies and played games and did all the mom things. After losing them, she shut down. Then my father came along."

"I'm sorry." Val moved slightly closer.

Stevie didn't stop to think; she moved closer as well. Before she could process what was happening, she found herself in Val's arms. It was too much. All of a sudden, their nice quiet lives detoured back into the turmoil that she had felt certain they had escaped. *We'll never be free!* her mind screamed. She gave in to the warmth that Val's embrace provided. Strong confident arms tightly held her. Stevie nuzzled closer, finally letting go and not pretending to be brave so Emma wouldn't know.

Comforting caresses began to circle her back. She knew she shouldn't be doing what she was doing. It felt damn good to just surrender. She couldn't remember the last time a woman held her. Val's touch bordered on intoxicating. She gazed up and saw dark eyes studying her. She reached up and cupped Val's face with her hand.

Her heart skipped a beat when Val tilted her head. The small distance between them evaporated. Stevie hungrily assaulted Val's lips. She was surprised by how soft Val's kiss was. Given the deputy's stoic demeanor, she expected her to be rough and demanding. Instead, she found gentleness.

She moaned softly and allowed Val's tongue to slip past her

lips. Her thoughts vanished as she gave into the seductive teasing. She ran her hands along the firm body pressed against her own. Her kisses turned hungry, fueled on by the feel of a hand gliding up and under the hem of her dress. Stevie leaned back, inviting Val to explore her body. Her breathing turned labored. She gasped when the buttons at the top of her dress were released. Every part of her felt alive. Her hands continued their own explorations. Suddenly, her hands stilled when her fingers brushed against cold steel.

"We can't," she heard Val gasp.

"I might agree," she desperately needed to give her body over to this woman. "If your hands weren't inside my dress."

"This is unprofessional." Val made a lame attempt at protesting.

Stevie might have conceded if Val's hands hadn't slipped deeper inside her garments. Her bra was released just before Val captured her in a hungry kiss. Stevie eagerly kissed her back while pulling Val's body down on top of her own.

"Get off my sister!"

Stevie shrank back. The booming voice was unmistakable. "Really?" She cringed, watching in horror as her sister turned away. She heard Caitlin's voice turn tender. "Your mommy needs to clean up a mess that she's made."

"Oh, she's a riot," Val said with a grunt while she fought to free her hand.

"She's talking to my daughter." Stevie groaned and pushed Val off of her.

They stumbled off of the sofa, and Stevie felt a fleeting

moment of panic when she caught the murderous look in her over-protective sister's eyes. An old tarnished image flashed through her mind. She was seventeen, caught messing around with her half-naked girlfriend. Her sister was supposed to be working a late shift; instead, she opted to come home early for some quality time with her baby sister.

"Stay with Auntie Caitlin just a moment longer," Stevie called out in a pleading tone while trying to adjust her clothing. "Sorry," she said to Val who was trying to distance herself from the situation.

"You better run." She heard Caitlin snarl the order at Val as she reentered the room. "You, fix your dress," she said to Stevie.

"I'm an adult," Stevie snapped, unable to control her temper. She checked her dress one last time while she fought against the strange feeling of being embarrassed at being caught in the act by her sister. "You can bring Emma in now." She tried to sound in control. Knowing that her face was flushed didn't help her cause.

"Keep your grubby hands to yourself," Caitlin whispered and cast one last warning look to the poor deputy who was cowering by the front doorway. "Emma, come on in. Mama's done cleaning up her mess."

Stevie was torn between feeling ashamed and being extremely angered by Caitlin's digs. "Very mature." Not a clever comeback, but it was the best she could come up with. She understood her sister's need to protect her. Still, at her age, it was annoying.

"Emma," she said, "wash up for dinner, your father will be here soon." She did her level best to sound and act as normal as possible. It was hard to maintain her demeanor with Val cowering by one doorway and Caitlin firmly planted by another. "Val, would you like to join us for dinner?" Her seemingly innocent question was greeted with mixed emotions. Val gaped at her while her sister growled. "Oh, for the love of..." She shook her head, annoyed with both women. "Caitlin, will you be joining us?"

"No, thank you. I need to get back to the station."

"I thought you were taking the rest of the day off."

"I was." The answer was slightly more subdued. "I have an identification and a toxicology report to deal with. Deputy, may I have a moment?"

Stevie cringed. On the surface, the request sounded polite. If it weren't for the look of pure hatred that clouded her sister's eyes, she might have relaxed. "Sis..."

"I just need a moment with my colleague."

"Right."

"It's all right." Val meekly crept across the room. "She has the right—"

"No, she doesn't."

"Stevie." Again, CC kept her tone on a polite level. "This is business. Deputy, why don't you join me on the other side?"

"Nice knowing you." Stevie shivered as she watched Val haplessly follow after Caitlin.

* * *

CC fought to control her breathing. She had picked up on the vibes Stevie and Deputy Brown had been exchanging since day one. The last thing she expected was to walk in on them messing around. She took a calming breath.

"This day sucks," she muttered, running her fingers through her hair in an effort to collect her thoughts. "I don't know what makes me want to kill you more. Wanting to use my niece as bait or catching you with your hands up my sister's dress."

"I wasn't suggesting using Emma as bait."

"Oh, so you have a very short operative that you can use in her place?"

"No, she'd be heavily guarded. We need to draw him out. She'd be completely safe."

"No, she wouldn't," CC somehow managed to say without exploding. "And even if she was, what about all of the other little girls in the neighborhood? The thirty-some six to eleven-year-olds that fit Bert's predilection. You got enough manpower to cover them?"

CC didn't feel any sense of relief when Val's shoulders slumped. "Didn't think that far in advance? I like that your main focus is on Emma," she said. "Life is hard enough without everyone knowing Emma's grandfather is a sick pervert. You're right. He's playing a game with us. Find another way to draw him out."

"He's not playing a game." Val's angry look troubled CC. "Someone else is pulling the strings, and we have no way to track them. He'll keep showing up for just a moment, then he'll be in the wind again. It's like a carnival fun house. All smoke and mirrors. We keep chasing him, and they do whatever it is they want to do to you."

"Me?"

"Yes, you."

"Why are you so certain this isn't about you?" CC couldn't help challenging her, but she wasn't dismissing the possibility that she was the focus.

"Because, I'm not supposed to be here."

"This wasn't your case?"

"No, I'm not even with the Connecticut office. I'm with the Capital Area Task Force." Val's voice was strained. "Truth be told, I'm supposed to be on vacation."

"Hell of a way to spend your downtime." CC once again ran her fingers through her hair. "So, what brings you so far from DC?"

"It was pure happenstance that I'm even here," Val said. "Good thing, too. I don't know what Deputy Finn's malfunction is, but if I hadn't bullied my way in, you'd just be finding out about this mess now. For the life of me, I cannot figure out why this guy didn't even want to look for Beaumont. On paper, he should have been an easy catch."

"Mark Finn?"

"Yeah. You know the guy?"

"You could say that." CC groaned as some of the pieces fell into place. "About seventeen years ago, he caught me with his ex-wife doing what you were trying to do with my sister. Oh, and before you say it, she was most definitely his ex at the time. The divorce was finalized that day. I was Cathy's celebration. Needless to say, I'm his malfunction. That doesn't let you off the hook for any of this. You're still on my list, Deputy Happy Pants."

"I swear, crossing the line was not my intention." Val sounded remorseful. CC almost felt bad for her. Almost. "I've never done that before. I mean, I've done that…"

"I get it." CC held up her hand in order to silence her. She had seen more than enough, adding more details to the encounter was not topping her list of things to do.

"I'm a professional, and what happened was against procedure, protocol, and completely out of order." Val was bordering on babbling. "I don't know what happened. We were talking, and she was so overwrought, and the next thing I knew I was holding her."

"Telling me that you pounced on my sister while she was vulnerable isn't helping you."

"You're right."

CC was pleased to hear the resolution in her voice.

"As for Finn," Val said, "it wouldn't have mattered if he did go by the book instead of sweeping this under the rug. All the tips were too little too late."

"I hate having my chain yanked, and I hate people yanking my sister's chain. Have I made myself clear?"

"Yes."

CC was more than a little thrilled when she caught a slight glimmer of fear in Val's eyes. "I need to get moving. But I'll be back. I expect you to have some answers regarding what you're planning on doing."

"I'm doing everything I can."

"Do more. For the moment, I don't care about the who or why behind this mess. For me and my own, this guy is the boogie man. Everyone seems to think because he failed in his attempts to rape us when we were children that somehow his actions were benign. Trust me, they were anything but. He robbed us of our childhoods. I won't have my niece go through that. Do your job and lock him up. You can leave through this side of the house."

Val accepted her words and departed, not bothering to say goodbye to Stevie.

Although she had no doubt that Deputy Brown would return, CC braced herself to see Stevie. She greeted Brad, who was chatting with Emma while Stevie was busy fixing dinner. CC didn't miss the fact that Stevie was purposely keeping her back to her. silence spoke volumes.

"Sis?"

"Chase her off?" Stevie muttered.

"No, I just sent her to work."

"Brad, I need a moment," Stevie said in an overly controlled tone of voice. "Emma, show Daddy how to work his new phone."

"Grown-ups." Emma sighed dramatically and snatched the gadget from her father's incapable hands.

CC was prepared for Stevie's outburst. She braced for a lengthy lecture as her younger sister dragged her back over to her side of the duplex.

"Okay, let me have it," she said before Stevie had the chance to blast her. "But before you do, let me remind you of something. A while ago, when Jamie first came back into my life, I seem to recall someone warning me about jumping into bed with her before we got a chance to get to know one another. You warned me about how we were caught up in the dangerous situation and old feelings."

"Yes, I did."

For a brief moment, CC was relieved to hear Stevie concede her point.

"I warned you that you were moving way too fast. And you're right, that ended horribly. No, wait it didn't. The two of you ended up happily married with no concept of what lesbian bed death is. Honestly, you can be such a jerk."

"I'm just looking out for you."

"I know, and I love you for that. However, I am an adult. Given the extreme situation we're in, finding a little comfort in a very sexy woman's arms wasn't the wrong thing to do."

"She needs to focus on the situation at hand, not bedding you." CC struggled against the urge to go completely ballistic. "Look, maybe all of us should get out town. We'll just wait until this blows over."

"You want to run?"

"Yeah." CC knew she should have felt bad about wanting to simply run. She didn't; all she could focus on was keeping her family safe. "There's something bigger going on. Jamie's at work, and I know she's safe there. How safe are you and Emma?"

"No." Stevie's voice was strangely quiet. "He isn't driving us out. He doesn't win this time."

Chapter 27

CC hated not having answers. Someone was out there playing with them. The unseen player held all the cards, "Except one," she wryly thought. The one wild card was Deputy Brown. She wasn't supposed to be there. CC hoped that she would, indeed, return. Having the deputy make a play for her sister was unacceptable, but having an armed guard with military experience camped out in Stevie's living room was a good idea.

In the meantime, she had work to do. She was at the morgue to deal with the least favorite part of her job. Billy Ryan's family had arrived and needed to make the identification so they could take him home. Marissa had called and said she needed to discuss the tox results with her and Max. In all likelihood, she'd sign off that it was an overdose and she and Max would turn the case over to vice.

Closing the file on Billy Ryan left her with one outstanding case. As she made her way through the corridors of the state forensics building, she asked herself once again if Annie Fraser's murder was behind all of this? She could feel it in her gut that Annie's death had nothing to do with the drama that had suddenly appeared in her life. Someone was making a big show out of making her chase her tail.

"All smoke and mirrors," she muttered before greeting Max who huffed and puffed to catch up with her.

"I hate these things," he said with a grunt.

"Yeah."

"Jamie holding up okay?"

"I think so." They approached three people who were

standing in the waiting area. CC was all too familiar with the defeated looks on their faces. "She stayed at work. I figured with all the police action going on there, it's the safest place for her."

"Good call."

"Mr. and Mrs. Ryan," CC said in soft, sincere tone. "I'm sorry for your loss. I'm equally sorry to have to ask you to do this."

"We understand," Mr. Ryan choked out. "In many ways, we've been expecting this for years."

"Billy's problems have been a long struggle," the younger man spoke. "I'm Jim Robixteau. Billy and I were in the same fraternity at UC San Diego."

"We asked Jim to join us." Mrs. Ryan's words were shaky. "He was at the last intervention. We thought sending Billy here for rehab would be good. He wouldn't be able to get in touch with any of his connections, like he did last time."

"Where was he getting treatment?" CC carefully inquired.

"McLean, it has a stellar reputation," Mrs. Ryan sniffed.

"Max, would you take them in, please?" CC handed the Ryans over to her partner while she and Jim stayed out in the waiting area. "It's nice of you to join them," she said to the tall, good looking young man.

"I had no idea Billy had gotten this bad," he said with a hard swallow. "I've been away. I ran into him at a funeral for another friend of ours. When his parents asked for my help, I was more than..."

"Where have you been?" CC asked when his words trailed off.

"Africa," he said without bravado. "Peace Corp. I did two terms."

"What was that like?"

"You've heard the ads, toughest job you'll ever love? It's true. If my family hadn't insisted it was time for me to come home, I'd still be there. I can't believe I'm going to another funeral. This will be the third one in a month. They say these things happen in threes."

CC digested the information. Jim was Billy and Simon's frat brother before they left UCSD.

"Can I ask you about Billy when he was at the university? He dropped out, didn't he?"

"Yes and no. The frat and the university asked him to leave. I made that happen. I figured it would be easier on his parents if he quit instead of being tossed out."

"Why was he on his way to being kicked out?"

"He had been on academic probation. Tag on his drug use and another thing that happened and his departure was imminent."

"What other thing? If you don't mind me asking?" She gently nudged.

"He and another brother were caught cooking up GHB." Jim turned pale. "Don't let his parents know. The other guy had good grades, so he transferred. I couldn't let it slide. I was the president of Delta. I hate the image fraternities have. You know, spoiled rich boys who party and won't take no for an answer. That's not what it's about. Maybe if I had reached out more to Billy…"

"It sounds like he made his choice. I know that isn't very

comforting. I'm sorry to ask you about all of this. It's just... the other guy. Was that Simon Fisher?"

"Yes." He was clearly taken aback. "How did you know?"

"I was the one who arrested him."

"Oh? I don't know very many details about Simon's troubles, since I was away. When my parents told me, I was shocked. Simon seemed to be truly grieving over Janie's disappearance. I even helped him organize searches. To find out it was him the whole time threw me. Then I thought about him and Billy cooking up a date rape drug during a time when he was supposed to be out looking for Janie. I can only hope he gets the help that he needs and perhaps finds his way."

"I can see why Mr. and Mrs. Ryan asked you to join them."

He seemed confused by CC's compliment, further bolstering her belief that Jim was a good person.

The identification was finished. They wrapped up the paperwork as quickly as possible allowing Marissa to release the body. Jim helped Billy's family with the arrangements.

"Seriously, that guy is bucking for sainthood," CC said.

"I don't buy anyone being that good." Max gave a snort.

"Come on, let's see what Vergas has for us before you canonize the guy."

"Nice of you to join us," Dr. Vergas tossed out a dig.

"I've been kind of busy." CC rolled her eyes, not in the mood for one of Marissa's tirades. "Let me guess. An overdose?"

"Yes and no."

"Okay." CC waved her hand in an effort to get Marissa to spit out the information before she was ready to file for retirement.

"The guy was shooting up with some very fine heroin and cocaine. The best money can buy. Which assisted in his death. The stuff was cut with some funky stuff."

"What kind of stuff? Tylenol? Baby powder? Laxatives?" CC was disappointed when each suggestion was dismissed. "Fine, let's see there's sugar, sleeping aids, powdered milk?"

"None of the above." Marissa had a smirk on her face. "Sodium hydroxide."

"Which is?"

"Drain cleaner. Sorry, it's a homicide."

"How do you figure?" Max asked. "So the dealer cut it with something dangerous. Nothing new there. These guys will cut drugs with anything."

"Hey, don't blame me. Calloway was the one who told me to be extra diligent. Good thing, too, or I wouldn't have done such an intense tox screen and just written it off as an overdose."

"Thank you, Calloway," Max said with a groan.

"Never saw anything like this before. The drugs were only cut with drain cleaner," Marissa said. "This stuff is pure grade. The kind of stuff you can only buy if your parents own a small nation or you're a big, and I mean really big, rock star. This grade of drugs can't be found on the streets. Not on our streets anyway. I've already checked with Vice. If for some idiotic reason you cut this stuff, why use something lethal? Someone wanted this guy dead. And they spent a small fortune to do it. No way he walked up to a neighborhood dealer and scored this stuff."

"Great," CC grumbled. "The hits just keep on coming. Okay, tomorrow we head out to McLean to talk to his rehab buddies. Everyone knows the best place to score drugs is in rehab. Thanks, Vergas."

"My pleasure."

"Is it me, or is she getting snotty?" CC asked Max once they were free of the smells of the autopsy room.

"Didn't you sleep with her?"

"Like a hundred years ago. I need to give Brooks a call."

"Oh no you don't. You are not turning this into a conspiracy. You have more important things to focus on. Take some time off. I'll ask the boss if he wants Mulligan to ride with me. If he wants to bring her over, this would be a good time to get her involved. I'm not buying that someone went out of their way to off this guy. Sounds like he just bought the wrong bag of drugs."

She chose not to argue. Brooks was right. Something was going on. But until her family was safe, she couldn't focus on anything else. "You know what? You're right. Let's head back and talk to the captain."

She did call Brooks and conceded that something really was going on. His excitement over her news died quickly.

"I can't connect the dots," CC said, "and I can't get caught up in this."

"What are you saying?"

"I have to sit this one out."

"Calloway?"

"I'm taking some time off. Once the dust settles, I'll be on this."

"I can't believe you're bailing on me!"

"My family is in danger."

"Shit, Calloway, why didn't you tell me? What can I do to help?"

"Keep an eye on Fisher. I don't need to be worrying about him." She felt a slight sense of relief. "Your friend Brown is working on the mess here in Boston. I meant what I said. Once this freaking nightmare is over, I'm all yours."

"Just be careful, Calloway."

"You, too."

* * *

Val sat in the conference room staring at the board. It wasn't that much different from the ones she had seen displayed in Calloway's home. Mills placed a fresh cup of coffee next to her. She nodded her thanks and offered Mills a seat.

"Mary Shelley. What an idiot," Mills said. "Although kind of appropriate."

"Think we created a monster?"

"I think we're the helpless villagers."

"Good. Most of them survive. It was Frankenstein's creator that got it in the end."

The rest of the team shuffled in. There were a few faces missing because they were working a detail; the only notable exception was Finn.

"Where's Finn?"

"Reassigned," a commanding voice said.

Val was the only one in the room who didn't jump when the lead field officer stormed in. "Oh." Val shrugged with an air of indifference. "And my new liaison will be?"

"I am." Chief Deputy Lester Ledger had a slight twinkle in his eyes. Val had briefly met the man when she first arrived. She liked him. Despite his small stature and graying hair, he possessed a strong presence. She finally felt as if her luck was turning.

"Because?" She didn't really care. She was happy to be rid of Finn; the guy was a slacker. Now that she knew the reason why he was dragging his feet, she liked him even less.

"When one of my people explains to me that it wouldn't have mattered if he had followed protocol because the perp wouldn't have been apprehended, I find that to be a piss-poor excuse."

Val stiffened ever so slightly when she spied the subject of their conversation entering the room. Detective Calloway was right behind him.

"My notes." Finn slapped a very thin folder down in front of her.

"Gee, thanks," Val said as she flipped through the three pages of nothing.

Finn ignored her jab and turned, almost running directly into Calloway.

"Mark," CC said in a taunting tone. He muttered something

under his breath that only Calloway could hear. Whatever it was made Calloway smirk.

"Three pages." Ledger was clearly disgusted as he flipped through the notes. "We've got a sexual predator roaming the streets, and he gives me three pages. Detective, please join us."

"Sure, Les." CC seemed to accept his terms. Val wasn't so certain. "Any more coffee?"

"I'll get you a cup," Mills merrily volunteered.

"Tell me again that Finn didn't do anything," Ledger tried to say to Calloway in a quiet tone.

Everyone in the room tensed up. The US Marshals had a zero tolerance for domestic incidents. It was one of the reasons Val chose to serve with them after her departure from the military. If Finn had stepped anywhere near going over the line when he busted up the little party, it would mean losing his silver star. No ifs, ands, or buts.

"No, he did not," CC said. The tension seemed to lift as Mills placed a fresh cup of coffee down near the still standing detective.

"Why not take a seat?" Val didn't enjoy the fact that Calloway was towering over her. She wasn't in the mood for a power struggle. She felt a small twinge of relief when CC shed her coat and took a seat next to Ledger. Val shook her head. Not a big power play, but a strategic move just the same.

"Detective Calloway is on temporary leave from the Boylston PD," Ledger told everyone. "We all know this case is hitting close to home for her. I've invited her here out of courtesy. Detective Calloway has worked with us on many occasions, and I don't see her as a threat to this investigation." He turned to CC. "That doesn't mean you are a part of this investigation. Is that understood?"

"Afraid I'll go all Dirty Harry on you?"

"Yes. I need to know that you understand that Deputy Brown is in charge. Now, let's get to work. Brown, tell me what we know and what we don't know. And do it quickly. Every second this piece of garbage is on our streets is one second too long. Understood?"

Val proceeded to explain the situation. How the tips came in just a little too late. The prepaid cell phones and the near misses they had encountered. She went over every detail and concluded with more questions than answers.

"That's it. We're guessing that someone is guiding his hand. The who or why is unknown. For the moment, our main concern is catching him, which is why we need to figure out where his next stop will be. I think he'll show up somewhere very close to the Calloway residence. As we all know since the Adam Walsh Act, the Marshal Service is responsible for sex offender tracking. Dropping the ball on this one isn't making the suits in the capital happy. That's why they've agreed to let me stay on."

"Why do you think, he'll show up near the Calloway home?" Ledger asked.

"All of his little guest appearances have been quick and almost without a sense of purpose." Val didn't miss the way CC winced. "Until now. When he showed up at Dr. Jameson's work, it was a clear indication that the stakes have been raised. He won't be stupid enough to show up at Detective Calloway's job. That leaves his daughter and granddaughter. There's a long weekend coming up. My plan is to place Emma Quinn, the granddaughter, somewhere safe. His daughter, Stevie Calloway, works from home and doesn't venture far from there. It makes sense that he'll show up in the neighborhood. It's accessible by your wonderful subway system. Easy for him to show up and duck out."

"How can you be sure he hasn't been there already? Or he'll

even be spotted if and when he does?" Ledger asked.

"Despite bordering on the city, it's a quiet neighborhood," Val explained, "with a good Neighborhood Watch. We've been tagged every time we've been there. You have some very observant neighbors, Detective. Even your mail carrier made us, which means we need to integrate people," she added, informing the team she was less than pleased that they hadn't managed to observe without being spotted. "Right now, Dr. Jameson is working at the hospital. Beaumont's ex-wife, Maria Gallagher, is home in her apartment in Waltham. Stevie Calloway is at home with her daughter along with her daughter's father, Brad Quinn. And Detective Calloway is gracing us with her presence. These are the key players. Some of you may have deduced that I like being the one in control. Up until this moment, some unknown factor has been running the show. That stops now."

"You have a plan?" Mills asked hopefully.

"I do. First we get Emma Quinn out of harm's way. Then we move at least one operative into the Calloway residence."

"Excuse me?"

Val could tell by the tone of her voice that CC was less than pleased.

"We want to do this without tipping our hand." Val fought to keep her voice as professional as possible. "As you astutely pointed out earlier this evening, Detective, every child in the area is in danger as long as Beaumont is on the loose. We'll need your sister's permission, of course. I'd like to move her with Emma."

"She'll say no."

"I know. For the moment, our team needs to review our

tactics so we can blend in. Starting with a new gardener. I noticed that your wife and sister maintain the yard work. Also, your new home needs work done. I'll go over the more intricate details later with you and your family."

"Not warming up to you," CC said with a snarl.

* * *

CC sat back and listened to Deputy Brown's plan. On paper, it wasn't half bad. The only problem was if it ended badly her family's well-being was on the line. She did her best to listen without interrupting, making only a few suggestions before she agreed to be there when Brown talked to Stevie.

After the meeting broke up, CC asked Val to join her for a private chat. It was time for the deputy to learn that she wasn't the only one with control issues.

Once inside a quiet office, CC held her breath, wondering if what she was about to do was pure genius or incredibly stupid. Val was studying a file with her back to CC. Quietly, CC drew her weapon and placed it against the back of Deputy Brown's head. Before she could cock her weapon, she was on the floor, her 9mm wrenched from her grasp. She struggled to catch her breath as she found herself kneeling on the floor staring up at Val's carefully aimed Glock.

"Have you lost your mind?" Val emptied the clip of CC's gun.

"Not just yet, but I'm getting there." CC held up her hand to show Val she wasn't going to try anything stupid. "I just had to be sure before I trusted you with the most precious thing in my life."

"About?"

CC remained calm, knowing that if she made one twitchy move she'd be dead.

"I had to know the phantom we are chasing isn't you. Like you said, you're not supposed to be here. That makes you a wild card. I did some digging into your past and couldn't find out a lot. Makes me wonder just what it was you did in the navy."

"You dug into my past?" Val asked with a laugh.

"Stevie tried to dig into your past."

"I figured as much, since you can't work your phone. Are you satisfied that your family's going to be safe in my hands? Or maybe I should kick the shit out of you first. You know, just in case you need a little more convincing."

"No, I'm satisfied." CC rose to her feet. "That makes twice you could have hurt me, or worse, and you didn't. I can trust you with my sister's life. Not her virtue, but her life. Can I have my gun back?"

"No."

"Why not?"

"Because I said so."

"Have it your way. I need to pick up my wife. If you're the detail that is supposed to be following me, you'd better hurry, because I drive like everyone else in this city."

* * *

Jamie was exhausted. Jack was more than a little displeased that he had administration on his back. Jamie couldn't fault the powers that be. If word got out that a child molester had been roaming the halls of the hospital, it wouldn't bode well. She looked at her watch. Tierney was late again. The girl was amazing. She had been warned, cajoled, threatened, and still she arrived later and later for each shift. Jamie went to Jack who was already in a foul mood.

"A moment?" she asked tentatively while taking a shy step into his office.

"You're not in trouble."

"I'm sorry your day turned into a train wreck."

"Jamie, you didn't invite this guy here, and thanks to you, we were prepared."

"Thank you." She accepted the compliment with a grain of salt. A part of her did feel guilty. "I have just one small matter to discuss with you. Dr. Tierney."

"Late again?"

"Yes. How did this girl get through med school? I like the kid, but she hasn't exhibited an ounce of professionalism. I think we need to cut her from the program."

"Done. Want me to be the bad guy?"

"No, I will. It's what you pay me for. That is, if she bothers to show up. Go home, Jack. I'll see you in the morning. Thanks again for everything."

Jamie wasn't surprised that Jack didn't seem to be in a hurry to head home. She couldn't imagine what it would be like to have to go home to an empty one bedroom condo. Just a few years ago, that was the way she lived her life. Now, the concept was inconceivable.

"Ah, Dr. Tierney." She found her errant resident hanging around the nurse's station. "Nice of you to join us. And just at the end of the shift."

"No, see," Tierney began to say. "You see there weren't any cabs. Then..."

"Don't you live a block from Sullivan Station?"

"Yes. I don't like going down there. Have you seen what the subway is like at night?"

"Yes, because most nights I ride it." Jamie rubbed her throbbing temple. "I find it interesting that you're afraid to ride the subway, when just last week I saw you put a junkie in a headlock."

"Yeah, that was something." Tierney had the bad manners to gloat. "I'll just get started."

"Don't bother." Jamie sighed heavily and waved for the younger woman to follow her. "My office, now."

Tierney didn't seem concerned; she simply followed Jamie to her office. "I know what you're going to say," Tierney said. "I'm buying a new alarm clock. The one I have must be defective."

"Stop. As entertaining as I find your little sagas, I can't let this go on. It isn't fair to the people in the program. We've had this little chat before. There are a lot of people out there who would kill to be in your shoes right now. You don't seem to care."

"I do."

"No you don't. I'm sorry, but you're done." Jamie stood firm. She hated it because the girl did make her laugh, but enough was enough. "I'll need your hospital ID, and you'll have to clear out your locker."

"I'm fired? For real?"

"Yes, for real. You can file an appeal with Dr. Temple. I have to warn you that he's already on board with dismissing you."

"Okay, so this appeal... when can I do that?"

"I'd try in the morning." Jamie once again wondered how this woman got through school. "He usually shows up around seven in the morning." Jamie was stunned when Tierney thanked her then happily sauntered out of her office after handing over her badge. "Seven A.M." She silently wondered whether Tierney would bother to be on time. "Unbelievable."

Jamie typed up her report and gathered her things. One last check, and she could wait for CC to come and get her. She hoped the excitement was over for the day. She couldn't help smiling when she spied a familiar figure lingering by the nurses' station. The nurses on duty seemed amused, and it only took Jamie a moment to figure out why.

"So, you're a cop? You guys have been busy here today," Murphy prattled on while the nurses giggled. "I'm a doctor." He emphasized his words by tugging on his lab coat.

"Yeah?" CC winked at Jamie, who was standing directly behind the young man.

"I get off duty soon," he said, completely unaware of how deeply he was stepping in it.

"Murphy!" Jamie barked. "A word of advice. Never hit on your boss's wife."

"Huh?"

"Hi, honey." She gave CC a quick kiss. "Murphy, get back to work."

"Yes, Dr. Jameson," he said in a squeaky voice while the nurses laughed hysterically.

"You could have warned him," Jamie said.

Stella laughed. "Where's the fun in that?"

"He seemed nice," CC said with a grin.

"You behave," Jamie said. "Stella, pull Tierney off the schedule."

"For tonight?"

"Permanently."

"You can't wait until next week?"

"Sorry."

"Had to fire someone?" CC winced.

"Yeah, the slacker I told you about. You okay?"

"It's been a long day." The smile CC had been sporting vanished. "And it's going to be a long night."

Chapter 28

Stevie was a nervous wreck by the time CC and Jamie arrived. Brad's constant pacing hadn't helped steady her nerves. Thankfully, Emma managed to have fun with her father before going to bed. Stevie's mood failed to calm when she caught the solemn looks on Jamie's and CC's faces.

Her pulse raced slightly when Val came right in behind them, huffing.

"You drive like a maniac," Val shouted.

"I drive like a Bostonian. Get over it," CC said. "Did you make your calls?"

"Yes," Val answered in a quieter tone. "Stevie, we need to talk."

"Last time a woman said that to me, she was walking out the door," Stevie said grimly. "Tell me that you aren't leaving us so soon."

"No, you're the one who's leaving." Val reached inside her blazer and pulled out her wallet. "You, Brad, and Emma. It's all been arranged. These are some friends of mine." She showed Stevie a picture of a younger version of herself along with four friends all clad in dress navy whites. "Ricky, Callie, Brenda, and Dave. We went through Annapolis together, and we all retired at the same time. Dave was with the DEA, Callie is Secret Service, Brenda is CIA, and Ricky is FBI. We're all still close."

"He's yummy." Brad was drooling over the picture. "Sorry." He gulped when he realized what he had said.

"Glad you like him. He's your new boyfriend."

"Lucky me."

"I'm not going anywhere," Stevie said. "My father isn't—"

"Stevie." CC tried to argue.

"I'm staying."

"Then at least send Brad and Emma," CC said. "These people are pros."

"We all live together in DC," Val said before Stevie could argue. "We also own a cabin in the middle of nowhere that is extremely secure. With our professions, we know a lot places you can hide without feeling like a prisoner."

CC picked up the argument. "You were already talking about sending Emma off with Brad to his family's place. The Feds are going to be covering this place. Mills is going to be fixing the roof, and—"

"And we have people posing as landscapers," Val said. "I'll be here."

"You can't come into my home and tell me to ship my child off!" Stevie was furious.

"Stevie, this is bad," CC said.

"I get that." Stevie fought against crying. "You trust her?"

"I have no choice." CC sounded defeated. "I'll be here. I've taken a leave of absence."

"What?" Stevie sat down when she felt her knees buckle. "You never..."

"He's coming, Stevie," CC said in a strangled voice. "He's back, and the only way to bag him is to set a trap. It's too dangerous to let Emma stay. I hate this just as much as you do."

"Fine. Brad, can you go?"

"Yes. I'll call the restaurant and the club and tell them I have a family emergency."

"Jamie?" Stevie looked toward her.

"I don't like it either." Jamie also sounded defeated. "But there doesn't seem to be another way. It's up to you and Brad."

"Stevie," Val said slowly, "right now, we can do this. We have the people. If he's on the run for much longer, they'll cut back. I'll be sent back to DC. You'll be left with this dufus named Finn."

"Cathy Finn? I thought she retired?"

"No," CC said. "Her ex-husband."

"Oh, the one who caught you with Cathy." Stevie almost laughed until she realized how bad things really were. "That wouldn't be good. The guy hates you."

"Who is Cathy?" Jamie asked.

"I kind of dated her." CC squirmed.

"Really?" Jamie bristled.

"Focus, please," CC said. "Stevie, the long weekend is coming up. We can do this now, and Emma will be safe. She'll be able to go on with her life without him ever getting near her."

"Stevie, we should do this," Brad firmly stated. "We can't risk—"

"Okay!" Stevie caved in. "When?"

"Now." CC reached over and held her hand. "Start packing her things and wake her up. Tell her that she's going on a trip with Daddy."

"Here." Val held out her phone and pushed a couple of buttons. Stevie almost laughed when CC jumped at the sound of her phone beeping. "It's copies so we haven't broken the chain of evidence," Val explained, snatching CC's phone. "Press here for Play and here to Delete. I got to say I love the phones you guys are sporting."

"I hate that everyone knows how to use my phone but me." CC snatched her phone back. She and Stevie watched in horror as the grainy black-and-white image played before them.

"My God, it's him." Stevie trembled. "That's my father. A little older, a lot pudgier, but that's him. Where was this?"

"Green Line." Val's stoic veneer cracked ever so slightly. "He got off at the Boylston Village stop."

"That's three blocks from here."

"That video is from the other day."

"I'll get Emma."

Stevie hated everything that was happening. She hated Val for coming up with a plan that would either make her run or be separated from her daughter. She hated that Emma was being fussy and she couldn't tell her what was going on. How do you tell a child that her grandfather was lurking around and that he's a bad man? She silently brooded while she tried to convince Emma that she couldn't pack her entire bedroom and that missing a couple of school days wasn't that big a deal. She hated feeling helpless, almost as much as she hated seeing her older sister, who had always been her protector, become helpless.

"I don't want to go," the still half-asleep Emma wailed as she stomped downstairs.

"It's only for a couple of days," Stevie said. "You'll be with Daddy and his new friend."

"There's a chess set there," Val said once Emma stomped into the living room and expressed her displeasure by tossing her backpack onto the floor.

"Daddy doesn't know how to play chess."

"It's true." Brad looked completely embarrassed.

"I do."

Stevie had been so caught up with dealing with Emma's tirade that she missed the three strangers standing in her living room. He wasn't tall, but he was a well-built, dark-haired Latino man with warm brown eyes. *Brad is going to be in heaven*, she mused.

"I'm Ricky," he said with a firm handshake. "And I love playing chess," he added, bending down to greet Emma.

Stevie only felt a small sense of comfort from his demeanor, and the fact that he was clad in a powder blue polo with an HRC logo embroidered on the breast. Just because he was family didn't mean she could trust him with her kid. She said, "See, Emma, it will be fun."

"Don't want to go," Emma screeched.

Stevie was at her wit's end when Caitlin stood and crossed the room. "Emma." CC knelt to meet Emma's eye level. "Stitch has a glitch." Stevie's heart broke as she watched her daughter's eyes widen with fear.

"Do you understand?" CC tenderly clasped Emma's shoulders.

"Yes." Emma jutted out her chin, doing her best to appear

brave.

"You can talk to us every day," Stevie said. "Even send videos on Daddy's phone. It'll be fun."

"Auntie Caitlin doesn't know how to use her phone."

"I'll learn, so you and I can talk every day," CC promised. "Everything is going to be all right. But your mommy and I need you to be brave."

"I will." Emma plopped her Orioles hat on her head and picked up her stuffed puppy.

"Don't forget to walk Dory," Stevie said while scooping Emma up in her arms.

"Dory?" Ricky asked.

"My practice puppy." Emma held up the stuffed animal. "If I do good with Dory, I get a real puppy."

"These nice people are going to take you on a very special plane ride," Stevie tearfully explained. "You be good for Daddy."

"I will," Emma said, breaking Stevie's heart when she clung tighter to her.

Brenda softly broke the moment. "We have to go. Sorry, ma'am."

After a brief flurry of activity, they were gone. Stevie's nerves were frazzled. She had just sent her daughter off to parts unknown with complete strangers.

"Jamie, do you still have that bottle of Disaronno?"

"I'll be right back." Jamie moved quickly, seemingly relieved to have something to do. "How many glasses?"

"I'll join you." CC slumped down on the sofa.

"I'm on duty," Val somberly added.

"As?" Stevie asked while Jamie retreated to grab the bottle of liquor.

"Oh, right," Val stammered slightly while CC glared at her. "I'm going to be posing as your new girlfriend. That way, no one will question why I'm hanging around or sleeping over. Unless, there's someone..."

"No." Stevie couldn't help notice that Val was sporting a slight blush. "Considering what happened earlier, did you think there was someone?"

"No, I just didn't want to assume."

"You failed to mention that your cover was going to be as my sister's lover," CC said with a snarl. "You could just as easily pose as a visiting cousin."

"It's a perfect cover." Stevie joined her sister on the sofa. A stifling silence descended over the room. Thankfully, Jamie returned with a bucket of ice, three glasses, and a large bottle of amaretto.

"Don't be shy with that pour," Stevie said. It wasn't her style to drink during a crisis. The past few days had just been too much for her to deal with. Jamie heeded her instructions and poured the drinks while Val lurked by the front window.

"Stitch has a glitch?" Val said, breaking the uncomfortable silence.

"It's a code," CC explained. "We have a bunch of codes to relate emergencies or to let Emma know that she's safe. Stitch has a glitch means there's danger and she needs to just do as we say. Or she can use it to alert us she's in danger without having to say it."

"Good idea, given the state of the world." Val moved slightly closer to the trio. "So, it works?"

"Up until tonight it was just a theory," Jamie said bitterly.

"Who's Stitch?"

"A Disney character," Stevie answered, fully aware that Val was simply trying to distract them. "I hate this day. At least I can track Emma with the family locator on her phone."

"The cabin is in Virginia," Val said. Once again, her voice sounded tense. "There's a lake and lots of stuff for her to do. They'll have a blast. That's where I was heading before my vacation plans fell apart."

"Deputy?" CC's strained voice interrupted. Stevie braced herself for the tirade her sister was certain to release. "Can I have my gun back now?"

Stevie's jaw dropped as she watched Val extract her sister's nine-millimeter pistol from inside her blazer.

CC held out her hand and impatiently snapped her fingers. "The magazine? I don't keep fifteen-round clips lying around the house."

"Fine." Val tossed the magazine at the grumpy detective. "It's not like you don't have a bug strapped to your ankle. I'm guessing a forty-caliber Smith and Wesson."

Stevie watched as her sister simply nodded and reloaded her gun. She was stunned to see CC holster her weapon as if it were no big deal.

"Yeah, this is making me feel better," Stevie said sarcastically. "You're drinking, which you almost never do, and you're carrying guns around the house. Care to tell me just how Val came into possession of your gun in the first place?"

"I had to be sure I could trust her."

"Speaking of which." Val stepped closer to CC. "The next time you aim your weapon at me, be ready to use it." The coldness in Val's voice sent a shiver down Stevie's spine.

"I'll remember that, for the next time you put your hands on my sister."

"Isn't this fun?" Jamie gave a snort and swirled the ice in her glass. "They're trying to out-butch each other. Another round, Stevie?"

"God, yes."

"Stevie?" CC started as Jamie handed her a fresh drink. "Not to add more stress to your evening..."

"Crap, there's more?"

"No." Caitlin pushed her drink aside. "I just wanted to tell you that in the morning I'm taking a trip to Waltham. I didn't know if you wanted to go."

"Visiting our mother?"

"Yes. I need to be sure she isn't involved with this."

"I'll pass." Stevie felt anger trying to spill over. "You go and do what you need to do. I have nothing to say to her."

"You're sure you're up for that, sweetie?" Jamie asked.

"Don't have a choice."

"You need sleep." Jamie stood and offered her hand to her wife. "It's almost dawn, and I don't know about the rest of you, but I feel like hell. Try to get some sleep, Stevie."

"I'll try. Don't forget to close the connecting door."

"I thought we might leave it open." CC seemed flustered while she glared at Val. "You know, to be on the safe side."

"Close the door," Stevie said. "The last thing I need is to hear the two of you. I swear you're worse than a couple of horny teenagers."

Stevie smiled when Jamie winked at her before closing, but not locking, the door that connected the two homes. She turned her attention to the brunette who was still stalking around her living room.

"So, Deputy Val. Now that we're dating, mind telling me where you're planning on sleeping?"

The question hung in the air as Val stood in the middle of the living room with her jaw hanging open. "I'm... I'm..." she stammered before she shook her head and managed to speak like a normal person. "I'm not."

"Oh?" Stevie poured herself another drink.

"I'm on duty," Val reminded her charge. In her heart, she was also reminding herself. "I won't be sleeping tonight. I'm here to ensure your safety."

"Thank you."

Val checked that the house was indeed secure. She told

herself she was performing her duty and not trying to avoid the attractive woman who was watching her every move. When she had checked and rechecked every nook and cranny of the modest home, she finally sat down. Stevie's brow furrowed when Val chose to sit as far away from her as possible without being in another room.

"So," Val absently said. Her mind turned completely blank.

"Yes?"

"Uh…" Val hesitated, still unable to conjure up anything remotely intelligent to say. "Uh," she repeated, feeling the heat of Stevie's gaze. "Were your parents Fleetwood Mac fans?"

The chuckle Stevie released informed Val it wasn't the first time someone had asked her that question. Val rubbed her hands along her slacks while Stevie just sat there looking at her.

"Yes," Stevie finally answered. "My mother is or was. I have no idea how her taste in music runs these days."

"Aren't you curious?" If Val were given the chance to see her mother again, she would jump at it.

"No." Stevie's head fell slightly back. She blew out an exasperated breath before continuing. "A long time ago, my sister was wounded. You probably already know that, since you've been checking us out."

"She was shot."

"At the time, I was living in Rhode Island with my parents. The department contacted them. I had no idea what had happened. They never said anything about it. The department called again. Caitlin wasn't doing well, and the doctors feared the worst. This time I answered the call. I told my mother, unaware that she already knew. She didn't care. I hitchhiked all the way up to Boston. I sat by Caitlin's bedside, praying for her. All through the ordeal, I tried repeatedly to get my mother to come and see her. She refused. The last time I tried, she hung up on me. I accepted something that day. Something that I had long suspected. It really was Caitlin and me against the world. So, no, I think I'll pass on seeing her. I don't really have anything to say to her. Are you planning on sitting way over there all night?"

"Yes."

"Why?"

"Let's see. I'm on a case, you're a little drunk, and you have a heavily armed, overprotective sister who already pulled a gun on me once."

"Is that all?"

"Works for me."

"She does have that effect on people." Stevie stifled a yawn.

"It's late." Val couldn't help feeling concerned for the overwrought woman. "Why don't I help you up to bed?"

"Now, that's the best idea I've heard all day."

"To sleep," Val quickly amended, while helping the slightly inebriated woman to her feet. "Like I said before, you're sobriety is in question."

"And you're on duty."

"I'm on duty." She helped Stevie climb the staircase. "Lead the way," she said, resting her hand against the small of Stevie's back. Internally, she told herself the action was only to ensure that Stevie wouldn't stumble. Deep in her heart, she knew it was a lie.

"This is my stop." Stevie leaned against the doorway to her bedroom. "I'd feel better if you stayed."

"I need to..."

"I know." Stevie held up her hand. Much to Val's joy and discomfort Stevie's hand came to rest on her chest. "You can watch over me just as easily from my bedroom as my living room. I just don't want to be alone. The house is too quiet with Emma gone. I promise, no funny business."

Val could only nod in response as she followed Stevie into the dark bedroom. She released a terse breath after she helped Stevie lay down. She tightened her blazer and shoved her hands in her pockets. She shifted nervously when Stevie gazed up with a curious look in her eyes.

"I wasn't planning on sleeping in my clothes." Stevie climbed off the bed.

"Oh? I'll just..."

"No need."

Before Val could bolt out of the room, Stevie lifted her dress over her head. Val willed her feet to move, or tried to at least look away. Stevie continued to undress, revealing her toned body. Val remained riveted to the sight. Her eyes scanned the length of Stevie's naked form. *Please just put your pajamas on!* her mind screamed while her heart raced. Val's stomach clenched when Stevie turned to her and climbed back into bed, forgoing the need to put on any clothing.

Val continued to stand there in the darkness long after Stevie had covered her body with the bedspread. Stevie rolled over onto her side and still Val stood there staring. She fought to control her erratic breathing. Nothing was working. All she could do was look down at Stevie who she prayed had fallen asleep.

"Are you just going to stand there all night?" Stevie's weary voice startled her.

She jumped when the younger woman moved and looked over at her. Val was unaware of what she was doing. Before her mind could catch up with her body, she had shed her blazer and climbed onto the bed.

"Take your shoes off." Stevie chuckled when Val stiffly moved beside her.

"Sorry." Val kicked off her shoes. She sat there for a moment completely at a loss. Stevie seemed unfazed by the events. She simply laid back down and curled up under the bedding.

Val clenched her fists before curling up behind the somber brunette. *I can do this*, she mentally chanted over and over again. She bit back a yelp when Stevie nestled closer to her.

"What's a bug?"

"Excuse me?"

"You said Caitlin had a bug strapped to her ankle."

"Bug." Val blew out a breath of relief. Shoptalk was something she could handle. "B-U-G is an acronym for a backup gun. Based on the size of the bulge beneath the cuff of your sister's jeans, I'm guessing her backup is a forty-caliber Smith and Wesson."

"Oh." Stevie yawned. "I know she owns a second gun. I've just never known her to wear it. Not around the house anyway. If Caitlin is scared, this has to be bad. I'm afraid," Stevie said with a sniff. She rolled over, and the fear in her eyes bore into the normally controlled deputy.

"Don't worry," Val said in an effort to calm Stevie. Her mistake was reaching down and caressing Stevie's arm. The feel of flesh prickling beneath her touch or perhaps the pleading look in

Stevie's eyes was her undoing. Her mind screamed for her to stop, but her body took over. Leaning down, she brushed her lips lightly against Stevie's soft, trembling lips.

It was meant to be innocent, she lied to herself. The feel of Stevie's arms wrapping around her body invoked memories of earlier that day. Memories of the two of them fumbling on the sofa. She gave into the feel of Stevie urging her closer. She moved slightly, half of her body now lying on top of Stevie's. The chaste, reassuring kiss morphed into a sensual exploration.

Val was lost in the feel of Stevie's tongue parting her lips. She gave into the sweet sensation. She returned the kiss with a passion she hadn't felt in a long time. Her hands refused to remain idle. She tugged the covers down, her body shivered from the feel of Stevie's naked body pressed against her own.

"You said you'd behave."

"I lied."

Instead of heeding the warning to remain professional, Val gave in to the desire that had been building since the first moment she had laid eyes on this woman. She cupped Stevie's breasts. She released a deep moan from the feel of Stevie's nipple hardening against her touch. She slowly explored the warmth of Stevie's mouth. Her hands tugged the sheet away from Stevie's body.

Val shifted and pressed her thigh between Stevie's legs. Their hips swayed in demanding rhythm. Unable to curb her desire, her kisses drifted lower. She took her time kissing and licking the supple curve of Stevie's neck. She was spurred on by the short needy gasps her lover released. Passion rolled off her body. Her lips blazed a determined path to Stevie's exposed breast.

Slowly her tongue circled the rose-colored bud, teasing it before capturing it between her eager lips. She suckled it eagerly. Pleased when she felt Stevie urgently rock against her, she nudged her lover's thighs farther apart. The scents and sounds of their passion filled her senses. Her body took over. She teased one nipple between her fingers while she taunted the other with her teeth and tongue.

If not for the sudden sound of displeasure from her lover, Val would have continued ravishing her. Startled, she slightly lifted her body. Her heart was pounding as she gazed down at the beautiful woman lying beneath her.

"This has to go," Stevie playfully demanded, tugging on Val's belt.

Confused for a moment, Val realized that her utility belt was the problem. "We need to stop." She tried to pull away.

"Just lose the gun." Stevie undid the offending belt that held Val's gun, handcuffs, and various other tools of her trade. Val was prepared to protest when she heard the thud of her equipment hitting the floor. Still she braced herself for an argument while Stevie tugged her white dress shirt out of her slacks.

Val was mystified as to why she wasn't stopping what was happening. Instead she gave in, allowing Stevie to undress her. Instead of voicing her objections, she let her clothing fall from her body. She failed to stop what could possibly be the stupidest thing she had ever done in her lengthy career. She slipped her hand between Stevie's quivering thighs.

Her lover's wetness pooling between her fingers drove away any objections of common sense. Eagerly, she glided her fingers along Stevie's swollen lips. She teased the opening of her warm, wet, center, before she began teasing her throbbing clit. Her heart beat wildly when her actions were greeted enthusiastically as Stevie passionately thrust against her.

Her pulse quickened from the feel of strong hands that ran down her back to her sides. Stevie's hands rested on her hips and drew her closer to the tantalizing body beneath her. Their lips united once again. Val was beyond thinking. Her body reacted solely on instinct. She teased her lover's engorged nub. Urgently, she thrust two fingers deep inside Stevie's wetness.

Her body shivered when Stevie cried out for more. Val answered her pleas, taking her harder. Stevie's body trembled as Val watched her ride against her touch. Stevie's body arched, and she cried out with pleasure as she climaxed. Val cast aside her doubts about what she should or shouldn't have done that evening.

She willing allowed Stevie to guide her down onto the bed. The last of her clothing was cast aside, and Stevie kissed and licked her way down Val's body. Val parted her thighs and guided Stevie lower, trembling from the feel of Stevie's warm breath caressing her thighs. She cried out when Stevie parted her with her tongue.

Val watched Stevie eagerly feasting upon her. She wrapped her legs around her lover's shoulders and gave all of herself. Stevie suckled her throbbing clit. Val begged for release. Losing the battle to hold on, she cried out before collapsing. She gathered Stevie in her arms, her heart still beating wildly.

"I swear, if you say this was a mistake..." Stevie murmured against her chest.

"I can't."

CHECKMATE

* * *

Next door, Jamie had escorted her wife up to the bedroom. She instructed her to secure her weapons in the lock box. CC complied and Jamie slowly undressed CC before removing her own clothing. She pulled back the covers and guided her to bed. Then she held CC and let her do the one thing she really needed to do. CC wept in her arms, finally allowing the floodgates to open. Once CC had cried herself out, she reached up and caressed Jamie's face. Jamie leaned into her touch.

It was like a dream, somehow being touched by this woman could wash away all her fears. She dipped her head and gently claimed CC's soft, inviting lips. Their bodies melted together. The kiss slowly deepened. There was nothing hurried in their movements. They explored the warmth of each other's mouth, while their hands slowly and softly caressed the other's body.

"I love you," CC softly whispered and drew Jamie closer.

"I'm yours." Jamie's hands glided along the supple curves of CC's body. Slowly she explored her way down then back up again. She laced her fingers through CC's long, silky hair. She suckled CC's bottom lip. CC leaned into her, and the feel of CC's exposed flesh brushing against her own drove her insane.

She relished the gentle exploration, yet her body demanded more. Instinctively, she understood CC's need to be held. To be loved. She lowered her own body and pulled CC down on top of her. Their tongues engaged in a duel for control as the kiss deepened. CC parted Jamie's firm thighs with her leg. Her body tingled as their bodies moved in perfect rhythm.

"I want you, Jamie. I need you."

"Take me."

Jamie guided CC's hand down her body allowing her to caress her along the way. She moaned when CC's fingers dipped into her wetness. Slowly, CC touched her and teased her.

"Yes." Jamie's body rose off the bed as CC entered her slowly. She felt CC's fingers reaching her very core. CC wiggled her fingers inside of her before retreating slightly. Jamie fought to steady her breathing, and her hands caressed CC's body. She smiled when she felt her lover tremble. She bit her bottom lip and gave in to the feel of CC steadily gliding in and out of her wetness. Not to be outdone, she cupped CC's mound and parted her, before mirroring her lover's ministrations.

Held captive by each other's fiery gaze, they pleasured one another slowly before giving in to the passion. Making love came so natural to them. They rode against one another, until they released strangled cries.

Chapter 29

Val awoke naked and confused. It was not a new experience for the world-weary deputy. Beside her, Stevie was caught up in a fitful sleep. The grim look on her face tugged at Val's heart. Val wanted to smack herself for being an idiot. Instead, she slowly slipped out of bed. Everyone would be there soon. She needed to make herself presentable. The problem was, she didn't have any clothing. Brenda had promised to drop some off while posing as a plumber.

She checked her watch. Brenda wouldn't be there for another hour or so. She glanced over at Stevie's closet. They were about the same height, and Stevie was more toned than the average stay-at-home mom.

She stole a pair of jeans and a plain blouse and went looking for the bathroom. She caught a glimpse of herself in the bathroom mirror. She growled. Anyone could take one look at her and know what she had been doing. *Her sister is going kill me.*

She took a quick shower, and filled with apprehension, she headed downstairs, pausing when she spied a familiar figure planted on the sofa.

"Crap." She quickly sought an exit plan.

"Might as well get down here." The harshness in CC's voice made Val fear for her life. "I can see you." Val stifled a yelp. No two ways about it, she was a dead woman. She learned a long time ago, that when someone tells you not to sleep with their sister, you should probably heed their warning.

Jamie stepped into view. "Honey, don't pick on her. Val, please join us? I've made coffee and Caitlin was just about to start breakfast."

"Thank you, Caitlin," Val said meekly and cautiously descended the staircase.

"Don't call me that," CC said.

"She has to call you something." Stevie snuck up behind her. "Stick with CC."

CC didn't buy the innocent smile Val offered. She returned it with an icy glare and stomped out of the room.

"Coffee ladies?" Jamie said.

"Yes, thank you."

"Thanks, James," Stevie said. "How pissed is she?"

"Let's just say I'm glad I have to go to the hospital and I hope that Val won't end up being one of my patients."

"I thought you were sleeping," Val whispered to Stevie while Jamie poured the coffee.

"Someone's banging on the roof."

"That would be Mills. She's posing as a roofer."

"Any chance she'll really fix the roof?"

"Knowing Mills, yes."

There was a knock on the door, and Jamie and Stevie froze. Val checked the window, and CC rushed into the room. Val waved that everything was all right.

"The plumber's here," she explained in as normal a tone as she could muster. She nodded for Stevie to answer the door. It was her friend Brenda, who was dressed in work clothes and toting a tool box and a couple of heavy bags.

"Miss Calloway?" She set her tool box and a bag down. She handed one to Val and dug out equipment. "I hear you've been having some problems." CC peered over Val's shoulder and nodded when she realized what was going on.

"Yes," CC said, "the dishwasher has been giving us trouble."

"Let's have a look at everything." Brenda gave Val a thumbs up.

Stevie looked bewildered. "What is..."

"The plumber needs to check things out," Val calmly explained. She felt a bit off center standing so close to the woman she had made love to only a few short hours ago. Val wasn't one for morning-after chitchat. Most of Val's dates ended with her leaving just before sunrise.

"More coffee?" CC smacked Val in the back of the head.

"Sure." Val wanted to kick the cocky detective's ass. She peered inside the bag she was holding and was shocked by the contents. Clothes. "What the f—" The sound of Dr. Jameson clearing her throat cut off her expletive. "Sorry." She took a moment to calm herself.

Brenda returned from scoping out the kitchen and moved upstairs. Val's ire grew as she looked over her new wardrobe. She couldn't figure out if Brenda was playing her or had simply lost her mind.

"It's clear," Brenda said and set her toolbox down. "Which is good, since you've already blabbed everything."

"No listening devices," Val said for Stevie and Jamie, who each sported a look of confusion. "What's with the new clothes?" She held out the bag that contained various items in pink or pastel.

"Everything in your closet has a navy insignia or US Marshal emblazoned across it. I know we're all married to our jobs, but hit the GAP every once in a while." Brenda turned her attention to Stevie. "Emma is fine. The trip went very smoothly. Bright kid."

"Thank you," Stevie mumbled. Val didn't miss the distant look in her eyes.

"You have a great security system in place," Brenda said. "3M film on all the windows so they won't break no matter how hard you hit them. Charlie bars on the sliding doors and basement windows. Security cameras all over the property, although, Miss Calloway, you need to turn yours on," she told Stevie.

Stevie simply nodded and set about powering up her laptop.

"I don't usually see this much detail with civilians," Brenda said.

"We had problems in the past," CC grimly informed her.

"Well, I might as well take a look at the dishwasher, since I'm dressed for the part. Then I need to get back to DC. Unless there's something else you need, Brownie?"

"Not at the moment. Thanks, Brenda."

She motioned to Val. "Why don't you join me?"

Val followed her, curious as to what was going on. She feared perhaps Brenda had found something she didn't want to reveal in front of the family. Val stood in CC's kitchen and watched Brenda fiddle with the dishwasher.

"What is it?"

"Have you lost your mind?" There was no mistaking the disappointment in Brenda's voice. "You slept with her?"

"How did... Never mind. Look, it was a moment of bad judgment."

"Never happened to you before." Brenda's eyes bored into Val. "Except that time in Milan when you slept with what's her name. Geez, Brownie, you'd think after that disaster—"

"I screwed up, okay?" Val cut off Brenda's tainted view of the situation. "Just for the record, this is nothing like that bi-curious wench from Milan, okay. Dimitra was a bored housewife."

"A bored senior officer's wife."

"How's the dishwasher?"

Val jumped when she heard CC's sharp tone.

"Seen better days. I can patch it up. You might want to start shopping for something new. I fixed the upstairs toilet while I was snooping around. Hope you got a good price on this place."

"We did. Short sale, but it needs work."

"No kidding."

"Is the place secure?" Val said in an effort to change the subject.

"Yes."

"You're not off the hook," CC said to Val. "But Stevie's over thirty. It's not like I can ground her." She turned to Brenda. "So what's it like working for the CIA?"

"Doesn't suck." Brenda finished patching up the dishwasher. "I have to go." She packed up her tools and brushed off her work clothes. "Brownie, call if you need me."

After Brenda's hasty exit, Val watched CC open the refrigerator and remove a carton of eggs. Her heart hammered in her chest as CC beat the eggs.

"What happened to Dave?" CC asked out of the blue while pouring the eggs into a skillet. Val stiffened, not wanting to answer the question. "You said Dave was DEA."

"Line of duty."

"Sorry."

"Part of the job."

"Doesn't make it easier."

"Yeah. Want to go over things for today?"

"No." CC waved her off while she finished throwing together a couple plates of scrambled eggs. "Jamie's going to ask her boss for the weekend off. I'm heading to Waltham. Other than that, I guess we're just sitting around and waiting."

"We've got troopers canvassing the hotels, mostly down around Beacon Street," Val said She couldn't understand why she felt a need to prove to CC that she was on top of things. "Everyone in the Boston area is looking for him. We released his picture to the local schools. I hit Emma's school first. I also put a couple of extra field officers around the main business areas. If he's near here, we have a chance of spotting him before he makes his way to your block."

"I'm not questioning what's being done. Nothing short of seeing him in chains is going to make me feel better."

"I also moved my vehicle into your garage. Having a black sedan with government plates parked out front wouldn't bode well."

A Cher tune echoed in the kitchen. "Jamie's idea," CC grumbled as she began to search for her phone. "She's programmed in all these ring tones. That would be Brad." She found her phone. "Hello? Hey there, peanut! I can see you."

"I know," Emma squealed. "This place is so cool. We're going fishing later, and I saw a deer this morning."

"Sounds like you're having a great time. Can you see me, or do I need to turn this around?"

"The old phones have the camera on the back," Emma said with a dramatic sigh. "Your phone has a camera on both sides. We can see you. Ricky made breakfast. He even caramelized the bananas."

"Did he now?"

"Yes!"

"Did you want to talk to your mother?"

"I called her first. I'm having fun, Auntie Caitlin. Love you."

"Love you, too."

Val stepped back to give CC some privacy. Needing to make herself feel useful, she gathered up the breakfast plates and took them into the other side of the house. Val offered Jamie and Stevie breakfast. She wasn't surprised that no one seemed interested in eating. She had endured some very odd mornings-after in her life, but not once had she offered breakfast to the woman she had spent the night with while making plans to hunt down her father.

"No eggs for me," Jamie said. "I had a bowl of Fruit Loops. Don't give me that look, Stevie. You know I think you're jealous because your sister never let you eat the fun stuff for breakfast." Stevie just stuck out her tongue. Val found it positively adorable.

"I need to get going," Jamie said when CC joined them. "I hope I can convince Jack to give me the weekend off. Maybe he'll pick them up."

"He didn't have plans?" CC asked while Val tried to disappear into the background.

"He might. I think he was going to try to get together with Joyce."

"I can't believe those two haven't worked things out yet."

"Jack doesn't seem to think there's a problem." Jamie's voice turned bitter. "In his mind, Joyce is overreacting. I'm off. You kids, play nice."

"We'll try." CC gave her wife a quick kiss. "Oh, Brenda fixed the toilet."

"The CIA fixed our toilet? Our lives are truly surreal."

CC watched Jamie leave in a fake taxi driven by an undercover cop. Then she stood in the middle of her living room with nothing to do. It was an unnerving feeling. In an effort to center her world, she checked and rechecked every nook and cranny of both sides of the house. Still feeling antsy, she climbed up onto the roof with a jug of water for the crew.

"How's it going?"

"Thanks for the water. Roof is coming along nicely," Mills said. "No sign of our guy."

"I can't take much more of this."

"Calloway, we're on it."

"I'm not doubting you. I'm just not good at sitting on the sidelines. Unless something comes up with the Stern case, I'm just in the way."

"Did she really fry his nuts?"

"Oh, yeah." CC couldn't help but laugh. "Never piss off a soccer mom."

"I'll keep that in mind. Sorry to do this to you, but you need to head back inside. Doesn't look good if you're up here hanging out with the help."

"Thanks, Mills."

CC scanned the street as she made her descent down the ladder. The normalcy of the view did nothing to calm her nerves. There was a storm brewing; she could feel it. Everything was being handled perfectly. Perhaps too perfectly. She gave the tree-lined street one last glance and returned inside.

"Hey, sis," she said. Stevie looked like she was ready to break down. "Emma sounded like she was having fun."

"She's having a blast." Stevie didn't look at CC. She just sat in an overstuffed armchair and stared out the front window. "I told her the pumpkins are rotting. I swear you carve them early, just so you can do them again."

"I do." The sight of Stevie slumped in the chair looking defeated tore at CC. "This will be over soon."

"I believe you. There's not much I believe in this world. Just you. So no lecture about last night."

"I won't. You found yourself in an extreme situation, having your daughter taken away in the middle of the night, and you found comfort. Not for me to judge you."

"She's a good person."

"Seems to be."

"Are you sure you want to see Mom?"

"I have to." CC suddenly felt nauseous. "Sure you don't want to go?"

"I have nothing to say to her."

"Fair enough."

"Tell me again that this will be over soon."

"You have my word. Like you said, he doesn't win this time. We have every federal agency and most of the cops in the city on our side. No offense to your genetics, but Bert isn't the sharpest knife in the drawer."

"None taken."

CC didn't know how to feel about anything. A part of her hated that she had to face her mother. Then there was the other part, the little girl that still remembered the good times, that wanted to see her mother.

"Come on, Deputy Doo Daa," she said to Val. "You're coming with me."

"Because?"

"Because you've already made contact with her." CC was relieved when Val nodded and yanked out her cell phone.

"Marino, give me a twenty on Gallagher." CC tapped her foot impatiently as Val listened to the response. "She's at home," Val informed CC. "The address is 372 Prospect Street. Do you know where that is?"

"I'll figure it out."

"You could just enter it into the GPS in your phone." Val tried to explain. "You don't even need to type it in you could just hit that symbol and tell your phone where you want to go."

CC stood there, stunned, as Val snatched the phone from the holder on her belt. Val's fingers furiously entered the data. CC's jaw dropped when her phone began speaking in careful detail, a crisp mechanical voice providing directions.

"See there's an app for that."

CC snatched her phone back with a sneer. "Everyone is a smart-ass today.

The drive over to Waltham was an eerily quiet affair. Which suited CC just fine. She had no intention of making idle chitchat with the woman who had bedded her sister the night before. Val kept herself busy with her own phone, while the GPS voice that CC had decided to call Mandy directed her towards her mother's address. Navigating the streets was easy for her except when Mandy decided to recalibrate because she felt CC should take another route.

"Starbucks!" Val shouted, startling CC. "They do exist."

"Yeah, there are a couple here and there."

"Can we please stop?"

"No."

"Why not?"

"Shall we start with you taking my gun or bedding my sister?"

"Which bothers you more?"

"My sister, you ass." CC zoomed past Starbucks. "What are you doing?"

"Checking the reports from my team."

"Don't get grumpy. You can do that on your phone?"

"I could do it faster if I had your phone. It's not fair. You don't even know how to use it."

"What are you, five years old?" CC wanted to smack the irritating woman. "Faster? Just how much technology do we need?"

"What are you, one hundred?"

"Not liking you."

"Fine."

"Fine."

"We're here. You take the lead."

CC was confused when they entered the apartment building. "This place is a retirement community."

"Yes."

"My mother is..." CC's voice trailed off. She had no idea how old her mother was. "Never mind."

CC's anxiety grew as they rode up in the elevator. When they stepped off, she hung back, feeling like a coward. She wanted to run.

Val's knock on the door was answered. CC could barely see her mother. The years hadn't been kind. Her mother looked worn and weary.

"Miss Gallagher?" Val kept her tone professional.

"Deputy." She stepped aside to allow Val to enter. "Any news? Please tell me you've caught him."

"I'm afraid, not." Val nodded for CC to follow. "We just have a couple of questions."

CC stood in the hallway with her feet firmly rooted. Finally, she exhaled and followed Val into the apartment.

"Cattie?"

"Yeah," she said in a clipped tone. She wanted to say more. To ask a litany of questions that might help her understand why her childhood had turned into a nightmare.

"My heavens." Maria sobbed and reached for CC before withdrawing her touch. "It's really you. I saw you on television last week. You look well."

"I'm fine." Finding her voice was a struggle. She couldn't look at her mother. Instead she looked around the simple setting that was her mother's home. The walls were bare, with the exception of an oil painting of Jesus. *Mom found Jesus. I wonder if she'll be pissed if I ask if he was behind the sofa.* She shook the random thought from her head. "I'm only here to be certain that you're not helping him."

"I wouldn't." Maria sounded offended. "After I accepted the truth, that was it. I filed for divorce and took off. I never want to see that man again. He ruined everything."

CC studied her for a moment. As far as she could tell, Maria was indeed clueless about Bert's whereabouts.

"No contact with him at all?"

"None. The only contact we had was through lawyers to finalize the divorce. That's it. You're married?" Maria pointed to CC's wedding band.

"Yes, five years now."

"And your husband?"

"Wife. My wife and I have been married for five years."

"Oh, so you're still that way?"

"Yes, Mother, I'm still a big lesbian." CC rolled her neck at the absurdity of the situation. "Always was."

"Oh." Maria's gaze moved from her daughter's face to the carpeting. "I suppose that's my fault as well."

"I'm gay, not defective. Honestly, given what happened… You know what? Never mind. Your shortsightedness isn't the issue at the moment. Have you felt like anyone was watching you? Anything strange happen here or at work?"

"No, Caitlin, I…"

CC tried to be patient as her mother searched for the right thing to say. It seemed like an eternity, just standing there waiting. Maria opened and closed her mouth several times, still not speaking.

CC was unable to endure the agony for any longer. "If you hear or see anything, contact Deputy Brown."

"Wait! Stevie is she…"

"Stevie is happy and healthy," CC said in a somber tone. Her original plan had included telling her about their lives. Maybe mentioning Emma, if she felt confident enough that Bert was truly out of the picture. *She doesn't deserve to know,* she silently concluded. If Maria Gallagher wanted to know more, she'd have to find out for herself. CC didn't waste time with goodbyes; she just walked out the door.

Deputy Brown could barely keep up with her as she charged towards the elevator. She needed to get out of there, breathe the fresh air, and forget everything. To her credit, Val kept silent. CC stormed outside the building struggling to breathe. Again, the deputy gave her space. CC paced around the sidewalk until she felt the tension ebb. Without a word, she climbed into her car and slammed the door.

Val had barely enough time to buckle her seatbelt when CC threw the Subaru in gear and sped off. She navigated the streets of Waltham until she found her way to Route 16. Back in what passed for civilization, she pulled into one of the few Starbucks. Val stared at her, almost as if she were waiting for instructions.

"Bring me back a spice pumpkin latte." CC wasn't really surprised at the stunned look Val was sporting. "What? I can be flexible."

CC sat there with the engine running and reviewed the short amount of time she had spent with her mother. She tried to be analytical and search for some clue of deception. She had to focus on catching Bert; her mother's ignorant attitude wasn't the issue. From what little had transpired, she doubted that her mother knew anything about Bert's whereabouts. Then again, she could be lying.

She was still pondering the possibility of her mother's deceit when Val returned with the beverages. "Your surveillance on my mother, did it turn up anything?"

"No." Val handed over a very large latte. "She works, she stays in her apartment, and every Sunday morning she attends mass at Sacred Heart Church down the street from her apartment. Other than that, she does nothing. Is it just me or did you feel like that painting of Jesus was watching us?"

"Watching, judging, hard to say." CC tried to shrug off the hurtful feeling of betrayal. "I don't know what I was expecting. Every day I meet people and mention my wife, and almost none of them think it's a big deal. I mean I work with die-hard good old boys, and they don't even blink. Somehow, I thought she'd react differently or at least have the good manners not to react. It's not like my sexuality is news to her."

"Detective, is there any chance your sister was adopted?"

"Huh? Oh." CC laughed. "I get what you're saying. Trust me, Stevie and I have asked ourselves that many times over the years. For the life of me, I still can't figure out how those two dingle berries brought her into this world. Sadly, they're her parents. I was there when she was born." Something didn't feel right. It was the same feeling she had been fighting since all this began. "I promised Stevie the day she was born that I'd look out for her. I'm not doing a very good job."

"Yes, you are."

"No, I'm not. There's something I'm missing."

"Catching Beaumont first is the right move. After we get that scumbag off the streets, we can figure out who hates you enough to pull this stunt."

"Not a short list."

"Given your stellar career, I'm not surprised."

"I'll tell you who tops the list." Deep inside, CC felt that she might be right. "But he's locked up in one of Southern California's finest institutions for the criminally insane."

"Fisher?" Val looked doubtful.

"His friends and family aren't faring well these days. In fact, they're dropping like flies. I just can't see how the little weasel could accomplish it. Brooks pulled his visitor logs recently, and the only people who have visited him from day one are his mother and whoever has had the misfortune of being his lawyer."

"Let's find Beaumont. If someone is playing cat and mouse with us, chances are he'll be playing peek-a-boo again real soon."

"I hope you're right. Because if you're not..."

"I'm not wrong."

* * *

Jamie strode through the emergency room, trying her level best to remain calm. Everyone was surprised to see her there so early in the day. She tossed out several lame excuses. She had no desire to reveal the real reason she was there. All she wanted to do was focus on the task at hand. She needed to talk to Jack and get time off so she could be with her family. If for some reason he said no, Jamie was fully prepared to quit her job. She stopped briefly to have a word with Randy Schumacher. In a not so subtle way, she reminded him of the back-to-back doubles she pulled for him a few months ago so he could sneak off to Vegas for a bachelor party his wife didn't want him to attend.

"A moment of your time, Dr. Temple?" she asked politely after she knocked on Jack's door.

"I hate it when you get all formal," he said and waved for her to come in. "It means I'm in for a boatload of trouble. Tierney not take her dismissal well?"

"Oh no, she was fine. In fact, she should have stopped by this morning to file an appeal with you. I told her you'd be here early this morning."

"You seem surprised that the resident you canned for being tardy couldn't drag her ass in here on time to appeal. I'm not surprised. Knowing that kid, she'll show up after the weekend whining and wailing. How that one got this far is a mystery to me. So, if it isn't our tardy resident or former resident, what brings you in here so early in the day?"

"I need to take some time off. I have a family emergency. I know you have plans with Joyce but..."

"You're good. Take as much time as you need."

"I thought you had plans?" Jamie had been prepared for some resistance. The last time she had spoken to Jack, he was eager to spend time with his wife.

"Joyce is out of town. She went on a cruise," he said in an incredulous tone. "To Alaska. I mean why would she want to do that?"

Jamie wanted to inform him that there were a great many reasons why Joyce would want to go on an adventure. Instead, she just accepted her good fortune and kept her mouth shut.

"When do you need to start your leave of absence?"

"Now, if that's possible. Schumacher is willing to fill in for me tonight and tomorrow night."

"Ah, finally cashed in on his little trip to sin city. I'll cover Saturday, Sunday, and Monday. Call me if you need more time."

"Thanks, Jack."

The faux taxi was waiting to shuttle her back home. She felt bad that things weren't working out for Jack. But she was relieved that she was able to be where she needed to be. When she arrived home, landscapers were busy, the roof was being fixed, and Stevie was busy working on her computer. Now that Jamie was home, she was at a loss as to what she should be doing. She went upstairs, changed her clothes, and failed to find anything else to do. She opted to bother Stevie.

"Working?"

"Ahead of schedule, but I didn't know what else to do."

"Any word from your sister?"

"No, which can't be good."

"Emma sounded happy."

"Yeah." Stevie smiled for the first time. She shut down her computer and turned towards Jamie. "She seems to like Ricky. Although she's a little confused as to why, if he's Daddy's new boyfriend, why did he sleep on the sofa?"

"How'd you explain that? Or did you just change the subject?"

"I changed the subject." She took Jamie by the arm. "Let's go outside, almost time for the mail."

"You could just ask Misty out. Or did last night change things?"

"Last night," Stevie said and flinched. "I needed..." Her voice trailed off. "Well, you know."

"Been there. It's just that Val seems like a nice person."

"I know." Stevie groaned. "They're back."

"And Misty is here," Jamie noted as Stevie raced outside. "This should be fun."

She watched as Val immediately went to Stevie's side, apparently much to Misty's displeasure. "Oh, boy." She turned her attention towards her wife who seemed to be sulking. CC held up her hand, a silent signal that informed her that she needed a moment. They'd talk later. In the meantime, she was curious about what was happening with Stevie and her not-so-secret admirers. She stepped outside to watch the show. Stevie looked terrified as she accepted the mail.

"Hi, I'm Val," the deputy said to Misty.

"Oh, uh nice to meet you," Misty stammered out before offering a fake smile. "Moving in?"

"No. Just visiting, for now."

"Oh." Misty shifted from one foot to the other. "Well, have a good day."

"Not nearly as entertaining as I hoped," Jamie said to herself before she went in search of her wife. "What smells so good?"

"I'm baking brownies," CC muttered from her spot by the coffee maker. "I couldn't figure out what to do with myself. Normally when I'm off I spend time with you or Emma. Or work on my honey-do list. Or fix something around the house."

"Honey-do list? Well, you do manage to get most of the errands accomplished during your downtime. Thanks for the brownies. How did it go?"

"She doesn't know anything."

"And?"

"She hasn't changed." CC feigned indifference. "She was over the moon just to see me until I mentioned my wife. She actually said 'You're still that way.' Like I have a sickness or something. She feels that somehow I've shamed her. Her marrying a sexual predator was nothing more than a minor lapse in judgment, but my being a lesbian is cause for scorn."

"She's an idiot." Jamie wrapped her arms around CC's slender waist. "You are an amazing woman, Caitlin Calloway. If she can't see that, then she's missing out."

"Thanks."

"What can I say? I'm crazy about you." Jamie stole a kiss. "Plus, the brownies help. I'm covered at work, and I have no idea what to do with myself. Are we supposed to stay inside or in the yard?"

"We keep out of the way. I'm not the lead on this one. Hell, I'm not even part of the operation. I'm just here. I feel useless."

"I can think of a way to make yourself useful," Jamie said in a saucy tone as she raked her nails along CC's arms. "Is the oven timer set?"

"Yes. You want a quickie while waiting for snacks?"

"Wouldn't be the first time."

"You're shameless."

"I'm a woman in love." She guided her wife upstairs. "And, I'm shameless. That's what happens when you hit the brass ring. All your dreams come true."

"I'm a dream come true?"

"Yes, you are. Now, if you'd be so kind as to take your clothes off, I'll show you how much I appreciate everything you do for me. Hurry, before the brownies burn."

Jamie's invitation was just what CC needed to hear. She tripped up the staircase as she raced after her wife.

Chapter 30

Stevie felt better knowing that Emma was safe. It didn't make her miss her any less. *Maybe I should have gone with her.* She instantly dismissed the idea. She refused to leave Caitlin and Jamie on their own. They needed her just as much as she needed them. Then there was Val. Stevie needed her in so many ways. But she wasn't staying. Which begged the question, just what did she expect from the enigmatic federal agent?

"Is there something going on with you and Misty?" Val's question was slow and direct. Stevie felt no malice hidden behind the words. They still made her feel uncomfortable.

"No. We've kind of flirted, nothing beyond that."

"I wasn't prying."

"Given how close we got last night," Stevie shifted nervously. "I think you have a right to ask a question or two. Can I ask you something?"

"Anything."

"What's with the tat?" Stevie was unable to stifle her laugh when Val blushed.

"About a decade ago, we had some downtime in San Diego," Val said. "We needed to blow off some steam. Heading down to Tijuana seemed like a good idea at the time. We found a little bar and started doing shots of the best tequila it has ever been my pleasure to wrap my lips around. The next thing I remember was waking up in my bunk, back at the base, with the mother of all hangovers and a mermaid tattooed on my ass. I still haven't gotten the full story. Brenda will only say it was funny and I'm happier no knowing."

"Oh, my." Stevie laughed. It felt good to laugh. But it didn't last long before she felt reality looming over her. "How did it go with my mother?"

"I don't get the woman. The first time I talked to her, she was all repentant. Today, she got all snippy because your sister is gay."

"That's Mom. During my custody hearing, when all the facts about dear old Dad came out, her only argument to keep me was my sister's homosexuality."

"What did the judge say?"

"'What's your point, Mrs. Beaumont?' I know a different judge might have sided with Mom. Thank goodness, this one didn't care. It probably helped that I had informed the judge that she didn't have to worry about my sister turning me gay. I was born that way."

"I can't imagine going through everything you and your sister have gone through. Only to have it all come back."

"I feel like I'm having a bad dream and can't wake up."

"I promise that I'm going to catch him and bring your little girl home."

The sincerity of Val's voice drew Stevie in. Before she could think, she was wrapped up in a warm embrace. She said a silent prayer that Val was telling her the truth.

"Thank you," she whispered, finally working up the strength to free herself from the tender embrace. "How about I start cooking something for dinner?"

"You don't have to do that."

"I need something to do. Knowing those two," she jerked her thumb towards her sister's side of the house. "They are otherwise engaged. Thoughts of food won't occur to them for hours. I'm assuming that ordering take-out isn't something you'd recommend given the circumstances."

"No, it isn't. Let me at least help you."

Stevie agreed, not certain as to how she should act around Val. She couldn't deny that she needed her there. Val jumped in while Stevie set about fixing a pot of soup. The weather had turned chilly, and she felt the soup would be a good idea. At least that's what she prattled on about. She admired the way Val really listened to her insane ramblings. The very diligent deputy did excuse herself every now and then to check in on her team. Stevie sensed that Val was going out of her way to make her actions seem innocent.

"Done." Stevie gave the chicken noodle a quick taste and removed biscuits from the oven. "Thank you for the help."

"I really didn't do anything."

"You were here, you listened to my babbling, and that kept me from going crazy."

"My pleasure. Do you smell chocolate?"

"Must be next door. I don't even want to guess what those two are up to."

"They have an amazing relationship. It's rare these days. Gay, straight, or indifferent, that kind of true devotion is hard to find."

"They're good together. I'm envious," Stevie said. "I haven't been able to find that all-knowing and giving thing. Until they got together, a part of me doubted it existed."

"You were in a long term before." Val blushed. "Sorry, I had to look into your past."

"That's okay. All part of the job, as my sister would say." She handed Val a piping hot bowl of soup. "Katrina. I thought she was the one. But I was wrong. Without going into detail, she left me for someone else. What about you, Deputy Val? Is there a trail of broken hearts out there?"

"Not really." Val tried to dismiss the idea. Stevie wasn't buying it. "I was career navy. Which meant I couldn't be out. Makes it hard to meet someone, much less build a life together. I entered the marshal service before I retired from the navy. I am very focused on my work. Again, doesn't leave a lot of room for a relationship. This was supposed to be my downtime. Now I have to put it off again."

"I'm sorry that your vacation plans got screwed, but I'm not sorry you're here."

CC and Jamie chose that moment to make their entrance. The couple were freshly showered and clad in T-shirts and loose-fitting sweatpants.

"Brownies?" Jamie cheerfully offered half a plate of freshly baked treats. "What smells so good?"

"Chicken soup. Join us?" Stevie accepted the plate of brownies. "Half a plate? Interesting, the other half must have vanished like the half plate of cookies you brought over last week."

"Someone ate the other half." CC bumped her wife with her hip. "Thanks for the soup, sis."

"I'm full, thanks." Jamie and CC joined Val at the breakfast nook.

"No small wonder." Stevie couldn't resist laughing. Her laughter died when she caught the melancholy look in CC's eyes. "This isn't your fault."

"I'm pretty sure it is." CC pushed aside her soup. Stevie didn't doubt that the topic of conversation had stolen her appetite. "Unless you have some interesting skeletons in your closet."

"What about me?" Jamie said.

"Sorry, sweetheart. They would have come after you directly. Using Bert is clearly personal. That means me."

"Or me," Stevie said.

"For what?" CC challenged.

Stevie searched her memory, hoping to stumble onto anything that would help ease her sister's pain. Nothing came to mind. She was a stay-at-home mom, who designed websites for mostly small businesses. Even her ex, Katrina, had long since moved on. Given the criminal nature of what was happening, that could only mean it was indeed connected to Caitlin.

"See," CC said when Stevie couldn't answer. "Back to me."

"Can't be helped, given the nature of your job," Val said. "I've been going over your past cases. Nothing is jumping out at me. Most everyone you put away is still on ice. You do good work."

"Thanks."

"I thought I had a couple of maybes, but they're dead. I'll keep looking."

"I told you who it is." CC stressed.

"He's locked up," Val countered.

"And nuts. And rich enough to pull this kind of stunt off." CC's words made Stevie feel very nervous. "Who else have I locked up that has the resources to bankroll this kind of operation."

"Who?" Jamie asked, her face tightening.

"Just a theory, James. Deputy Brown is right, I don't know anything." CC immediately tried to backpedal.

"Fisher?" Jamie asked.

"You are way off base, Calloway," Val said with a heavy sigh.

"The guy is locked up twenty-two hours a day. One hour outside alone in a metal cage. One hour of therapy, by himself. He isn't allowed to attend group therapy anymore."

"Because he managed to get his hands on a lab coat, and because he can walk the walk and talk the talk, he almost waltzed out the front door." CC wasn't going to be persuaded.

"No phone calls," Val continued to say, completely unmoved.

"The only two people who bother visiting him are his lawyer and his mommy. Do you honestly think Cynthia Fisher, the matriarch of the clan, is behind the scheme to aid and abet a fugitive? You know, I can see it, she attends the garden club meeting, then checks on the child molester she set up at a posh hotel in Boston. Happens all the time."

"You don't have to be so snippy," CC snarled. "I know what I feel. My gut has gotten me this far. I don't know how, but that weasel is involved."

"Well." Val seemingly backed away from her earlier tirade. "When we catch Bert, we can ask him."

"Sadly, it's the only plan we've got."

Stevie could hear the heartache in CC's voice.

The room took on an eerie silence. Everyone sat around the table playing with their food, except for Jamie, who had begun to drum her fingers on the table. Stevie smiled at the nervous habit that her sister usually exhibited. You really do become one another. She shook her head in wonderment. The slight distraction did nothing to ease the steadily growing tension. Everyone jumped when the theme song for Dragnet blared out.

"You really need to stop screwing with my phone," CC informed her wife. She snatched the device from the leather holder clipped to the waistband of her sweatpants. "Yes, Max?"

"You're having way too much fun reprogramming that gadget," Stevie said to Jamie with a snicker.

"I can't help it. It's fun and it bugs her. Emma helped me pick out the tunes." Jamie gloated.

"Max and Leigh are on their way." CC ended her call. "They claim they need to talk about a case. I suspect they just want to check on us."

"Probably." Val readied her own phone. "I'll alert my team."

Stevie felt a shiver pass through her. Little things were adding up in a disturbing manner: Having visitors monitored, just in case. Having the house watched. All of the protective measures made her nervous. It was the knowledge that they were a necessity. Stevie was accustomed to CC's job being risky. She had lived through far too many close calls with her. She was never certain if it was the high risk of Caitlin's career, or if just maybe her sister had a propensity to attract trouble.

After CC had cleared and cleaned the dishes, she was left with nothing to do but sit and wait. Her fingers drummed out a catchy little tune on the table. She knew it was driving Stevie and her wife nuts. She just couldn't stop. She blew out a terse breath when she heard the knock at the door. Even though she had told Max they'd be on Stevie's side of the house, she still checked the monitor. It was Max and Leigh, and she let them in.

"Coffee?"

"Sounds good," Max said as they made themselves comfortable. "How are you holding up?"

"Sitting around waiting for something to happen doesn't suit me. What's going on with Wayne? Maybe we should go next door?" She thought Stevie and Jamie might not want to hear the gory details of their latest case.

"Stay here," Stevie said. "It will give us something to talk about."

"She's right, honey."

"How about you, Deputy Dawg?" Leigh teased. "Up for a little shoptalk?"

"Deputy Dawg? Do you guys sit around trying to think of these clever monikers?"

"Yes."

"Any reason why?"

"It's your whole Fed need-to-know bull," Leigh said, her eyes narrowing. "You blow into town and only tell us anything when you deem it necessary."

"We could have been on top of this long before now, if you

had just paid us a visit," Max said. "Instead, you follow our partner and her family before you let anyone know what's going on. I don't like it."

"All right." CC felt proud at the way Max and Leigh were determined to cover her back. "But we're all on the same page now. What can you tell me about Billy?"

"The head nurse at MacLean is like a drill sergeant," Leigh said excitedly. CC had to admit the lady was eager. "Like most consolers, she's recovering herself. Doesn't take any crap. Ryan lasted longer than she thought he would. She really didn't have any patience for a spoiled rich white boy from California. Ryan stuck it out for a while, whining the whole time. Then he decided enough was enough, and he walked out. He wasn't there under a court order, so he was free to go. According to Nurse Nancy, good riddance. She's not interested in wasting her time on someone who's just doing enough time to get his platinum card back from Mommy and Daddy. She did confirm what Vergas had said. He didn't score that quality of blow from anyone there. She keeps her ear to the ground, and she hasn't heard of anything remotely close to that high grade being out on the streets."

"Billy boy didn't have any money," Max said. "The room he was staying in was prepaid last week. Too low rent for cameras. Desk clerk, who's nothing more than a strung-out teenager, doesn't remember who paid for the room. It might have been Ryan or Bat Man. That's it. What's happening on your end?"

"We're waiting for the devil," CC said grimly.

"How long was this guy clean?" Jamie asked. "Sometimes, after being clean for a period of time, an overdose is common."

"Less than two weeks," Max said. "And this guy has been

using since he was a teenager. I'm surprised he's lived this long. Then again, cutting heroine with drain cleaner..."

"Drain cleaner?" Jamie's eyes widened. "I've heard of a lot of funky things added to drugs to spread the batch out, but drain cleaner? That had to hurt. Not to mention it's insane."

"No kidding," CC said. "Could a person survive that?"

"If treated right away, sure," Jamie answered after thinking about it for a moment. "But that would depend on how much drugs he had done."

"He was shooting up a lethal level of speed balls. And he kept shooting up, despite the fact his intestines were probably twisted in knots."

Jamie groaned with disgust. "If he had stopped after the first injection, drank some milk, and got medical help, he might have had a chance of living. But the high is more important than any pain they're going through. Someone knew how to get to this guy."

"Like offering a kid a pony."

"I doubt he enjoyed the ride," CC added her two cents, not missing the way Stevie had withdrawn from the conversation. She couldn't fault her. Everyone else at the table was accustomed to chatting about these matters the way most people discuss the latest reality show.

"Stevie why don't we—" she began to say, eager to change the subject. Stevie had been through enough. There was no need to expose her to anymore. CC's pesky cell phone decided to blare out another tune. "Yeah, Brooks." She didn't bother to hide the fact that she was miffed. "We were just talking about Billy Ryan."

When she had informed him about Ryan's death, Brooks sounded just a little too excited. She was about to explain that the guy did indeed die of an overdose, in hopes to cool his jets. She had no intention of mentioning the drain cleaner. If there was something to her theory, there was a chance Brooks could get overzealous and blow it. When they had Beaumont where they wanted him, then and only then, would she be able to focus on the who and why.

"I've got another one," Brooks said before CC got the chance to update him. "Happened about a week ago. Professor Archibald Harden. He taught at the University of Wisconsin."

"Our boy didn't have any ties there," CC said quickly, purposely not using Fisher's name.

"Harden taught at the University of Texas back when Simon was a student there after he left San Diego," Brooks blurted out. The guy sounded absolutely rabid. "In fact, Simon almost failed his class. Naturally, Simon blamed the professor for ruining his GPA. Harden complained to the dean that Simon tried to set his office on fire. There wasn't any proof, so Simon walked. But Harden has testified at Simon's hearings a couple of times."

"I think I remember him. How in the hell did you dig this one up?"

"I'm looking under every rock," Brooks explained. "It's like he's working down a list of everyone who's ever pissed him off."

"Since nothing in his life has ever been his fault, that can't be a short list. How did the professor pass on?" CC's head throbbed. She tried to convince herself to just ignore the information.

"Carbon monoxide poisoning."

"I see." She thought about it. Between the location and the lack of trauma involved, as much as she wanted to, she couldn't see the connection. "Was there an investigation?"

"No. The cops blamed it on a faulty flue in the fireplace. The thing is, the guy lived in faculty housing and the batteries for the detector were missing."

"Oh, come on," she said. "You know how that goes. People are always forgetting to replace those things, or the remote goes dead, and instead of dragging their fat asses out to the store they clip the batteries from the smoke or carbon detectors. They always plan on replacing them. They never hurry because deep down we're all convinced we'll never need them. If we didn't have a small child in the house, I doubt we'd be as diligent as we are."

"I guess." Brooks sounded reluctant to accept her explanation. "I'll let you know if I hear anything else."

CC said her goodbyes and returned her attention to the group who were staring at her. She shifted uncomfortably. She hated being the center of attention. Lately, it seemed to be a constant. She didn't like it one bit. She just wanted to enjoy her life, spending time with her family and doing everything she could to ensure the snarky Mrs. Stern spent the rest of her natural life behind bars. If CC could ensure Stern's prison employment consisted of cleaning the toilets for the next sixty years, that would be a bonus. Instead, CC was hiding, and everyone including herself was wondering just who she had pissed off enough to exact this over-the-top revenge. Once again, only one name came to mind.

"Brooks thinks he's got another one. A professor who keeled over from carbon monoxide poisoning," she said.

"He knew your boy?" Val asked.

"Yes, he was in his class at the University of Texas."

"Simon didn't fare well in his class?" Jamie's tone was crisp, alerting CC she hadn't been fooled by the attempt to keep Simon's name out of the conversation. The edge in Jamie voice made her nervous, but CC couldn't fault Jamie for being uneasy. After all, at one point she had been Simon's teacher. Needless to say, his being arrested instead of becoming a doctor probably was topping his list of bad days.

"Apparently not." CC wanted to let it go at that, hoping it would put Jamie's fears to rest. She didn't like to think about the alternative. If Simon truly was the big bad guy behind this scheme, in all likelihood Jamie could be next on his list. "Look, it's ridiculous." CC pretended to dismiss the idea. "We have a bigger problem to deal with. First, we're out of brownies."

* * *

The next couple of days passed quickly. CC almost felt like she was on vacation. Except Emma wasn't there, and an abundance of law enforcement officers wandered about pretending to be laborers. The upside was the roof was finished. Mills and her team did a great job. The only hiccup being they finished far too quickly. Now the team was hanging about just pretending to work.

"Those workers you hired are amazing!" a voice said.

CC jumped when she heard the excited utterance. She had been wandering around the yard, trying to find something to keep herself busy. She blew out a sigh of relief when she spied the Birkenstocks standing on the edge of the lawn. She pondered whether Birkenstock was indeed their last name or just a weird coincidence.

"Yes, they are good," CC said to her neighbors. "We were lucky to get them."

"You must give us their card," Freda, the shorter of the two, said.

"I'll get it to you." CC wondered how she was going to get around this one. "I can't promise anything. They have a waiting list."

"Good roofers are hard to find," Ethel said. "We're thrilled at how much work you girls are doing. The old place really needed it. Poor Mr. Spivey just couldn't keep up, and he was too stubborn to hire anyone. Where has little Emma been?"

"On a trip with her father."

"That's nice," Freda said. "Word has it, your sister has a new friend," she added with a wink.

"Wow, no secrets in this neighborhood." CC had to laugh. At the condo complex, they had met their neighbors but rarely socialized with them. Normally, it was just a nod or a quick hello.

"Not many," Ethel said. "You'll get used to it. No one is overly nosy, but it's good to know you have friends who'll be there for you. I have to say, seeing another gay couple move into the neighborhood was great. Not to mention, it really boosts the property values."

"What?" Jamie asked, seemingly joining them from nowhere.

"Didn't you know?" Ethel laughed. "When we take over a neighborhood, the real estate prices go through the roof."

"Learn something new every day." CC shook her head. "So, yes, Stevie is seeing someone new. Val, who's with the EPA. That's why you've been seeing a sedan with government plates rolling around the neighborhood. Not to worry, she pays for her own gas. Don't want you to think she's using your tax dollars to court my sister. She's been trying to convince us to put in solar panels."

"Oh, you should," Ethel said. "We did. Every little bit helps.

"We're thinking about it."

"It's nice to have family so close," Ethel who was obviously the chatty one of the two said. "There was a time when everyone hid under a rock."

"Not you," Freda said with a snort.

"Good Lord, woman." Ethel waved off her comment. "It's been over fifty years since I was a wild child. Let it go."

"More like sixty years," Freda playfully corrected. "CC, you get that information to us when you get a chance. We need to finish our walk."

"My God, that really is going to be us some day," CC wryly said as they waved goodbye to elderly women who were shuffling down the street.

"What information?"

"They want to hire our roofers." CC couldn't help but laugh.

"Can't say that I blame them. Mills and the team did a great job."

"Don't get me wrong," Jamie said. "I love spending the long weekend with you, and getting all this work done on the house is great, but—"

"But the reason behind it sucks."

"More than I can say."

"I know, James." CC took a deep breath, fearful she would say something wrong. Her shoulders slumped, and she couldn't look at Jamie. The guilt she felt was overwhelming.

"This is not your fault," Jamie said as if she were reading her mind. "None of this is your fault. Maybe you should make an appointment with Dr. Miller. You can't tell me that you don't need to vent."

"My therapist is going to love this," she said in a low voice.

"What?"

CC jerked her head up, and her heart skipped a beat when she spied Val standing a mere three feet away from them. Based on the uncomfortable look on the woman's face, she knew that she had heard the comment. "That is not for publication," CC said.

"I get it." Val kept her voice low. "Detective, I'm not going to tell anyone. Given everything you've been through in your life, if you hadn't sought help somewhere along the line, I'd be concerned."

"I didn't go through the department."

"Understood." Val held up her hands, seeming to let the subject go. "We have an issue."

"The Birkenstocks hired Mills and her crew away from us?"

"No, but they did try. We've got a couple of possible sightings."

"Possible like before, where they were real and you chose not to tell me until I already knew?" CC wasn't in the mood for games. "Or possible like, it's a maybe, maybe not?"

"Maybe, maybe not. The Holiday Inn on Beacon Street and Coolidge Corner."

"He's still lurking around the neighborhood." CC felt completely frustrated. "Okay, why don't we head down to the Holiday Inn and check things out?"

"If it is him, he's out," Val tersely explained. It was evident she didn't appreciate the help. "Which means he could be lurking around. What I need you to do is stay inside. All of you."

CC shifted uncomfortably. She was unaccustomed to being told what to do. Normally, she was the lead. Everyone turned to her. Handing over complete control with so much at stake frightened her. She was prepared to argue. But she knew in her heart this was one of those times in life when she needed to just shut up and listen.

"Come on." Jamie tugged on her sleeve. "Have you forgotten that we're out of brownies?"

CC nodded compliantly. She pointed at Val. "You keep me in the loop."

"I will. If he turns up at the hotel, you can suit up, but remember, you're just along for the ride. Oh goodie, it's time for the mail." They watched Stevie dart outside. "Are you sure there isn't something going on with them?"

"Geez, you slept with her again?" The blush Val was sporting was all the confirmation CC needed. "Will you stop doing that? As for Misty, no, there isn't anything going on between them. Stevie's too shy to ask her out," she said against her better judgment.

"Shy?"

"Yes." CC shook her head then it hit her.

"Oh?" The groan Jamie released confirmed her suspicions. CC loved her kid sister. If Stevie had one flaw, it was the way she treated women. When she cared about someone, she was shy; but if all Stevie was seeking was a little fun, that's all there would be. CC almost felt bad for the clueless woman standing in front of her. Almost. "Yeah, well you kids can work this out after the case is over."

She felt a twinge of regret as she and Jamie hurried into the house. "I think she's falling for Stevie."

Jamie shuddered as she began to putter around the kitchen. "I think she's already fallen for her. But Stevie will have to deal with this. You have enough to worry about. How about a game of chess? I'll let you be the Heroes. I know you secretly wanted that team."

"Of course I wanted them. Their pawns are cute little Dalmatians," CC groused. "Mine are the Hyenas from the Lion King, and my queen is Cruella DeVil. How much does that suck? Thanks for the offer, but Emma and I still have a game going. I'm a couple of moves away from checkmate."

"You don't have to sound so happy about it. Remember she is only seven."

"Going on thirty."

Chapter 31

Jack Temple set off for his daily walk along the beach. He was taking his evening stroll later than usual after filling in for Jamie. The good thing about being the boss was being able to delegate. He wanted to help, but working his part of the day plus the overnight was a bit much for him. Nolan was more than happy to cover the overnight portion of Jamie's shift. Then again, Nolan wanted Jamie's job. He had felt slighted when Jack went outside the hospital to recruit Jamie for the position.

Jack drank in the scent of the sea air. Living so close to the ocean, he was determined to enjoy it while he could. He'd be home soon enough. Not quite as soon as he thought he would. He didn't understand why Joyce just up and went on a cruise with a bunch of friends. It just didn't make any sense to him.

Much to his relief, thanks to the chill in the air and the darkness, the beach was devoid of panhandlers and lovers. He did spy one lone figure sitting by the bandstand. Based on the small stature, he assumed it was a woman. He just hoped it wasn't one of the ladies from Shirley Avenue. The last thing he was in the mood for was being propositioned by one of the neighborhood working girls.

* * *

"Why do you keep staring at her ass?" CC asked Jamie after Val had left the room.

"I am not."

"James." CC groaned, already frustrated by being held under house arrest. Now her wife was checking out another woman's backside. Normally, these things didn't bother her. The both of them appreciated attractive women. So long as the admiration remained at a distance, there wasn't a problem. Jamie always reasoned it didn't matter where you built your appetite so long as you ate at home.

"Okay, fine. You won't believe this, but according to Stevie, the big bad deputy has a mermaid tattooed on her ass."

"I didn't need to know that."

"Then why did you ask?"

CC felt thoroughly frustrated. She tried to formulate an argument. She hadn't asked. Then again she had. Which in her mind didn't explain why Jamie was staring at Val's backside. It wasn't as if she'd be able to see it. No matter how long Jamie stared, CC doubted that she would suddenly develop X-ray vision.

"You know," she slowly began to say, fully prepared to inform her wife that staring wasn't going to accomplish anything, when Val burst into the room.

"Do you have a Kevlar vest?"

"Yes."

"Here?"

"Yes."

"Suit up."

CC nodded and sneaked a peek at Val's backside. With a shake of her head, she headed up to her bedroom with Jamie close behind.

"You know you can't see it just by staring," Jamie annoyingly pointed out.

"You should know, since you've spent most of the morning

staring at her ass." CC donned a long-sleeved T-shirt with the Boylston Police Department logo emblazoned on it and slipped on a comfortable pair of jeans. She checked and put on her utility belt that held extra handcuffs, mace, a small Maglite, and a blackjack. Then she strapped on both of her guns. She covered up with her Boylston Police blue windbreaker.

"I hate this," Jamie said.

"I know. I'll be safe. Chances are they won't let me anywhere near him. Hopefully, this means we've got him and our lives can go back to normal. Or what passes for normal with us," she added as a joke. Jamie wrapped her arms around her and held her tightly.

"Be safe," Jamie whispered before finally releasing her hold.

"I promise."

"Say it again."

"I promise I will be coming home to you."

* * *

The teams arrived at the Holiday Inn on Beacon Street without any fanfare. Val pulled around back and joined the others. Once again, CC found herself in the odd position of having to stand in the background. Ledger went to great lengths to remind her that her presence was a favor, and she was not a part of the operation. CC felt a small sense of comfort that a team had been left behind at her home. If for some reason they got it wrong, Jamie and Stevie would still be safe. She was ready. Her heart raced as she followed the team up to the fourth floor. Thankfully, Beaumont's room was at the end of a hallway next to a fire exit. One team discreetly, or as discreetly as they could manage, went in the front. CC followed the second team up the stairwell. The third and fourth teams positioned themselves around the back and front of the building.

CC said a silent prayer that Bert was indeed in his room. If he was out and about, there was no way he could miss the extreme police presence. She fought to control her breathing while she followed after the team all clad in black and armed to the teeth. She added another prayer that this was really it and she'd be able to keep her promise to Jamie. She was left behind at the entrance of the fourth-floor staircase.

"Room Service!" Val pounded on the door. The marshals had fanned out so they wouldn't be seen through the peephole.

"I didn't order anything," a graveled voice shouted from within.

CC trembled, and her knees began to buckle. After all the years, she still recognized his voice. She steadied her 9mm in front of her, and a fear born from her childhood threatened to choke her. She listened to the banter as Val tried to convince the occupant to step outside so he could sign a waiver saying it was the wrong room.

"Hey, I get it." Val sounded at a loss. "I just don't want to lose my job. Come on, I have a kid to support," she added, almost pleading.

"All right," the voice barked from inside and the door opened ever so slightly.

It was the only opening they needed. In a rush, federal agents filled the room. "Albert Beaumont. US Marshals!" Val announced as a scuffle ensued.

CC couldn't see what was happening, but she knew the sounds all too well. Val ordered him down on his knees and to interlace his fingers behind his head. All the while, Bert was shouting that they had the wrong guy.

"Check my ID on the table." He sounded pathetic. "My name is Mike Buanoma."

"ID checks," one member whose voice CC failed to recognize confirmed.

"Fingerprints will tell us all we need to know," Val said. "Now stay still, or I will hurt you. We do have a quicker way to confirm your identity. Send her in."

CC nodded when Ledger waved to her. She kept her gun properly positioned in front of her but pointed down. Her lungs seized when she saw him. He was sitting on the double bed with his hands cuffed behind his back and his ankles chained together.

"Hello, Bert." She felt the old anger rising to the surface. "What's new?"

He turned pale and suddenly the room was filled with a sour odor. "Eww," Marino said. "Maid is going to hate you."

CC just shook her head as she approached him. All this time, she had feared the very thought of him. Instead of the monster she remembered, here sat a pudgy old man in shackles, who soiled himself after hearing her voice.

"Go ahead," he choked out with a nod towards her gun. "You know I deserve it. Do it." The last part was offered as a desperate plea.

She looked around the room, and not for the first time in her life, she knew she might be able do what he was asking and be allowed to walk away. Instead, she cast an evil smirk down at him and holstered her gun. He flinched when she leaned in close to him.

"Just so we're clear," she said in a gritty voice that made him squirm. Encouraged by the look of fear in his eyes, she leaned even closer to whisper the words she had wanted to say for decades. "You're not worth it." She enjoyed watching him tremble. CC stood up straight, her cold stare never lifting from his cowering form. "Deputy, this man is Albert Beaumont."

"Good enough for me. Albert Beaumont," Val said, "you are under arrest for violating your probation and being a jackass. You have the right to an attorney who could fight your extradition back to Connecticut." She prattled on with the required Miranda warning and lifted him to his feet. "Before you call for a lawyer, ask yourself how much time you want to spend in a Boston jail cell."

CC didn't miss the way she looked directly at her or the gloating tone in her voice. "You could just tell us who sent you here," CC told him.

"I don't belong in prison," Bert said. "I'm sick."

"A minute ago you were begging me to blow your brains out because you deserve it." CC almost laughed at the absurdity of the situation. "Now you want therapy?"

"Take him down to the van," Val told her crew. "We need to do a sweep. I'm sorry, Detective, but you can't be here for this part."

"Understood."

CC didn't want to do anything that might help Bert in any way, shape, or form. She headed to the privacy of the stairwell and called home. Her message was short, "We got him." After she made the call, she felt a huge weight had been lifted. She understood there was more and she wouldn't like it. For the moment, she allowed herself to enjoy the brief taste of freedom. It felt good, and she was determined to enjoy the feeling for as long as she could.

* * *

Val and her team had done an extensive search of the room. They found only an odd assortment of clothing, a bundle of cash, the fake ID, and a cell phone. While being processed, Bert couldn't make up his mind on whether or not he wanted legal representation. He seemed relieved when he was placed in an interrogation room instead of a jail cell.

CC watched the interrogation from the other side of the mirror. After several hours, Bert offered very little. He claimed not to know anything. He said he wasn't allowed to contact his unknown benefactor and simply followed instructions.

"Think you can get him to be a little more candid?" Val asked after leaving Bert alone in the room.

"He doesn't know anything." A slight tremble of anger surged through CC. "I'll try, but I got to go with him being too stupid to pull this off."

"He said the last text gave him directions to Crescent Street," Val said. "He was just about to head over there when we showed up. He was on his way to your home."

"I wonder if he knew it was my house he was being sent to. His boss isn't going to be happy that he screwed up." CC mulled everything over and still came up with the one name. "Good thing you've managed to keep this quiet. The lack of press will work for us. Wish me luck?"

"Like you need it."

"Hey, Bert," she said in an overly cheerful tone. "How's your day going?"

"You were always a little bitchy."

"Can't be helped." She was no longer filled with fear and loathing. The moment he wet himself in the hotel room, he turned into every other skell she had dealt with since graduating from the academy. "Why were you planning on visiting me?"

"Why would I do that?"

"Three Crescent Street?"

"Great." He buried his face in his hands. "Look, I was simply following orders."

"That excuse didn't work for the Nazis." She couldn't resist the jab. "Face it, Bert, you've stepped in it big time. Things will be much easier on you if you just tell us how you got mixed up in this mess."

"I told that other bitch I don't know anything."

"You want to stop talking? Your mouthpiece is on his way. Say the word, and we'll send you down to a nice cozy cell."

"Yeah, right. You'd like that, me locked up with a bunch of mean sons of bitches while my useless fat-ass lawyer takes his sweet time driving up here. I'll tell you again. I was at work and someone dropped off a package with my boss. The boss said it was from Stevie."

"Did he mention Stevie by name?"

"No, he just said it was from my kid. Inside the box was a little cash, a cell phone, and a note to turn it on. The cash was enough for a train ticket. On the phone there was a text waiting for me. It said if I followed instructions, I'd be given a new identity and enough money to start over again. All I had to do was follow instructions, and I'd have a new life. It also said I should never try to contact the caller. If I did I'd be sorry, that part was explained in great detail."

"Did you save the original note?"

"No, and I trashed the cell phones every time I was sent a new one. Just like I was told to do."

"Yeah, we found your last one. Dumping it in the hotel trash wasn't the brightest move. So your last instruction was to swing by my house and hang out for no longer than ten minutes?"

"Yes, then I was to park my ass in the hotel room for at least a week."

"Okay, that's it I guess. You sure you don't want us to try to hurry up that lawyer of yours?"

"Why? So I can stay here in Boston with all of your friends looking out for me? No thanks. How is Stevie?"

"You don't get to know."

"She's my kid! You turned her against me."

"You sure that was it? Not you trying to put your hands in her pants when she was a kid?" CC felt it all coming back to her. "The same crap you pulled on me and God knows how many other young girls." She punctuated her point by knocking over her chair when she stood. "Enjoy your stay in Boston. The one thing that makes me happy is that, by running, you've guaranteed that you won't be seeing daylight for a very long time."

"See, there's that bitchy tone again." He wagged his finger at her. He quickly withdrew it when she leaned down and flattened her hands on the table.

"You want to see bitchy?"

"No," he said and gulped.

"I didn't think so."

After she left Bert quaking in his boots in the interrogation room, she took a moment to thank everyone who worked on the case. On the way home she called Max.

"We got the son of a bitch."

"Are you okay, kid?"

"I feel good. Seeing him in chains was the best thing I've seen in years. I'll fill you in on everything later. For now I need to get home."

She was a little curious if Val was going to swing by and offer her goodbyes. Not to her, but to Stevie. Or had she picked up on Stevie's indifference to the situation? Stevie's attitude wasn't new. Still there was something, in her eyes whenever Val was in the room. The look didn't jive with Stevie's blasé demeanor.

Stevie was waiting for her as she entered the house. "It's over?" Stevie nervously asked, her arms folded tightly across her chest.

"It's over. Emma will be home in the morning."

* * *

Jamie yawned before trying to steal the blankets back from her slumbering wife. CC was a notorious blanket thief. Jamie secretly loved the way she had to wrestle the blankets away from the sleeping woman who would later deny taking them. Just as she had managed to snuggle back under the covers, her cell phone rang.

"Really?"

After a blissful night, the frantic morning phone call was a rude interruption. For the first time since she had been employed at

Boylston General, Jack had failed to show up for a shift. He not only failed to arrive, he didn't call, which was odd since he had a habit of calling even when he was running a few minutes late. Jamie found it strange, and the staff was freaked out. Jamie begged Stella to do what she did best, handle things until she got there.

"I'm sorry," she said to CC who awoke when the phone rang. "I can't believe Jack is a no-show. They've tried calling him. He was only covering part of my shift. He had Nolan covering the later part. I guess the overnight was too much for him."

"Nolan? Your biggest fan."

"I know the guy's a jerk. I'm used to it. I hope Jack is all right."

"Why don't I swing by his condo? He's living at Waterfront at Revere Beach right?"

"Could you? I'm worried. This is completely out of character for him."

"It's not a problem. I'll go right after Emma gets back."

"I can't believe I'm going to miss the little peanut coming home."

"Now that this mess is over, we can get back to our lives."

"It's not really over, is it?" Jamie felt her stomach clench when CC failed to answer her.

* * *

When Jamie arrived at the hospital, it was a flurry of activity. The long weekend meant families had time together. For certain families, time together wasn't a good thing. For those clans, gatherings normally ended with a trip to the emergency room. Normally, even with the sudden influx of people, the staff handled it with ease. With no one in charge, however, mayhem could easily take over.

"Thank God for you, Stella." Jamie watched the nurse easily handle the staff. "Bring me up to speed?"

"Head trauma in bay four, rash in bay six." Stella rattled off every bump and bruise as she handed Jamie a stack of files.

"There's a fresh pot of coffee in your office. Grab yourself a big cup after you check on Mr. Kasbe. He's in bay five."

"Right, the guy who can't get it up. Thank you, Stella. I'd be lost without you."

Jamie handed out assignments then heeded Stella's advice and grabbed a cup of coffee.

Chapter 32

CC and Stevie were on their second pot of coffee. The morning had been exhausting. The slightest noise had them lurching towards the front door, in hopes they would find Emma waiting on the other side. After what seemed to be an eternity, a nondescript black sedan pulled up in front of the house. CC braced herself when Stevie almost knocked her over trying to reach the front door. CC stood back proudly, watching Stevie swing little Emma around while Brad and Ricky dutifully unpacked the car.

"I don't recall her taking so much stuff with her." CC helped the two men with the luggage.

"We did some shopping," Ricky said sheepishly.

CC watched Brad and Ricky dance around one another. There were definitely sparks flying between the two. She suspected that Ricky kept things primarily professional. She wondered how long it would take for both men to make excuses so they could go off and be alone. She hugged Emma who prattled on and on about the lake and all the animals she had seen.

"Ricky told us ghost stories while we ate s'mores by the fire," Emma chatted away without taking a breath.

"Were they scary?" Stevie asked.

"No. Sorry, Ricky."

"It's okay," he said and smiled brightly.

"Where's Auntie Jamie?"

"She had to work, peanut."

"I thought..." Ricky began to say.

"There was an emergency at the hospital."

"Is anyone hungry?" Stevie was excited as she headed toward the kitchen.

"Sorry, Stevie," Brad said. "We stopped at IHOP. One last treat before the trip was over."

"I had a pancake that was as big as my head!" Emma exclaimed, almost drowning out the knock at the front door.

"Oh, lookie," CC said when she greeted Deputy Brown. "Come on in." CC was fully prepared to harass the deputy, but something in her demeanor told CC to back off.

"Ricky, thanks for the help," Val said in crisp tone.

"Anytime. I had fun," he replied.

"Now maybe you can start your vacation." CC tried to gauge what was going on. The case was over, which should have made Val happy. The chilly air that swept in along with the stoic brunette was unsettling.

"Not just yet. I came to pick up my stuff and..."

"Right." CC assumed she needed a moment alone with Stevie. "Hey guys, why don't we take Emma next door and—"

"That's okay," Val said. "Maybe the boys can take Emma next door and check out the chessboard? Your aunt thinks she has you cornered."

"Okay." Emma sighed dramatically. "Time for grown-up talk. Come on, Ricky, you'll love this chess set Auntie Caitlin bought for me. It's Disney."

"That kid doesn't miss a thing. Sorry about the interruption," Val said once the three of them were alone. "Something has come up."

"I gathered that." CC was truly miffed that Val had spoiled Emma's homecoming. "Did you get a lead that might direct us to whoever has been pulling Bert's strings?"

"Aiding and abetting is a felony but not my job. I only go after them when they run," Val said. "I'm still going to look into it. My job is done or was. I don't know how to say this, so I'll just spit it out. Albert Beaumont died this morning."

"What?" CC was shaken. This news was the last thing she expected.

"How?" Stevie asked.

"He was being moved to what we thought would be a more secure location and was shivved."

"Someone stabbed him on the way to the bus?" CC couldn't believe it. Based on the look on Val's face, she was troubled by the situation. "Stevie, are you okay? I know he was who he was, but he was still your father."

"I should feel something. Right now all I can focus on is Emma being home and safe. As far as Bert goes, I'm numb."

"Deputy, do you want me to follow you downtown or are you going to insist I ride with you?"

"Wait," Stevie said. "What the hell's going on?"

"I'm in a position to make his death happen," CC said. "I didn't," she added for Val's benefit. "But Deputy Brown would be remiss in her duties if she didn't question me in a formal setting. This happened on her watch, and she has to do everything by the book."

"Cops." Stevie looked and sounded indignant.

"We can take my car," Val said.

"I'll be right behind you," CC said. "I'd like to get this over with as quickly as possible."

CC didn't miss the curious look Val gave her. She didn't feel a need to expand on why she was in a hurry. She simply headed out to her car and sped towards downtown.

During her drive, she tried to wrap her mind around the fact that Bert was dead. She didn't miss or grieve for him; she was more curious about the circumstances than anything else. The only thing she could come up with was whoever Bert was working for more than likely thought of him as expendable, more so after he got caught. CC was hopeful that whoever stabbed him held the key to the mysterious mastermind.

"Are you carrying?" Val said once they had reached the federal offices.

"No, I am not carrying a weapon. With my niece coming home I secured my weapons. You can search me if you'd like." She opened her long gray trench coat.

"No need." Val seemed apologetic. CC wondered whether her demeanor was real or was she just putting on a show. The higher the body count got, the fewer people she trusted.

"Hey, Frank," she cheerfully greeted the older man. "They brought you in as well? What, no Mac C, or haven't you gotten around to him yet?"

"A barroom full of cops verified that he was unaware

Beaumont had been apprehended," Val said drolly. "Detective Donnelly has been cleared as well. Can we get things started, Detective, or would you like to contact your union rep first?"

"I don't need legal advice. I'm anxious to get this over with. Frank, would you mind waiting for me?"

"I'll be right here, Cattie."

"Thanks." She followed after Val, who once again was giving her a curious look as they entered the interrogation room. "I understand that I have the right to remain silent and the right to an attorney. I also understand that this interview is being recorded." She took a seat.

"You in a hurry?"

"I thought I made that clear. Is the recorder on?"

"Yes." Val announced the time, date, and their names for the record. "Detective Calloway, after you left the federal building yesterday afternoon, where did you go and who did you talk to?"

"After you apprehended Albert Beaumont, I called my wife and sister to inform them that my stepfather was in custody. I also called my partner, Detective Sampson. Would you like my cell so you can check the call logs?"

"As much as I love your phone, just your permission to run a check on the number will be more than enough."

"You have my permission. Now back to my activities on the day in question. Later that day I confirmed with you that my niece could come home. After Beaumont had been processed, I went directly home and spent time with my wife and sister. We called it a night around eight thirty. My sister may have waited up a bit later.

She might have been expecting a visitor."

"Oh, um..." Val stammered. "I guess that's it."

"Who did it?"

"Lawrence Cha... Charanski."

"It's pronounced Sharkansky." CC's shoulders slumped. "Damn it."

"You know him? Isn't that just great."

"Shark? We grew up together. We were in the same classes, until he started being held back. He finally dropped out around my junior year," CC said. "Nice guy, even though he was the neighborhood thug. His sister used to be Stevie's best friend. After they started school, Carol seemed to be following in her older brother's footsteps. She ended up turning her life around. She's a social worker for DSS now. She's done a lot for the kids in this city. I'm guessing it doesn't look good for me that the guy who stabbed my stepfather was a former classmate of mine."

"No it doesn't look good. You not only hated the victim, you had one helluva motive for wanting him dead. The only thing working in your favor is that you spent most of yesterday in the company of federal agents. Now I get to question all of them."

"Add yourself to the list, since I spent most of my time with you. Look, I didn't have anything to do with Bert's death. I don't doubt that a lot of people would sympathize with my motives if I had. Crossing that line isn't who I am. Also, with Bert dead, I might never find out who targeted me and my family in the first place. Now if I promise not to leave town, am I free to go?"

"Yes." Val snatched up her files and left of the room.

CC didn't like the sound of hesitation in Val's voice or the abrupt way she ended the interview. She wasn't in a position to start an argument, but she did want some answers. CC chased after the deputy, fighting to keep in her ire in check.

"Is Shark here? If it's okay, I'd like to talk to him. You can record the whole thing," CC said as Frank approached them. "I cooperated with you, and there's a chance I might be able to get him to talk."

"You're still a suspect."

"When was I out of the task force's watchful eye? I didn't have the time to mastermind a hit."

"Do it," Frank said, "or I'll tell everyone that I lied about you having Ted Williams's number tattooed on your arse. Don't think I'm bluffing. I'll toss you right into the Sevens and let Mac take it from there."

"Oh, that's not what she has on her ass." CC enjoyed the sight of Val's eyes bugging out.

Val gulped. "Okay, but we videotape everything."

CC knew it wasn't fair, but she did enjoy seeing Val squirm. She even had the bad manners to snicker when the deputy darted off to set everything up.

"Thanks for sticking around, Frank, and for the backup."

"Anything for you, Cattie."

"Do you still have connections in Revere?"

"A few. What's up?"

"My wife's boss is missing." CC didn't like the gnawing

feeling in her gut. "He lives in a condo across from the beach. It's probably nothing, but it's out of character for him to not show up for work."

"I'll make some calls."

CC thanked him just as Deputy Brown made her approach. Val told her everything was in place. She could have a short informal chat with the suspect while it was being videotaped. Val and Ledger would be watching from the other side of the mirror. CC agreed to the terms, anxious to find out if her old classmate knew why Bert was running around Boston yanking her chain.

"Shark!" She greeted the burly bald man shackled to the table. She made certain that she pronounced his name the proper Revere way, which was to drop the "r" and say it loudly.

"CC!" He tried to stand, only to be halted by his chains and the deputy standing behind him. "Sorry. I'd give you a hug, but I'm all tied up. How the hell are you kid?"

"Same old Shark." She smiled and took a seat in the uncomfortable plastic chair on the other side of the table. "Damn, it's been forever. I miss those days when you'd drop off a bag of fried clams from Kelly's when I was working the overnight at that gas station."

"It was nothing." He waved her off.

"Yeah, like it was nothing giving me a ride home after my shift and not blabbing my real age to the owner."

"I heard you'd become a cop." He smiled and quickly changed the subject. CC found it interesting that he didn't seem to mind being chained to a table because he had just murdered someone, but talking about his sensitive side made him uncomfortable.

"Carol said you're doing good." He seemed to enjoy the impromptu reunion.

"So is she."

"Yeah, she turned it around. I'm proud of her. Even when she keeps harping on me to get my shit together."

"Ever think of listening to her?"

"This is who I am." He shrugged as if sitting there in chains clad in an orange jumpsuit was nothing out of the ordinary. Then again, given his long history with the legal system, this probably was the norm. "Heard you married a hot blonde," he added with a wry grin.

"That I did." CC couldn't refrain from laughing.

"Damn, CC you really got it going on," he complimented her. "Good for you."

"So, Shark, hate to throw a wet blanket on the party." The uneasy feelings she'd had earlier resurfaced. "Want to tell me why you killed my stepfather?"

"Oh, that? Didn't like him."

"Neither did I," CC said. "But shanking him? That's a bit much."

"Carol is doing good, isn't she?"

"Yes." CC was confused as to why the conversation returned to his kid sister.

"Yeah, I'm proud of her."

"You should be. What happened, Shark?" Her voice shook as

she asked the question.

"When?"

"This morning, when you killed a man." CC wasn't fooled by his stalling tactics.

"Not much of a man, if you ask me," he responded with a shrug.

"I'm inclined to agree with you. Still, it doesn't explain why you went to all of this trouble." CC tried to keep calm.

CC patiently waited for him to answer. He just sat there with a bored look. If it weren't for the turmoil she felt was lurking just below the surface, she would have been convinced that nothing was amiss.

"Would you like for me to get in touch with Carol?" She threw out just to get him talking again.

"Nah." He blew off the suggestion as if she had offered to buy him a cup of coffee. "She doesn't need to be bothered by this crap."

"I think she's going to hear about this. Better she hear it from a friend."

He sat there for a moment, just studying the dilapidated table. CC thought she had lost him. Just as she was about to say her goodbyes, Shark looked up. There was a pained look in his green eyes as he held her gaze.

"I asked her how she got it together," he said. His tone was still light, but his eyes betrayed his true emotions. "You know about all the trouble she got into when she first started school."

"Yeah. Things started to go wrong for her around the time

she stopped hanging around with Stevie."

"I never understood it," he said, the tension finally showing in his voice. "Out of the blue, she just changed. After she cleaned up her act, I asked what had happened. She told me that she got therapy and that helped her pull it together. Now she helps a lot of kids."

"She's great. The kids in this city are lucky to have her. Still doesn't answer my question."

"To change like that all of a sudden," his tone turned grim. "She stopped eating, talking, and wouldn't hang out with her friends. Then she started acting up. I thought she was just being a pain in the ass."

"Oh, my God." CC felt her world collapsing.

"She told me what happened."

"No, I watched him. I made sure—"

"He stayed away from Stevie," Shark finished for her. "It was just before school started. She was outside playing in the yard. He drove up and offered to take her for an ice cream. She knew not to go with strangers, but this was Mr. Beaumont."

Shark hesitated for a moment. "I found out he was doing a stretch down in Connecticut. Sadly, I don't have any juice down there. I was working on it. Then I get word my fish is swimming right up here in Boston. A little infraction, good timing, and it was like Christmas came early."

"I didn't know." CC felt like she was going to throw up. "I thought I kept everyone safe."

"Geez, CC, you were just a kid yourself. I heard you went to the cops long before Stevie was born. You're not the one who dropped the ball."

"A jury might be sympathetic," she tried to reason with him.

"No jury." He dismissed the idea with an air of indifference. "I did it. I'm pleading guilty. I'm all for saving the taxpayers money. Don't do the crime if you can't do the time. Good thing it happened up here. No death penalty."

"Shark, you're talking about life without parole."

"I did it. I planned it. I acted alone."

"I doubt that."

"All on me," he said with a brilliant smile. "I know you don't agree, but some folks just need killing, and the guy who molested my baby sister tops that list. At least with the long weekend, I get a couple of extra days up here enjoying the peace and quiet."

"Then back to Walpole forever?" CC still couldn't believe what was happening.

"Not that much longer than I was already looking at." He shrugged. "Truth is, when I'm on the inside, I stay clean, sober, and work hard. On the outside, I'm looking for the easy way to make a buck. Instead of working, I steal or sell drugs. If the loudmouth next to me in the bar bugs me, I'll punch the shit out of him. I just don't handle being out well. Inside, I'm a straight arrow with focus. Don't argue with me on this. The bastard got what he deserved. This has nothing to do with you. This is on me."

"Damn it, Shark. This doesn't have to end this way."

"Just do me one favor? Watch out for Carol." He grimaced. "She's gonna be pissed when she finds out. She told me to let it be, said she visited him down in Connecticut and got closure, whatever that means."

"I never understood the concept. I'll keep an eye on her for you, and maybe I'll even visit you."

"Uh, I'd like that, but having a cop show up to say hi wouldn't be good for my health." He laughed. "How about a Christmas card or some clean socks on my birthday? Just let me finish this my way."

"Are you sure there isn't anything else about this you want to share? Like how you knew he was here, or how you managed to get so close to a federal prisoner?" He just sat there with a blank look on his face. "Nothing huh? Okay then, have it your way. Take care and watch your back."

"You do the same."

She felt the urge to hug him; instead, she waved and walked out. She wasn't surprised when Ledger and Brown met her outside the room. "You got everything you need?"

"That should wrap this up," Ledger said.

"He had to have help to organize this," Val tried to argue.

"No way he'll rat out anyone." CC explained. "Shark's an honorable guy. He'll do what he said. He isn't going to recant. He'll go in for his arraignment on Monday and plead guilty, because he didn't like Beaumont."

"Tuesday, long weekend," Val corrected her. "You sound certain he won't decide that life in prison is more than he bargained for."

"He'll do his time and keep his mouth shut. Like I said, for a thug, he's got a strong sense of honor. Now, if you're done with me, I have something I need to do." She walked away, not waiting for a response, and caught up with Frank who was sporting a very grim look.

"I've got bad news. They pulled a body off the beach this morning. John Doe with sketchy details. Might not be your guy." She wanted to believe him. She just couldn't shake the feeling that things had just gone from bad to worse.

Chapter 33

The beach looked gloomy. CC had fond, and not so fond, memories of Revere Beach. It was a long stretch of beach just down the street from her childhood home. As a little girl, she played there with her brother and parents. Later, she would take Stevie there under the guise of having fun. In truth, CC often used the outing as an excuse to get out of the house.

In high school, it was a popular hangout. Later, when she lived in a rat-infested rooming house, it was her refuge. Now the city had cleaned it up as well as most of the surrounding neighborhood. Still, an unsavory element clung to the low-rent businesses and homes.

She tightened her coat around her body when she stepped out of the car. The October wind storming off of the ocean was freezing. Frank was already waiting for her by the seawall. They ducked under the bright-yellow, crime-scene tape just in time to catch State Medical Examiner Timmons. CC recognized the trooper in charge, Sean McManus, a good guy.

"Calloway." He tipped his hat. "Would you mind?" He motioned to the body bag.

"Body is slightly bloated," Timmons said as he unzipped the bag. The smell of decay assaulted her at once. The stench of a rotting corpse was something she would never get used to. His face was indeed bloated from being in the water. But there wasn't a doubt in her mind.

"That's him." She sighed wearily, wondering when all of this was going to stop. "Dr. Jack Temple. He lived right over there." She pointed to the tall building located across the street. "We should check out his place," she said as the body bag was re-zipped.

McManus agreed with her suggestion, and the three of them, along with a CSU tech made their way across the busy street.

"How did it happen?" CC asked during the elevator ride up.

"Don't know," Timmons flatly stated. "Drowned, that we know for sure. But it appears he was only in three feet of water. Facedown, that's all it takes. I'll know more when we get him back to the lab."

"I know he liked to go for a walk along the beach every night," CC said. "Still doesn't explain how a smart guy like Jack ended up drowning in a couple feet of water."

"You never know with these things." McManus sounded grim.

"You know this guy well?"

"He's my wife's boss at the hospital."

"Does he have family we should contact?"

"He and his wife are separated." CC was fighting to hold it together. "She's on a cruise at the moment. His sons are in the area. My wife should have the contact information."

"Thanks for the help on this one," McManus said sincerely as they stepped off the elevator. "Without an ID, it might have taken a good while before we found out who he is."

"This is it," the manager gruffly announced while unlocking the door to Jack's one-bedroom condo.

"Do you need a key to lock and unlock the door?" CC asked before they stepped inside.

"Yah." He wiped his nose on his shirtsleeve.

"Portrait of a middle-aged man in the middle of a divorce," McManus said when they stepped inside.

"Very little furniture and a big-ass television," Frank noted as they took in the Spartan surroundings.

"Jack was a bit of a neat freak," CC added to the conversation.

"What's that?" She pointed to two objects lying in the middle of the living room floor.

She and McManus slipped on latex gloves as they began to search the empty surroundings while the tech snapped off a series of pictures. Frank hung back by the front door to ensure that the manager left and no one else entered, disrupting the search.

"We have a woman's scarf and a Charlie Card," McManus said and bagged the objects CC had pointed out. "The card has a photo on it. A woman."

"Empty bottle of vodka sitting by the sink," CC said while searching the tiny kitchen area. "You might want to bag that as well." She paused for a moment to look inside the refrigerator. It was a collection of healthy food that had been ignored in favor of takeout. Inside the freezer, she found nothing but a couple of trays of ice and another bottle of Kettle One. She used her phone to take a quick picture of the bottle of vodka. "There's another one in the freezer you might want to bag as well."

"Okay." McManus didn't seem to agree with her suggestion, but he bagged the bottles. "Nothing else here," he said after they checked everything. It didn't take long. Jack seemed to be getting by with the bare essentials. His phone was sitting in the charger, clothes with dry cleaning tags hung in the closet, and his keys were in a bowl that rested on a well-worn table by the front door.

"Where are his keys?" CC asked, confusing her companions.

"Right there," McManus grumbled and pointed to the bowl.

"I meant the keys to the condo." Without touching the keys in the bowl, she pointed to the interlocking rings. "These are his car keys. Those are the hospital keys. You can tell by the way they have 'Do not duplicate' engraved on them. The rings interlock and have clips so they can be attached to a belt loop or a lanyard. There should be a third set with his house keys."

"And you know this how?"

"My wife has the same key ring." She pointed to the hospital logo. "It allows the staff to exchange keys without having to hand over their personal keys. It also makes it easy to just grab the set that you need."

"Well." McManus rubbed his chin. "He would have had them on him. Otherwise he wouldn't have been able to lock the door when he went for his little walk. I'll have CSU look for them. He might have dropped them when he fell. They could be anywhere by now."

"I know you don't have to..." CC hoped she wasn't about to overstep her bounds. "But if you could keep me in the loop, I'd appreciate it."

"No worries, Calloway."

She and Frank left McManus to carry on with the investigation. She asked him for one more favor, and he agreed. She left Frank and headed straight to the hospital. With a flash of her badge, she brushed past the reception desk.

The emergency room was in full swing. Jamie was tied up

with a patient. CC decided to wait in Jamie's office. Just as she was about to enter, a doctor stopped her. She recognized him.

"Dr. Nolan, I'm Detective Calloway." The surly man had been introduced to her on several occasions. He stared up at her with a blank expression. "Dr. Jameson's wife." She could never figure out if the guy was forgetful or simply rude. Given his chosen profession, she hoped for rudeness. She ignored his curious stare and waved him off. She made herself comfortable in Jamie's office, curled up on the sofa, and watched the sunset. If it hadn't been for the horrific events of the day, she might have appreciated the view.

* * *

Jamie hated the day she was having. The ER was overflowing with patients, and the staff was worried about Jack. Adding to her troubles was Dr. Nolan crawling up her butt. It was painfully obvious he was using Jack's unexplained absence to move himself up the food chain. If she caught him yakking about hers or Jack's lack of professionalism one more time, she was going to shoot him up with a healthy dose of Haldol. An evil smirk crossed her lips when the thought of drugging the annoying man played out in her mind.

"Jamie?" Stella waved her over.

"What now?" She snapped without meaning to.

"Didn't Nolan tell you?"

"That he's a big pain in the ass? He didn't have to. I figured it out all on my own."

"We all knew that long before you started working here," Stella said with a snort. "No, did he tell you that your wife is waiting for you in your office?"

"What? No. For how long?"

"Over an hour."

"Great." Jamie knew full well that Nolan had intentionally failed to inform her. "I'll be in my office."

"Sorry, Jamie," Stella said. "He said he'd tell you. I should have known better."

Jamie rushed to her office, which was down the hall from the emergency room treatment area.

She rushed inside, ready to apologize. She found the love of her life sprawled out on the sofa, snoring like a moose in heat. She couldn't help thinking how tired CC must be if she fell asleep on a sofa that was a good couple feet too short for her. She hated waking her, but it had to be done.

"Caitlin?" She gave CC's shoulder a gentle shake. She jumped back when CC bolted upright.

"What? I'm awake."

"Yeah, right." Jamie almost laughed. "You look exhausted."

"Today sucked."

"I'm sorry I took so long." Jamie winced, still troubled by the weary look in CC's eyes. "Nolan failed to mention you were here."

"The guy's a dickhead."

"Language," Jamie said, although she wholeheartedly agreed with CC's assessment. "What happened today?"

"I got a late start checking on Jack because I had to go downtown and answer some questions." CC seemed reluctant to talk, which made Jamie even more nervous than she already was.

"Bert is dead. I had to go through an interrogation. It was brief. No one thinks I was involved."

"Wait, he's dead? How?"

"Someone didn't like him. Turns out I went to high school with the guy who killed him. He's doing time for some very nasty stuff. Apparently, Bert molested his kid sister."

"How old were you when this happened?" Jamie knew CC was blaming herself.

"I was a kid. Logically, I know that there was nothing more I could have done. I still feel guilty. That's not the worst part. In fact that's the good news for the day."

"Geez, what's the bad news?"

"We found Jack."

"And?" Jamie was shivering, already sensing the answer.

"I'm sorry," CC choked out. "His body was found at the beach. It appears that he drowned."

"Are you sure?" Jamie knew it was the truth; part of her needed to be absolutely certain.

"I saw the body. It was him."

"I don't understand." Jamie was fighting to keep her tears at bay. "In the middle of October, he decided to go for a swim?"

"We don't have the details." CC wrapped her arms around Jamie's trembling body. "The state troopers promised to keep me in the loop. We'll know more after his autopsy. Baby, I'm sorry. The troopers will probably be calling you soon, to get his contact information."

"My God, poor Joyce. I contacted his son, Mike. He said he stopped by and saw Jack early yesterday morning. He dropped off some mail that had been piling up at Joyce's place. I can't believe this."

Jamie couldn't hold it together any longer and began sobbing. CC held her tightly until Jamie forced herself to stop.

"Crap," she said and sniffed. "I need to get back to work."

"Baby, you need to take a moment."

"I can't." Jamie brushed the tears from her face. "Today has been insane enough. I have to call Mike, tell the staff, and I have no idea when I'll be home. I'm second in command without him..."

"Easy." CC once again wrapped her arms around her sobbing wife. "Take a moment."

Jamie gave in to the comfort of CC's embrace. She started crying once again. Then she allowed herself to simply be held. When she felt a little steadier, she pulled herself together. She took a moment to wash her face and gave CC one last embrace before she set off to face what would probably be the longest day of her life.

CC kissed her goodbye and asked Jamie to call if she needed anything. Feeling a little more composed, Jamie made her way back into the emergency room. She entered during a lull and just in time to hear Nolan talking about Jack's lack of professionalism.

"Dr. Nolan, zip it."

He jumped at her hostile tone and kept his mouth shut.

"Get any and all available staff together in the lounge, now," she ordered him.

"Excuse me?"

"I said now." It was a rare occasion when she reminded a member of the staff that she outranked them. When she did, no one, not even Nolan, questioned her.

Jamie took a moment to catch her breath. Then she went down the hall and entered the break room. Anyone who could be pulled away from what they were doing mingled around, awaiting her arrival.

"I'm sorry to pull you away from your duties." She felt the weight of the world pressing down on her as everyone in the room watched her. "There's no easy way to say this. I don't have any details, yet. Dr. Temple has passed away. Apparently, he had an accident late last night or early this morning. Again, I don't have any details. When I do, I'll let you know." Her mind went blank. She had no idea what she should say next. After a couple of decades of informing immediate family members of the passing of a loved one, she had no idea how to tell the staff about Jack.

"But—" one of the residents began to say.

"Dr. Jameson will post the funeral information when she knows more." Stella effectively cut the youngster off. "In the meantime, as sad as this moment is, we do have a responsibility to our patients. Isn't that right, Dr. Jameson?"

"Yes, this is an extremely sad day, but we have to keep the ER running." Jamie felt herself slipping into work mode. "As I said, when I have more information, I will let you know. If anyone would like to take a moment to go to the chapel or catch their breath, I understand."

The staff was clearly shaken as they shuffled out of the

room. Nolan lingered behind. Jamie knew the wheels were spinning. He wasn't concerned about the how or why of Jack's passing. She hated thinking it, but she knew Nolan was thinking about who was going to fill Jack's seat.

"Doctor?" She shook her head when she saw him flinch.

"When did it happen?" He seemed at a loss. Jamie hoped that just perhaps he was moved by Jack's passing and not mentally calculating the perfect time to submit his resume.

"I'm not certain," Jamie answered. "The police are doing an autopsy. He was discovered on the beach. At this moment, it's anyone's guess."

"So you found out from the family?"

"No." Jamie mentally counted off at least a dozen times during that hour CC was waiting that she and Nolan had not only crossed paths but had spoken as well. "My wife, the police officer, told me. I'm curious as to why you failed to inform me that she was waiting in my office."

"I didn't know." His voice squeaked a school girl's. "I thought it was personal."

"It was," Jamie said furiously. "I considered Jack to be a good friend. Even if CC was stopping by to say hello, why not tell me? You know what? Never mind. We have work to do."

"Who's going to be in charge?" he asked.

Jamie paused for a moment, choosing her words carefully. She wished she could smack him around. "It's the weekend. We carry on just as we would during any other long weekend. If you would like to go home, you are more than welcome to. Come Tuesday, I'm certain the suits will assign someone to handle things during the interim. For the moment, you're free to go if you want to, and you don't need to come in tomorrow either."

"I see."

Jamie didn't miss the leery tone of his voice. He thought she was making a power play. The truth was, she hadn't thought about who would handle what. Her only concern was for Jack's family and keeping things running. She didn't want Jack's job. She liked being in the thick of things and practicing medicine. She found the administrative aspect of her job frustrating.

If Nolan wanted it, then more power to him. Although, it would mean he would be her boss, which was not something she was looking forward to. Still, given the choice of having Satan as her boss or being chained to a desk, she'd opt for Satan. *First do no harm,* she silently reminded herself.

He stood there, obviously weighing whether he should leave and spend time with his trophy wife or stick around in hopes of advancing his career. Jamie could see the fear in his eyes. He needed to show the powers that be what a good team player he was, when in reality, he only wanted the accolades and prestige without having to do the work. Jamie didn't care about his dilemma. Her focus was on the here and now.

"If you'll excuse me, Doctor." She brushed past him, eager to get away from him. "I have work to do."

Jamie hoped that by immersing herself in work she would be distracted. It only slightly helped ebb the pain. Much to her annoyance, despite the fact she had told everyone she didn't have any details, everyone pestered her with questions regarding Jack's passing. Since she didn't know anything, she had nothing to say.

Around midnight, she retreated to her office in hopes of

catching a quick nap or at least a moment of peace. Stella barged in without bothering to knock. Since she came with cookies and coffee, Jamie opted to overlook the faux pas.

"You look like crap. Eat something."

Jamie did as she was told while the two of them made themselves comfortable on the sofa. "Nolan's still lurking around."

"We could use the help," Jamie said, not really believing her words.

"He's not helping." Stella's snort made her disdain evident.

"He hasn't seen a single patient. All he's done is trawl for information. He could care less about what happened. He wants Jack's job."

"He's welcome to it."

"Don't you dare stick me with that prick."

"I don't want the job."

"Why not?"

"Because I like playing doctor." She couldn't resist teasing the older woman.

"That must make CC happy." Stella giggled before her face turned somber. "I can't believe he's gone."

"I know. It just doesn't seem real. He loved the beach and his nightly strolls. How did he end up drowning?"

"In that neighborhood, there could have been a thousand things that happened." Stella shook her head. "I'm sure the condo is nice. But that area doesn't have the best reputation."

"For all we know, he had a heart attack. I feel so bad for

Joyce. I know she wanted to spread her wings, but she really loved him." Jamie shivered, fearful of what might have led to Jack's death.

"Poor thing," Stella said. "Could you do me one favor?"

"Anything."

"Get Nolan out of here before I kick him in the balls?"

"I don't know." Jamie found herself smiling. "I'd like to see you kick him in the privates."

"He isn't doing anything but bothering my nurses."

"Fine. I'll get rid of him."

* * *

Val grimaced when she pulled in front of the house. She looked at her watch. It was far too late for a visit. On the drive over, she had convinced herself that she simply wanted to pick up her belongings. She still couldn't believe that she had forgotten to grab her bags when she came over earlier that day. Ricky would say she did it accidentally on purpose. There was a light on, indicating that Stevie might still be awake.

"And what do I say?" The only action she had managed to achieve since pulling up to the curb was limited to shutting off the car engine and putting the keys in her pocket. "I should keep it casual. Sorry for dropping by so late, I just needed to get my things. Oh, and I'm sorry for taking your sister in for questioning." She cringed at the last part. She had no idea where she stood with Stevie. Based on the look Stevie was sporting the last time she saw her, she was less than pleased.

"You going to sit out here all night?" CC's cocky question

startled her.

"Geezus!" Val clutched her heart. "You scared the shit out of me. I must be losing my touch."

"Or my sister has you so uptight you don't know whether to wind your watch or spit." CC laughed. "You should see your face."

"Knock it off." Val valiantly tried to slip her cool facade back in place. "For your information, I'm not sitting here worrying about your sister. I'm just collecting my thoughts. It's been a long-ass day."

"I know. If it makes you feel better, after I left you I had to identify my wife's boss's body. Then I swung by the station to let the brass know that I'm ready to return to duty."

"Whoa, back up. Whose body?"

"Dr. Jack Temple apparently drowned last evening," CC said. "I can't help wondering if Brooks might be right."

"Brooks? Not this again."

"When Fisher was Jamie's student, he started crossing the line of a professional relationship and invading Jamie's personal life, Temple had him bumped from Jamie's team and moved to a different shift. Simon didn't take it very well. After that, he went from stalking to menacing."

"I still think you and Brooks are way off base."

"Doesn't matter," CC said. "So, again I need to ask if you're planning on sitting out here all night. Because in another six hours, Emma will be up and raring to go. Which is not for the faint of heart. Stevie just got her to bed a little while ago."

"Stevie is awake?" Val tried to sound nonchalant but knew she had failed miserably. The bright light inside Stevie's home was a dead giveaway.

"Yes, Deputy, she's awake and probably calling the cops because a strange car is sitting out in front of her house."

"I just need to get my stuff," Val gruffly said, finally getting out of the car. "Sorry about hauling you downtown."

"It's procedure. If the roles were reversed, I would have done the same."

"Detective?" Val cleared her throat. "When I was first looking into your background, I came across something I thought you might be interested in. Did you know a guy by the name of Terrence Donovan?"

"Yes, he was an enforcer for the Winter Hill Gang." CC quirked her head, her interest clearly piqued. "Died from cancer back in the early nineties before everything in Southie unraveled. Why do you ask?"

"According to the Feds, he gunned down a guy outside of the Quiet Man Pub. You might know the guy he hit, Scotty McIntire," Val carefully explained not certain how the information would be received.

"McIntire put two bullets in me, so yeah, you could say I knew him. Thank you," CC said warmly. "I've spent a lot of time wondering if someone I knew thought they were doing me a favor. Good to know it was just the mob doing what they do."

"It can't be confirmed since everyone who was at the bar that night claims that they didn't see a thing, but the bureau is fairly certain McIntire's hit was ordered by the Winter Hill Gang."

"Yeah, well the name of that place is more than a reference

to a John Wayne movie. The Winter Hill boys didn't like rats. It really pissed them off when they found out the boss was the biggest rat in the nest. Still is from what I hear. Thanks for telling me."

"There's something else. While we were booking Beaumont, another tip came in."

"Just after he would have taken that stroll through my neighborhood." CC shook her head. "We may never know what was going on. For the moment, I'm planning on enjoying the peace and quiet. If you want to know what is what with Stevie, I suggest you knock on the door and talk to her."

"It was casual. She's made that clear."

"That's what she's said." CC pursed her lips. "Still, I get the feeling that maybe that isn't entirely true. Take it from an old married woman, if you don't ask questions, you don't get answers."

"Just how is it you met your wife?" Val asked, her heart beating faster the closer they came to the house.

"I gave her a speeding ticket."

"Really? Wait, you would have been in uniform. How long have the two of you been together?"

"Which time?" CC laughed. "I told you if you don't ask questions, you don't get answers. Trust me, I know. Go talk to Stevie. I'm going to bed. Frankly, this day sucked."

"You feel bad about Shark, but you obviously don't approve of what he did."

"When cops break the rules, it makes us become 'them.' I prefer locking up the bad guys, not becoming one." She knocked loudly on Stevie's front door. "Have a good night, ladies," CC said and snickered when Stevie opened the door.

Suddenly Val felt as if she couldn't breathe. She was standing there, being glared at by a woman who did not look happy to see her.

"I just came to get my stuff." Val felt lame when she offered her reason for being there at such a late hour.

"In the corner where you left it," Stevie said calmly. "Right before you carted my sister downtown."

"I had to."

"I know. Caitlin repeatedly explained your reasons." Stevie did not sound happy. "Something about Bert dying on your watch. I get it. I guess."

"I just had to have her give a statement. She had motive."

"Along with a lot of other people, including myself."

"You were never without a federal agent nearby." The harder Val tried to explain, the more she felt like she was skinny-dipping in quicksand. "If you want to give a statement, you're more than welcome to. We have the guy, and he's made it clear that he acted alone."

"I can't believe Shark did it. Did he say why?"

"Uh..." Val hesitated, quickly catching on to the fact that Calloway omitted that part of the story. "He said he didn't like him. With inmates, sometimes that's all it takes. What sucks is that he was able to get to him while Beaumont was in federal custody. I have some explaining to do."

"That's what Caitlin said. She also said there was a good chance that the state was going to contact me regarding arrangements. Is that possible?"

"Yes." Val's heart sank. "You were Beaumont's only living relative that we know of. His mother is still alive, but we couldn't trace her. After Beaumont went to jail, she fell off the radar."

"His mother? I thought she was dead." Stevie grimaced. "I guess I'll wait to see if anyone calls. I thought this would fall on my mother."

"They're divorced."

"Lucky Mom," Stevie said with a lingering hint of disgust.

"You must be anxious to start your vacation."

"It's still on hold for the moment."

"Oh?"

Not the enthusiastic response Val was hoping for. "I have to stick around until Mr. Chagrin…"

"Shark."

"Shark is arraigned." Val was still fighting against the tightness that had been building up in her chest since the moment she decided to drive over to see Stevie. "When I get back to DC, I'll throw myself on the mercy of my boss. I might still get that vacation. Chances are I won't."

"Oh?"

Again with the monosyllabic response that could be interpreted a thousand different ways. Val had never found herself at such a disadvantage in her entire life.

"If by some miracle I do, I was thinking of heading to the cabin or…"

"Or?"

"Or," Val said, feeling slightly encouraged. "I've been thinking of taking my car out of storage for a little road trip. It's a nineteen sixty-seven Corvette Roadster."

"Nice ride."

"Thanks." Val was embarrassed by the blush she felt creeping up on her. "I restored it myself. I had hoped maybe you could join me, then I realized it's a sports car and there's no backseat."

"Emma." Stevie nodded.

"Not something I've had to consider in the past."

"Half the women I meet run because I have a daughter," Stevie said quietly. "The other half are far too into me because they think I'm offering an instant family. One woman I went out to dinner with was planning Emma's future before the appetizers arrived. She hadn't even met my daughter. Another one, who I swear all I did was join her for a cup of coffee, showed up the next day with a gift for Emma. I love my daughter, and we are a package deal, but I want someone who loves me and my kid."

"Look, I know I'm uneasy around Emma," Val said. "The simple truth is, I haven't spent a lot of time around kids since I was one."

"I know." Stevie smiled and brushed Val's arm tenderly. Val couldn't suppress the shiver that ran through her. "You're the right mix. You want to get to know me and Emma."

"There's a but coming." Val's body was quivering from Stevie's innocent caress.

"But—"

"You see I knew that was coming," Val said, half-joking in an attempt to lighten the mood. "But this was just casual for you. I get it."

"No, you don't." Stevie's dark brown eyes misted up. The sight tugged at Val's heart. "I need to keep this casual."

"Because?"

"Your job." Stevie looked embarrassed. "If it wasn't for what you do for a living, I'd be looking at this moment completely differently."

"My job?" Val didn't believe it, despite the look of sincerity in Stevie's eyes.

"I already pace the floor at night," Stevie blurted out, her voice trembling. "I'm very proud of my sister and what she does, but it scares me to death on a daily basis. I've already sat by a hospital bed once, wondering if she was ever going to wake up. What you do is even more dangerous. Which sucks because you are an amazingly sexy woman. But…"

"But you have enough excitement in your life." Val wondered if Stevie was just letting her down easy. The look in Stevie's eyes and her demeanor screamed that she was telling the truth. Val strode across the room and grabbed her bag. She paused for a moment, kissed Stevie on the cheek, and walked out the door. She tossed her bag in the car. She felt like an idiot for letting her guard down. Never again, she promised herself and sped off.

Chapter 34

CC sat in the living room, flipping through the more than six hundred TV stations. She could see the light was still on next door. She wondered if Stevie was seducing Deputy Brown or breaking the poor woman's heart.

Deep down, CC was hopeful that things would work out. Stevie had been alone for far too long. Before Jamie had reentered her life, CC had lived in a similar manner, content to drift from one woman to the next. All of that changed with one feisty little blonde doctor. She smiled at the memory and made her way upstairs to her office. She might as well get work done since sleep was still eluding her. She flipped the boards over.

The Stern case was done. It was time to just wait for the trial and the circus to begin.

On the other two boards were Bert's movements and the mysterious deaths. With Jack's accident, she couldn't help feeling there was a connection. She tried to study the boards, but her mind kept wandering. Frustrated, she flipped over the board for the Stern case, which only seemed to be a distraction. She sat back down and then she saw it. For the first time, everything was perfectly clear.

"My God, Brooks was right the whole time. This is bad, a mad man who has nothing but time on his hands thinking of ways to get even with the people who have wronged him. How in the name of God is he pulling this off?" She shuddered at the possibilities and was frustrated by not knowing how things had been set in motion. She made a list of the information she needed but might not be able to obtain: the phone logs from Bert's phone, all of the autopsy reports, and the official police reports.

Thinking of the one person who might be willing to help her, she phoned Brooks.

"I know what's going on, and you're right. Now tell me how we can prove it?" She blurted out the words before he could properly answer the phone. "I need to see the files, and we don't have jurisdiction."

"I know," Brooks said. "It's been like spitting in the wind. Everyone thinks I'm crazy. But I can feel it. There's no way this many people who have a connection to that little weasel just dropped dead."

"Maybe we should just let him out, have them declare him sane. Texas still has the two bodies found on I-20. Don't forget about the one in Ft. Lauderdale, before he got savvy with forensic evidence. Maybe we should just let them have him now."

"Smartest thing you ever did was run his DNA after he was locked up."

"I just made sure it was entered into the data bank." She sighed. The need for sleep was finally catching up with her.

"Wouldn't you hate to be his lawyer? Can't say he was crazy at the time, because then the prosecutor can mention the other victims. Juries hate it when rich little whiners get away with hurting women. Leave out the crazy defense, and we have the pubic hairs that match his DNA."

"Good plan, except he isn't due for another competency hearing for a good while."

"Yeah, I know."

CC promised to keep him up-to-date and finally called it a night. She climbed under the covers, and the bed felt cold without Jamie there. Thankfully she was so exhausted, she was able to fall asleep.

CHECKMATE

* * *

Feeling utterly miserable, Val dragged herself to her hotel room. The only upside was, she had managed to get Ricky booked in the room next to hers. She needed him. After everything they had been through together, Ricky was the only one who would understand. Her heart sank when she spied the Do Not Disturb sign on the door. She chose to ignore it, lying to herself that he just needed a good night's sleep. She knocked on the door with a loud pounding. She was surprised when it took a few moments for him to answer the door. Given their background, both were light sleepers. When he appeared in the doorway wearing nothing but a sheet, she understood. She almost laughed at the way he covered the doorway to prevent her from seeing inside the room.

"What's up, Brownie? I thought you'd be packing so you can head back to Connecticut."

"My prisoner had the bad manners to get shanked."

"Who did it?" He was suddenly all professional, seeming to forget that he was standing in the middle of a hallway wearing nothing but a sheet.

"Another inmate who had good reason."

"Then you're all wrapped up." Ricky gave her a curious look. "So why are you here and not shacked up with Stevie?"

"Wasn't in the cards. I can't wait to get out of this town." Val didn't know if she should feel dread or envy. "Ever since I've been here, I feel like people are pissing on my boots and telling me that it's raining."

"I understand," Ricky said.

"Doesn't matter anyway. The doer is being arraigned on Tuesday morning. He said that he's pleading guilty. I'll be heading back to DC right after that."

"They always say they're going to come clean," Ricky said.

"Never do. All of a sudden they're recanting, and their lawyer is screaming police brutality."

"I don't know." Val wanted to agree. She had seen it time and time again. Still there was something about Shark that told her Calloway's assessment of the situation was spot on. "It's late. Go back to doing whatever it was you were doing. I'm raiding the mini-bar and looking forward to a gin-induced coma."

"Good night," Ricky called after her.

When she got to her room, she flung off her shoes and snapped open the honor bar. She poured herself a healthy dose of gin with a splash of tonic. While she sipped the potent cocktail, she decided to flip through her notes. In two days, her work on this case would be put to rest. Whoever was aiding and abetting Albert Beaumont would fall on someone else's shoulders. Normally, that would be fine by her, but someone had been yanking her chain, and she didn't like being played.

"I need answers," she muttered. She sprawled the file out on the bed. "I need to know who did this." She took a healthy swig of her drink. "I need ice and lime," she added with a grimace and a cold stare at her beverage. Without venturing down to the bar, which was closed anyway, lime was out of the question. She grabbed the ice bucket and set off in search of the ice machine. The giggling she heard coming from Ricky's room irked her. She was jealous. If things had gone differently, right at that moment instead of roaming the hallways of a strange hotel searching for the ice machine, she'd be wrapped up in Stevie's arms.

Val tried to relax and let it go. In the past she had been to places that most definitely qualified as hell, and she survived. One little brown-eyed computer geek was not going to get the best of her. Several teeny tiny bottles of Tanqueray gin later, she found herself dialing Stevie Calloway's number. Her last working brain cell pleaded for her to hang up. The advice came too late. Before she could disconnect, Stevie answered the call.

"Hey, Val."

"Oh, crap," Val said, realizing what she was doing. "Sorry, I shouldn't be calling."

"Ah, someone has the drunken dailies. Does this mean you'll be sporting a new tattoo in the morning?"

"Christ, I hope not." Val's head suddenly throbbed. "I should be safe. The only mate I have in town is next door making time with your baby's daddy."

"Uh-huh." Stevie sounded tired.

"Did I wake you?"

"No. I'm still keyed up from having Emma home. She kept me running around most of the night. Then she wanted to wait up for Caitlin and Jamie. She got a bit cranky when she found out Jamie wasn't coming home tonight. I'm exhausted, but I've never been so happy to have her home. How are you doing besides a little on the buzzy side?"

"A little?" Val barked with laughter. "Me? I'm just trying to wrap things up. Once your buddy Shark is arraigned, I'll be on my way. A quick stop in Connecticut, then it's straight down to DC."

"And possibly a vacation?"

"Don't really care anymore."

"Val, I'm sorry." Even with the gin clouding her senses, Val could hear the sincerity in Stevie's voice. "I never meant to hurt you, and I'd be lying if I said I didn't want to see where things might go from here, but…"

"But my job isn't what you'd hope for."

"You're doing something you love. It's just so dangerous. I can't. Which sucks, because you are sexy as hell."

"That is not fair." Val muttered. "You tell me this now, when I'm way across town and drunk so I can't drive over there and ravish you."

"I tried to tell you before." Stevie's tone turned timid. "I should stop now. I don't think either of us should be stringing the other along."

Val couldn't think, much less speak, at that moment.

"You still there?"

"Yes," Val reluctantly admitted. "I get it, Stevie. As much as I would love to spend every free moment with you until I leave, it would make leaving that much harder. I guess there's nothing left to say."

"Val?"

"Just promise me you'll take care of yourself and the munchkin."

"I promise, if you promise to do the same."

"I don't have any munchkins."

"Cute." Stevie's throaty chuckle sent a jolt down Val's spine.

"Promise that you'll be careful."

"I promise."

Val hung up, accepting that it was the end. She found it funny that they never really had a beginning, yet there was most definitely an ending. She packed up her files, dumped the last of her drink down the drain, and crawled into bed. She wanted nothing more than to get as far away from Boston as she could.

* * *

A familiar touch caressed CC's stomach. "You better stop that. My wife could be home any moment now." She didn't bother to open her eyes.

"Will she now?" Jamie purred into her ear. "Then we better hurry."

"Have you no shame, woman?" CC chuckled and finally blinked her eyes open. Much to her delight, Jamie stole a lingering kiss. Instinctively she wrapped her arms around Jamie's waist. Eagerly she began to remove the pale blue scrubs Jamie was wearing. By the way they smelled, Jamie had been wearing them all night.

"No time," Jamie gasped as the kiss came to a reluctant end.

"Tease."

"Sorry, gorgeous. I need a real shower and to change. After a quick, and I do mean quick, nap, I have to head back in."

"What about that dufus Nolan? I thought he was there to help."

"He was there and no help." Jamie climbed off of CC. "I

finally told him to help or get out of the way. He chose to get out of the way. Not before he pissed off everyone in the ER. You're going to love this. I called Peterson, Jack's boss, to let him know what had happened. He already knew because Nolan called him about the accident and to inform him that he was running the ER."

"Snake."

"No kidding." Jamie yawned. "I wouldn't mind if Nolan had stepped up to the plate. I certainly didn't appreciate him lying to the powers that be."

"Why would he do that?"

"He wants Jack's job." Jamie removed her underwear. "Which he can have."

"You don't want it?"

"Would you be happy sitting behind a desk?"

"No." CC watched Jamie move around the room without a stitch of clothing. "Need help in the shower?"

"Normally, I'd be all over that, lover. If I let you in the bathroom, I might not make it back to work."

"Spoilsport."

CC had fallen back to sleep before Jamie finished her shower. The next thing she was aware of was the alarm clock chiming and Jamie cursing. She promised to make coffee and allow Jamie another few moments of sleep. She threw on a pair of boxers and a Red Sox T-shirt and made her way downstairs. She fought against the barrage of yawns while she waited for the coffee to brew. The constant thumping and giggling next door alerted her that Emma was wide awake.

"I've missed that," she said and opened the adjoining door. "Good morning, peanut." She gave Emma a squeeze.

"Mama said I can have a puppy," Emma said with a squeal of delight just as Jamie entered the kitchen wearing a fresh pair of pale blue scrubs. "Auntie Jamie!"

It melted CC's heart to see Jamie bend over and hug Emma tightly. "Can we play today?"

"I'm sorry, kiddo. I have to work. There are a lot of sick people today. Did I hear someone say something about a puppy?"

"Mommy said I can have a real one."

"Really? Hooray!"

"Yes, I did," Stevie said. She looked at CC. "By any chance are you free today, sis? I could use some help when I go to the shelter."

"I need to stop by the station." CC handed Jamie a cup of coffee. Then she poured a very large one for herself. "If I get out early enough, I'd love to go. Why not take just Emma?"

"Because then instead of getting one puppy, we'd end up with twelve."

"Mommy." Emma giggled.

"Hmm." CC hummed in agreement and studied the chessboard. "Well, my certain victory doesn't seem so certain."

"You taught me that move." Emma grinned at CC.

"Yes, I did." CC scrunched up her face, disconcerted at being outwitted by a seven-year-old. "I need to get back up to speed with my cases. Max and Leigh agreed to meet with me. Hopefully it won't take too long."

"Good." Stevie pulled CC aside. "Is it true what Val told me? Mom found Jesus?" she asked in an amused tone.

"Apparently."

"Did you ask her if he was behind the sofa?"

"I wanted to." CC couldn't help laughing. She loved that she and her kid sister shared the same twisted sense of humor. "She was already being snotty about my marriage. I let it slide. A little faith might be what she needs right now."

"I got the call this morning from the Department of Corrections."

"About Bert's remains?" CC glanced over at Emma who was chatting Jamie's ear off. She smiled and returned her attention to Stevie. "I'll support whatever you decide to do. If you want to just let the state handle it, that's fine by me. If you want a funeral or to have him cremated, I'll help you."

"What would we do with the ashes?"

CC shivered at the thought of Bert lying around in a drawer somewhere in the house.

Jamie broke free of Emma. "I have to go, sweetie," she said. She walked to CC and kissed her on the cheek. "Stevie, I caught a little bit of the conversation. You might want to consider donating his body to science."

"Excuse me?"

"Med schools and labs are always looking for healthy bodies. It's too late to harvest his organs for transplant. Still, if you donate his body, it can be used for training med students or medical research. You're not responsible for a grave or what to do with his ashes, but you can still give him dignity. I can handle the paperwork and fax it over to you. That way you don't have to do anything. You can say goodbye if you want."

"I don't want." Stevie shook her head with disgust. "But I don't want to just dispose of him. This sounds perfect."

"I married a very smart woman," CC said before stealing a kiss.

"Yes, you did," Stevie agreed. "Thanks, Jamie."

"Auntie Caitlin." Emma disrupted the discussion. "The pumpkins are rotted. We need to make more."

"And we will."

Jamie made her departure, and CC settled into a relaxing morning. She played with Emma as they made plans for the new, improved pumpkins. It felt good. Normalcy was slipping back into place. If it weren't for the lingering feeling that just below the surface all hell was planning on breaking loose, CC would have truly enjoyed her day. After she dressed and said her goodbyes, she went to the station.

"Both of you here on Sunday, how sad is that?" She handed coffee to Leigh and Max.

They set about going over the files. With the late Billy Ryan, they had nothing. The motel room, like the ones Bert had stayed in, had been booked with a prepaid credit card, then paid off with a money order. The money orders were purchased in small stores, and the tapes of the purchaser were long gone. CC had nothing to go on but a creepy feeling.

The Stern case was much easier. Both the DA and her lawyer tried to convince the soccer mom to take a plea. Still feeling she had done nothing wrong, she refused. CC was grateful for her arrogance. Now that Mr. Stern had filed for divorce, the court case was ready to move forward as quickly as the wheels of justice would allow.

"That's it," Leigh announced with a loud sigh. "We still don't know where the drugs came from."

Mills chose that moment to show up. CC waved her over.

"Okay, I'm off," Max said. "I'm going to look at a boat."

"A boat?" CC blinked with surprise. "Shouldn't you wait until you get to Florida to buy one of those? I mean you don't even know how to drive one."

"I'm going to wait. Or not. Someone on Facebook is selling a beauty, dirt cheap. I'm just going to look." He was off before CC could say anything more.

"Shirley's going to kill him," CC said as she offered Mills a cup of coffee. "I need some information. I don't want to jam you up, but I'd like to see everything you've got on Beaumont. Most importantly, the phone records, texts, tower locations, the whole nine yards."

"Calloway, you know I can't do that," Mills said with a soft smile. CC really enjoyed her easygoing, country attitude. There was something refreshing about Mills that put her at ease. "Hey, can I see that fancy phone of yours?"

CC unclipped it from her belt and handed it over without question. She was becoming accustomed to people being fascinated by the new gadget. "Good thing you're so tall," Mills said. She punched the buttons on both her phone and CC's. "You can video an entire crime scene without taking it off your belt. Here you go." Mills returned the phone.

"Thanks." Confused, she thanked Mills for her time and Mills made her departure. "Okay, that was helpful." She pursed her lips.

"May I?" Leigh held out her hand for the cell phone.

"Sure, why not? Everyone else plays with it." CC handed the phone over before draining the last drop of coffee from her cup. "I need more caffeine."

"You need to look at this." Leigh handed the phone back.

CC looked at the screen. She blinked with surprise. Clearly displayed on the screen was all of the information she had requested from Mills, plus a few added goodies she hadn't been brave enough to ask for. "Just as I suspected. Everything lines up. How is he doing this?"

"How is who doing what?"

"Every tip on Beaumont was made right before someone made Brooks' death list, and all the people on that list only have one thing in common."

"Which is?"

"Simon Fisher. There was Fisher's father, his next-door neighbor, the woman who stole his girlfriend, an English professor who gave him a bad grade, and now Jack Temple who bumped him to a different shift when he started stalking his supervisor. They're all dead due to very explainable circumstances. They only share two connections. Simon Fisher, and right before they died, the Feds got a tip where Beaumont was lurking around. I need information that is out of my reach, and thanks to Mills, I have something to start with."

"Know any Feds who might owe you a favor?"

"I think my credit isn't as good as it used to be. Feel like some real coffee? I'll pay if you hit Dunkies." CC curled her lip in distaste and turned her attention to her computer. There was another little matter she wanted to look into. Leigh agreed to do another coffee run, while CC toiled away.

"And who is Dr. Nolan?" Leigh asked after she returned with fresh java.

"Schmuck who is making my wife's life a living hell. He wants Dr. Temple's job and Jamie out."

"Didn't the guy just die?" Mulligan was clearly disgusted. "Got anything on him? Not that it's right to use the department for personal use," she added with a sly grin.

"I was hoping for parking tickets or something," CC said. "Damn MD plates, they can park anywhere. All I got is the guy lost a fortune in his divorce. Probably because he bought his second wife a new rack."

"Wait, how did that cost him in the divorce?"

"He bought them before he and the first wife broke up."

"That would do it. Are they nice?"

"Her tits?" CC laughed. "Nolan definitely got his money's worth. The guy is clean other than living beyond his means. Two Mercedes cars, expensive home in Chestnut Hill, and I've seen his young bride wearing very garish dead animals everywhere."

"Fur? In this day and age?" Mulligan huffed. "Okay, so they live on credit and are not even close to being politically correct. That gives you nothing. Bummer."

"The bills seem up-to-date as far as I can tell," CC said. "It's not like I can tap into his bank records. Bummer is right. I was hoping for something that would ruin his day."

"Not that I want to encourage your bad behavior, but I've got an idea." Leigh dialed her phone. "Danson? It's Detective Leigh Mulligan from Boylston PD, we met at the MS fund-raiser. I'm calling because I came across something that might interest you. The guy isn't in any trouble or anything, but something looks hinky."

CC leaned back and listened to Leigh give out Nolan's information. "Do I want to know what you just did?" she asked when Leigh wrapped up the call.

"Loreen Danson is an agent for the IRS."

"Geezus." CC gaped at her, completely amazed. "You're having him audited? Remind me never to piss you off."

"You said it yourself. The guy took a bath in the divorce, but his bills are up-to-date even though he lives beyond his means. I feel it is our civic duty to report this suspicious activity."

"Again, remind me never to piss you off." CC grinned, fully appreciating Leigh's creativeness. The ringing of her telephone disrupted what she was about to say. "Calloway," she said to her caller. She listened carefully. "Hey, Shirley, no he's not. He just stepped out to look at a—" Leigh's frantic waving of her arms alerted her that she was about to make a mistake that was going to make her partner very unhappy. "A file. He needed to look at a file. I am not lying. Max has a Facebook page? Really, why?" Shirley didn't offer an explanation she simply and firmly instructed CC to tell her husband to get his butt home without a boat in tow.

"You don't have a Facebook page?" Mulligan looked bewildered.

"Why would I want one?"

"To keep in touch with people."

"Trust me, if I want to talk to someone, I'll find them. I need to let Max know he's in deep doo-doo."

"Doo-doo?"

"My wife is always on me for talking like a cop." CC dialed Max's cell number. "Like some of the crap I've heard come out of her mouth is dainty. Come on, pick up." She could feel her irritation growing when she was kicked to voice mail. "Max, turn around. Shirley is on to you."

Leigh and CC decided that Max had fair warning. If he didn't listen to their warning, then he deserved Shirley's wrath. They called it a day. Despite wanting to pursue her hunch, CC was eager to take Emma to the shelter to find a puppy. When she returned home, both she and Emma were disappointed that they had missed the shelter's closing time.

"I honestly don't know which one of you is pouting more," Stevie said after they had finished cleaning up after dinner. "You or my daughter."

"I was looking forward to it for Emma." CC's cell phone rang. "No fun ring tone?" She snatched her phone off of her belt. "Oh, no." She grimaced when she saw that the number was Max and Shirley's home number. "He must be in the doghouse if he's calling me this late. Hey, Max?"

"CC, it's Shirley."

"Oh?"

"Max isn't back yet. I've been calling him, and he hasn't called me back. I was hoping he was hiding out with you."

"No." CC felt a tightness in her chest. "He's probably hiding at the track." She tried joking. "Did it say on that Facebook thing where he was going?"

"Yes, it was in his messages." Shirley's tension seemed to be growing. "He wasn't very clever when it came to picking out a password. Someone by the name of Bunny said to meet him at the old Ballard Restaurant to look at a boat docked at the Fox Hill Yacht Club."

"Bunny? Hold tight, Shirley. I'll go check it out."

"What's up?" Stevie asked.

"Max is ducking his wife." CC tried to sound unconcerned. "I have to see if I can track him down."

Chapter 35

Val was still feeling the effects of her misspent evening cuddled up with tiny bottles of gin. She hadn't gotten drunk in a very long time. At least this time she didn't wake up with anything permanently stenciled on her body. She finally dragged herself out of bed and went back to work on her case files. Since Ricky still had the Do Not Disturb sign latched on his doorknob, she set about wrapping things up. It got late and her stomach was growling, but the thought of eating made her feel queasy. She decided to skip it. Instead, she headed out to Waltham for one of her last chores.

It was chilly by the time she arrived at Maria's building. When she knocked on her door, she didn't care if she was waking the older woman up. Val flashed her badge at the peephole when she heard shuffling.

"Deputy?" Maria seemed nervous as she looked up and down the hallway. Her face drooped when she didn't see anyone else. "You're alone?"

"Yes." Val was determined to keep this little get-together as professional as possible.

"I was hoping Cattie was with you. Things didn't go very well with her, did they?"

"It's not for me to say. I'm here to inform you that Albert Beaumont has been apprehended."

"Thank you, God. He's locked up. You have no idea how worried I've been."

"I have other news. While in custody, he was murdered." She stopped there, not certain what to say next.

"Oh, my! Was it one of those gangbangers I hear about on

the news?"

"No." Val's internal voice once again cautioned her to just wrap things up and get out of there.

"Then who?"

She knew she shouldn't say anything, but she couldn't stop herself. "It was another inmate. A family member of one of his victims."

"Someone from Connecticut?"

"No." Val decided to continue since she had already said far too much. "One of his victims from here."

"Here? No, that's not possible. We were married then and there is no way—"

"It's the truth." Val had no idea what Maria Gallagher's reaction was. She didn't bother to wait for it. She just made her way towards the elevator before heading over to the marshal's office to finish up her paperwork. In the morning, Mr. Sharkansky would be arraigned. If Calloway's prediction was true, Val's work in Bean Town would be over and done with. She could be on the road before lunchtime.

* * *

CC pulled into the dilapidated parking lot of what was left of the old Ballard Restaurant and Fish Market. The once popular venue had closed months ago, and the buildings were fully in disrepair. By the look of things, they were going to be torn down. She grabbed her Maglite and began to look around. She circled the block and around the Fox Hill Yacht Club that was just a couple doors down. No sign of Max or his car could be found.

"I swear to God, Max, if you've got your fat arse planted on a barstool so you can duck your wife, I'm going to beat the snot out of you." Something about what was left of the buildings caught her eye, just as blue and white lights lit up the parking lot.

"Great, more fun." She lowered her flashlight and unclipped her badge from her belt. "Officers," she said to the two patrolmen.

"Detective." One of them nodded.

CC squinted in the darkness to see if she recognized him. "Sully, it's been a long time." She smiled brightly.

"That it has, CC," the older police officer said. "What brings you out here? Heard you were tied into the floater they found at the beach the other morning."

"I knew him. I'm out here because my partner is AWOL and his wife is calling me every ten minutes asking for him. He was supposed to be here looking at a boat."

"We had a call," Sully said. "There was an alarm at the car lot across the street. Turned out to be a false alarm. Wrapped it up a while ago. Just to be on the safe side I thought I'd swing back around. Then I noticed your car and someone prowling around."

"Sorry about that. So nothing hinky at the car lot?"

"Probably just kids. These empty buildings have been busy since they shut down the old restaurant. The old place is coming down completely on Tuesday. We've had our share of looters. Mostly kids partying or folks looking for copper piping."

"See an eighty-seven Buick roaming around?" CC still hoped Max was just laying low until Shirley calmed down. "Black. The plate is PBJ12."

"I haven't seen it, but let me call it in," Sully said while his partner seemed content to lean against the cruiser.

While Sully called in Max's plates, CC turned her flashlight back on and returned to her superficial search.

"Whatcha' doing?" The youngster who had been napping against the cruiser suddenly came to life.

"Cool your jets, kid," Sully told him. "This here is Detective CC Calloway from Boylston. She'll forget more about being a cop than you'll ever learn. If she wants to look around an old building, we let her."

"Thanks, Sully." CC nodded with appreciation.

"Got nothing on your partner's plates. Sorry."

"Do you mind if I go inside? I noticed the door has been pried open." CC neared what was left of the back of the building.

"Probably looters, like you said, but I just want to make sure before I call it a night."

"No problem. Covering your partner's ass is all part of the job." He directed the last part toward the kid who had returned to his position against the cruiser.

"Is he old enough to shave?" CC whispered to Sully who had grabbed a flashlight and was following her lead.

"I doubt it. The kid's not gonna make it past his probation, if he doesn't pull his head out of his ass."

The battered old door creaked and teetered on its hinges when they pulled it aside. Even with the dim lighting from the flashlights, CC could tell the place had indeed been ransacked for anything and everything that might be of value. She wasn't filled with confidence when the stairway they walked down buckled beneath them. She doubted Sully felt any more secure than she did. The basement reeked of mold and dust.

CC was thankful when she reached the bottom of the staircase without it caving in. Sully released a terse breath from behind her. The cold darkness along with a stronger stench was making her nauseous.

She shivered as a new scent invaded her senses. She knew the coppery smell anywhere. Blood. She and Sully shone their flashlights wildly across the expansive basement. Her heart leapt when she saw the outline of Max's battered old trench coat. The same coat he had worn for almost as long as she had known him.

"Max!" She rushed towards the body lying on the dank cement floor.

* * *

"Having any luck?" Mills asked Val who was buried with an endless stream of paperwork.

"With?" Val groaned. She felt completely disgusted.

"Beaumont's partner in crime?"

"I've got nothing."

"We had another call."

"They don't know we nabbed him." Val grinned, finally feeling a small degree of satisfaction. "Or that he's dead. Did we get anything useful this time?"

"The voice is indistinct as always." Mills frowned. "Call came in at 1730. We traced it to a payphone at Logan airport."

"According to Calloway's theory, we'll have another body

soon." Val gave a snort, not liking anyone in the Calloway clan at that moment. "She's probably right. Not that it matters. Feel like taking a trip to the airport? Maybe they have something on tape that will be helpful."

* * *

"Max?" CC placed her fingers against his neck. "Sully, call for a bus. We've got a pulse."

"Thank God." Sully reached for the microphone attached to his collar. "Officer down. We need a bus, now."

"Make sure they send him to Boylston General."

"Kind of far."

"If it was your partner?" CC defended her actions. Everyone knew that Boylston had a far better reputation than the hospital that was closer.

"BGH, it is." Sully made it clear that Max was to be transported to Boylston General. "Any clue as to what happened?" He shined his flashlight around the scene.

CC's nerves were beyond frayed. "Looks like someone clocked him from behind. Look at the nape of his neck."

"Burn marks? Geez! Just who in the hell have the two of you been pissing off lately?"

"I have no idea." In her heart, she knew. In all the years she had been wearing a badge, there was only one candidate. She began to search Max. The flashlight teetered while she was performing the task and dialing her cell phone. "Shirley, it's CC. Get to Boylston General. He's fine. Nothing but a bad bump on his head. The ambulance is on its way, and we should be there soon."

"CC?" Shirley tearfully began to say.

"It's okay. Just ask for Jamie when you get there." She disconnected the call before she lost control. Her next move was to call Jamie. "His piece is missing," she said to Sully.

"Son of a bitch."

Sully was busy calling it in while CC was being connected to her wife. "Jamie, Max has been hurt."

"My God, where are you?"

"Saugus. The ambulance is on its way." CC's chest tightened when she extracted a baggie out of Max's pocket. "We're taking him to you. Someone is seriously trying to piss me off."

"Is he breathing?"

"Yes. But he's lost a lot of blood. It looks like someone smacked him in the back of his head."

"Show me on your phone? You remember the button for video?"

"Yeah." CC fiddled with her phone. "Can you see him?"

"Can you shine more light on the gash?"

"Uh-huh." CC's stomach flipped. Somehow she did as Jamie requested. "Can you see?" She gulped and prayed she wasn't about to throw up.

"That's not good," Jamie solemnly said just as the EMTs barreled down the staircase.

"The EMTs are here."

"Give them your phone, and let me talk to them."

CC did as she was told. Her body ached as she stood. She turned away. The sight of Max lying face down on the musty cement floor was making her sick.

"I put an all points out on his car and an alert that his gun is missing," Sully grimly told her. "What did you find in his pocket?"

Reluctantly, CC handed over the bag filled with small amber colored vials.

"Coke?" Sully looked as if he were going to pass out.

"Someone is setting him up."

"Good thing you came looking for him. No one would have looked down here until Tuesday. That's if they bothered to check the basement before they began tearing the place down. How do you want to handle this?"

"We've got a case where high-grade cocaine was involved. The Feds are working it with us. Play it by the book. I don't want anyone thinking the wrong thing."

"You do know how to liven up your weekend. Okay, I'll bag and tag it, and we'll connect with your people."

One of the EMTs handed her phone back and informed her that they were ready to transport Max. She shuddered as she watched the staircase buckle from the weight of the gurney.

"Told him to lose weight," she couldn't refrain from saying.

"I'll be following with lights and siren. His wife will be there by the time you arrive." She turned her attention to Sully. "I'll keep you in the loop. If you could do the same, I'd appreciate it."

"You don't even need to ask."

* * *

Before the ambulance arrived, Jamie had assembled the best of her team together. "I know we're all tired, but I need you to focus," she said. "This is a police matter. Pay attention to anything our patient may say." Her staff was indeed weary, but they seemed eager to get to work.

Nolan had made the mistake of showing up that evening. Once again he failed to perform any duties other than annoying everyone in the building.

"Dr. Jameson." He interrupted her while she was listing Max's vitals off to the doctors. "You seem to be spread pretty thin. Perhaps I should step in on this case?"

"I've got this one." Jamie knew he was only interested because the police were involved. For Nolan, that meant a chance at giving a press conference. "But if you're eager to work, there's a woman in bay three that needs an ultrasound."

"What?"

"Or the little boy in bay five with a fever."

"But..."

"Doctor, you did say you wanted to help. We have a lot of people who are in need of medical attention, and we have a lot of students who could benefit from your many years of experience. Stella, give Dr. Nolan a chart," she said before he could voice his objection. "Okay, now back to business. We are awaiting the arrival of a fifty-eight-year-old man. I've been in constant contact with the EMTs."

She continued right up to the moment Max was wheeled

through the doors. "On my count, one, two, three." Her nerves calmed once they had moved Max onto the bed. "CBC, chem-lab. Alvarez, clean and prep his head wound. Where is the portable X-ray?"

"On its way." Stella stepped right into the fray.

In all the years Jamie had been dealing with the harshness of emergency medicine, nothing had prepared her for working on someone she knew. When CC had called, she had a bad flashback to her mother lying in a hospital bed withering away. Dying from the cancer they had failed to discover until it was too late. Jamie had sat by her bedside feeling helpless. She barked orders at the nurses, doctors, and anyone else that had the misfortune of being around her. She was a doctor. She needed to do something, anything, to make her mother's suffering stop. Now she found herself responsible for Max's life. The pressure nearly overwhelmed her.

Jamie took a calming breath and went to work. She tried to pretend that this was a stranger, not the man who had been like a father to her wife. She instructed her team carefully. Stella was there jumping in whenever the pressure got to be too much.

"Good job," she said with relief. "Get him downstairs for a cat scan. Don't wait for transport, let's just get him moving. Thank you, everyone." She patted Stella on the shoulder. "A moment?"

"You did good," Stella said once they were alone. "He's going to be okay."

"I hope so. You never know with head injuries. Stella, is God in town?"

"Yes. Not only is he in town, he might still be in his office. Why?"

"I need the mother of all favors."

"I'll call him."

"You have his direct line?"

"Oh, yeah." Stella grinned and picked up the extension that was mounted on the wall. "Dr. Bradford, this is Stella. I'm good, and you? Look, Dr. Jameson needs a moment of your time." Stella smiled as she listened. "Good, I'll let her know." She hung up. "He's on his way down," Stella brightly said to a very stunned Jamie.

"I could have gone to him." Jamie gasped.

"He said he was on his way out to a dinner engagement and he'll meet you in your office. You better hurry. For an old fart, he can move pretty quickly."

Jamie darted out the back way and straight to her office. Stella wasn't kidding. Seated at her desk was Dr. Hamilton Winthrop Bradford. At Boylston General, and all of the partner hospitals, which covered most of the state, he was the man in charge. One word from him, and your career soared. On the other hand, if you crossed him, chances were you'd never practice medicine in the United States, Canada, United Kingdom, and most of Europe. In the world of health care, this Mayflower descendant was indeed God.

"Sir," Jamie nervously began to say.

"Jamie, cut the 'sir' crap." The silver-haired gentleman waved her off. "I feel old enough."

"I need a favor." Her heart suddenly pounded with fear. She didn't take offense when he motioned for her to sit in the chair in front of her desk. After all she was the one who had requested an audience.

"As long as you're not quitting, you can have a kidney if you need it," he said with a hearty laugh. "You must know how much we need you right now." He held up his hand before she could object to his statement. "Trust me. I've more than enough people informing me who the person is that's keeping the ER running like a well-oiled machine. I also know who is a useless sack of poo just hanging around trying to further his career. Just let me make a quick call, before we go any further."

Jamie nodded in agreement. On the inside her heart was racing.

"Deval? It's Hamilton." He smiled brightly as Jamie felt her stomach clench. "I'm going to be a little late for dinner." He rolled his eyes as he listened. "I know, but as you know, the business of health care is not a nine-to-five job. I'll be there as soon as I can." He seemed to be gloating as he wrapped up the conversation.

"I'm so sorry," Jamie said fearfully. "I wasn't aware that you were meeting with the governor."

"He'll wait. Now what can I do for you?"

"I have a patient, a police officer with a head injury. There's a chance that his case is connected to an ongoing investigation. In fact, it might be connected to what happened to Jack, I mean Dr. Temple."

"Pull up the file." He stood so she could access her computer.

"I'd like to put Detective Samuels in a secure location where he can be given the medical treatment he needs. But I also would like to keep him safe."

Jamie's hands were shaking while she typed in the information that brought up Max's file. If Dr. Bradford was annoyed by her request, it didn't show. He simply reviewed the file. Then he closed it and reopened it, using his own password. Jamie stepped out of the way. She didn't have the nerve to ask what he was doing. She simply returned to her place in front of the desk. Unconsciously, she began to tap her foot while Bradford picked up the telephone.

"Martin? It's Bradford," he said in a stern tone that sent a shiver down Jamie's spine. "I need a bed on PH22. No access except medical personnel and the police."

"His wife?" Jamie was still reeling from what she was hearing.

"And his wife," Bradford added. "Zuckerman will be his attending. How quickly can you make this happen? He's down having a cat scan right now." Bradford typed away on the computer before shutting it down. "Good. I just sent you the file. Dr. Jameson from emergency will be up with him ASAP." He didn't stop there. As soon as the call was over he was already dialing a second number. "Bruce, it's Hamilton. I just assigned you a new patient. I sent you the file. He'll be in Phillips House, twenty-two. I expect you to check on him as soon as possible." He didn't bother to wait for an answer, he just hung up. "That should about do it."

"More than I had expected." Jamie gaped at the man who simply oozed power. "I can't thank you enough."

"No need." He shrugged as if he had bought her a cup of coffee, not moved mountains to ensure Max's safety and good health. "Did you know that Detective Samuels and your wife solved the murder of Whitney Cabot about fifteen years ago?"

"I'm not familiar with that case."

"I am." He stood while straightening his jacket. He bent over to scribble something on a note pad. "This is the name Detective Samuels is listed under."

Jamie accepted the slip of paper and almost burst out laughing. She stuffed the slip of paper into her pocket.

"My grandson is at that age. It is just about the only thing he says," Bradford said with a wry smile. "Good luck, Dr. Jameson. I'm off to give the governor an earful."

As soon as Max was back, Jamie informed her team that his file had been red-flagged, which meant they were not to discuss his treatment with anyone. She stressed the point again before grabbing Alvarez and Stella. The three of them used the back elevators to wheel Max upstairs. Phillips House consisted of three floors where dignitaries, rock stars, and other people who commanded privacy were treated. Most were listed under fictitious names. To enter the unit you had to be buzzed in after being viewed on camera. Jamie slid in her key card then buzzed.

"Dr. Jameson with Seymour Butts."

No one answered verbally, the buzzer simply buzzed and the three of them scurried to get Max inside. "Dr. Jameson, Dr. Zuckerman is waiting right this way." A middle-aged nurse with a no-nonsense attitude led her through the pristine hallway. They guided Max into a room with a large plasma television, mini fridge, large comfortable bed, desk, and a comfy sofa for visitors. With the assistance of the floor nurse, they skillfully moved Max into his bed.

"Dr. Jameson." Dr. Zuckerman didn't bother to offer his hand.

"I have Mr. Butts's file, including his X-rays and the scan. Is there anything you need to add to the information?"

"No. I'll be returning soon with his wife."

"Very well. That should give me time to examine him,"

Zuckerman said. "What's his real first name? If he wakes up, I'd like to perform some standard tests."

"Max."

Dr. Zuckerman nodded and dismissed them with a wave of his hand. The trio left the unit as quickly as possible.

"That place is nicer than my apartment," Alvarez said. "I never knew it existed."

"The three floors that make up Phillips House are very restricted. You need the right last name or an Academy Award to get in." Jamie carefully explained.

"So, how did you…"

"I asked for a very big favor. Remember, you can't talk about this," Jamie said. They exited the elevator. "Thank you, Alvarez. Go home, it's getting late." Alvarez hurried away. "Thank you, Stella. I've always known that you were the one who is really in charge, but to have God on speed dial, now that is impressive."

"Oh, please. Ham? I've known him since he was a wet-behind the ears intern."

"You lead such an exciting life," Jamie teased. She left Stella and went in search of CC and Shirley.

Spotting her wife was easy. CC stood out among the crowd in the waiting area. She seemed to be in a very animated conversation with the police captain and an older pot-bellied man who was obviously a cop. The tacky necktie and cheap suit jacket gave him away.

"Shirley?" She approached Max's wife and tenderly offered her arm. "He's going to be okay. He's up in a secure room." The poorly dressed detective stomped over and flashed his badge. Jamie ignored his intrusion and continued speaking to Shirley. She nodded to CC and the captain when they sauntered over. "The doctor assigned to his case is the best." Once again, Mr. Bad Suit flashed his badge. Again, she ignored him. "I'll take you upstairs," she said to Shirley.

"Hold on." The pushy man flashed his badge again.

"Yes, it's very shiny. Thank you for showing it to me," Jamie said curtly. "Now, if you will excuse me, I'm taking Mrs. Sampson to see her husband."

"I don't think—"

"That's more than apparent," Jamie cut him off. "I'll be back. You can have a seat."

"I'm going with you," he said, working Jamie's last nerve.

"Are you a relative?" Jamie asked, pleased when his jaw dropped. "I didn't think so. I suggest you find something to occupy yourself until I return."

"This is a police matter."

"This is a medical matter. I will call security and have you removed."

"She'll do it, too," CC said bluntly.

"Who do you think you are?" Detective Whiney asked.

"At this moment, I'm the acting head of emergency medicine at this hospital and one of Detective Sampson's physicians."

Jamie didn't bother to stick around. Her only concern was for Shirley and Max. Shirley was trembling until Jamie informed her of the alias Max had been assigned. Then she wailed with laughter. Once inside, Jamie translated Dr. Zuckerman's diagnosis for Shirley that boiled down to mean Max was going to be just fine, but they needed to keep an eye on him.

* * *

"If you think you're going to cover this up, you have another think coming. Understand, Calloway?"

"I understand that you're acting like a jackass." She sneered.

"What's with that doctor? I need to talk to Sampson, and I need to do it now."

"I wouldn't push Dr. Jameson's buttons, Palmucci," the captain informed him. "Just simmer down and wait. We've offered you full access to our files and lab."

"I'm telling you, those drugs are going to match the stuff we found in Billy Ryan's room," CC tried explaining for what seemed like the one hundredth time. "All I'm asking is that you tell the press you found an unidentified body at The Ballard."

"I won't be part of a cover-up. Your partner was found with drugs in his pocket. How do I know he didn't take them from your crime scene?"

CC was exasperated. She had already spelled out everything for Palmucci over and over again. "There's no cover-up. Investigate to your heart's content. I'm just asking you to list Max as a John Doe. Trust me, someone is going to call in and tell you who he is. In the meantime, he stays here and gets medical treatment. I'll bet you fifty bucks that not only do you get the call, but the drugs are a match and we won't be missing a single gram."

"Fifty? You have a lot of faith in your partner. I can't help wondering if you're in it just as deep as he is." His superior tone was working her nerves.

"I'm telling you it has to do with this case we fell into. Max Sampson is clean. Hell, he's getting short. Why risk everything to start dealing?" She tried once again to get through to him.

"Maybe that was the incentive. You did say that he's shopping for a boat."

"Yeah, Max is dirty. That's why he's driving a Buick that's almost two decades old." She threw her hands up in frustration.

"Found his car." Palmucci sucked air through his teeth. CC hated when people did that. It was not only annoying, it was disgusting to boot.

"And?" the captain said.

"Suffolk Downs." Palmucci snickered. "Probably where he set up the deal."

"Or where the killer hid it," CC said. "The track is a perfect hiding place, and it's in Boston."

"Yeah?" Palmucci scratched his head, clearly confused. "It's not far from the scene. He could have walked."

"Really? It's what… four, five miles maybe more down the highway? There's no way Max could have managed without stroking out." CC doubted that Palmucci would fare better. "As for Max's car, Boston PD will tow it to our garage, not yours."

"I knew it. A cover-up." He shouted startling everyone in the waiting area.

"You know diddly squat," CC said just as Jamie returned. "How is he?"

"At the moment, he's resting comfortably," Jamie said in a cool, professional tone. CC cringed when Palmucci again shoved his badge in Jamie's face. "Yes, I've seen it. Your mother must be very proud." Jamie brushed his gold shield aside. "Given the situation, he's been placed in a secure location under a pseudonym."

"What?" Palmucci was, indeed, a clueless wonder.

"Single room, fake name," CC slowly spelled out for him. "We need to put an officer outside his room."

"I figured as much," Jamie said. "You need to have them checked in by someone on the list, which is limited to me, Shirley, and his doctors."

"Fine. I'll have one of my men over in a minute." Palmucci glared at CC.

"Fine by me." CC was pleased when he looked surprised.

"Now, Detective..." Jamie said to Palmucci.

"Palmucci."

"Palmucci," she repeated clearly annoyed. "Detective Sampson has suffered a serious head injury. He didn't say anything relevant other than knowing his name and his wife's name. Just the basic stuff. I asked him what happened, and he has no idea. Short-term memory loss isn't uncommon in these situations. Get your officer here, and I'll escort him up to the detective's room."

"I'll see him now." Palmucci announced giving his belt a jerk as if he had just won something.

"No."

"What?"

CC held back a snicker as she watched Palmucci's face turn

beet red. Palmucci was basically a good cop, but when he got something stuck in his head, it stayed there. The guy had the bad habit of developing tunnel vision. It had cost him dearly over the years. He lost some big cases, and his family, for nothing more than being pigheaded. Jamie just stood there, not flinching no matter how hard Palmucci tried to intimidate her. CC couldn't have been prouder.

"If you need anything else, you can contact Detective Sampson's physicians, Dr. Hamilton Bradford and Dr. Bruce Zuckerman." Having had her say, Jamie spun around and walked off.

"Oh, I'll be contacting them alright," Palmucci said. "That bitch has no idea who she's dealing with."

"I'd let it go." CC didn't feel the need to inform him that Jamie was her wife. Based on the grin he was sporting, Captain Rousseau approved of her suggestion. "We've agreed to cooperate fully. Are you going to do the same? It'll give you the freedom to investigate without everyone knowing he's a cop."

"Fine. Fine." Palmucci was already barking into his cell phone, trying to locate the two doctors Jamie had mentioned. "I'll be in touch," he added with a triumphant smirk, dismissing CC and her boss.

"He thinks he's won something." CC led the captain around the corner.

"Palmucci is always thinking he's hit the case that will make him famous."

"He should just try doing his job."

"I know, and I'm trusting you on this one."

"You don't think Max is dirty, do you?"

"No."

"Good."

"I trust both of you."

CC cast a glance at her boss. The poor guy had been dragged out of a party because one of his people had been found with his head bashed in and a stash of drugs in his pocket. She was willing to bet this wasn't the way he had planned on spending the long weekend.

"Give me two days," CC said as they approached Jamie's office. "Then all of us, including Palmucci, will sit down, and I'll tell you everything. If you still think I'm a lunatic, then so be it. Personally, I'd love to be proven wrong."

"That is never good," Rousseau grumbled while CC knocked on the door. "Whenever you don't want to be right, usually everything goes to hell."

"Have a seat." Jamie waved at the chairs when they entered her office.

"Jamie, good to see you again. Just wish it was under better circumstances."

"Me, too. Okay, so now that Detective Smart Mouth is busy trying to get in touch with two of the most prestigious doctors in the country, I can fill you in. Max suffered a severe subdermal laceration and another laceration that led to extreme blood loss."

"Someone hit him in the head, which cut him, so he bled a lot." CC ran her fingers through her hair as she translated what Jamie was saying.

"Before that," Jamie said, "he received an electrical shock. In addition to his head injury, he suffered cuts and abrasions."

"Someone zapped him with a stun gun and tossed him down a flight of stairs. I saw the burn marks."

"He struck his cranium on a hard surface."

"Smacked his forehead on the cement floor."

"Then someone used a blunt object and struck him in the back of the head," Jamie said. "He seems to be doing well. He knows his name, what year it is, and his wife's name. However he has no recall of this afternoon's events. With this type of trauma, it's not surprising that he's blocked out what happened. His short-term memory should return soon, but nothing is certain. His doctor, who literally wrote the book on the subject, is very optimistic. We should know more in the morning. Given recent events, I assumed that you wanted him kept somewhere safe. So, he's in the private ward under an alias."

"How private?" Rousseau asked.

"You have to be buzzed in. He's on the floor where rock stars go to dry out and the Kennedys go for whatever they need. Very secure, and the staff is well versed in keeping their mouths shut. Shirley is up there with him now. The two of you can wait to see him in the morning."

"James..." CC began to protest.

"Caitlin, let him catch his breath. He's in good hands. I wasn't kidding, Dr. Zuckerman wrote the book on this subject. The hospital wooed him away from the National Head Injury Institute."

"Thank you." CC felt as if a huge weight had been lifted from her shoulders.

"Don't thank me. Dr. Bradford arranged everything."

"Isn't that the guy you're always referring to as God?"

"Around here, that's exactly who he is. He seems fond of you and Max. So, it wasn't hard twisting his arm."

"Really?"

"Hamilton Bradford," Rousseau repeated the name slowly. He smiled when the answers came to him. "The Ivy League murder. Of course. He's one of those Bradfords."

"Whitney Cabot," Jamie said.

"That's right. He's her second uncle or something like that," CC suddenly recalled. "That poor girl."

"Murdered?" Jamie cringed.

"By her boyfriend." CC clenched her jaw as the image hit her of Whitney Cabot's remains scattered in a dumpster. The horrific memory still made her sick. The body had been mutilated so badly, it took almost a month to identify her. "Derrick Peabody Adams, from another fine old New England family. His hobbies included rowing, tennis, golf, domestic violence against the women in his life, and he was rather fond of date rape. Now, he's spending the end of his days in a five-by-nine cell at Walpole. I'd add him to my list of people who hate me, but why would he bother killing people on the West Coast?"

"If either of you want to visit Max tomorrow, I can take you up," Jamie said. "It will have to wait until after three. Jack's services are in the morning. I'll try to make time for the cranky detective. With a disposition like that, no small wonder he's divorced."

"How did you know he's divorced?"

"What woman would let her man leave the house dressed like that?"

CC was thoroughly amused by the look of pure disgust plastered on Jamie's face. "I'll go with you to the services," she offered.

"Then you'll need to go home and get some rest."

"Yes, ma'am."

She nudged her boss before giving Jamie a quick kiss. She felt spent as they wandered back out to the parking garage and searched for their cars.

"You know what I find amazing?" Rousseau threw out.

"What's that?" CC yawned and clicked the remote for her Subaru.

"You *can* follow instructions."

"Only hers."

He laughed and went on his way. CC climbed into her car and pulled out her cell phone. She sent a picture email and smiled. She was really getting the hang of the new gadget. She had her doubts in the beginning. Still she did feel that all she really needed to do was make phone calls. She hit speed dial while searching through her CDs.

"Wayne," she barked at the poor technician. "I sent you a photo."

"I know! Did you know this is my day off?"

"Look, I don't have a lot of time on this one," she pleaded.

"You never do."

"Run the bar code on that bottle of vodka. I want to know where and when it was purchased, and by whom."

"You don't ask for much. Again, my day off," he groused.

"Then I need you to break into Max's Facebook account and find any messages from someone named Bunny. Track down the sender and get back to me ASAP. Got that?"

"Day off, and if you want to know about Max's personal life, just ask him."

"Can't right now. Someone tried to kill him." She grimly informed him.

"What? Okay, I'm on it. I'll get back to you as soon as I can, just tell me that he's all right."

"For now, he's doing okay. I need you to keep this quiet."

"Anything. I'll have what you need in about a half an hour."

CC thanked him. She didn't miss the sound of fear in his voice. She still hadn't started her car. Instead, she made a series of phone calls. Most led nowhere. Since it was a holiday, the information she desperately needed was on hold. "Stupid Columbus Day," she snarled and headed home.

Chapter 36

The morning was dismal. The chilly dampness was just what CC would expect for a funeral. She stood by Jamie's side trying to comfort her. Nothing in their lives made sense at the moment. It was all she could do to keep it together. Somewhere out there somebody was getting a kick out of their misery.

After the services, she cast a glance at Joyce Temple. She hated what she needed to do next. The first was to leave Jamie's side. She felt a pang of guilt despite Jamie's reassurance that it was all right.

"I have to get back to the hospital anyway," she said and sniffed. "I've already paid my respects to the family. Jack's family are being complete jerks to Joyce, just because they were separated when it happened."

"Grief does have a way of turning people into assholes. Sorry about the language."

"No worries, it's the truth. I know you need to talk to them. I'd rather be on the road when you do that."

"See you tonight?"

"I don't know."

"Be careful and call me later. I love you."

"I love you, too."

CC paid her respects and carefully asked some questions. She also watched the crowd for anyone who didn't belong. She hated using a funeral as a way to gather information. She always hoped that she wasn't adding more grief to an already unbearable situation. When Joyce gave her a quick hug before she left, she felt mildly relieved.

She left the gathering at the cemetery and drove directly to the courthouse. After fighting to find parking, she finally caved in and paid to park in one of the city's many garages.

After showing her badge in order to explain her firearms, she entered the courthouse. Leigh and a few others were waiting for her.

"The captain told me what happened. How is Max?" Mulligan asked.

"According to Jamie, he's doing all right." CC wanted as few people as possible to know about Max. She was still uncertain what she was going to tell Leigh. Not knowing who she should trust disturbed her. Then again, it was naive to think word wouldn't get out. She took comfort from the fact that Max was tucked away where no one, not even another cop, could get to him.

"Do you know what happened?" Leigh was clearly concerned.

"Not sure yet," CC hedged. "Deputy Brown, so nice of you to join us."

"I just need to see Mr. Sharkansky arraigned, then I'll be on my way."

There was a hint of disdain lingering in Val's voice that troubled CC. She could only hope the bitterness had something to do with her kid sister. She quickly excused herself when her phone began to vibrate.

"Talk to me, Wayne."

"One bottle of Kettle One vodka, purchased by Dr. John J. Temple at Jobo Liquors on Cambridge street, five thirty-five p.m. on

September 30. I know this because the good doctor used a credit card. Next, I broke into Max's Facebook account, which took all of two seconds. The guy uses his badge number as his password. He did receive messages from a person named Bunny Trails. Bunny isn't one of Max's Facebook friends. In fact, Bunny has no Facebook friends. The only thing Bunny has done is send Max three messages about a boat that he or she is selling. The e-mail address is one of those free accounts where you can enter anything for your personal information and it goes through."

"That would explain the name."

"According to the information I got, the accounts were set up last week. Bunny's address would place him or her in the middle of the Potomac River. I traced the IPO for the last message. It's a pay computer located at Logan Airport. The user used a prepaid credit card, the kind any schmuck can pick up at your local supermarket. How is Max?"

"Hanging in there. Can you find out which supermarket our schmuck used?"

"I'm on it and anything else you need." Wayne ended the call.

CC stared at her phone for a moment, trying to make sense of everything. Realizing that nothing was making sense, she returned to Leigh and Val who had been joined by Trooper McManus.

"They don't really think Max is dirty?" Leigh said, clearly upset.

"I don't know."

"The Globe ran the story that you wanted, the body of an unidentified man discovered in a vacant seaside restaurant."

"Good, that means Palmucci isn't being a total idiot." CC ran her fingers through her hair in an effort to calm herself. "I can see his point."

"Come on, this is Max."

"But if it wasn't," CC said. "He's about to retire, his car is found at the track, and he's found in an abandoned building down the road with drugs in his pocket. I can't fault Palmucci for thinking he has something. Now let's prove him wrong. What have you got for me, McManus?"

"Dr. Temple drowned."

"No kidding."

"No sign of a struggle. His blood alcohol clocked in at .16, twice the legal limit."

"Good thing he wasn't driving."

"Not very conducive for swimming." McManus cleared his throat. CC noticed that he seemed nervous. "Also, there were traces of hydrocodone."

"Which is?"

"Vicodin."

"Vodka and Vicodin. That can't be a good mix."

"According to Niezwicki, it will make you loopy as all hell. Checked the bottle like you asked. According to our guy in the lab, there were traces of vodka."

"And?" Her brow furrowed. There just had to be more or why else would McManus bother coming to the courthouse?

"Vicodin." He seemed reluctant to reveal this information "It was in a powder form. Someone crushed it up and added it to the vodka. We ran the bar code, like you suggested." He referred to his notepad. "It was purchased on the day he died, at Blanchards on Revere Street at five past three. Cash sale, and before you ask, the store tapes automatically rewind after seventy-two hours. The sale has already been taped over. The guy popped a couple of pills and washed them down with vodka and ended up taking a swim. That's it."

"Okay." CC's jaw clenched. She was unhappy that McManus was ready to dismiss the whole thing as an unfortunate accident. "Let me run a couple of quick questions by you before you finish typing up your report. Would a doctor know not to mix Vicodin and booze?"

"Come on, you've seen it, some of them are worse than the junkies."

"True. Still, why not just take the pills? Why crush them up?" It was clear by the blank look on his face he didn't have an answer. "Next question, why walk several blocks to buy a bottle of vodka on a cold night when you have an unopened one sitting in your freezer? Before you answer that one, tell me how he bought the bottle when he was still at the hospital, filling in for my wife? What did you find out about the Charlie Card?"

"Uh, yeah, that's a bit hinky. It's a special needs card. It has a picture because the user gets a discount on public transportation. Ran the name, picture, and prints. It belongs to June Devlin. She has a long rap sheet, for drugs and prostitution. She lives on Shirley Avenue."

"A crack-addicted prostitute who lives on Ho' Row. Isn't that a shock," CC said. "How did her stuff get into Jack's condo? His son was there bright and early that morning to drop off some mail. Mike

Temple swears the place was as pristine as ever."

"She couldn't have," McManus stammered before he continued. "Ms. Devlin was busted outside the Squire on Friday night. She won't have any money until the third of the month when her disability check comes in, so she couldn't post bond. Because of the holiday, she wasn't arraigned until this morning."

"So you're telling me Dr. Temple bought a bottle of vodka while he was at work, even though he already had one in his freezer." CC carefully spelled out everything for McManus's benefit. "Then he put crushed up painkillers in his vodka, even though it would be easier to just wash the pills down with the vodka. He also had a visit from a working girl who was in jail. Then he strolls down to the beach and passes out in the water. Is that what you think happened? Did you locate his keys?"

"No," he said. "The keys inside his condo were what you said, car and work. We never found the other set of keys. Why are you so interested in his keys?"

"Because you need a key to lock or unlock the door, and someone locked up that place. Honestly, does any of this sound plausible to you?"

"No."

"How about this?" CC took a calming breath before continuing. "Jack took his evening stroll, which was his habit. Somewhere along the line we don't know where or how he had a couple of drinks, unaware the vodka was laced with a little extra something. He was dumped in the water. Drunk and medicated, he drowned. It looks like an accident. His drinking buddy goes back up to his condo and plants the now empty bottle and the lady's belongings."

"Why?"

"That I don't know."

"If he drank an entire bottle of vodka, his blood alcohol level would be much higher," Mulligan said astutely. "Add in the Vicodin, and he wouldn't have been able to walk down the hallway much less to the beach."

"The only prints on the bottle were his," McManus tried to argue.

"I have no doubt," CC said. "The guy who set him and Max up is smart. Cold night on the beach, a person wearing gloves wouldn't look out of place."

"Bad luck does seem to follow you around," Val grimly noted. She jerked her thumb at the doors of the courtroom, alerting everyone that it was time. "I'm sorry to hear about your friend, but the clerk is calling us in."

CC's stomach churned. She hated the way things ended. Shark could have had a much different life. The sight of him there in his orange jumpsuit in shackles broke her heart. As kids, they had the same advantages and disadvantages. Her life, after a series of troubles, went one way and his another. She found it strange that as he stood there at the defendant's table he seemed at peace. The case was announced, and still Shark stood there looking completely serene. "How do you plead?" Judge Dillard asked in a bored tone. Everyone expected the standard "not guilty" everyone offers before allowing the wheels of justice to turn.

"Guilty," Shark said with a sly smile.

Dillard blinked, clearly surprised. Even the court reporter paused. Dillard flipped through the file and gaped at Shark.

"Are you certain?"

"Yes, I did it," Shark said.

"Because?"

"I didn't like him."

"Okay. We can schedule sentencing in—"

"Now works," Shark said. "Why waste time?"

"Is there a plea bargain in place?" Dillard questioned clearly confused.

"No, Your Honor," the ADA answered equally befuddled.

"Your Honor." The weary-looking public defender finally spoke up. "My client, against my advice, has made it clear that he doesn't wish to waste the court's time or money."

"I did it," Shark repeated. "I heard he was here. I got transferred up here. I made a shank out of my toothbrush. The guards almost found it. They're very good. This isn't a reflection on them. I got close to Beaumont, and I stabbed him. Is there anything else you need to know?"

"It's not even my birthday," Dillard whispered, apparently astonished by the morning's events. "The victim?" He turned his attention to the prosecution table.

"Mr. Albert Beaumont was a federal prisoner," the prosecutor said. "Recently captured by the marshal service for violating his probation in Connecticut."

"And what was the victim on probation for?"

"Lewd act with a minor," the ADA explained. "Mr. Beaumont was classified as a level three."

"I see." Dillard nodded. "A little jailhouse justice. Mr.

Sharkansky, you do know that if I sentence you now, this is it? Based on your record and the nature of the crime, you're looking at life without the possibility of parole."

"I know," Shark responded with a hint of a smile. "It's okay. I understand that I won't be getting out."

"I must say, that in the thirty years I've been sitting on this bench, this has never happened before. The court accepts your guilty plea and sentences you to life to be served consecutively with your present jail term."

"Huh?" Shark turned to his lawyer.

"That means, you start this sentence after you've completed the time you are serving for, let's see, assault and possession with intent to distribute a controlled substance," Judge Dillard carefully explained.

"Oh, okay. Thank you." Shark was led out of the courtroom through the side door.

"I don't believe it," Val said. "Never saw anyone just say, yeah I did it."

"Told you." CC couldn't help gloating.

"I guess that's it for me." Val sighed as they exited the courtroom.

"Wait." CC couldn't believe she was trying to keep her there. "What about who helped Beaumont?"

"Aiding and abetting is a big deal," Val wearily explained. "But as I've explained before not listed under the scope of my duties. I just catch them. The agency will assign someone to check into it

Detective Calloway, it's been an adventure."

"Right," CC nodded sensing that there was nothing she could say that would change Val's mind. "I'm guessing next time you'll just go on vacation."

"I think I will."

"Good luck, Deputy." CC offered her hand. She was pleased when Val reciprocated the offer. *She looks like an abandoned puppy,* CC couldn't help noticing. She wondered just what it was Stevie did to the poor woman.

"We need to get to work." Leigh nudged her.

"We don't have a case. I should go see Max."

"That would be a case. I'll start on the West Coast cases," Leigh eagerly volunteered. CC was more than happy to give Leigh Brooks' number. Having another ally might be just the push they needed.

Mulligan said, "I got a call this morning from my friend with the IRS. Your pal Nolan is already being investigated by the Newton Police."

"Really?"

"A pharmacist in Four Corners tipped off narcotics that he's been writing far too many prescriptions for oxycodone and other controlled substances."

"Now we know how he's maintaining his lifestyle." CC shook her head with disgust.

"Newton and the IRS are working together. Rumor has it something is going to go down soon."

"One less headache." CC was slightly relieved about having

Nolan audited. "I'll see you back at the station."

"Give Max a hug from me."

* * *

"Dr. Jameson to see Seymour Butts," Jamie said after buzzing for entrance to the private ward.

"Seymour Butts?" CC laughed. "Good one."

"I swear the boss came up with that one. I thought you'd like it. Max is much more responsive. That pushy detective hasn't been up to see him, yet. I think he's having trouble getting through to Max's doctors."

"Jamie, he needs to talk to him," CC cautioned.

"And he will," she said as they entered the ward.

"Thank you."

"No need."

"I'm serious, honey." CC paused just outside of Max's room. "Having Max stowed away is a big help."

"I trust you," Jamie said. "If you think Max is in danger, I'll help any way I can. You're my brass ring. Following your instincts has saved our lives more than once. If you say someone's in trouble, I believe you."

"I hate that all of this is coming back to haunt us. I hope that I'm wrong."

"I wish for that, too." Jamie's words were overly cautious for CC's liking. "But if you're convinced it's Fisher, I think we should at least rule him out before making any rash decisions. Go have a chat with Max. I'm sure Shirley could use a break."

CC flashed her badge to the cop who was sitting outside of the room looking completely bored. She didn't recognize him; the only thing she noted was that he was a Saugus cop. Palmucci might have had problems getting up to talk to Max, but Jamie had made good on getting an armed guard for his room.

"Hey, knucklehead," she teased Max after giving Shirley a big hug. "Just what kind of trouble did you get yourself into this time?"

"Wish I knew." He shrugged and rubbed his forehead.

"Shirley, Jamie wants to take you downstairs for lunch," CC said. "I'll keep an eye on this Jack wagon." Once Shirley had made her departure, CC's smile faded. "Seriously, what happened?"

"I honestly don't know." Max rubbed his head again. His pale complexion and agonized expression spoke volumes. "I went to look at a boat. The price was good. Too good to ignore. I figured if it lived up to the hype, Shirley and I could sail it down to Florida. Kind of a second honeymoon."

"Even though you don't know how to sail," she couldn't refrain from pointing out. "Did you ever talk to the seller on the phone?"

"No, just a couple of messages on my Facebook account." Max's voice was strained. He seemed to be struggling. "A guy lost his job and had to sell his boat because he really needed the money. I figure what the hell I'll take a look."

"Did Bunny Trails give you any information about who he really was?"

"No the name cracked me up, but people are always coming up with silly shit online."

"Another reason to stay away from it."

"I guess he knew I was looking for a boat because I've talked about it a lot on my wall."

"Okay, so you set up a meet, then what?"

"It was late," Max said slowly, still struggling. "By the time I got to the Ballard, it was dark. The place looked abandoned. I got out of my car and checked the time. Next thing I know, headlights are shining in my face. The only thing I remember after that is a searing pain and hitting the deck. That's all she wrote until I woke up here and my name was Seymour Butts. Thank you for that, by the way."

"Thank Jamie." CC chuckled. "The good news is Dr. Zuckerman says that your thick skull is just fine."

"Thank you," he grunted. "Always a smart ass. What is it?" He asked noticing the pensive look on her face.

"The bad news is there were drugs in your pocket and your gun is missing." She reluctantly answered.

"They got my gun? What do you mean drugs?"

"Palmucci from Saugus is investigating."

"Palmucci? Great, someone is trying to make me look dirty and I have that slimeball on my case."

"Relax. You need to stay calm so we can get back to work."

"Drugs," Max growled not heeding her advice. "I see those wheels spinning. What are you thinking? Other than I'm beyond screwed."

"Drugs planted to disgrace you." CC tried to formulate her

thoughts. "Dr. Temple was drunk and had painkillers in his system. Add a hooker's belongings were strewn across his condo. If that gets out, it won't make him look good. Billy Ryan probably would have died from the purity of the drugs he was shooting up, but someone added drain cleaner, making certain it hurt. Seems like someone is going to a lot of trouble to make a point. It has to be Fisher."

"Come on kid," Max grumbled. "He's under lock and key. How could he pull this off?"

* * *

Jamie was beyond the point of exhaustion. Working her job and Jack's after saying goodbye to him that morning was taking a toll on her. The only bright spot on the horizon was the holiday weekend was officially over. Once the board had a chance to get together, they could address the situation and, at the very least, name a new acting head of the emergency room. Then she could go back to her old routine. Of course that would depend on whether or not people would stop dying or being attacked. Out of the corner of her eye, she spied Nolan lurking around. Not in the mood to deal with his snotty attitude, she ducked out a side door and made a beeline for her office.

"Grace," she said to Jack's secretary. The poor woman's eyes were still red from the day's events. Jamie had told the kindly, overly organized woman to take the day off. Grace insisted that she needed to keep busy.

"There are two police officers waiting to see you."

"I'm a popular girl today." Jamie slid into her leather chair. "Send the cops in, if you don't mind."

"They're not together. One is that Detective Palmucci, who has been calling nonstop. The other one is a Detective Hiller." Grace handed Jamie his card.

"From Newton." Jamie scrunched up her face and flipped the card over. "Send him in first."

"It would be my pleasure."

Jamie got the distinct impression that Detective Palmucci had worn out his welcome with the entire staff of Boylston General.

"Detective." Jamie politely greeted the slightly pudgy man. "How can I help you today?"

"Thank you for seeing me." He smiled brightly. "I was looking for Dr. Temple."

"I'm sorry, Dr. Temple passed away a couple of days ago." Jamie fought not to get choked up. "I'm kind of filling in until his replacement is named."

"I'm sorry for your loss." He sounded sincere.

"Thank you."

"I have a warrant."

"Oh?"

"Nothing drastic," he said. "In fact, the only reason I have a warrant is to ensure all the legal bases are covered." His smile returned as he handed her the official-looking document.

Jamie scanned it. "You need patient information?"

"Not treatment. Just if they were treated here, when they were treated, and by whom. The names and addresses are all listed."

"I see that." Jamie set the legal papers aside so she could power up her computer. "All of these people have Newton addresses." She couldn't help noticing the ritzy addresses. She typed away, seeking the requested information while Detective Hiller made himself comfortable. "According to our records, not one of these people has ever been treated at this hospital. According to the Gateway information, almost all of them have only gone to where their primary care physicians are located. Which would be Newton Wellesley. Would it be rude of me to ask what this is all about?" She handed him the warrant and a printout of the information she had obtained.

"Sorry, I can't comment on an ongoing investigation." Again, his tone seemed earnest. "Thank you, Doctor…"

"Jameson, Jamie Jameson." She offered her hand. "Trust me, I understand the rules."

"Jamie Jameson? I think you would." He laughed. "Sorry. CC and I go way back. I gave her a hard time back when she was still in uniform. She got me back though." He laughed again. "Thanks to her, I always check my jock before a game. Uh, sorry."

"That's quite all right. I accept that at times the person I married is an overgrown juvenile delinquent."

"My wife says the same thing. Thanks again, Doc."

After Detective Hiller made his departure, Jamie buzzed Grace to send in the insufferable Detective Palmucci. He stomped into her office looking like an angry water buffalo. She offered him a seat.

"I'd rather stand."

Jamie made herself comfortable behind her desk. She assumed he was making some kind of power play in an effort to assert his authority. Jamie didn't care; she just wanted to get back to work and then hopefully see her home and her family.

"What can I do for you today?" she asked in a bored tone.

"You can stop yanking my chain."

"Trust me, that is the last thing I'd want to do."

"Where are you hiding Max Sampson?" The veins in his neck bulged.

"Don't you have a uniformed officer babysitting him?" she asked with concern. If Palmucci hadn't sent the guy sitting outside Max's room, then who was he?

"Yeah, yeah." He quickly dismissed her comment. "I can't get to see him. I also can't get in touch with those doctors you sent me chasing after. Enough bullshit, Doctor. I need to question him."

"Sorry to hear that. Dr. Bradford and Dr. Zuckerman are important men around here." Jamie yawned, clearly not intimidated by his snarky attitude and bad language. "I'll take you upstairs, then I need to get back to work."

"I've been upstairs. They said Sampson isn't there."

"Not under that name. Given the circumstances, everyone thought it best to keep Detective Sampson's stay here quiet." Jamie stood and waved for him to follow her.

"I don't get it," Palmucci said. "Why all the cloak and dagger? That Bradford fellow is a pain in the ass. His secretary refused to put my calls through. Told me he was at dinner."

"The night this happened, Dr. Bradford was having dinner." They exited the elevator. "With the governor," she added as they were buzzed into the private ward.

"What?" The color drained from his pudgy face.

"Here you are." She led him into Max's room. Shirley had

returned and still looked haggard. CC was comfortably reclined, but she had a worried look written across her face.

"Ronald, about time you showed up," CC taunted him. "Anything back from the lab?"

"Not yet." He gave a snort. "Sampson, we need to talk."

"Excuse me." Shirley stood and made her exit. Jamie caught up with her, deciding that both she and Shirley needed another cup of coffee. She wrapped her arm around Shirley's shoulders and led her downstairs to the cafeteria.

"It's going to be okay," she said to reassure the trembling woman.

"Max is alive. That's all I'm focusing on."

* * *

CC gave Palmucci a sly grin when he turned to her. His bushy gray eyebrows furrowed as he cast a disgusted look down at her.

"You don't mind do you?" she said in an innocent tone. "I mean, if Max is dirty, as his partner I'm next on the list. Might as well get this over with so we can focus on our jobs."

"I've been getting the runaround since this went down. I don't know how you got the doctors around here to join the party, but I'm sick of being bullshitted. Look at this room. It's nicer than my apartment."

"No doubt." CC was pleased by his unkempt appearance and lack of balance.

"Yeah, Jamie is a miracle worker," Max said, unaware of Palmucci's displeasure. "This place is pretty swanky. You'll never guess who I saw in the room down the hall."

"You're on a first name basis with the ER doc? I thought you were out of it when they wheeled you in?"

"Jamie?" Max blinked with confusion. "Of course I know her. She's Calloway's wife."

CC smirked. "Did I forget to mention that? My bad."

"Your wife?" Palmucci said. "Well that would explain why you insisted that Sampson be brought here."

"Would you want your partner treated at a clinic in Lynn?"

"No," Palmucci reluctantly agreed.

"As for the digs, Dr. Bradford set that up," CC said. "A thank-you for the Whitney Cabot case."

"The blue blood murder?" Palmucci seemed impressed. "That was a good catch. I thought for certain that arrogant pissant was going to get away with it."

"So did he," CC said wryly. "Miss Cabot was a member of Dr. Bradford's family. Keeping Max comfortably under wraps is his way of saying thank you. You found Max's car at Suffolk Downs?"

"Yeah." Palmucci stiffened up.

"Again, based on the piece of crap he's still driving, you think he's dirty?"

"Heh?" Max said. "That Buick has gotten me—"

"From hell and back, I know."

"He was buying a boat," Palmucci said.

"Looking at boats," Max corrected. "Come April, I'm off

duty."

"Might be nice to have a little something put aside." Palmucci tried to play him.

"Seriously?" CC couldn't help laughing. "That's what you got? Once the lab reports come in, and your techs match the drugs to our case, you'll see the light."

"What about the fifty Gs that showed up in his bank account last week?" Palmucci gloated.

"What?" Max and CC asked in unison.

"Fifty grand sent by wire transfer from a numbered account in the Cayman Islands. Care to explain that?"

"I didn't know about it." Max groaned miserably. "All I know is I got a message on Facebook, someone talking about a boat. The guy said he was having financial trouble and would let it go for a song. I figured it's worth a look. It was dark by the time I arrived. The parking lot looked empty, except for all the construction vehicles. I got out of my car. I was blinded by a set of headlights. I felt a sharp jolt running through me. Next thing I know, I wake up here. That's the whole enchilada. I know it sounds lame, but that's what happened."

"And the money?"

CC fought against the urge to stand up and start pacing. She knew Max was being set up. She knew why. What she didn't know was how to prove it.

"What money?" Max suddenly looked bewildered.

"The fifty grand?"

"Palmucci," Max said, "what are you doing here?"

"Max..." CC was about to prompt him when Jamie entered the room with Shirley in tow.

Max looked at CC. "Calloway, what brings you by? Shirley, put on a pot of coffee for my partner."

"What the—" The question died on CC's lips when Jamie touched her shoulder.

"Not again," Shirley wearily uttered, looking to Jamie for help.

"Max," Jamie said slowly, "do you remember where you are?"

The way he paused made CC's heart lurch. Palmucci just narrowed his gaze in CC's direction. Max leaned back, seemingly unaware of what was going on.

"Max?" Jamie prompted him once again.

"Hey, Doc."

"Max, where are you?"

He thought for a moment, and his face turned grim. "Happened again?"

"Can you tell me where you are?" Jamie asked while checking his pulse.

"Hospital. I saw the headlights and then I was here," he answered, slurring his words slightly.

"That's right," Jamie said in a terse voice and hit the call button. "Everyone out."

"Hold on," Palmucci began to protest. Surprisingly it wasn't

Jamie or CC who silenced him, it was Shirley. She grabbed the grumpy detective by the arm and dragged him out of the room. He wagged his finger at CC. "What are you playing at?"

"My husband hit his head on a concrete floor. Would you like to take a guess what that did to his skull? The doctors are amazed that he didn't end up in a coma." Shirley punctuated her point by poking Palmucci in the chest with her index finger. "I've seen the X-rays. He's lucky to be alive. If you want to talk to him, go through his doctors. I won't risk his health." She only stopped jabbing him in the chest long enough to allow the medical team inside the room.

"I thought he was doing okay." CC felt completely helpless.

"For what he's been through, he is doing okay," Shirley tried to explain. "Jamie says that sudden gaps with his short-term memory aren't that surprising, but Dr. Zuckerman wants to keep an eye on him."

"Head injuries are like that." Palmucci suddenly softened up. "Had a partner back in the seventies who took a tire iron to the back of his head. He was never right after that. Calloway, do you know somewhere quiet where we can talk?"

"Shirley?" CC didn't want to leave her alone.

"Go, and figure out who did this to my Max," Shirley said. "Then kick the snot out of them."

"It will be my pleasure." CC grinned. "Come on, Ronald. We have work to do."

She dragged Palmucci downstairs to a small area with a coffee bar. He sat there sipping his coffee. He was refusing to make eye contact with her.

"What's on your mind, Ronald?" It was the second time she

purposely used his first name. "Do you really think Max is dirty?" Her question was quiet, not filled with accusations.

"On paper," he said slowly, still not looking up from his coffee, "I've got a case that points to a dirty cop."

"What's your gut telling you?"

"Don't get snotty with me." He finally looked up at her. "I've known you since you were in diapers. If you weren't Joey Calloway's kid…"

"I know you knew my old man. You even slept on our sofa after your wife kicked you to the curb."

"You remember that, huh?"

"The sight of you first thing in the morning is hard to forget. I have to be honest here. As much as I want to help move things along and clear Max's name, right now I'm worried about his health. What I just saw happen upstairs scared the crap out of me. Ask me what you need to ask me, so I can get back upstairs and check on my partner."

Palmucci sat there for a moment, and his bushy eyebrows wiggled up and down. CC sipped her coffee and tried to enjoy the moment of peace and quiet. She knew it wouldn't last long. Palmucci proved her right. First he cleared his throat three times and then looked her directly in the eyes. He seemed troubled but calmer than he had been for the past couple of days.

"Calloway," he tentatively began to say. "If I pulled Max's name off the file and handed it to you, what would you think?"

CC didn't answer; she just ran her fingers through her hair. She held his gaze and hoped he would get to the point. She didn't doubt for a moment that he was using this to further his lagging career.

"An off-duty cop," he said, "nearing retirement, is found in an abandoned building scheduled for demolition. His head is bashed in, and he has a pocket full of drugs. What's your conclusion?"

"Dirty cop," she regretfully agreed. "But he's not."

"I have to follow the evidence, same as you would."

"I get it. I just want you to get to the truth and soon. Someone tried to kill my partner. Max has had my back since day one."

"Listen, kid, off the record, you're Mac C's blood. If Max had money troubles, I don't doubt your uncle would extend a little generosity to the man who held Joey Callaway's little girl in his arms while she was bleeding out on Dunster Street. What I think and what I can prove are two different things."

"I'm familiar with the feeling."

"I did get a call this morning, after the story about our dead John Doe hit the paper."

"Yeah?"

"The caller wished to remain anonymous."

"Man or woman?"

"Couldn't tell." He gave a snarl and his aggravation showed.

"They disguised their voice. Could have been either. They did inform me that the body was that of Detective Max Sampson from Boylston. No, excuse me Boylston Village Hills."

"They stressed the BVH?"

"Oh, yeah." He snickered.

"I told you, it's a setup."

"I asked the caller to come forward." He sounded more than a little cocky. "They were afraid. I told them they didn't need to be afraid of Sparks or the Sea Side boys. My caller went off the deep end, saying of course they were afraid of Sparks and the Sea Side boys. They'd killed a cop. The caller added that Sampson was an idiot for getting involved with them. I offered protection. That's when my informant hung up."

"Who are Sparks and the Sea Side boys? You got gangs running around Saugus now?"

"No," he said proudly. "I made it up."

"But your caller knew who they were, and more importantly, they knew Max's name." CC couldn't help smiling at his ingenuity. "Well played."

"Not well enough. Couldn't trace the call. Just short enough to be useless. We've got nothing except your uncanny ability to come up with a well-placed hunch. I'm still not convinced the call was legit. It could have been anyone trying to throw me off track."

"What can I do to help?"

"Tell me what's going on?" He seemed to be pleading. "Given the circumstances I don't think it is too much to ask for."

"You've got it. I need help, not just from you. I'll set up a little chat with my boss and the Feds. Hopefully we can get to the bottom of this."

"I want in on this," he said gruffly. "If this is something bigger than a dirty cop, I don't want to be left out in the cold. If it's a dirty cop, that suits me just fine."

"Need a check in the win column?"

"Who doesn't these days?" He exclaimed. "Max got a sweet retirement package. Not because he was thinking of leaving. He got the offer because they need to make space. Turns out they didn't need to. Your buddy Andy got an OUI over the weekend."

"Crap."

"It's not like the old days," Palmucci said. "You hit your lights, and the dashboard camera lights up. You can't just call a buddy and make it go away. That makes two openings in your department."

"You job hunting?"

"I might have to be if the budget cuts come down." He sounded desperate, which made CC nervous. "But if I have a front-page bust before the next city council meeting, I could just sit back and do my job."

"I need a couple of days. I promise you'll be in on this." CC was troubled by his attitude. Sitting back and doing your job just didn't jive with her. Palmucci needed to close this case. The truth didn't seem to be an important piece of the puzzle.

He agreed to go along for the moment, yet he stressed that he was still following all leads in the case, which included the possibility that Max had gotten his hands dirty. CC told him she understood. She excused herself and headed back upstairs. She was halfway to the elevators when her cell rang.

"Now what?" She stepped away from the crowded area and found a quiet spot as she answered the call.

"Calloway," she briskly answered the unknown number.

She slumped down in a chair by the vending area after she finished the unsettling call. She buried her face in her hands, trying to catch her breath. Once she felt somewhat steady, she made a call.

"Hey, it's me. Any chance I can convince you into coming back to Boston?" CC yanked the phone from her ear when the tirade began. "Before you say 'screw you' again," she interrupted the cursing, "there's something you should know. Someone tried to kill my partner, and now Brooks is dead."

Chapter 37

Val's head was pounding, and she momentarily hated her life. She missed the days when all she had to worry about was some scumbag shooting at her.

"Ready to drop me off at the airport?" Ricky merrily exited his room.

"Change of plans. I'm dropping both of us off at the airport. I need to go to California. Care to join me?"

"What in the hell did you get yourself into this time, Brownie?"

"Damned if I know."

* * *

Jamie finished her rounds with her students and headed back upstairs. She ran into her wife just as she entered Max's room. Her heart sank the moment she caught the troubled look in CC's eyes.

"Honey? Did you do something nasty to Detective Hiller's athletic supporter?" Jamie felt slightly better when Max and CC burst out laughing.

"He had it coming," CC said wryly. "How did you know about that?"

"He was here earlier, on official business."

"Oh?" CC looked confused before she smiled. "Yeah, that."

"What?" Jamie didn't like the tone in CC's voice.

"Nothing."

"Don't lie to me."

"They can lie to kingpins in the mafia, but they can't lie to us," Shirley said with delight.

"Out with it, Calloway. She'll find out," Max added his two cents.

"Just something I heard." CC tried to avoid answering the question, but Jamie wasn't going to let her off the hook. She just glared at her wife until she cracked. "About Nolan."

"Tell me you didn't have him investigated!"

"Technically, no."

"What does that mean?"

"I was looking for something. I didn't find anything, except what I had already learned from the hospital gossip. Nolan's first marriage broke up when he bought his girlfriend new boobs. He married the girlfriend after the wife cleaned him out. He lives way beyond his means. The nurses here are a wealth of information."

"I know," Jamie said.

"Leigh thought his income, or lack of income, was interesting. She called a friend from the IRS."

"You had one of my coworkers audited?"

"No." CC drew the word out. "Leigh merely suggested that the IRS take a look at his finances. They started to, but the discovered he was already being investigated by the Newton cops. See, I didn't do anything."

"Oh, no." Jamie rolled her eyes. "Look, the guy is an idiot.

That doesn't mean you can investigate him."

"Someone else already was."

"What department does Hiller work for?"

"Narcotics. He's working with the IRS on the case. I don't know the details. But I can guess."

"So can I," Jamie said grimly. "Hiller had a list of people who have never been treated at this hospital. Nolan doesn't have privileges anywhere else."

"Privileges? Oh, that's where you're allowed to treat patients at other hospitals," CC answered before Jamie could. "You can do that just about anywhere in the state."

"In the medical field, I'm higher up the food chain," Jamie said. "That's one of the reasons he hates me. It's still no excuse for you investigating him. Just because someone is rude to me doesn't give you the right to have them audited."

"I disagree, and again, it wasn't me. It was Leigh."

"Uh-huh." Jamie narrowed her gaze. There was a time when the look would frighten CC. Jamie was disheartened to discover that was no longer the case. "Well, at least he won't be my boss. Sounds like he's supplying his neighbors. Suburban junkies are the worst. They pay more for drugs and are downright stupid about it. They don't think that they're addicts or doing anything wrong just because they have a prescription. The brass is going to be pissed when this gets out." Jamie was disgusted by what Nolan might be involved in. "Max, nice to see you doing better."

"Thanks." He sighed, and his eyes drifted shut. Jamie paused for a moment. She needed to be certain he had only fallen asleep.

"I need to get back downstairs." The long hours and stress

were draining her.

"I'll walk you out," CC said.

The stroll out of the unit and to the elevators was a quiet one. "Sorry, about Nolan," CC finally said before Jamie had a chance to call for the elevator.

"Not your fault he's a jackass."

"Yeah, but you don't need any more crap right now." CC wrapped her arms around Jamie's waist. "I miss you."

"I miss you too, baby." Jamie leaned her head against CC's chest. "When this is all over, we need to take a long vacation."

She lifted her head and sighed at the worried look in her wife's eyes. She reached up and laced her fingers in CC's long hair and drew her down for a lingering kiss. "I'm afraid that will have to hold you until I can break out of here."

"Is Max going to be okay?"

"He should be, but there's no guarantee at the moment. You saw his injuries and all the blood."

"Earlier when he started slurring his words, I thought he was going to stroke out."

"I won't lie to you. It could happen. He's getting the best care possible. We just need to have a little faith."

"What are you going to do when they offer you Jack's job?" CC brushed her fingers against Jamie's cheek.

"If they do, I'll say no and hope for the best. Chances are they'll just combine my job with his. Which means I not only get to deal with all the bureaucratic crap and insurance companies, but I'll have to bump someone to nights and move to mornings. I'll never see you."

"We'll cross that bridge when we come to it. What can I do to make this better?"

"Just take care of yourself. Promise me you'll be careful."

"I promise."

* * *

Val was oddly calm only because of the years of training she had endured. From the moment she drove across the Massachusetts border, her life had begun a downward spiral.

"She is a crazy person," Val grumbled. Ricky squirmed in his seat as she hit the gas exiting the hotel parking garage.

"What if Calloway is right and this is an inside job? We need to find a place where we can do a little research without leaving a trail. The public library is too iffy."

"I think I know where we can access a terminal. What do you want to look at?"

"Start at the beginning." He grinned. "If Calloway isn't insane, then whoever is doing this has to be paying some heavy debts to make this scheme happen. I say we follow the money. Where are we going?"

"We need to find a safe computer," Val answered as she parked her sedan in front of the familiar house.

"I hate to bother you," Val said in a haggard tone. She was standing in the last place she wanted to be. Thankfully, she had Ricky there for backup. "I need a favor."

CHECKMATE

"Okay?"

Val was encouraged when Stevie stepped aside and allowed Ricky and her to enter her home.

"We're in a bit of a hurry, and I need to use your computer."

"And you can't use yours because—"

"Keystroke program," Val said while she avoided looking at Stevie. "Oddly enough, the government likes to keep tabs on what we're doing with the toys they let us play with."

"My computer can't help you. I installed a similar program."

"Why?"

"I have a seven-year-old daughter who is very curious about everything. I can't watch her every second she's on the computer. With the program, I can keep track of what she's looking at and typing in. It's a big bad world out there. I have no desire to let the bad guys into my home."

"What about your sister's computer?" Ricky asked.

"Caitlin's? It's an antique. It was all I could do to get to stop using dial up." Stevie quickly explained. "She suffers from a phobia when it comes to technology."

"Do you think she'd mind if we use it?"

"I don't see why she would." Despite her reassurances, Stevie sounded leery.

"Please? This is very important." The sense of dread that had been consuming Val since her arrival dissipated slightly when Stevie ushered them to the other side of the house and up to her sister's office.

Val didn't waste any time, she just plopped down in CC's chair and powered up her computer. "Sorry about this. This is the only place where we felt safe." Her skin prickled as Stevie watched over her shoulder.

"Here, it's for Emma." Ricky handed Stevie a small package.

"Thank you. Where are you off to?"

"Airport. I have to see someone." Val typed furiously.

Stevie gasped. "Oh, my God."

Trying to ignore Stevie's shock, Val kept typing and plugged a flash stick in the drive. "Got it." She started to download the information.

"Can't use it in court," Ricky said. "But Calloway was right. It's a setup."

"I know, but it gives us the upper hand." Val erased her steps from the World Wide Web.

"Not to be nosy," Stevie said, "but what is it you did in the navy? And don't tell me nothing much. I just watched you bounce off of two dozen IPO addresses, some in countries I've never heard of. Then you accessed information from a numbered bank account."

"A good way to track a crime is to follow the money," Val tersely explained. Her body still tingled from the feel of Stevie leaning dangerously close to her. "The money I just tracked led us to Max Sampson's bank account."

"Max?"

"Everything's going to be fine," Val told the frightened woman. "It isn't where the money ended up, it's where it started, and this pile of cash started just where your sister thought it would."

"Don't worry, no one will be able to track what we did," Ricky added as Val typed in another code and the screen went blank. Stevie gasped when the computer rebooted.

"How did you?"

"Simple program. The closest anyone will get to the trail is Budapest, possibly Myanmar." Val innocently quipped.

"What the hell did you do in the navy? Should I be worried that the men in black are going to show up on my doorstep?"

Val rubbed her fingers through her short, dark hair. "I drove a truck." She offered her standard answer.

"You drove a truck? Of course you did. After graduating from Annapolis, you drove a truck." Stevie scoffed at the ridiculous answer.

"I worked for the government. Who knows why they do what they do?" Val tried to shrug it off.

"And how about you, Ricky? Did you drive a truck as well?"

"No. I was a glorified office clerk."

"Nice try." Stevie groaned with disgust. "Sure, that explains everything."

"We have to go." Val looked at her watch. "Tell your sister I'll be in touch and to watch her back."

"What is going on?"

"Hopefully, nothing."

* * *

CC pulled Jamie closer and stole another kiss. She needed the feel of Jamie's body pressed against her own. The simple comfort of holding her wife in her arms made her feel centered.

"What aren't you telling me?" Jamie murmured against her chest.

CC hadn't planned on telling Jamie just yet. Her feisty wife was already on edge. CC took a step back; the determined look in Jamie's eyes informed her there was no way to dodge the question.

"Brooks died."

"When?"

"Last night. Heart attack."

"You believe that?"

"The guy chain-smoked for over thirty years."

"But he quit smoking and drinking and started working out months ago."

"Yeah, but the damage could have already been done, right?"

"Caitlin, keep your promise." Jamie struggled with her words. "Watch your back. There's no way I can make it without you."

"I promise." CC tried to reassure her by explaining that it was probably a coincidence. Explaining to her wife, the doctor, that someone just up and had a heart attack didn't fly. "Okay." She finally just gave up. "But you promise me that you'll be careful as well. I need you by my side more than you know."

They shared a quick kiss before finally getting on the

elevator. CC took small comfort by holding Jamie's hand during the ride down to the first floor. They exchanged a quick goodbye in the lobby, and CC headed out to the parking lot. Surprisingly, she spotted Shirley running after her.

"CC!" Shirley huffed, clearly out of breath. "There's something you should know."

CC's stomach flipped. She felt uncertain if she wanted to hear what Shirley was going to say. "I could explain it better if we had a computer," Shirley said. "There must be a café nearby where we can go online."

"Will this do?" CC nervously handed Shirley her cell.

"Oh, this is nice." Shirley touched the screen, and the phone came to life. "This is the new model isn't it?"

"You know that fancy gizmo shop on Newbury? Stevie took them on as a client. Now I have a fancy new phone that I have no idea how to work." CC watched in wonderment as the older woman confidently pressed images on the screen. Then Shirley smiled and handed the phone back to her.

"Shirley, what is this?" CC was convinced she couldn't be reading the numbers correctly.

"My bank statement. We've been keeping it quiet. If that Detective Palmucci dug a little deeper, he would have found that we didn't need the money. Remember last year when my father passed away?"

"Yeah, I thought he and Max didn't get along."

"My dear father mistakenly assumed that a lowly cop was below his daughter's standards." Shirley snorted with disgust. "In the end, Dad admitted that Max was the best thing that ever happened to me. We weren't expecting anything from his estate. That came as quite a surprise. Between my retirement package and Max's, we would have gotten by. Still, each of us would have had to put in a few more years. With this, we had no reason to keep working. That's why we can afford the move and Max finally gets the boat of his dreams. I've saved it in your files. You just need to download it and print it out. Think it will help?"

"This most definitely helps."

On the way to the station, CC made several phone calls. Each with the same message, "I need your help." There was only one way to get to the bottom of things. She was smart enough to know that she couldn't do it alone. There were resources that needed to be tapped, doors opened that she had no way of entering. She doubted that anyone was going to be happy about working together. She also doubted that anyone would believe her. She couldn't blame them for their skepticism. She doubted Brooks when he had first called her. Now he was dead, and Max was lying in a hospital bed, with an uncertain future.

* * *

"I can't believe I let Calloway suck us into this," Val said. "I'm seriously beginning to hate that wench."

Ricky just nodded. They had flown commercial, something they rarely did, only to spend a few chilly hours in Wisconsin.

"What brings the Feds into my backyard?" the surly sheriff asked.

"Just looking into a case that might be connected to an aiding and abetting job," Val said. "About Professor Harding. I understand he met with an unfortunate accident."

"Carbon monoxide poisoning. Faulty flue in the fireplace," the sheriff explained clearly not enjoying their company. "How could this poor guy's death have anything to do with your case?"

"Probably doesn't." Val shrugged. "But the boss, well you know how it can be."

"That I do." He finally smiled.

"I really hate wasting your time with this stuff." Val prayed that she sounded sincere. "Was there anything unusual about his death? It sounds pretty cut and dried."

"No." If it weren't for the slight crackle in his voice, Val might have believed him.

"Now you just lied to me," Val playfully said. "If you do that, I'll never be able to get out of your way. Did your team find anything odd with the flue?"

"The flue? No, but it had been recently installed. I guess there will be a lawsuit."

"No doubt," Val agreed with a slight sigh. "So what did you find at the scene that's making you uncomfortable?"

"I knew this g-guy," he stammered. "I never suspected he was into anything kinky."

"Kinky?"

"When Archie was found, things weren't quite normal." He averted his eyes. "He was sitting in his living room, with a fine glass of scotch nearby, and…"

"And?"

"And he was wearing a blonde wig and more makeup than a working girl."

"Excuse me?" Val hadn't read anything about that in the initial report. "Anything else?"

"His pants were down around his ankles and his, you know, was in his hand." The sheriff blushed.

"You know?" Val groaned.

"You mean his penis?" Ricky said.

"Yeah, that's what I mean. I had no idea he was twisted."

"Okay." Val shook her head in an effort to process the information. "So, he was a transvestite?"

"He must have been," the sheriff said grimly. "Or someone tricked him into it. We didn't find anything else."

"Such as?"

"Makeup, women's clothes, there wasn't even one of those heads for the wig."

"No makeup?" Val asked.

"Nothing. I've been wondering if maybe he hooked up with a woman who was into some strange stuff. The coroner thinks it's possible Archie was posed after he died."

"It would make sense," Val slowly began to say. "Except if someone else had been there, they'd be dead, too."

"I know. I just keep hoping."

"If there was another person, that could be the one we're looking for," Val said. "Would you mind e-mailing us all the files on this case? I know it's a lot to ask, but if we can clear your friend's name, it might be worth a look."

The sheriff seemed eager to help clear his friend's name. After Ricky downloaded everything to his tablet, they were back at the airport, this time heading for much more civilized weather.

"I swear if she sends us down the wrong street again, the bitch is going out the window." Val aimed her tirade against the GPS that was badly leading their rental car around San Diego. She had been spewing her displeasure all the way from Boston.

"A favor, she asked for a favor?" Val's disgust grew steadily. "A favor is will you help me move, not some cross-country, wild-goose chase."

"Enough!" Ricky finally yelled. "Do you want to find out what happened to Brooks?"

"Ricky, I knew the guy." Val seemed to calm down just a little. "I liked him, even if he did suffer from tunnel vision when it came to Fisher."

"In the end he was right about the guy."

"The first time. This new thing he and the crazy lady from Boston are fixated on is just ludicrous. Every time I met up with Brooks, the guy burned through two packs in less than an hour. The guy dying from a heart attack isn't a surprise."

"Everyone at the funeral seemed surprised. He had quit smoking, and I heard more than one person say that he was getting in shape."

"Yeah." Val clenched her jaw. "There's something going on. Something no one wanted to talk about."

"Then we have work to do, so quit your bitching," Ricky said. "We were damn lucky the ME and his partner agreed to meet with us."

"I doubt that I'd be up for a little interagency chitchat if I had just lost someone on my team. Sorry about my attitude," she forced herself to say. "I'm not used to feeling this way. This thing with Brooks on top of being dumped, I'm not myself. Personally, I am convinced that they put something in all that Dunkin Donuts coffee they forced me to drink back in Boston. Tell me something, Ricky. When you did that background check on Calloway for me, did you find out where marksmanship ranked?"

"Above average."

"How far above average?"

"Marginal. She's a good shot, but not by our standards. The few times she's had to discharge her weapon in the field she's hit her target."

"Ever kill anyone?"

"No."

"How about physically. Is she in good shape?"

"The same, above average but not extraordinary. You took her down, what do you think?"

"I think she's in good shape, but her strengths are her street smarts and intuition. If she's right about any of this, those aren't going to help her go up against a hired gun."

"You're worried?"

"Me?" Val scoffed at the notion. "I just think we need to find out whatever we can and get back to Boston as soon as we can."

Three hours later, they were waiting not so patiently in a conference room at San Diego Department of Forensics. They had been sitting, waiting, and waiting. When they arrived, the greeting they received was anything but enthusiastic. There was the usual rumbling and grumbling about Feds interfering with a local case. After repeatedly explaining that they were simply doing some background work on an aiding and abetting case, they were shown to a conference room.

"What's on your mind, Brownie?" Ricky asked.

"First Calloway's partner and now Brooks," she said, grinding her teeth. "Think there's a chance she's just having a bit of bad luck?"

"What exactly happened to her partner?"

"If anyone asks, he's dead." Val scanned the room in an effort to see if their conversation was being observed. "He was dumped in an abandoned building. They found a stash of high-grade coke on him."

"That doesn't jive with the background check you had me do," Ricky said in a hushed tone.

"I don't know. The guy was heading south after buying a new house, and from what I hear, he was shopping for a boat."

"He could afford it," Ricky said.

"On a cop's salary?"

"On his wife's inheritance. Her old man owned a very successful brokerage firm. Guy had a knack for picking winners. He died last year and left most everything to his only child and her husband. After Sampson and his wife paid off the taxes and enormous fees, they pocketed a cool three point six million."

"That guy is rich, and that's how he dresses?" Val sputtered.

"Yeah, they paid off their bills, made a couple of investments, bought a place in Florida. Other than that, they haven't touched the money. Probably don't want anyone to know. How many times has someone hit the jackpot only to have long-lost friends and family crawling out of the woodwork? Based on his history and the fact that he has more than enough money tucked away, I don't see him peddling drugs. Had to be a setup. Speaking of setups, how long do you think they're going to leave us sitting in here?"

"Maybe they think if they leave us in here long enough we'll just take a hike." Val did some research on her laptop. Ricky kept pace with his tablet.

"They could have at least offered us a cup of coffee."

"Sorry about that." A booming voice cut through the room.

"I'm Detective Loomis and this is Dr. Hutchinson. Can I ask just why you are looking at cases that have no federal jurisdiction?"

"Can we have some coffee?" Val couldn't resist tweaking the weary-looking detective. "Kind of falling asleep here."

"Coffee?" Loomis barked while the young Doctor Hutchinson chuckled. "Yeah, answer my question, and you can have all the java you want."

"We're working an aiding and abetting," Ricky said. "We might have a connection to a couple of your cases. Now, about that coffee? I like mine black, and Deputy Brown likes hers light with one sugar."

"Sure." Loomis rolled his eyes and stormed out of the room

"I love seeing him frazzled." Hutchinson chuckled once again and took a seat. "Still you have to understand that today is not the best day."

"I understand. I knew Detective Brooks. Can you tell us what really happened to him? Or perhaps shed some light on these other cases?" Val nodded towards the stack of files the good doctor had placed on the table.

"I have to wait for Detective Loomis."

"I won't tell, if you won't tell."

"I'll tell."

"Coffee!" Loomis slammed down two paper cups.

"Not bad," Val said after taking a sip.

"This is still California. None of that government issue crap."

"Glad to hear that. Now, down to business. I just spent a long stint in Boston. The reason I was in Boston and the reason that I'm here is because I was tracking a child molester. This creep skipped out of his halfway house."

"Halfway house for a piece of crap like that? God save us. Did you catch the guy?"

"Yes, but someone was helping him."

"Someone who might be connected to your unusual deaths," Ricky added, giving Val a chance to grab another well-needed sip of coffee. "It's a maybe, but we need to check it out."

"How so? I mean a child molester and our deaths don't sound like a match. No one here was involved in anything like that."

"No one in San Diego, or no one in your department?" Val asked, and her stomach suddenly turned.

"I don't know what you think you're looking for," Loomis barked.

"Look I'm working with a maybe here. If there's a chance you know something," she quickly cut in in an effort to calm him down. "I'd like a shot at the person who was helping this guy."

"So would I." Loomis snarled the anger still evident in his eyes. "What's the connection? I'm telling you right now Brooks was clean."

"Brooks? Hold on." Val asked. "I knew the guy. We worked a couple of cases together. I thought he was a good guy. The way you're acting is making me feel sick. What happened?"

"Brooks was a good guy. One of the best. He had a heart attack plain and simple. It's just that when they found him…" Loomis's voice trailed off while Val held her breath. "He was in bed naked, and there was a DVD playing. It was kiddy porn."

"No!" Val pounded her fist on the table. "I don't believe that Brooks was into something sick like that."

"Now you have my undivided attention," Loomis said with relief. "It had to be a setup. Now that I know that you aren't here on some kind of witch hunt, how about you tell me what you need to know? Better yet, tell me what you know."

Val hesitated for a moment. This is where things would get tricky. In her mind, everything added up. Saying it out loud, the entire theory sounded ludicrous.

"When I was chasing my scumbag, we kept getting tips on where to find him. The tips were a day late and a dollar short. They originated from a burner phone pinging off a cell tower in this area.

More precisely, in the areas of where your deaths occurred."

"That's it?"

"It's all I've got," Val said with an exasperated sigh. "I just need a little info on Brooks' death. Also, Bitsy Marsden, Malcolm Fisher, and a junkie by the name of Billy Ryan. Whatever you can tell us might help exonerate Brooks and put away the person who used a child molester as bait."

"That's a compelling argument," Loomis finally said. "The first tip-off we had was the Marsden case. On the surface, it seemed like your usual random act by a group of thugs. The only hiccup was our thugs were all the way up in East LA. It just didn't seem likely that someone would travel all the way down here just to attack a woman at random and then hightail it back up to LA with her car."

"It does beg the question as to how they got all the way down here." Ricky said while he made notes.

"It bugged me," Loomis conceded. "The choir boys who were nabbed using her credit cards ended up having an alibi. That's when we started looking into Ms. Marsden's life."

"What was their alibi?" Ricky asked.

"At the time Ms. Marsden was attacked, they were at St. Agnes attending choir practice."

"Oh, so they were literally choir boys?" Ricky stifled a laugh.

"Uh-huh." Loomis snorted. "They went from choir practice to the local skateboard park. Hung out there for a few hours. On their way home, they spot the BMW. Keys in the ignition, wallet in plain sight. They jacked the car. Dumped it at the local chop shop. The following day, they started their shopping spree. They got pretty far, until the system caught up with the cards. LAPD had them in custody by dinnertime."

"What did you dig up on Ms. Marsden's personal life?" Val asked.

"Marsden worked for a very conservative financial firm, and she was about to be fired."

"Why?"

"She was about to be named in two sexual harassment suits. Both complainants were under her direct supervision. One was a married man, and the other was her female personal assistant. The old man who owns the company was not pleased."

"I take it you looked at her disgruntled staff members?"

"Both of them had alibis, and the lawsuits were about to be quietly settled."

"The case that caught my attention was Malcolm Fisher," Dr. Hutchinson eagerly added. "He was already dead by the time the EMTs arrived, but he should have been fine. On the surface, the case did seem routine. I dug deeper than I normally would in a case like this one. One of the EMTs bagged the EpiPen."

"Our labs guys ran some tests," Loomis said. "Everyone expected to find nothing, other than perhaps the pen had malfunctioned in some way."

"And what did the boys in the lab find?"

"Instead of traces of epinephrine," Hutchinson said, "they found bee venom. I also found a substantial amount of bee pollen in Mr. Fisher's tissue samples. In addition, there was bee venom in his blood work. Instead of receiving a shot of medicine, he was injected with the one thing in the world he was deathly allergic to. Very clever if you ask me. Detective Loomis retrieved the sports drink he had been drinking that day from his golf bag. The lab found large amounts of bee pollen."

"According to his caddy, he was drinking from the bottle from the time he teed off," Loomis explained while Ricky furiously scribbled on his notepad.

"The pollen set off a reaction," Hutchinson excitedly told them his theory. "The pollen alone wouldn't kill him, just make him uncomfortable as hell. When he was injected with the venom, that was what sealed his fate. The high dosage shot directly into his system caused his breathing to be obstructed and his heart to seize. His death was very painful but thankfully very quick."

"What about Ms. Marsden?"

"It looked like a sexual assault," Loomis grumbled.

"But it wasn't," Hutchinson said. "Her clothing was in disarray, but the only injury she suffered was the large gash across her throat. She bled out in a matter of minutes."

"Detective Loomis, is there anyone you can think of that would go to such lengths to kill her and try to make it look like an attempted rape gone wrong?"

"Other than the trouble at work, nothing else was evident in her life." He seemed to lose his patience. "Listen, tell me what's going on, or get the hell out of my house."

"That's what we're trying to find out," Ricky said. Val smirked when she spied the veins in Loomis's neck bulge. "What did you discover when you performed the autopsy on Detective Brooks?"

"Back up." Loomis slammed his fist against the table. "I want to know who the hell is behind this?"

"At this moment we don't..." Ricky began to say.

"Bullshit."

"They have one person in common." Val decided to be up front. The theory was so farfetched Loomis would probably laugh them out of the state.

"Who?"

"A skell by the name of Fisher."

"Fisher? Simon Fisher? He's locked up."

"Yes, I know." Val didn't even blink when he waved dismissively at her. "His original alibi was Billy Ryan wasn't it?"

"Yeah, we could have saved some lives if that little junkie had told us the truth," Loomis growled. "Didn't 'fess up that he couldn't account for Simon for the whole weekend until after Fisher was locked up. Junkie putz. All he had to do was tell us he was partying all weekend and we would have looked at Fisher right off the bat. Instead, we were chasing shadows."

"Ryan's dead. Overdosed."

"What a surprise." Loomis snorted with disgust. "This is what you've got?"

"Brooks thought Fisher was worth looking at," Val said coldly. "Now he's dead. Doctor what did the autopsy reveal?"

"It was troubling."

"Because?"

"He had a heart attack." Hutchinson shifted in his chair. "But, thanks to living a much cleaner lifestyle for the past few years, he was in very good health. I couldn't find any sign of heart disease."

"He died of a heart attack, but his heart was healthy?"

"Yes."

"Did you find anything else? Toxins or some other explanation?"

"Nothing except a blemish on his neck."

"Blemish?"

"A bruise consistent with an injection, but I can't be certain."

"By his carotid artery by any chance?"

"Yes."

"Air embolism?" Ricky rubbed his face.

"I can't prove it."

"That's the beauty of an air embolism," Val groaned. "Just inject a bubble of air in his carotid artery, and there's no trace evidence to prove that it was murder. What about the tox screen?"

"Nothing except traces of diazepam."

"Let me guess. There was just enough to knock him out?" Val felt as if she were trying to swim upstream. Nothing made sense. On the surface, all of the so-called cases could easily be explained, until you lined them up next to one another and took a good hard look.

After another hour or so of going over the case files, Val didn't feel any better. When they announced they were finished, Loomis couldn't wait to rush them out the door.

"We don't have a case," she growled as Ricky hurried to catch up with her.

"It's just too much of a coincidence," Ricky tried to argue.

"Why don't we touch base with Calloway and head up to San Francisco? Dr. Logan has agreed to meet with us."

"Fisher's father, Marsden, Ryan, Sampson, and Brooks. If it is this punk, I don't get his motivation. Seriously, what's the point?"

Val silently reviewed what little they knew all the way up to San Francisco.

* * *

"Thank you for meeting with us, Dr. Logan." Ricky shook the athletic-looking doctor's hand. Val followed and allowed Ricky to take the lead.

"I'm afraid I don't have much time," the doctor apologized. "I am intrigued that the FBI decided to pay me a visit."

"We're involved in a case that may or may not pertain to Elizabeth Pryce's death."

"Speaking of intriguing, Ms. Pryce's passing is the most interesting case I've worked on in a very long time. I was clueless as to what caused such a painful death in an otherwise healthy woman. I was convinced that she had come in contact with some form of poison. All the tests I ran for the usual toxins came back negative."

"I understand," Ricky said. "Unless you know what you're looking for, you can't test for it."

"Thankfully, her home hadn't been touched since her death," Dr. Logan continued. "Truthfully, after the way she passed, no one was anxious to go near the place. There was a fear of coming in contact with something contagious. The only things that had been removed were her body and her cats. The cats were in perfect health. Which further convinced me that it was poison. I went back with the CSU team suited up and prepared for anything. We took anything that she might have touched or tasted. I tested everything, and I found it. The tissue samples I had saved confirmed my findings. She was poisoned."

"With?"

"Hemlock and white oleander."

"That's a bit old school," Val noted with surprise. "How did someone manage to slip her that?"

"We found the culprit in the form of a gift box of tea and honey. The tea had white oleander and the honey was laced with hemlock. Very effective and extremely painful," Dr. Logan said.

"Who sent the gift?" Val asked.

"It was traced to a nonexistent company. No prints and the only clue we have is that the postmark was from Los Angeles. I hope this helps. I want to see whoever did this to that poor woman get what they deserve."

Dr. Logan broke protocol and gave them copies of all the lab reports and his notes. Val and Ricky downloaded the information onto their tablets.

"Remind me again what Elizabeth Pryce's connection is to Fisher?" Val asked once they had checked in at the airport.

"His girlfriend's roommate," Ricky said. "Your buddy Brooks discovered that Janie dumped Fisher to be with Elizabeth."

"Right, broke the case open." Val reviewed her notes. "Brooks said it was Calloway who steered him in that direction. When was the last time you heard of someone being poisoned with hemlock?"

"Socrates."

"The killer had a good shot of getting away with it." Val carefully began. "He could have grown the hemlock himself and mixed the yellow resin in with the honey to mask the bitter taste. According to Dr. Logan's notes, it takes one gram per kilogram of body weight. Elizabeth weighed just over one hundred twenty-five pounds, but the killer used sixty kilograms. Enough for a person at least twelve pounds heavier. The symptoms include nausea, emesis, and abdominal pain. Due to the rapid onset of symptoms, treatment is rarely successful. Add the white oleander that was mixed in with the tea, and the poor girl didn't stand a chance. Does this bolster Calloway's theory? What do we know about Elizabeth's personal life? Did she have an ex-lover from hell who liked to garden?"

"Worth looking into."

"I never thought I'd be anxious to get back to Boston," Val grumbled. "I can't shake the feeling that all hell is about to break loose."

Chapter 38

CC didn't know how to feel about how eager Leigh was to assist her. They commandeered one of the conference rooms and went to work. CC's fingers had black smudges from the magic marker she had used to write on the whiteboard that resembled the ones she had at home.

"I can't believe it." Leigh studied the work. "When you lay it out side by side like this, it seems obvious. Still…"

"It's a far-fetched theory, and we have no proof," CC concluded for her. "How do you conk Max on the head and make it all the way to California to kill Brooks? I always knew the little bastard was smart. I just never suspected he could have pulled something like this off."

"How and why?"

"If I had the answer to that, I'd be sleeping at night."

"They're starting to arrive," Leigh noted looking towards the hallway. "I know I'm not Max. I just want you to know that I've got your back."

"I appreciate that more than you know."

CC organized the photocopies she had prepared. She had made over two-dozen phone calls before checking in to the station. Now that everything was laid out, she felt certain of two things. First, she was right, and second, almost no one was going to believe her. The stellar reputation she had developed over her long career would only go so far.

"This is quite the little powwow you've gathered," Rousseau said as he took a seat.

"Yes, sir." She nervously looked around the room.

She had managed to gather her boss, Mills, McManus, Palmucci, and Wayne. She had Dr. Richards waiting on the speakerphone, and Val and Ricky had just arrived. CC couldn't shake the feeling that this was one of those moments that could sink a cop's career.

She felt a twinge of guilt when she saw both Val and Ricky were dressed casually in street clothes. At her insistence, they came to the station directly from the airport. She guessed that sitting in a squad room was the last thing they had planned on doing.

"I'm sorry for this," CC meekly apologized while Leigh made certain that everyone had a copy of the files CC had put together. "I'll tell you what I've got, then all of you can tell me I'm nuts. Or help. Your call."

She felt her stomach clench. "Up on the board here, I've made three charts. The first is reported sightings of Albert Beaumont, the child molester that the Fugitive Task Force caught last week. Next to that is a list of dead bodies, or in Max's case, presumed dead. Last is the connection between the victims and Simon Fisher."

"Fisher?" Rousseau said. "You can't be serious."

"I wish I wasn't."

"Hear her out, sir," Leigh asked. "I know it sounds crazy, but people are dying."

"I get it," he said. "If this proves that Max was set up I'm all for it."

"Oh, please," Palmucci scoffed. "Then explain the fifty grand."

"Here." CC shoved a sheet of paper across the table. Much to her annoyance, Palmucci didn't bother to look at it. She ran her fingers through her hair and took a calming breath before she dared to speak. "Let's start at the beginning." She pointed to the boards. "Malcolm Fisher died of anaphylactic shock. Supposedly, he was stung by a bee. Ricky, you and Val talked to the medical examiner in San Diego. Can you tell everyone what you found out?"

"Malcolm Fisher did indeed die of anaphylaxis," Ricky said while flipping through his notes. "The troubling thing is his caddy gave him a shot of epinephrine. According to the medical examiner, there were no traces of epinephrine in Malcolm Fisher's system. However, although the amount of bee venom in his system would lead us to believe he was attacked by a swarm of bees, there wasn't a mark on him."

CC picked up the thread. "Around that time, the Connecticut US Marshal's office was informed by an anonymous caller that Albert Beaumont had skipped town. The caller's voice was hard to identify."

"We couldn't," Val said. "We were simply told that Beaumont would be arriving in Boston via a Peter Pan bus. He arrived by train hours ahead of us."

"But you went looking for him," CC said. "Another tip of his whereabouts came in. On that day, Elizabeth Pryce died. Ricky, what did the San Francisco ME tell you?"

"At first, Dr. Logan was clueless as to what caused such a painful death in an otherwise healthy woman." Ricky paused to clear his throat. "After searching her home and running a battery of tests, he determined that she was poisoned."

"With?"

"Hemlock and white oleander."

"Hemlock?" McManus said. "Geez, where do you get that these days?"

"You can grow it." Ricky shrugged. "The CSU team checked out Ms. Pryce's home. They found that she had received a gift of tea. The hemlock was in the sample of honey, and the oleander, which grows wild on the West Coast, was in the tea. The police tried to track down the company that sent the free sample. They found out the company was bogus. If Dr. Logan hadn't been so diligent, the death would have been written off as a stomach virus. Dr. Logan is more than happy to cooperate with our investigation."

"What investigation?" Rousseau asked in a demanding tone.

"Who are these guys?"

"US Deputy Marshal Val Brown and FBI Special Agent Richard Samaria." CC made the introductions. "They are investigating an aiding and abetting case."

"You called in the Feds?"

"I-I..." she stammered, knowing her boss was pissed that she had breached the thin blue line that said locals don't play well with Feds. "I did. They can get information that is out of our reach."

"You mean your reach. So far I haven't seen anything that warrants our involvement."

"I guess I do." CC's heart sank. "In which case, I guess I should keep going. On September 29, the Fugitive Task Force received another call alerting them that Beaumont was roaming around Copley Place. At the same time, Bitsy Marsden went for a jog in San Diego. A few hours later, she was discovered with her throat slashed and her sweats down around her ankles. LAPD arrested two upstanding citizens when they tried to use her credit card. They later found what was left of her BMW in a chop shop in East LA. Turns out the kids they arrested didn't kill her."

"But they had her stuff," Palmucci tried to argue.

"They also ended having solid alibis for the time of Ms. Marsden's murder," Ricky explained. "I personally find it hard to believe that someone would hitch a ride all the way down to San Diego just to steal a car."

Palmucci responded with a grunt and roll of his eyes that was worthy of a teenage girl.

"Next we have another tip that sent us chasing after Beaumont, during which time Professor Archibald Harding died of carbon monoxide poisoning in Wisconsin. The police blamed it on a faulty flue in the fireplace. Thing is the fireplace had recently been refurbished. Also, the good professor was naked from the waist down. He was wearing makeup, and he had his Johnson in his hand."

"So? He went happy," Palmucci said. "Freaky but happy."

"According to the coroner, he was standing at attention," Ricky said. "He was fairly certain that his body had been posed postmortem. He just can't prove it."

"Also," CC said, "the police never found any traces of makeup in the house."

"And?" Palmucci once again snidely broke in. "So he had a playmate, big hairy deal."

"A playmate who didn't die of carbon monoxide poisoning? I doubt if he had a friend who played dress-up and left him sitting there jacking off." CC was pleased to see him slump down in his chair. She hoped that would be the end of his outbursts. At that moment, she was very tempted to slap him around.

"Next on the hit parade is Billy Ryan. He checked himself out of McLean and went straight to a prepaid hotel room. He shot up the purest heroin and cocaine on the planet and overdosed. The quality of the drugs alone would have killed him. Billy got the added bonus of having his drugs cut with drain cleaner. Our ME confirms that Billy died a horribly painful death. About the time Billy was jacking up, another tip came in that Beaumont was spotted lurking around Boylston General."

CC paused when there was a knock on the door. She took a moment to grab a sip of coffee while Leigh answered the door. Leigh seemed upbeat when she handed CC a FedEx envelope.

"I got your package, Dr. Richards," CC announced, confusing everyone in the room.

"Good," Dr. Richards acknowledged over the phone. "You should continue, Detective. I get the feeling you are surrounded by skeptics."

"Isn't that the doc who did the profile on Fisher?" Her boss's face was beet red as he asked the question. "She's been listening this whole time?"

"Yes, sir," CC said and she watched the vein in Rousseau's forehead bulge. She was in it deep, and there was no turning back.

"More Feds?"

"Yes, sir. There was another tip. Once again, the caller's voice was ambiguous. At the same time, Dr. Jack Temple went for a stroll on Revere Beach. He had consumed vodka laced with painkillers. The empty bottle of vodka was found in his kitchen. Jack also had an unopened bottle in his freezer. Wayne ran the bar codes on both bottles."

Wayne said, "The bottle in the freezer was purchased at Jobo Liquors on Cambridge Street two weeks ago, and Dr. Temple paid with his Visa card."

"Jobo is down the street from the hospital," CC said. "Dr. Temple would have passed it along his walk to the Bowdoin T-stop."

"The second bottle," Wayne continued, "was purchased with cash at Blanchards Liquors on the day that Dr. Temple died."

CC once again stepped in. "It was also purchased while Dr. Temple was at the hospital. He wasn't supposed to be working that day. He was filling in for someone else. McManus, did you ever find Dr. Temple's keys?"

"No. The only keys that we found were his car and work keys."

"Dr. Temple," CC told them, "had a nifty little interlocking key ring that hooked to a clip and a lanyard. It's designed so you can keep different sets of keys separated. Dr. Temple was wearing the clip and the lanyard when he was found. No keys. The only way to lock or unlock the door to his condo is with a key."

"They could have washed away," Rousseau argued. "The guy drowned."

"This key ring is very sturdy," CC answered. "A gift from a pharmaceutical company. My wife has the same setup. When Jamie is at work, she locks her personal keys in her desk and only carries hospital keys around. To unlock one of the sets, you need to twist the metal bar, bend it up, twist again, and then detach it. Not something that would just wash away."

"Also, we found something interesting in Dr. Temple's condo," McManus said without missing a beat. "His son had visited that morning. The place was neat as a pin. Apparently, Dr. Temple was a very organized man. When we entered the locked condo, we found a woman's scarf and a Charlie Card. The card was for special fares, since the owner is on disability. We have her name, June Devlin."

"What's her disability?" Palmucci asked.

"Junkie, prostitute."

"Isn't that grand," Palmucci said and snarled. "And we get to pay her rent. The road to hell is paved with good intentions and democrats."

"Don't make me smack you. " CC couldn't suppress her anger. "McManus, where was Ms. Devlin at the time of the murder?"

"What murder?" Palmucci interrupted once again. "Did I miss something?"

"No," Val said before CC had the chance. "But if you'd shut up and listen, you might learn something. I swear you make one more snotty comment, and I'll be shoving my foot up your ass."

"She'll do it, too," Ricky said with a sly smirk.

"You think you scare me, little lady?"

"Seriously, you don't want to push her," CC told him. "Just let me get through this, then you can tell me what a jackass I am."

"Fine." Palmucci folded his arms tightly against his chest. Everyone else in the room sighed in apparent relief.

CC doubted that they agreed with her, but Palmucci did have a way of pissing people off. "McManus, if you don't mind?" she said to the amused trooper.

"Ms. Devlin was incarcerated for solicitation," McManus explained. "Locked up over the long weekend. When Dr. Temple went for his swim, she was sitting in jail. She wasn't arraigned until Tuesday morning when she posted her forty-dollar bond and went on her way."

"The kick in the pants on the day of Jack's death is the tips kept coming in." CC pressed on, determined to explain everything.

"Beaumont, like the fair Ms. Devlin, was in custody, thanks to Deputy Brown and the task force. Another tip came in around the time Max took a header down that flight of stairs," CC said. "The tips haven't stopped, even though Beaumont is dead."

"If I may ask?" Palmucci cleared his throat. "Who in the hell is Albert Beaumont?"

"The miserable sack of poo my mother had the misfortune to marry after my father died."

"You mean Bert? The sorry son of a bitch." Palmucci was clearly disgusted. "You should have slammed that loser with a baseball bat."

"Been, there, done that, didn't take. Doesn't matter. He has fallen victim to a little prison justice."

"He deserved it."

"Even though he's dead, the task force is still getting calls," CC said, ignoring Palmucci's grunts and groans. "After Max was attacked, Palmucci leaked a story about a John Doe being found in an abandoned building."

"Yeah, I got a call identifying the body as Sampson," Palmucci said. "He could have had anyone make that call for him, and it still doesn't explain his car at Suffolk Downs."

"Come on, that's at least four miles from the Ballard, and there's no way Max could have walked that." CC handed Palmucci a photocopy. "But someone wants us to think Max is dirty. Drugs in his pocket, car at the race track, and the fifty grand you found in his account. You might want to look at that paper I gave you."

"What is it?"

"A bank statement." CC fought against the urge to shove it down his throat. "This is from Shirley Sampson's bank account. Shirley's father, who passed away last year, was an investment banker. As you can see, he was damn good at his job. That's how Max could afford to retire. After his father in-law's will cleared probate, he and his wife were set for life. He didn't need to sell drugs. Just after Max took his spill, Detective Brooks of the San Diego PD died of a heart attack. He was found naked in bed with kiddy porn in the DVD player."

"This is what you've got?" Rousseau seemed less than pleased. "You've got nothing."

* * *

It was getting late. Jamie sat at her desk, wondering how much caffeine was too much. Thanks to one of her students, it would be hours to go before she could even think about heading home. A loud knock on her office door disrupted her plans to search for more coffee.

"Come in."

She wasn't surprised when Murphy stormed in, his shaggy blonde hair mussed from the long night he had endured. Jamie leaned back and motioned for him to have a seat. He paced for a moment before accepting her offer. While he shifted nervously in his seat, Jamie dug through the stack of files sitting on her desk. She extracted the ones she knew she would need for the confrontation she sensed was coming.

"Dr. Jameson, I need to speak to you." The young man was clearly upset. Again, Jamie wasn't surprised. Murphy had just spent the last several hours sitting by the bedside of a woman with a nasty case of diarrhea and an equally nasty disposition. "I feel you are being unfair to me."

Jamie opened one of the files. "Do you understand the gravity of the mistakes you've been making?"

"My patients would have been fine if my instructions were followed." His indignant tone irked Jamie to no end. "I didn't need to be assigned as a babysitter."

"Dr. Murphy, you need to focus. You want to be a doctor, then you had better start learning what that means. Day one, I told you first do no harm. Trust me when I tell you that the slipshod way you've been handling your patients is harmful."

"Excuse me, Doctor Jameson, but I have to disagree," Murphy arrogantly began to say. "It's more than obvious that Alvarez is your favorite."

"I don't play favorites. I want each and every intern, resident, and student who comes into this hospital to learn as much as they can." Jamie was thoroughly annoyed when Murphy rolled his eyes. She managed to hold her anger at bay and picked a file from the stack that had been sitting in front of her when Murphy decided to pay her a visit.

"Fine, you need convincing?" Jamie went over Murphy's cases one by one and pointed out the errors he had made. She closed the folders and addressed Murphy, who was squirming in his chair. "In just over an hour from now, instead of heading home and seeing my family, I get to go before the board and explain why someone of your caliber is making so many rookie mistakes."

"The board?" He gulped.

"Because of your error in misdiagnosing Darren Beauchamp, his mother hired a lawyer. There's a very good chance the hospital will be facing a lawsuit," Jamie said. "Take what I am about to tell you, not as good advice but as the gospel. C.Y.A. Cover your ass. For some doctors it means to do just what you've been doing, nothing. For me it means to be diligent. So pull your head out of your ass, do your job, and try to learn about what it means to be a doctor. If you don't, you're out of the program. Have I made myself clear?"

"Yes." He clenched his jaw as he spoke.

"In the meantime, there's a woman in bay seven I want you to treat. Her name is Diane Stone. She's a flight attendant from Indiana with a very nasty rash. I expect you to be diligent with her."

Murphy stood silently for a moment before he stormed out of her office. Jamie doubted he had seen the light. With a yawn, she glanced at the clock and felt sick. She wanted to be home, sleeping beside her wife. Instead she was about to face a very early morning meeting with the board.

"Putz," she couldn't refrain from muttering. She picked up the phone and hit speed dial. "Stella, it's Jamie. I just sent the boy wonder over to you. I've assigned him the flight attendant. The one with the STD, who insists that it's impossible for her to have a sexually transmitted disease because she only associates with nice men. Make certain he is focused and gloves up. I don't want the little dweeb to contract anything." Jamie listened as Stella assured her that she would be on Murphy's case. After she wrapped up the call with Stella, she was about to get up and brew herself another pot of coffee when another knock on her door stopped her.

"Come in."

"Hey, Dr. Jameson." Tierney greeted her with a bright smile. "Got a second?"

"Barely. What can I do for you?"

"Well, I came by to see Dr. Temple, I know I'm early but—"

"No, you're late." Jamie sighed wearily. "Why didn't you come in on the day I told you to?"

"I was going to, but I ran into trouble with this cab driver and—"

"Kris, there's no easy way to tell you this, but Dr. Temple passed away."

"For real?"

"Yes. Look, standard procedure is that you file a grievance with my supervisor. There's a problem with that since I'm filling in for Dr. Temple."

"Makes sense. You'll be taking over his spot. I mean who else are they going to get?"

"Anyone but me. The problem for you is, I'm the one who fired you. I can't review your grievance. Here is what you can do. Go down to HR and beg them to let you fill out the paperwork. I'll take it to the board and let them decide who will handle your complaint. If you want back in the program, you will go downstairs, right now. Don't stop to socialize. If you're lucky, there will be someone in at this hour. If there isn't, stay outside the office until someone shows up. If you do everything right, you might get back in for the nex rotation."

"I can't come back now?"

"No, you've already missed most of the rotation." Jamie felt her head spinning. "Go, now. Don't stop for coffee, a donut, or to chitchat."

"Okay. Thanks, Dr. Jameson."

"The girl is an idiot," Jamie said aloud when Tierney finally left her office. "I need coffee." She gathered the files she would need for the meeting. Since she no longer had the time to brew a fresh pot of coffee, she opted to stop at the coffee express booth in the main building. She rushed over and managed to purchase a large hazelnut coffee with time to spare. Her glee was short lived when Dr. Nolan cut her off at the elevators.

"Dr. Jameson, a moment of your time?"

"We'll have to talk in the elevator," she said curtly. "I'm heading upstairs."

"This won't take long. I'm here on the behalf of Dr. Murphy. It has come to my attention that you are singling out this fine young man. Using him as some sort of scapegoat as it were."

"Good heavens, this is his plan B?" She grumbled as they entered the elevator. "Look, the kid stepped in it. Either he shapes up or he's gone."

"I think you're overreacting. Making him examine a woman with a nasty infection on her genitals. Don't you think that was a little extreme?"

"Emergency medicine isn't pretty." Jamie wondered when was the last time Nolan examined a patient? "If he wants glamour, he can specialize as a nip-and-tuck man. For the moment, he's in the middle of his ER rotation. I shouldn't need to explain to you how lackluster that can be at times."

"I think you're being unduly hard on him. In fact, I'll vouch for him. After all, I was the one who accepted him into the program. I will gladly take over as his instructor."

"Fine, he's all yours. I hope you can be an inspiration to him." Jamie willing conceded.

"Thank you." Nolan seemed surprised.

"Oh, don't thank me." A thought occurred to her. "I'm on my way to see the board. Would you care to join me?"

"Yes." He was visibly stunned, yet he jumped at the chance.

"Let's go then. I believe they're waiting."

Two hours later, Jamie and Nolan emerged from the conference room. Despite her exhaustion, she felt elated. Nolan had been so desperate to show off, Jamie allowed him to present Murphy's case. It only seemed fair, since he had vouched for the young man's character. Nolan prattled on and on about how Murphy was a fine young man with a bright future. Nolan went into his version of how he felt that Jamie had intentionally been treating the upstanding doctor unfairly because he was a man.

Jamie sat there patiently while Nolan postured to prove his worth and Jamie's lack of professionalism. He did everything he could to toss Jamie under the bus, which is why she silently sat there when Dr. Flanagan inquired about what went wrong with the treatment of little Darren Beauchamp and his emergency surgery.

Nolan just stood there, having never taken a seat, and his mouth hung open. When Dr. Flanagan looked to Jamie for the answer, she explained Murphy's error and the need for closer supervision. Nolan's body shuddered as he fell into his chair. Jamie adeptly answered all of the board's questions regarding the numerous other mistakes Dr. Murphy had committed during his rotation. For the first time since she had met him, Terry Nolan was speechless.

Jamie felt a sliver of regret for allowing him to assure the board that he would personally be overseeing Murphy. He even had gone so far as to vow that he would groom him in an unbiased manner, something he strongly felt Jamie had neglected to do.

"You sandbagged me!" Nolan bellowed once they were inside the elevator and away from everyone else.

"Did I?"

"You know you did!"

"Only because I think the kid is a train wreck. You're the one who has faith in him, and as his self-appointed mentor, you needed to be there when the board determined his fate. Give yourself some credit. If not for your passionate plea regarding his character and the promise to personally look after him, they wouldn't be allowing him to stay in the program. I'll have Grace give you a copy of his file."

They stepped off the elevator.

Nolan huffed and puffed all the way to the ER. Jamie made a couple of detours in an effort to distance herself from Nolan's wrath. Sadly, he dogged her every step of the way until she stopped to hand Stella a cup of coffee.

"Want to tell me why Nolan's panties are in a twist?" Stella asked.

"You'll see." Jamie smiled when she spied Murphy rounding the corner.

CHECKMATE

"You!" Nolan screeched. "Get over here, now."

"Dr. Nolan?" Murphy smiled brightly while waving as he hurried over. "I take it things went well."

"You neglected to tell me a couple things when you came sniveling into my office. I didn't find out until I had already promised the board that I'd be your keeper. Prepare yourself to give a deposition."

"Uh, yeah, I kind of heard that. I really have to talk to a bunch of lawyers?"

"You knew and didn't tell me?"

"My God, Nolan's head is going to explode." Stella giggled while she, Jamie, and the entire nursing staff watched the scene unfold.

"Listen carefully, Murphy," Nolan said, fuming. "From this moment on, your ass is mine. First thing you can do is fetch me a latte. Mocha with a hint of crème, and a light dusting of nutmeg." Murphy stood there with his jaw hanging open. "Did I stutter, or do you need to write this down? Go."

"But—"

"I said go."

"It's a shame that kid didn't pay attention to what goes on around here." Stella laughed. "Can't believe he thought Nolan was going to be his savior."

"I hope he pulls it together," Jamie said. "He does have potential. All he needs to do is focus and work his ass off."

"If he doesn't, I pity anyone who ends up being treated by

him."

"Dr. Jameson, you're needed in reception." Grace interrupted the party.

"Grace, what are you doing back here so soon?"

"Couldn't sleep. That detective from the other day is out front and would like to speak to you."

"Which one?"

"The nice one."

"And the hits just keep on coming." Jamie groaned.

"What's going on?" Stella asked.

"Stella, you and the girls are going to have plenty to talk about today."

Jamie clung to the hope that Hiller had been barking up the wrong tree. As much as she disliked Nolan, she didn't want to see him ruin his life. Her heart sank when she entered the reception area. The grim look on Hiller's face spoke volumes.

"I'm guessing this has nothing to do with whatever it was my wife did to your athletic supporter."

"I'm afraid not." His mood only darkened.

"How can I help you?"

"I just need to ask you a few questions."

"I'll tell you what I can." Jamie braced herself, already filled with a sense of dread.

"Does Dr. Nolan have privileges at any other hospital?"

"No."

"Does he have a private practice? Or practice medicine anywhere else?"

"No." Jamie's stomach churned. "Dr. Nolan is an attending in our emergency room, and this is the only place he's allowed to practice medicine."

"Thank you. That's all I needed to know."

"Is this what I think it is?"

"I don't know. What do you think?"

"You're with narcotics, aren't you?"

"Yes."

"I see."

"You wouldn't know where I can find Dr. Nolan, would you?"

"He's in the treatment area," Jamie said. "I'll page him. I'm assuming you have a warrant for his arrest."

"Thank you. I'd rather not do this in front of a lot of people who came here for help."

"Bridget, would you page Dr. Nolan and ask him to meet me out here?" she politely asked the bored looking receptionist.

"Thank you again. You're Nolan's boss, aren't you?"

"For the time being."

"Well, you might want to tell the suits that the hospital has nothing to worry about. Everything is on Nolan."

"Still won't look good in the press."

Nolan stormed out of the treatment area. Judging by the scowl he was sporting, his mood had failed to improve. "Now, what do you want?" he barked at her, unaware of the three uniformed police officers behind him.

"This is Dr. Nolan," she said to Hiller who smiled. "Dr. Nolan, this is Detective Hiller. He would like a word with you."

"Yes?" Nolan snarled. "I am very busy, so make it quick."

"Oh, I will. Please turn around."

"What?"

"Dr. Terrence Nolan, I have a warrant for your arrest."

"What for? Is this your doing, Jameson?"

"No, your problems are your own."

"Oh, so it was your bitch wife?"

"If you're referring to my good friend CC..." Hiller spun Nolan around and placed handcuffs on him. "I suggest you zip it. In fact, Doctor, you have the right to remain silent. Anything you say can be used against you in a court of law. You have the right to an attorney. If you cannot afford one, one will be appointed by the court. Do you understand your rights?"

"Ouch!" Nolan squealed when Hiller gave the cuffs one last pinch.

"Doctor, do you understand your rights?"

"Yes, I'm not an idiot. Now tell me what this is about."

"Selling prescriptions." Hiller spun Nolan around. "As for Detective Calloway being involved, I hate to burst your bubble, but

I'm from Newton. For someone smart enough to become a doctor, you'd think you'd be smart enough to tell your pill-popping buddies to spread their refills around. The fifteen clients that we know about all went to the same pharmacy in Four Corners. The pharmacist thought the frequency of refills suspicious. When you get your one phone call, you might want to mention to your lawyer that the IRS has frozen your assets."

"What?"

"Didn't anyone tell you that you don't get to keep the money from selling drugs?"

"I didn't sell drugs."

"No, just the means to get drugs." Hiller gave him a little push. "Same thing. Dr. Jameson, thanks again. Best to CC."

Nolan was led out the front door in handcuffs, crying like a baby. Jamie blinked when she saw Murphy standing there helplessly with a cooling latte in hand.

"Is he coming back?" Murphy's voice squeaked.

"Doubtful. We'll need to get you reassigned." Jamie tried to reassure him.

"But I was on his team."

"You were his team. Dr. Nolan isn't an instructor."

"But he was on the panel that accepted me."

"Yeah, he loves joining committees," Jamie said and yawned. "Most of us try to dodge those. Since Dr. Nolan doesn't have a whole lot to pad his resume with, he volunteers for any committee that will have him. Murphy, are you about to hyperventilate?"

"No. Maybe." He suddenly gasped.

"Calm down, you'll be fine."

"Can I come back to your team?"

"No. You tried to throw me under the bus, young man. I'll find you a suitable position. In the meantime, either drink that coffee or toss it out. You can finish rounds with my team. Someone will call you with your new schedule."

"Thank you," he blurted out as he made a mad dash back inside.

"That was funny," Bridget said.

"Hysterical." Jamie dialed a now familiar number on her cell phone. "Dr. Bradford? Sir, I have bad news."

Chapter 39

"At least, my father died doing what he loved. Nothing meant more to him than a good day out on the golf course."

"What?"

"Rewind it."

"How in the hell?"

The comments kept coming when almost everyone in the conference room caught, Simon's slip. Leigh paused and reset the DVD.

"Dr. Richards?" CC's voice trembled as she watched the DVD replay.

"I told Brooks." Dr. Richards sighed. "I guess he didn't share this with you."

"In the beginning, I didn't buy into his theory."

"You never told Fisher?" Leigh said when the DVD finished playing.

"Could another inmate or a guard have told him?" Palmucci was scratching his head.

"No," Dr. Richards said. "Simon is isolated twenty-three hours a day, unless he has therapy or a visitor. He had neither that day. The guards weren't informed as to why I needed to see him. I only treat six inmates at that facility. The only reason I'm involved with their cases is because I wrote the profile on each of them. Thankfully, I videotape all of my interaction with them."

"So, you're not so much treating them as you are studying

them," Val said.

"What did I miss?" Wayne asked.

"Simon shouldn't have known his father died on a golf course," CC explained for him. "Since no one told him how or where his father died, he was either in on it or psychic."

"I still say someone tipped him." Palmucci gave a huff.

"There wasn't enough time," Dr. Richards said. CC fumbled with the remote control trying to rewind the DVD.

Leigh snatched the remote from CC's grasp. "Where do you want me to cue it?"

"The beginning," CC said sheepishly. "There, look at the way he's sitting when he's alone. He knows why he's there. That's the same cocky attitude the little prick had when we had him in the box. Max almost broke him, then all of a sudden he was all smiles just like at the end of this interview. I'm telling you, he knew Daddy was dead and all the details."

"You can't prove it," Rousseau argued. "All you have is a handful of unfortunate incidents."

"Not entirely." CC felt queasy when her boss challenged her theory. The dubious looks she was getting from everyone else did nothing to help calm her nerves. "First we have Simon's father, who turned his back on Simon and controlled his trust fund. He died from bee venom. Yet there wasn't a single mark on his body. The woman who stole the love of Fisher's life, Elizabeth Pryce, was poisoned. Billy Ryan, who at one time was Simon's alibi, until he confessed he was far too wasted to know what was happening that weekend. Professor Harding ruined Simon's GPA. Bitsy Marsden, who all throughout their teen years shunned Simon's advances, ended up with her throat slashed and lying almost naked for everyone to see.

Max, who almost got him to crack by playing the father figure, got his head bashed in and was set up to look like a dirty cop. There's one more that we just found out about. A prisoner guard named, Fernandez, who was trying to make Simon's already miserable life even more miserable, was crushed to death. Then we have Detective Brooks, who chased Simon for years. Every time we got a tip to chase after Beaumont, someone who pissed Fisher off died. Everyone on that list, at one time or another, testified against him at a competency hearing."

"Can you prove all of it?" Rousseau asked. "Or any of it?"

"No."

Val clenched her jaw. "On paper, all of these events appear to be nothing more than happenstance. I, for one, don't believe in coincidences. What I want to know is who is next?"

"Simon is probably working a short list at the moment," Dr. Richards began to say. "Based on his belief that everyone is out to get him, I would put Dr. Watkins, who is the head psychiatrist at the facility, and myself, on his list. I did the profile that helped catch him. I also wrote about him in one of my books. I listed everything from animal mutilation to setting fires and that he was a bed wetter up until he was fourteen."

"Fourteen?" Palmucci gave a squeal. "This guy couldn't fit the pattern of a serial killer whack job any better if he tried."

"No kidding," CC said. "I'm sure I'm on his short list."

"And your wife," Dr. Richards added. "After he clears his major obstacles, those of us who have testified against him, he will start with the lesser evils. I'd guess anyone who has been his legal advisor. At the moment, he seems to be focused on clearing the path. He wants his freedom."

"Maybe we should give it to him?" CC eerily suggested.

"What?" Rousseau barked.

"We could get him on the I-20 murders. After Fisher was incarcerated, I entered his DNA into CODAS. His profile was a match on three bodies. The murders happened less than a year after he killed his first victim. He was a little sloppy in those days."

"And I'm just hearing this now because?" Rousseau asked.

"Not our jurisdiction." CC squirmed in a futile effort to duck her boss's angry glare.

"Yeah, right."

"This little prick is a smarmy little bastard," Palmucci said, still watching the interview that Mulligan had been playing over and over again. "Look at him. He knew that the old man bought it on the back nine."

"When the doc failed to react, he thought he won," CC said. "Fisher's fatal flaw has always been that he assumes that he's smarter than everyone else. Look at the way he watched for a reaction. When there wasn't one, he just leaned back and smirked. I hate this guy."

"How in the hell are you ever going to prove anything?"

It didn't escape CC's notice that Palmucci was dumping the problem squarely in her lap.

"Dr. Richards," Ricky said before CC had the chance to admit she was completely clueless. "During the time frame we're looking at, who has visited Fisher?"

"Just his mother and his lawyer."

"Lawyer's name?" Val and Ricky began making notes and flipping through files.

"Eunice Cockburn."

"Really?" Val said. "Geez, anyone else willing to bet she spent high school being stuffed in her locker?"

"Probably," CC readily agreed. "She's an odd duck. I only met her once. It was during Simon's last competency hearing. She barely asked any questions."

"Simon has run through a lengthy list of legal representation," Dr. Richards said. "Scraping the bottle of the barrel isn't that uncommon for someone who has been in the system as long as he has."

"Does he have any friends inside?" Ricky asked.

"Not anymore. He had managed to convince a great number of his fellow inmates that he was a staff member. When they found out the truth, they didn't take it well. His neighbors aren't the most stable group. For the past couple of years, he's been restricted to the locked ward. He's only allowed out for one hour of exercise, meetings with his lawyer, and therapy."

"How about mail, any pen pals?" Ricky was furiously typing on his tablet.

"He gets very little mail, only from his mother now and then. His case has never been publicized, so he doesn't have the usual groupies. Lately, he has received newspaper clippings with no return address cartoons, recipes, daily events kind of a mixed bag, they appear to be harmless."

"Can you fax those to us?" Ricky asked.

"Yes, they were collected after he had a chance to read them."

"There's a fax machine here in the conference room," CC said, confused as to why anyone would be sending Fisher recipes. "The number is six-one-seven-five-five-five-nineteen-forty-six."

"Front and back," Val said. "Send us copies of both sides."

"What are you thinking?" Ricky asked her.

"Barcelona."

"Right." He smiled knowingly.

"Tell me again how you were just a glorified file clerk in the navy." CC narrowed her gaze. "Anything else for the good doctor?"

"I'd like to see Fisher's profile and any other notes you have on him," Ricky politely requested. "You can send it to my e-mail at the bureau. It will go straight to my Blackberry."

"I'll do it right away."

"Dr. Richards?" CC said. "I have one more request."

"Yes?"

"Get the hell out of town. Go someplace no one would ever think to look for you."

"I was about to suggest the same thing to you. I'm sending all the information. I would appreciate being kept up-to-date. I'm heading back to Quantico in the morning. I think I should be safe there."

Dr. Richards hung up. Everyone sat around drinking coffee and reviewing the files. Ricky studied the files on Simon on his Blackberry and tablet while the fax machine started spitting out papers. Rousseau just sat there with a sour look plastered on his face. CC couldn't sit down; she kept pacing while she silently prayed for a miracle.

"Keep going," Leigh whispered her encouragement.

"Bees and keys," CC lamely began to say, "Two instances that prove those two deaths weren't the unfortunate events they appeared to be."

"You've got nothing," Rousseau repeated.

"On the surface, no I don't. When you put the pieces together, we've got murder."

"I'm not so sure," Palmucci said.

"Why don't we take a look at Fisher's mail?" Val suggested before Palmucci could further express his displeasure.

As they flipped through the fax sheets, CC felt defeated. They were indeed benign: nothing but recipes, random articles, and comic strips. She couldn't understand why Val and Ricky seemed excited.

"Want to share with the rest of the class?" CC asked them.

"It's a simple system," Val carefully explained. "Here we have a copy of the comic strips from the San Diego Times. Nothing noteworthy, unless you look at the back." She held up the paper. Everyone leaned over squinting and no one seemed to see what she was excited about. "Bottom right hand corner." She pressed the paper closer.

"Memorial services for Malcolm Fisher," CC read aloud. "It cuts off there."

"Now look at this one, the recipe for banana nut bread." Val thrust another sheet of paper across the table. "On the front we have a recipe and on the back..." She flipped the page over.

"There it is," Leigh exclaimed. "Alumnus attacked at the university training track. Bitsy Marsden, class of... it cuts off there."

Frantically, everyone began sifting through the printouts. The room filled with murmurs as they discovered the blurbs carefully hidden on the back of each newspaper article.

"Clever son of a bitch." CC was disgusted. "On the surface, it looks like he's reading something completely lame."

"On the back, just a snippet small enough to slip under the radar," Val said. "Just enough information to let Fisher know the job had been done."

"Just like I told you, Palmucci," CC said. "This is why your mystery caller was determined that you identify Max as the victim."

"Proof of death from the hit man?" Palmucci shook his head. "You still haven't explained the why."

"Fisher is a typical sociopath. Nothing is his fault."

"But how could he hire a hit man when he's locked up?" Wayne sounded completely bewildered. "He's in a secure mental health facility. It's the super max version of a booby hatch."

"Sadly, the best place to find a criminal is in prison. Granted, Fisher isn't in your typical prison, but he is surrounded by criminals," CC wearily explained. For someone who worked in law enforcement, Wayne could be extremely naïve at times. Much to her frustration, the room grew quiet.

"Look at the time line." Leigh was clearly frustrated by the lack of enthusiasm. "A tip comes in, and someone who knew and betrayed Fisher dies. Although the burner phone couldn't be traced, the calls all came from the same areas where the murders took place. Beaumont was an excellent decoy. News of his untimely passing will be public knowledge soon. That's going to make our enforcer more than a little edgy. We need to move quickly."

"Officially, all I can do is assist the US Marshals with the aiding and abetting," Mills said. "Unofficially, I'm with you."

"I don't know how long we can stick it out," Val said. "None of our bosses are thrilled, so we don't have a lot of time."

"Understood."

"Flying by the seat of your pants has never stopped you before," Rousseau said to CC.

"Whatever you need," Wayne promised.

"Same here," McManus said. "I'm working a suspected homicide. That might give me a little leverage."

"Palmucci?" CC was curious as to which way he would lean now that he had all the facts and it looked like a lost cause. Palmucci had already made it clear he needed a winner. CC doubted if he cared how he got his win.

"I always said you had balls, Calloway," he said gruffly. "Someone tried to kill a cop in my backyard. That doesn't fly with me. I'm in."

CC wanted to believe Palmucci. She just didn't trust that he wouldn't jump ship at the first sign of trouble. As for the others, she had to have faith that they had her back. The meeting wrapped up, and everyone went on their way with the notable exception of Rousseau.

"I'm stepping outside for some fresh air," he said. "Join me."

CC understood that by fresh air her boss meant he needed a smoke, which meant he was stressed. Filled with a sense of dread, she followed after him as he huffed and puffed his way out of the building. It took time to reach a designated smoking area. Rousseau took a seat on a wooden bench located next to an ashtray. CC tightened her long coat around her body and joined him.

Her nervousness grew when he just sat there, lighting up one cigarette after another. On paper, cops weren't allowed to smoke anymore unless, like her commanding officer, they joined the force prior to 1986. Still they weren't supposed to be seen smoking while in uniform. CC suspected that was why the dingy hidden area cleared out when the boss showed up. He snubbed out his third cigarette and was lighting up his fourth when he finally looked at her.

"You never smoked?"

"No, sir. I was afraid I would set a bad example for Stevie."

"My wife quit about fourteen years ago. She didn't want us to smoke around our grandkids. Can't smoke at home. Can't smoke at work. I don't drink, so how am I going to relieve my stress? And now I have to walk to Rhode Island just to light up. What kind of sense does that make?"

She was about to make a smart-ass comment but thought better of it. She just sat there with her hands shoved in her pockets and waited for the axe to fall.

"Damn clever."

"Making people smoke out by a smelly dumpster?" She questioned nervousness growing steadily with each passing moment.

"Not that. When I was watching the tape, I could see he's

the same cocky son of a bitch he was when you first had him in the box. Bastard is still too smart for his own good. Talk about your perfect alibi. He's locked up in a federal loony bin. The victims seem random. Their deaths, for the most part, appear to be mishaps. Until you had people look closer."

"Not just me," CC said. "Cops in Wisconsin were really bugged they didn't find any makeup in that house. The ME in San Francisco couldn't let it go, and Brooks was on it from the get-go. I should have started looking sooner. The whole time I was chasing Beaumont, I knew someone was playing me and I still chased after him."

"Don't beat yourself up for going after a child molester. Now impress me with how you're going to catch this cocksucker?"

"I'm in the same spot I was in a decade ago. I've connected the dots, I know in my heart that it's him, and just like the last time I went after this bastard, I can't make a case. I doubt I can get him to cough out a confession a second time. I know my career is on the line."

"I'm not worried about your career. Right now, you and Mulligan are working a suspicious drug overdose. Palmucci is investigating an assault and battery case. McManus is looking at a suspicious drowning. The Feds are working a fugitive case. On paper, none of these cases are connected. If you happen to chat with one another and find connections, we can just chalk it up to interagency cooperation."

"If you're backing me on this, what has you worried so much that you're blowing through a pack of smokes in record time?"

"I'm not worried about you making the department look bad. I'm afraid you're going to get yourself killed."

CC couldn't respond. It was a very real possibility. Rousseau fired up another cigarette while CC contemplated her fate.

"I'm glad Mulligan has your back," he said in a quiet tone. "I'm moving her over this week."

"So soon?"

"Andy's gone."

"I heard about his little mishap."

"Mishap? That's being polite. I spent the morning with him and his union rep. Both of us bent over backwards trying to get him to take the retirement package. The stubborn jackass wants to fight it. I've got Crowley waiting in my office. I'm not looking forward to having my ass chewed out."

"Crowley." CC gave a sneer and groaned before she thought better of it. "Sorry, I know he was the number-one badge in this town forever. I also know that even though he's retired now, he still carries a lot of weight."

"Not as much as he thinks he does."

"I just can't get past his lack of understanding that this is the twenty-first century. I heard what he said after I was shot. 'The stupid slit licker got what she deserved.' He thinks that the only use the department has for women is as file clerks and meter maids."

"I know. He's a dinosaur who thinks the only good cop is an Irishman. Hate to say it, but there are still cops who agree with him. But not as many as you think. The bastard is stewing in my office, convinced that he'll order me to take Andy back and I'll just do it."

"What are you going to do with Andy?"

"He's screwed up more times than I can count. He's

suspended without pay pending a hearing."

"Damn."

"Compared to worrying about you walking around with a target on your back, Andy's bitching and moaning is nothing. Calloway, promise me you will be careful. I mean it. Fisher's had a hard-on for you from the get-go. The guy is locked up and had his father whacked on a golf course. Promise me, no heroics."

"I promise."

* * *

After dealing with her unusual day, Jamie had a late meeting with her staff. She hated being in charge. She knew she didn't possess one tenth of Jack's poise. He could handle the suits, the insurance companies, whining doctors, clueless interns, and arrogant residents with ease. Jamie, on the other hand, often resorted to threatening to set someone on fire. Even she had to admit it wasn't a very diplomatic approach.

"Okay." She felt very uneasy. The people who surrounded her were her peers. Very few of them would be eager to follow her lead. "I think we can all agree that this week has been an exercise in insanity." The wry comment seemed to put the others at ease. "If you haven't heard, during the interim, I'll be running the ER while still maintaining my position."

"And you sleep when?" Dr. Butler asked with concern.

"Rarely," Jamie honestly answered. "Look, I don't want to be sitting in Jack's chair. Not now, or in the future. Hopefully, the suits will name his replacement soon. In the meantime, we have to keep going. Our biggest problem at the moment is scheduling shifts. I've been reviewing the intern and resident hours and things just don't jive. We have some kids that are busting their butts. Alvarez has worked back-to-back doubles for a week straight. I put her on a schedule that would allow her to work around her home situation. I know everyone has life that, for some of these kids, includes another job. So why is it I see that Jessica Huggings has failed to work a single night or weekend, and quite often, she's out the door by mid-afternoon?"

"She's my problem child," Schumacher said. "Her work is adequate at best, mostly because she's convinced she knows more than everyone else. I told her to work her assigned shifts. The little darling went behind my back and traded shifts. She keeps trading until she's free and clear for the weekend."

"I'll swap with you," Jamie said. "I'll take Huggings, and you get Murphy. He was supposed to go to Nolan but..."

"Yeah, what happened?" someone asked.

"Dr. Nolan has been a very bad boy. Dr. Bradford has suspended him indefinitely, which means we need to not only work out the students' schedules, but our schedules. Nolan is going to leave a gap."

"Not much of one," one of the doctors said. There was a collective snickering around the table. "I swear the caliber of students dipped after he became chair of the selection committee."

"Okay." Jamie bit her tongue before she could agree. "Let's get through this."

"What about you, Jamie?" Schumacher asked. "You can't keep doing twenty-four seven. As much as we appreciate you busting your butt, you need some downtime. Chances are you're going to end up on days."

"I'm not taking Jack's job. I'm certain the board already has several qualified candidates in mind."

"So, if one of us put our name in, you wouldn't be offended?" Dr. Marcia Jacobs asked. "I think most of us didn't because…"

"We assumed it would be you," Dr. Carver finished for her.

"If any of you are interested, feel free. But I'd do it soon. The suits want to get things back to normal as quickly as possible."

"I heard Nolan put his name in before Jack's body was cold."

"Basically, and just so we are perfectly clear, I have already declined the position."

"You told God no thanks?"

"Pretty much, now let's finalize the schedules."

Jamie managed to get through everything and clear the conference room in quick fashion. She glanced at her watch, wondering if she had time to swing by the house. She didn't.

"I think you're making a mistake," Marcia noted when she caught up to Jamie who was giving Grace the new schedules and a list of instructions. "If you don't take the job, God knows who we'll get stuck with. They might even bring in some pencil pusher from the outside."

"That's how I got here."

"You were a well-sought-after ER doctor. Jack scored with the brass when he got you to sign on."

"And now I have a home and a family here. No way I'm going to allow this place to swallow me whole. Put your name in, Marcia.

Quite frankly, I'll just be happy going back to working my normal hours and teaching my kids."

Marcia offered her thanks and dashed off. Jamie looked at her watch. She could grab lunch or dive into whatever drama had been brewing while she was in meetings. She was afraid that if she went home, she'd be tempted not to return.

"Why don't you just take a break?" Stella's face was filled with concern. "Catch your breath. The madness will still be here when you get back."

"That's what I'm afraid of." Jamie thought she just needed to clear her head. "As sage as your advice is, with everything that's going on, I need to stay."

"Since you won't listen to me, I can't be held responsible for when you snap," Stella said lightheartedly.

* * *

Jamie sat in her office and tried to dig her way out of the mounds of paperwork that had magically appeared overnight. She looked up when Dr. Bradford entered without bothering to knock.

"This can't be good," she grumbled as she offered him a seat.

"It's not as bad as it could be," he said with a halfhearted smile.

"The hospital is settling with the Beauchamp family. The standard lump sum and a nondisclosure agreement."

"Good. I'm sorry about that. I should have been more hands-on with that kid. I feel like I'm letting my students down. I'm not there to keep them from screwing up. Some of them have shined, but the rest aren't getting the education they signed on for."

"There's a simple solution. Step into Jack's shoes permanently."

"Give up teaching and practicing medicine?" Jamie groaned. "I'm sorry, sir. But as I told you the other day, I'm not savvy enough to deal with the politics. You seem to forget my little habit of threatening people. I love teaching. I love emergency medicine. I'm not cut out to be a pencil pusher."

"You could do both. Fiscally, the board would be thrilled."

"I'd be doing half the job on both fronts. These kids know enough to pass the boards, but they don't know how to be doctors. Despite being a hard-ass, I'm very proud of my students at the end of their rotation. I'd like to think they are prepared to be doctors."

"It's why we hired you. There's no way I can talk you into accepting the job? Jamie, you've earned it."

"I'm an ER doc with a surly reputation. That I've earned. You need someone who can not only save a dying man, but schmooze the suits. Trust me. I'd be out on my ass in a week."

"You are blunt. Well, I've got a stack of applicants to sift through. One less since Nolan got himself locked up. Heard the wife left him the moment the IRS put a lien on everything. I have to say, I am not sorry to see him go. Speaking of which, Murphy dodged a bullet this time. Just so we are clear, the kid is hanging by a thread. He committed a cardinal sin. He cost the hospital money. Is he back on your team?"

"No, I traded him for another problem child. I'll give his supervisor a heads-up."

"Just out of curiosity, do you have any suggestions as to whom you'd like to see become your new boss?"

"As a matter of fact, I do."

Chapter 40

Ricky and Val were in awe as they drove up the long driveway bordered by a sprawling landscape.

"How do you get this much green in the middle of San Diego?" Ricky said as they parked the rental car in front of the stately home known as Greystone. The less than humble manor had housed members of the Grayson and Fisher clan for longer than California had been a state.

"I know the kid came from money, but this is ridiculous." Val shook her head in awe.

"I'll bet you a twenty a butler answers the door."

"It will be the maid."

Ricky's mood turned sour when they announced themselves to the maid. They were escorted to the sitting room and waited for the lady of the house. Unable to sit still, Val paced around the room. She inspected every knickknack, hoping to find a clue that would explain how a life so well provided for could go so horribly wrong.

"Good morning," a frail-looking woman said. Cynthia Fisher's voice was tired, befitting her vacant grey eyes. Val noticed the lady of the house seemed far more interested in looking at the hardwood floor instead of drawing her attention towards her guests. Val was curious. Was the lady simply rude or was there something fascinating about the floor? The only thing Val noticed were a series of divots dug into the fine wood, which seemed out of place with the rest of the pristine home.

"An eyesore," Mrs. Fisher said to Val. "It took me months to pick out the perfect wood for this room, Brazilian cherry. Malcolm strode in wearing his golf shoes. Day in and day out, he'd stroll in and ruin the floor. I'd replace it, but what sense would that make? He'll only do it again. For the life of me, I'll never understand why he loves that game. Chasing a little ball around all day long. Seems somewhat futile when you think about it."

"Men can be infuriating," Val said in an attempt to placate her.

"We hate to disturb you during this difficult time."

"You are here about my son. Why can't you people leave us alone?"

"We have a few questions regarding your husband's passing." Val began not certain Mrs. Fisher was aware that her husband had died.

"He went to play golf and didn't come home."

The finality in her voice disturbed Val. "Yes, so tragic."

The woman seemed completely bewildered.

"It's a shame your son wasn't allowed to attend the services."

"You people are responsible for that."

"When your husband passed away, what was his relationship with Simon?" Ricky carefully posed the question.

"Simon blamed his father for turning his back on him. Now they will never have a chance to make peace. Something else I blame you people for. Now, if you don't mind, I would like you to leave my home."

"Understandable, to say the least," Val said as gently as she could muster. "Just one last question. When your husband passed away, did Simon take control of his inheritance?"

"Other than his legal fees, what would he spend his money on?" She gave a dismissive wave. "If you have any further questions, talk to his attorney. Don't bother me again."

* * *

"You're really getting the hang of that phone." Val yawned, exhausted from the constant traveling and sifting through files. The only thing she learned from their visit with Simon's mother was that the woman was broken. Down the road it might help them. At that moment, all it provided was proof of how much damage one person could inflict. She and Calloway were videoconferencing. Val was hoping for some insight regarding Simon Fisher.

"Yes," CC said. "Tired?"

"Exhausted. We haven't learned anything that we didn't already know. I've been going through Dr. Richards's notes and the profile she did on Fisher. There was a shrink back in his prep school days. He refused to talk to us, although he did say that he wasn't surprised when Dr. Richards informed him of Simon's fate. Any hints on how I should handle him?"

"Don't. In fact, stay out of the room." CC carefully instructed. "Ricky will have a better shot. Fisher feels entitled. Everyone is beneath him, especially women, with the exception of his mother. If he suspects that you're gay, he'll shut down. Ricky won't have an easy time, because he's Hispanic, but he'll fare better than you will. What you need is an old white guy who reminds him of Daddy."

"Didn't you get to him by flaunting your sexuality?" Val questioned.

"No, I irked him because he thought I was trying to steal his girlfriend. At times, his anger towards me was more of a hindrance than an edge. At his hearings, it's an edge. Simply showing up and flaunting my relationship freaks him out. The board gets an up close and personal view of just how big of a whack-a-doodle he is. The way I got him was to catch him at a moment when his guard was down. For the first time that we know of, his intended victim escaped. He wasn't thinking clearly, and I used it to confuse him even further."

"Dr. Richards agrees. Still, I'd like a chance to rattle his cage."

"You could always flash him the mermaid on your ass. Might turn him on."

"My what?"

"Hey, I wish I didn't know about it, but I do. That's what you get for sleeping with my sister."

"Get over it. She did."

"I'm not so sure."

"What?"

"Nothing." CC quickly backed off. "Let's just focus on Fisher. You can deal with your love life later. Just be careful. Fisher's biggest asset is that he's smart. Fortunately, it's also his biggest downfall."

"Thanks for the advice. We'll let you know how it goes." Val groaned and disconnected the call.

"After reviewing everything," Ricky said, "including Fisher's history of bed-wetting that continued past puberty, possibly arson, the college professor's belief that it was Fisher who set fire to his office, and let us not forget the neighbor's pets turning up dead and mutilated, what surprises me the most is that this guy didn't start killing sooner. It's like he took a course on how to grow up to be a serial killer."

"There has to be something we can use to get the little freak to crack," Val said. "The only things I can think of would be considered illegal not to mention inhumane. Did you dig up anything useful on his fellow inmates? Somebody had to help him find a gun."

"Nothing. I'll keep looking. I'd really like to know how some dill weed in a maximum security booby hatch pulled this off. How do you want to play this? Calloway told you to stand down."

"I know. He's smart and narcissistic. I can't believe I get to spend the day with a self-centered know-it-all. Then again, that could work." A sly smile emerged on Val's face. "Since he's so much smarter than us, let him prove it. There's nothing a know-it-all likes better than explaining things to the rest of us idiots. I think we play it as unconcerned cop and inept cop."

"Can I be…"

"No, you're inept. Break out those dweeby glasses. You know the ones. Dorky black frames and coke-bottle lenses."

"I hate you."

"You love me. Come on, let's make this weasel sing. My vacation is on the line."

"You only have yourself to blame. If you had just dropped off that perp in Connecticut and come home, you'd be all rested and relaxed by now. But, no, you just had to jump jurisdiction."

"Couldn't help myself."

* * *

"Are you certain you don't want to link with Calloway? I can wear my earpiece and stream her in via video. Fisher would never know."

"Ricky, no." They made their way through security. "We can handle this guy. You forget she only bagged him the first time because she got lucky."

"I don't know if I'd call it luck. Sounds more like persistence."

"Looks like every other federal lockup," Val said once they made it through security.

"What did you expect?" The guard who was with them asked. "I'm Lt. Ronan. I'll be your escort."

"Thank you for your assistance, Lt. Ronan," Ricky said graciously. "What can you tell us about Simon Fisher?"

"He's a bucket of fuck. He landed himself in Candy Land in record time."

"Candy Land?" Val already sensed the answer.

"That's the nickname for the lockdown unit. He's locked up by himself in a five by nine cell. He's allowed to go to therapy and gets one hour in the cage. That's the four by twelve fenced-in area he gets his recreation time in. Unless he gets a visit from his lawyer or Mommy, the douche bag is restricted to his cell."

"Sounds like you don't like him very much, or do you just dislike all your charges?" Val pressed.

"I treat everyone with respect if they respect me. Fisher tops my list of pissants who think the world owes them a favor."

"How's his diet?" Val smirked as the lieutenant escorted them to a conference room where they would be allowed to interview Fisher.

"Same as the others. Burgers, pasta, chili-mac, and water. All meals are served on Styrofoam trays, and his only utensil is a thin version of a spork."

"No soft drinks, bottled water, or coffee?"

"Not in the budget."

"Sounds like fine dining," Val said as a jest.

"It's what he's earned." Ronan glared down at the paper cup Val held. "Best finish that coffee. Waving it around is like poking a bear."

"We'd like to videotape our interview," Ricky said as they entered the sterile room.

"No problem." He nodded. "Seriously Deputy finish your coffee. You do not want to get the little freak to get his panties in a twist."

"You don't say," Val casually answered.

"Wait here. I'll have Fisher brought up as soon as possible," Lt. Ronan said with a knowing look in his eyes.

"Thank you."

Val flipped the lid off the cup of gourmet coffee she had fought tooth and nail to bring in.

"Smells great." Ricky looked through the files he had stacked on the table. "That all part of your master plan?"

"Fisher's multiple infractions include causing a ruckus over not being able to get a decent cup of coffee. Smelling this ought to get a rise out of him."

"Taunting an inmate with coffee when he's only allowed tap

water?"

"You know me, Ricky. I will use whatever I need to get the job done. If I had to, I'd bring in a half-naked hooker waving a fresh-baked apple pie. Lucky for us, Fisher is accustomed to the finer things in life. Like a good cup of Joe."

The door opened, and Ricky quickly donned the thick, clumsy eyeglasses. While Val slumped down in her chair and plastered a bored look on her face, Ricky frantically flipped through his files, appearing to be helpless.

"I'm not saying a word without my lawyer," Simon said once Lt. Ronan shackled him to the table.

"Fair enough," Val said and yawned. "Come on, Dick, the man wants his lawyer."

"Deputy, need I remind you that this is my case," Ricky sputtered in a squeaky voice. "Just drink your coffee if you're not going to help."

"I need to let it cool off." Val stretched her arms above her head. "Can't rush a good cup of coffee. Isn't that right, Doc?"

"The lady is correct," Fisher said. "Hawaiian?"

"Jamaican blue mountain."

"Excellent choice." Fisher licked his lips.

"Would you like a sip?" Val casually offered.

"Deputy! You can't offer him any beverages. Good heavens, woman, don't they teach you people anything?" Ricky screeched.

"My mother taught me not to raise my voice when it wasn't necessary. Why don't you be a good boy and call the doctor's lawyer? And be quick about it. I have dinner reservations."

"Don't waste your time, Agent," Fisher said. "My attorney is out of town."

"Seems like we've wasted your time, Dr. Fisher." Val smiled and nudged her coffee closer. Fisher reached for it, only to fail when Ricky snatched it away. "Now, that was rude," Val said. "It's only coffee. What did you think he was going to do, caffeinate us to death?"

"A hot, scalding beverage! Your lack of common sense is appalling."

"You know what I find appalling? The FBI wasting my time with this malarkey you call a case." Val emphasized her point by making quotation marks when she stressed the word *case*. "I can't believe that our government wastes money on crap like this. Oh, by the way, Dr. Fisher, this session is being recorded."

"That's quite all right. As I stated before, I won't be answering any questions without my lawyer. Since she's out of town, I guess you can save the taxpayers' money and be on your way."

"You heard the man." Val popped out of her chair. "I told you from the get-go, this was a waste. Thank you, Dr. Fisher. Sorry for intruding on your day."

"No worries. It isn't like I have anywhere to be."

"Good point. Sad to say, the only way to extend this little visit is if you waive your right to legal counsel." Val nudged her coffee just a little closer. She was delighted when Fisher appeared to be salivating. She felt her stomach churn when he leaned back.

"I don't think so." He had a smug expression. "Nice try."

"That means we can go. Come on, Agent Dick, I need to get

ready for my dinner date at Stromboli's."

"Stromboli's?" Fisher gulped and his beady eyes glazed over. "Nice place."

"Yes it is." Val couldn't resist smirking. In reality, she'd be lucky if she and Ricky had a chance to stop at Burger King. "I already have my meal planned. I'm starting with oysters on the half shell. For my main course, I'm going for lobster ravioli in a white cream sauce. If I survive, the triple chocolate expresso truffles are to die for."

"I know." Simon sighed, and his confident posture slipped.

"The food here must leave a lot to be desired." She prodded him.

"It is pure unadulterated swill, and that's just the coffee. The rest is a mess of overcooked starches. Not fit for a pigsty."

"This is what happens when you murder innocent women." Ricky wagged his finger.

"If I had committed such horrible acts, I would deserve this vile treatment. I happen to be innocent."

Val sat down and reclined in the uncomfortable chair. She watched Fisher out of the corner of her eye when she slid her coffee closer to herself and took a sip.

"Mr. Fisher," Ricky said, "on March twenty-seventh in two thousand three you were busted for having a laptop in your cell."

"I don't see my lawyer." Simon easily dismissed Ricky. "And it is *Dr.* Fisher. Don't you have anything to add?" he asked Val who was yawning.

"No. Your innocence or guilt isn't my concern. If you're guilty, then you are where you belong. If you were wrongly convicted, you have a lawyer, one I'm certain you're paying a very high price for."

"You have no idea. Then why are you here?"

"Bureaucratic horse manure. I'm supposed to be on vacation. But thanks to this yo-yo here." She jerked her thumb at Ricky. "I'm stuck following his sorry ass around."

"Dr. Fisher," Ricky said. "You seem to have accumulated quite a few infractions during your internment."

"Big deal," Val said. "The guy is locked up. He has to do something with his time. I'm certain the officials here are more than capable of handling it. If I had to guess, I'd be willing to bet you spent your time at Quantico watching reruns of the X-Files. I don't care what that bitch back in Boston said, the good doctor can't even get a decent cup of Joe, never mind hatch some convoluted scheme to make her look bad."

"I have to agree with the lady, Agent Dick. This does seem like a waste of time, not to mention the taxpayers' dollars."

"Dr. Fisher, if you are that eager to get back to your cell..." Ricky tersely began to say.

"Not at all." Fisher laughed, once again reclining his posture and beaming.

Val took one look at Fisher's smug expression, and it was clear that he would love to spend the day yanking Ricky's chain. Thankfully, Ricky had decided not only to allow the facility to record the session, but a small camera had been added on the lapel of his blazer. Pleased with the way things were going, Val took another sip of coffee, fully aware that Fisher was watching her every move.

"So, Agent Dick," Fisher said in a snarky tone, "is this why you came to see me? To tell me the government is wasting time and money listening to the ramblings of a crooked cop? Just what is she trying to frame me for this time?"

"These are very serious allegations," Ricky began to say.

"Oh please," Val said. "A mugging gone bad, some pervert cross-dresser, and a dirty cop. You know, I think she was in cahoots with her drug-dealing partner."

"You should listen to the lady, Dicky." Fisher had a confident smirk. "My neighbor was attacked by a gang of vicious thugs. As for my former professor, I always said there was something wrong with that man. Don't even get me started on how corrupt the police are in Boston."

Val didn't react; she just stretched and took another lazy sip of her coffee. Ricky ignored the statement and perused his files. Fisher was watching their every move. When they failed to react to his knowledge, his confident smirk only grew. Everything she had learned about Fisher was true. He not only thought he was the smartest guy in the room, he needed to prove it. On the surface, it appeared that her plan just might work.

"Hey, Dicky boy, you've got a question for the doctor? Tick tock. Stromboli's won't hold my reservation."

"Hold your water." Ricky managed to look lost. "On February eleventh, two thousand three, you were cited for having a cell phone in your possession. Care to tell me how you got it?"

"Really?" Fisher laughed. "I'm in prison. Well, not your ordinary prison. Some of my neighbors here are really off the charts. Still they are criminals, and some do possess certain skills." Fisher looked from Ricky to Val, his contempt clearly evident. "He doesn't seem very organized."

"No kidding." Val gave a grunt. "How's the appeal going?"

"My lawyer is working night and day. Once I'm out of here, I'm suing the lot of them, the keepers in here and that dyke cop who framed me."

"Framed you?" Ricky said.

"Did you see my mug shot? I was beaten to within an inch of my life."

"Wait," Val said. "I think I glanced at that. Weren't you attacked by Janie? She claimed she was defending herself."

"Poor Janie. That dyke twisted her thinking. Janie has nothing to fear from me. It was that cop who was sniffing around her. I need to get out of here to protect her from those kinds of people."

"You just never know with that kind." Val nodded in agreement. Internally, she wanted to smack Fisher. Calloway had been right. Dr. Simon Fisher was just as crazy as he was smart. Something Val found to be a very dangerous combination. She gave Ricky a nod to inform him that it was time to go. Fisher had already told them what they came there to find out. He was involved, and there was no way they could prove it.

Ricky peered over his goofy eyeglasses, and his look begged for more time. Val shrugged, not feeling confident that anything would come of it. Ricky pursed his lips before returning his attention to the stack of paperwork.

"Dr. Fisher, at what age did you stop wetting your bed?"

Fisher barked out a laugh. "That's the best you got? Please. Dr. Richards should write fiction. In fact she already does. My father,

God rest his soul, was confused, and she manipulated him."

"Actually, the statement regarding your little problem came from your mother. That's how she referred to it, 'Simon's little problem.'"

"What?" Fisher's face turned beet red. "No, it was my father. Mother still sees the truth. She knows I'm an innocent victim."

"Innocent victim?" Ricky enunciated slowly.

"I know your associate doesn't care one way or another, but I was framed."

"You keep telling yourself that, Doc." Ricky snorted with disgust. "Just like you keep insisting that you didn't set Professor Harden's office on fire after you almost failed his class."

"Why would I bother? I took the class again and fared much better with a more enlightened professor. One who, I might add, wasn't a pervert who liked to play dress-up."

"Different class at a different college. You switched schools a lot. Why is that?"

"I expect the best," Simon said. "I was extremely disappointed in the education, or rather lack thereof, I was being offered."

"You've been getting some interesting mail lately. Planning on baking a cake?"

"Agent Dick." Simon chuckled. "The outside world is filled with crazy characters. I can't stop some poor lonely woman from sending me mail. The guy in the next cell, Tim Doriean, is in here for killing his pregnant wife. Bolted her inside the household freezer. Kept her there for over a year before someone figured it out. At least once a week, he gets a letter from some misguided woman begging him to marry her. There are some seriously deranged people out there."

"I've got a question for you, Dr. Fisher," Val said casually and took another sip of her coffee. "If you're innocent, then why did you confess? This has nothing to do with the case. I'm just curious. It sounds like you got a raw deal."

"I didn't confess." Simon scoffed at the idea. "Haven't you been listening? I was framed by a jealous dyke. I've warned Janie time and time again to stay away from those people. Just not natural."

"No kidding." Val pretended to agree. "You must be worried. Janie's back in Boston under the influence of that deviant, and you're stuck in here."

"I don't know why she doesn't listen to me. That will change once I'm out of here."

"I hope you're free very soon. I'd hate to think about someone I cared about hanging around with that type. Agent Dick, are we done yet?"

"No."

"Dr. Fisher has informed us that he has nothing to say. Until his lawyer is available, we're wasting our time. Hell, even if his lawyer were here, we'd be wasting our time."

"Fine." Ricky pretended to fuss before he called for the guard.

"Holy crap," Val said once Simon was escorted from the room. "Now I understand why Calloway called for the clown wagon instead of letting it go to trial."

"No kidding." Ricky gulped. "He's nuts. This guy really believes that Janie is alive. We need to drop in on Fisher's lawyer. She's in LA. I want to wrap this up before we find another body."

"I agree. Now that we've tipped our hand, he knows that we know. Calloway has to be number one on his hit list. I'd like to be in Boston, if anything happens. This guy let a child molester run wild. I want to be the one to grab him by the short hairs."

"You believe Fisher is behind this?" Ricky gloated.

"So do you. The guy knew too much. Pity we can't use it. Even if we got the tape in, Fisher can just claim his lawyer or his mommy told him about the unfortunate events. It doesn't help that the guy is a couple clowns short of a circus."

"I'll send a copy of the video to Calloway, then we can hit the road."

"Hurry. It will take her forever to figure out how to play the video."

"Done, let's go."

* * *

It did take CC a good amount of time to open the video message. Thankfully Leigh Mulligan intervened and loaded it onto her laptop.

"Look at the cocky bastard," CC said with disgust as they watched the video at her desk.

"Janie Jensen fought back?" Leigh asked, the confusion evident in her voice.

"Not that we know of. The only victim we know that fought back was the surviving victim."

"Who was that?"

"My wife."

"But Brown said Janie?"

"The twitchy little freak thinks she's alive. He confuses his victims with Janie. My wife *Jamie* really confused him. It's the reason we took a plea. The little bugger really is nuts, legally nuts. The truth is, we never had enough evidence to ensure a conviction."

"And yet you still got him. Amazing. Okay, so other than tipping her hand, what did Brown accomplish?"

"Now that he knows that they know, he'll step up his game."

"That would be interesting if it weren't so freaking insane."

CC looked up at Leigh, who was studying the board she had created. "We had to push him." CC tried to reason with her new partner. "Worst-case scenario, I've been moved way up on the hit parade."

"What is the best-case scenario?"

"I've been moved up on the hit parade. That or Simon's goon will take an interest in Ricky. Either way we'll be on the alert."

"Seriously?" Leigh sputtered. "The best and the worst outcome is a target on your back. I don't know."

"Honestly, neither do I. We're just playing a hunch. Maybe the background check on Fisher's playmates will give us a leg up."

"A leg up on what?" Palmucci entered the conference room.

"Who kidnapped the Lindberg baby. Got any ideas?"

"You're a real smart-ass, Calloway. What's going on with your grand plan? So far all I've seen is nothing but smoke and mirrors."

"Best I can do."

"If that's your best, we're all screwed. I got a good case against your partner."

"Take your best shot, Palmucci. In the meantime, Leigh will play you a video we've been watching. I need to talk to my boss, but he's locked in with Crowley."

"That cannot be good." Leigh cued up the tape for Palmucci. "Didn't Crowley retire a few years ago? Why is he butting in on this business with Andy?"

"Because he can. He was the number-one badge in this city forever and as backward as the day is long. He still thinks that women shouldn't be on the streets."

"The first time I met him, he referred to me as a greasy wop," Palmucci said. "Unless you're an Irishman, Crowley doesn't think you should be wearing a badge."

"Nice," Mulligan said. "So he's in there chewing the captain a new one because Andy is a good old boy?"

"Yes." CC glanced over to the Captain's office. "I'm glad you're here, Mulligan. But I have to say I miss the coffee the guys were bringing me every morning."

"It's no secret that almost everyone wanted Max's seat."'

"I hate this little tool!" Palmucci slammed his fist on the desk. "He did everything but say that he's in on it. The little dingle berry needs to have his arse kicked."

"I couldn't agree more."

Everyone in the squad room jumped when the door to the captain's office flew open. Crowley stomped out, his face red and the veins in his neck bulging.

"Listen to me, you stupid Canuck. You do what you're told."

"Or?" Rousseau confidently challenged. "If you'd like to testify on Andy's behalf, feel free."

"Shove it." Crowley stormed out of the squad room.

"Like a breath of fresh air, isn't he?" Palmucci returned his attention to the video. "Hey, what's the word on Mac C? I need to get my bets for Sunday in."

"I can't get through to him," CC said. "Keep it down about Mac if you don't mind."

"Try him again," Palmucci grumbled.

"Fine," CC snapped unclipping her phone. Quickly her mood turned surly when she was unable to get it to dial her uncle's number.

"Here, let me." Leigh snatched the cell phone from CC's grasp. "You were streaming real-time video to him."

"Great. I'm putting my career in the hands of a woman who can't work her phone." Palmucci shivered. "Oops, your CO does not look happy."

"Calloway, my office, now!"

"Sucks to be you." Palmucci gloated.

"No kidding."

"Tell me you have something!" Rousseau said before she had a chance to close the door.

"Nothing we didn't already know."

"Not what I was hoping to hear."

"We've just confirmed that all of the unfortunate mishaps weren't mishaps. Fisher probably knows that we're on to him."

"Oh, goody. Any other happy news?"

"No, sir."

"Calloway, what's going on with you?"

"I wish I had a better foothold on this." She confessed. It feels just like the last time I went up against this little puke."

"It would help if we had a clue who we're looking for."

"True enough. Right now I don't know who to trust."

"You think there's someone on the inside?"

"Wouldn't surprise me. At this moment, I trust you and Max. Everyone else involved with this farce is new."

"The Feds sure, but what about Mulligan?"

"I'd like to trust her and Brown, but let's not forget the boatload full of Feds that showed up out of nowhere, Palmucci, and the rest of the lot. Everyone came on board right about the time Beaumont showed up. I'd like to think I'm not working with that psycho's handyman, but how can I be sure?"

"You can't," he said grimly.

"Please don't make me promise to watch my ass, again."

"Just do it. Keep me up-to-date on everything, and I mean everything."

"You say the sweetest things."

"Get out of here. Go see your wife."

"Good advice. Maybe the break will clear my head."

* * *

CC didn't make it past her desk when Wayne rushed in waving his hands frantically. CC surmised that he was either on to something that might be important or he had finally snapped.

"Credit card." Gasping, he almost fell over when he caught up with CC.

"Wayne, catch your breath," CC said as Mulligan joined them.

"Credit card."

"Yeah, you've said that."

"Okay." Wayne fought to control his breathing. "The prepaid credit card that was used to book Billy Ryan's room was used to book another hotel room."

"That's the best news I've heard in weeks. Where was it used?"

"The Beachside in Revere."

"I know where that is. It's right across the street from Blanchards Liquors." CC's heart pounded against her chest.

"The room was booked the night before Dr. Temple died."

"Wayne, this is great." CC felt a jolt of exhilaration. "We'll swing by and find out if anyone at the hotel can help us with a description of our mystery man."

"He's still there."

"Come again?" Mulligan asked.

"Whoever used the card hasn't checked out yet."

* * *

"Good afternoon. Is Ms. Cockburn in?" Val asked as she and Ricky showed their badges.

"No," the petite, bored-looking woman said.

"We need to speak to her regarding one of her clients." Val kept her tone polite as she tucked away her badge.

"Simon Fisher?"

"Yes. How did you know that?" Val leaned closer, sensing that the young lady wouldn't object.

"Ms. Cockburn never has more than one client at a time."

"Really? I'm Val by the way."

"Leila." The slender woman giggled slightly. "It's true. She never has more than one client at a time. Which is good because she's always running around. I had no idea estate planning was so complicated."

"Is that her specialty?"

"It's all she does."

"With only one client, how does she manage to keep you

busy?"

"I have to do all sorts of stuff, background checks, booking flights and hotel rooms. You wouldn't believe the errands she has me run."

"When is she due back?"

"Don't know. She called the other day to let me know that she had to extend her trip. I'm just enjoying the peace and quiet, and I get home in time to watch *Ellen*."

"A real slave driver, huh?"

"She's always sending me all over the place to pick up weird stuff."

"Like what?" Val took a seat on the edge of the desk.

"One time I had to pick up a snake. Not just any snake, a rattlesnake. I almost peed my pants the whole drive back to the office. I mean it was in a box, still I was terrified."

"A rattlesnake?" Val was taken aback.

"Swear to God." Leila held up her hand to emphasize the point. "What can I do? She pays mad money. Plus I have a company car. She pays for the gas, my cell phone, and lots of other things, so long as I hand in the receipts. She's a real stickler for receipts. I guess lawyers have to be that way."

"We have to go." Ricky handed Leila his card. "Thank you for your help. Just let Ms. Cockburn know that I need to speak to her."

* * *

"Feels good to be heading back." Ricky yawned once they

were in the air finally flying back to the East Coast. Val tried to take a nap while Ricky powered up his computer.

Ricky interrupted her attempt to sleep. "I got some info on Fisher's mouthpiece. It doesn't add up. From the looks of it, she was a professional student for a long time. Graduated from law school in Canada then here."

"Why both?"

"She's American, but get this, her father was the junior ambassador to Canada."

"That's a real job?"

"That's not the hinky part."

"It isn't? Seriously? Why in the name of our tremendous deficit would we need a junior ambassador to Canada? What else you got on her?"

"Her specialty is estate planning."

"If she's an estate lawyer, why in the hell is she working Fisher's case? Or need to buy a rattlesnake?"

"That would be the hinky part. It seems the closest she has come to entering a courtroom was when she represented Fisher at his last sanity hearing. I don't like this."

* * *

It hadn't taken long for CC and Leigh to assemble a team. Her first call was to Mills, who gladly brought in her crew. Dark vans surrounded the nondescript motel that was conveniently located across the street from the very same liquor store where the mystery bottle of vodka had been purchased. CC, Leigh, and Mills took the lead. First they needed to speak to the desk clerk.

"Officers, what can I do for you this evening?"

"We need information." CC shoved a slip of paper at him, not surprised when he jumped back. "We need the name and room number of the person who used that credit card."

He stood there staring at the paper as if it held the mystery of life.

Leigh pushed past everyone. "This is taking too long." She snatched the paper from the clerk's hands. She nudged him aside and made herself comfortable at the computer located on the counter.

"Can you, I mean, should you be doing that?" The boy suddenly looked worried. "Don't you need a warrant or something? Maybe I should call my boss."

CC challenged him with a firm clasp to his shoulder. "Be a good boy and stay out of our way."

"Got it," Leigh said. "Room thirteen twelve, a Ben Dover."

"Are you serious?" CC asked as the boy chuckled.

"Bend over. I didn't get that at first. That dude must have some issues."

"No doubt," CC wryly remarked.

"No car." Leigh printed the information.

"Okay, kid, sad to say we need your help." CC snapped her fingers in his face in an effort to get him to stop laughing at the suspect's unfortunate name. "By any chance, did you photocopy Mr. Dover's driver's license or some other form of identification?"

"Yeah, we have to." He shrugged then he simply stared out into space.

"Get it," CC said with a fierce growl. Her ire grew when the boy failed to move. "What's your name?"

"Kyle Johnston," he answered before he seemed to drift off again.

"Yo, Kyle, get the paperwork for Mr. Dover."

"Bend over." Kyle stumbled over to a file cabinet located behind them. "Here you go." He handed CC a single sheet of paper.

"There's no picture," CC said.

"Yeah, it's Canadian." Kyle shrugged.

"You know what else it is?"

"What?"

"Expired. It's out of date. Just so you know, Canada changed their driver's licenses. They have pictures now. This expired back in eighty six."

"Bummer."

"Yeah, bummer." CC gave a snarl while Mills alerted the teams as to where the suspect's room was located. "Okay, Kyle. How about you give us a room key? Then you need to just sit here and do nothing."

"I have a feeling he won't have a problem with that," Leigh said with disgust. "According to the computer, the room has been accessed twice. Both times were the day Dr. Temple drowned. Housekeeping hasn't been in the room. There was a notation that the Do Not Disturb sign was on the door each time housekeeping stopped by."

"All that was in the computer?"

"Yes. The one hiccup is the computer only records when a keycard is used to open a door, not when someone exits."

"According to the floor chart," Mills said, "the room we want is at the end of the hallway next to the stairwell. The location isn't a surprise. The last room next to a stairwell is almost always out of camera range. Plus with the stairs right there, you can avoid the elevator." They exited the lobby and began to organize their people.

"Also, camera free." CC tightened the tether on her Kevlar vest. "Okay, Mills, this is your area of expertise. We'll follow your lead."

Mills separated the teams, covering every entrance and exit of the modest motel. She, Leigh, and CC led a team dressed in black and full battle gear to the room. Mills knocked on the door to announce their presence. CC's heart was pounding. If the mysterious Mr. Dover was in the room, they didn't have probable cause to search his room much less arrest him. For a brief moment, CC feared that she had just ended all of their careers. There wasn't an answer to the announcement that they were the police. She motioned for her team to prepare themselves, and she slid the keycard in.

In a burst of activity, the door flew open and the tactical team stormed into the empty room. The team searched everywhere: the bathroom, behind the curtains, even under the bed. The room was empty and in pristine condition. The small room consisted of a tiny closet, a big-screen television, a nightstand, and a king-size bed.

"The bed hasn't been slept in," CC grimly noted.

"The bathroom hasn't been used either," Sgt. Glasheen, a member of Mills' team said. "This room hasn't been used."

"It was just a pit stop," CC concluded. "He hit the liquor store across the street and hung out here until it was time to catch up with Jack Temple."

"Maybe we'll get something from the bogus license." Mulligan's tone betrayed her lack of confidence. "We'll run the name through the database. Maybe we'll get a hit."

"On bend over? Seriously, it's not even a convincing alias." CC threw her hands up. "Might as well let CSU have a crack at the room. Maybe we'll get lucky." She looked around the room and felt defeated. Hotel rooms could have hundreds of random prints, hair strands, and fibers. The chances of the forensic team uncovering something that would lead them to the man behind the gun were slim to none.

Chapter 41

The only thing CC wanted after they wrapped up at the motel was to head over to the hospital and see Jamie. Instead, she was summoned to the captain's office to receive a royal reaming, courtesy of her superior officer and a very cranky ADA. They failed to see the logic of storming into a civilian's hotel room without probable cause or a warrant. ADA Ketchum made a point of informing her that she should kiss his ass since he was the one who woke up the manager and ended up having the corporate headquarters grant the police full access before the crime scene unit had begun processing the room.

CC offered him a humble thank-you and took her lumps. After Ketchum stormed out with a look of superiority, the captain began his own tirade. After he finished, he asked her one last question, "Why in the name of God did you ignore the basic rules and storm in like you were Clint eff-ing Eastwood?"

"This guy has already killed one cop and tried to kill another," CC said. "And don't bother telling me that my judgment is clouded. The cop this bozo missed was my partner. So, yeah my judgment is off."

"Tread lightly, Calloway, or this time your instincts are going to blow up in your face."

* * *

After being called on the carpet by her boss, CC tried to make her escape. Just as she was ready to grab her coat, the phone rang. She and Leigh were needed at a crime scene. She was tired of looking over her shoulder while spinning her wheels. Leigh jumped right in, eager to get started. The case failed to provide a distraction. It was a murder-suicide. Henri Fitzgibbons came home from work and shot his wife then himself. It took very little detective work to uncover that Mr. Fitzgibbons was unemployed and had amassed a large gambling debt.

It was a grim scene that was quickly becoming a sign of the times. Faced with an ever-increasing debt, unable to stop gambling because he was under the delusion that the next bet would score the big payoff, Mr. Fitzgibbons opted to end it all. He couldn't leave his wife behind to endure the stigma of his failure.

The police were left with cleaning up the mess. The hardest part for CC was the miserable task of informing the Fitzgibbons' relatives and friends. The only thing left after the coroner's wagon pulled away was to go over everything one last time before preparing themselves for a long night of paperwork. CC's exhaustion grew with each passing moment. To her credit, Leigh had a head start on the paperwork. The woman traveled nowhere without her tablet or Blackberry.

"Coroner won't have anything for a couple of days," Leigh said wearily as she hung up her phone.

"Peachy." CC tried to finish typing up her initial report. "This one seems pretty cut-and-dried. The bullet holes in their heads kind of told the whole story. I just don't understand how people can feel so helpless that they think that murdering their family then eating a bullet is the only option left. Then again, I've seen the sorriest excuses of why one person decides to kill another."

"Speaking of sorry excuses," Leigh said, "I have a little something I dug up for the Stern case. A few years ago, Mrs. Stern was involved in an assault and battery. Apparently, she decked a fellow patron at the IHOP on Soldiers Field Road."

"Any particular reason why, other than she's an angry spazz?"

"The other patron took the last booster seat."

"Well, then she was just asking for it. The victim didn't press charges?"

"No. Mr. Stern intervened via a huge apology and monetary compensation."

"Send it over to the DA. I'll be a happy woman after that one goes before a jury of her peers."

"In her mind, she doesn't have any peers. Any word from our nomadic Feds?"

"They'll be back sometime in the wee hours." CC released a hearty yawn. She glanced down at her watch and blinked with surprise. "Geez, where did the night go?"

"Christ, my cats are going to be pissed," Leigh said.

"Go. I'll finish this up and head over to the hospital. I feel like I haven't seen my wife for weeks."

After Leigh had sped off to tend to her furry little friends with a promise that she'd be back to help with the paperwork, CC wrapped up her share of it. She paused for a moment to take a quick look at the boards in the conference room. Her conversation with her captain troubled her. Without Max by her side, she honestly didn't know who she could trust.

She stared at the names and dates in an effort to ease her troubled mind. Leigh had appeared just when things had been set in motion. She claimed she was making a career move. CC had worked with her here and there over the years. Still she really didn't know a lot about the enigmatic blonde, only that she was divorced. Her story was plausible with budget cuts looming and her being teamed with a first-class spotlight-hogging numbnuts. If she were in Leigh's shoes, she'd be looking for a new assignment. It was the timing that made CC uncomfortable.

Next she had Deputy Brown, who appeared to be a no-nonsense, kick-ass-and-take-names-later, Fed. Her list of friends seemed to fill the alphabet soup that comprises national security. It wasn't a group CC wanted to piss off. Given Brown's mysterious background, it wouldn't be much of a leap from US Marshal to sophisticated assassin.

Rounding out the list of possible threats was her merry band of colleagues. Any number of people in her department could have turned rogue. CC didn't want to consider the possibilities. Palmucci was most definitely someone to keep an eye on. She doubted he possessed the intelligence to be the killer, yet his stupidity on its own made him dangerous.

She grabbed her coat, unable to shake the feeling that she had wasted the past couple of days and had learned very little. All she knew for certain was that people were dying.

By the time she arrived at the hospital, she could feel the walls closing in. She exchanged greetings with the staff and set about tracking down Jamie. She finally found her in her office buried under a stack of paperwork.

"That can't be good."

"It isn't." Jamie smiled up at her and removed her glasses. "What brings you by?"

"I miss you."

Jamie bolted from behind her desk and captured CC in a fierce hug. She smiled and gave in to the warmth of Jamie's bone-crushing embrace. Jamie snuggled closer, while CC ran her hands down Jamie's supple curves. She loved the feel of her wife's body. She shivered when she heard the soft moan her touch elicited. In the back of her mind was the agonizing reminder that if things went badly this would be the last time she held Jamie in her arms. She needed the moment to last, and time was of the essence.

She fiercely captured Jamie's lips. Her tongue darted into the warmth of Jamie's mouth. Jamie rubbed against her body, encouraging her to take more. CC reacted quickly, fearful that either of them could be called away at any moment. She aggressively guided Jamie down onto the sofa, one of the features CC loved about the fairly new office.

"Baby?" Jamie whimpered.

CC ignored the husky whisper as she was far too busy trying her best to feel Jamie's flesh. She pushed the top of Jamie's light blue scrubs up. She hesitated for a brief moment when she felt Jamie resisting. Her hungry kiss quickly quelled her wife's objections. She ran her hands up along Jamie's naked torso. Jamie's needy pleas encouraged her. She cupped her firm full breasts. Jamie wrapped her legs around CC's waist and drew her closer. She knew there wasn't time, but still she couldn't resist pinching and teasing Jamie's erect nipples.

Jamie started to beg for more. CC's hands abandoned Jamie's breasts and glided down her supple body. CC's body was humming with desire. Her hunger grew when she captured one of Jamie's nipples between her eager lips. She suckled the swollen bud urgently as Jamie's body arched beneath her.

CC wove her long fingers in the fabric of Jamie's waistband. The thin blue material was quickly yanked down to her knees. CC suckled harder, taunting and teasing Jamie's nipples. Her fingers brushed against the thin material of Jamie's panties.

"Now?" Jamie desperately groaned.

CC abandoned her lover's breasts and moved her lips slowly higher. She enjoyed the taste of Jamie's flesh and captured her wife in a searing kiss. Her tongue darted between her quivering lips, while her fingers slipped inside Jamie's underwear. With her kiss, she taunted and teased her wife while her fingers dipped inside her wetness. Slowly she explored her swollen lips and brushed against her clit. Jamie rocked insistently against her; CC's demanding kiss prevented her from speaking.

In the back of her mind, CC knew that time was running out. She tried to savor the feel of Jamie's body riding against her own in a steady rhythm. She was forced to suppress her need for tenderness and plunged two fingers deep inside of her wife. She felt Jamie's body tighten against her touch.

CC moved urgently, stroking Jamie's engorged clit each time she plunged in and out of her. Jamie shuddered beneath her as CC took her harder. CC leaned back and watched Jamie quiver as she guided her closer to the edge. After all these years, it still amazed CC as Jamie's body exploded. The sight of her lover falling captive to her touch was sheer beauty. CC smiled, watching Jamie convulse, her words lost in a haze of pure bliss. While Jamie recovered, CC simply enjoyed the sense of peace that filled her.

"What?" Jamie asked when she reached for her wife only to have her advances brushed aside.

"We'll have to finish this later."

"Brat."

"I love you."

"I love you, too. You're still a brat." Jamie climbed to her feet. "Get me all hot and flustered then call it a night. Now I have to find an empty room and grab a shower. Be forewarned, when I get you alone you're mine."

"Anytime."

They exchanged quick kisses and promised to finish expressing their love later that day. Silently CC was worried that the moment would never happen.

* * *

With her heart still beating rapidly, CC quickly cleaned up in the ladies' room and headed upstairs, hoping to catch Max awake. She was buzzed in, despite the fact that it wasn't even close to visiting hours. Much to her surprise, she found her partner wide awake and cussing at the television.

"What did it do?"

"There's nothing on," he groused and waved for her to join him. "What are you doing here at this ungodly hour?"

"Too much to do and nothing to do."

"Hit the wall did you?"

"Something like that. You know me. I fly off the handle with a crazy idea, then I'm shocked when it doesn't add up."

"It will. You have a way of pulling things out of your ass."

"Thanks, I think."

"Still no word on my gun?"

"No."

"Not the way I wanted to end my career."

"It won't be," she said. "I'll be pulling something out my ass anytime now. How are you feeling?"

"Better. The headaches and gaps have subsided. Just wish I had gotten a look at the scumbag that popped me."

"You remember not seeing the perp. That's good."

"How is that good?"

"You're remembering. I hate to admit it, but you really had me worried."

"I don't remember that much. I pulled up to the restaurant or what's left of it. I wasn't that late, but it was already dark. The only things I could see clearly were the sagging buildings and a big old backhoe parked in the middle of everything. I heard a beep. I had to shield my eyes from a pair of high beams. I thought I heard gravel grating against the ground. Next thing I know, I'm in pain and everything is spinning. I smelled something burning. Must have been me, getting zapped. That's it, except in my haze I could swear someone was singing, well not really singing."

"Your attacker gave you a concert? Who hit you, Lady Gaga?" CC tried to joke, hoping it would help ease Max's frustration. "What were they singing?" she asked when her joke fell flat.

"*Humpty Dumpty*. Humpty Dumpty sat on a wall. You know the rest. I heard humming in between the lyrics, and I could feel gravel or rocks scraping against my back. That's it."

"*Humpty Dumpty?*"

"Yeah, like being blindsided wasn't embarrassing enough, this bozo had to add insult to injury."

CC sat there for a long agonizing moment. Something Max had just said made her skin prickle. She felt as if she were trying to answer one of those annoying word puzzles. When the answer was just within reach...*It can't be that simple*! The truth was suddenly clear as day.

"Max, you are a genius!" she said gleefully.

"What did I say?"

"You, my friend, just solved the case. I'd kiss you if you weren't so butt ugly."

Max lay back and looked at her as if she had lost her mind. She smiled and jumped to her feet. In one brief moment, everything fell into place and she couldn't waste time. She waved goodbye to Max and sped off towards the nearest elevator. She grabbed her cell phone and began dialing what she hoped was Wayne's number. The answer was so simple, she couldn't believe she hadn't accepted it before. Each member of the team had mentioned the possibility more than once. It just seemed ridiculous. Now it seemed obvious.

She was still fumbling with her phone when she reached her car in the parking garage. Frustrated by the wonder phone, she gave up on Wayne. She decided to try to call Deputy Brown and Leigh. She wanted to talk to all of them at the same time. She knew her phone was capable. She, on the other hand, was confused by it. Blaming her gloves for her inability to complete the simple task, she started banging on the screen. Convinced she had failed, she conceded defeat and slid the phone into the holder on her belt.

Embarrassed by her inability to successfully make a phone call, she muttered a string of obscenities under her breath. She dug her keys out of her pocket and remotely unlocked her car. Once she had the car heated up, she'd try again to make her calls.

"Ring around the rosy, pocket full of posy."

She had almost reached her car when she heard the song begin. Instinctively she reached for her gun, but she was a moment too late. Her fingertips brushed against the leather snap just as she felt a searing pain. It was the last clear thought she had.

* * *

CC awoke blindfolded and tried to move, but her hands and feet were bound. She was in a moving car and knew by the feel of her hip and ankle that she had been stripped of her weapons. She tried to call out, but her mouth was taped shut. Feeling nauseous, she shivered from the cold. The only thing she knew for certain was she was in a car headed towards a very uncertain future.

Her stomach clenched when the car come to an abrupt stop. She held her breath. Was it just a traffic light or her final destination? The answer came quickly as she was jerked from the back of her own car. The soft fabric that had covered her eyes was torn from her face. It took a moment for her vision to clear. She wasn't surprised when her captor was revealed to her.

CC's mind raced in an effort to formulate a plan that would ensure her escape. She never had the opportunity to make an attempt; the stun gun fired against her chest halted any possible action. Rendered helpless and squirming with pain, she was dragged through the woods. Another jolt of electricity left her lying on the ground, only capable of groaning. Her restraints were removed along with her long winter coat.

Left on a pile of dirt, her body twitching in agonizing pain, she had no concept of how long she laid there curled up. Eventually, she did manage to uncurl her body and roll into a kneeling position. Her abductor remained silent while she struggled to move her body. Finally able to stand, although she teetered, she was impressed that she was on her feet. Her captor sat a good seven feet away pointing a gun at her. Once again CC tried to formulate a plan. She spotted a small camping shovel. Eunice Cockburn had made herself comfortable on a fallen tree. She cocked the gun and aimed it directly at CC's heart.

That can't be good.

"Start digging."

Chapter 42

While she dug, CC summarized her version of events, skimming over a few details that she didn't feel Cockburn needed to know. One detail was that the lawyer should have taken CC's phone when she took her guns. When she began digging, she noticed not only was the phone still resting on her belt loop, but it appeared to be recording. Anyway, CC hoped it was doing that.

"The keys were unavoidable," Eunice said with a wistful sigh. "I needed to get into Dr. Temple's apartment to frame the hooker. I couldn't risk going back to the beach just in case someone had already stumbled upon him. I dumped the keys in the trash at the subway station. In hindsight, I should have left the vodka bottle on the beach. I thought someone might snag it. I thought I needed it in plain sight, making it obvious that he had been drinking. Then again, if I had known my friendly little hooker was locked up, I would have handled things differently. The good doctor himself made my job easy. All I had to do was hang out at the bandstand looking forlorn and lost. I spun my woeful tale of how my marriage broke up. He listened and sympathized with my plight. How could he not? It was so similar to what was happening with his own marriage. I offered to share my vodka, which just happened to be his favorite."

"You certainly do your homework."

"Success stems from looking for the small details. Don't you agree? As for the bees, that was perfect."

CC couldn't help correcting her. "You used too much bee venom. It tipped off the medical examiner. Although, everyone was impressed that you managed to tamper with the EpiPen. From what I understand, it isn't easy."

"It was a bitch. But we needed Simon's daddy out of the way to free up his money. He was more than eager to have his father whacked. There just might have been some animosity between those two."

"You think?"

"The others proved to be just as easy. Little Billy Ryan, for example. All that took was a smile and the promise of drugs. Your partner was a snap as well. Seriously, did he really think he could score a boat like that for fifty grand? After I set up the meeting, I boosted a car from the lot across the street. Flashed the lights with the remote and tossed good old Max's fat ass down the staircase. I returned the car before I took off with his."

"You dumped it at the racetrack."

"And hopped on the Blue Line right back to my cozy room at the Hilton."

"Conveniently located at the airport."

"Comfortable and easy."

"I can't believe you know how to hot-wire a car."

"I don't." Eunice waved her hand in a dismissive manner. Unfortunately for CC, it wasn't the hand that held her gun. "I broke into the sales office and simply took the set of keys I needed. The most important thing I needed was a car with a keyless start. I needed to shine the lights in Sampson's eyes."

"Very methodical." CC felt queasy, not seeing a way out. The only good sign was that her captor was still talking.

"I do apologize. This wasn't supposed to be your final resting place. Originally, I had planned on dumping good old Albert here."

"Oh, yes, my distraction. Must have pissed you off when we

caught him."

"Good help is hard to find."

"After all your hard work, that had to irk you. You busted your butt flying all over the country. All Bert had to do was follow a few simple instructions."

"I'm inclined to agree. I took out Professor Harden without breaking a sweat. I simply tracked him down. The guy's security system was crap. Rigging the flue to malfunction was easy enough. I just had to hide in the basement with a gas mask and wait for the carbon monoxide to do its job. I posed him and walked out the front door. Fernandez was another walk in the park. You'd think someone who works in corrections would be more safety conscious. I had everything perfectly timed, and that idiot Beaumont couldn't show up on the right street corner at the right time. How hard can it be? I flew all the way to San Diego, slashed little Bitsy's throat, drove her beamer all the way up to LA, dumped it in downtown hell, and was back in my office before the sun set."

"Although you did make mistakes."

"Keys, bees, you wouldn't have gotten me on just those. What else did you find? Might as well tell me."

"It was all I needed," CC lied. She couldn't let this lunatic know that Max was alive and well.

"So you say."

"If you don't mind my asking, what were you planning for me?"

"I had something devilishly clever in mind for you." Eunice almost cackled.

CC couldn't help wondering who was the most bat-shit crazy,

Simon or his lawyer?

"I was going to kill Beaumont and dump him here. My theory was that you wouldn't stop looking for him after he disappeared. There was a good chance he wouldn't be found. If he was discovered, it wouldn't reflect well on the late Detective Sampson or you."

"Because?"

"I was going to kill him with this gun."

"My gun?"

"No, dear heart, this isn't one of your guns. This is your late partner's gun. Originally, I had planned on putting you in storage. There are some dandy storage units along McGrath highway that are climate controlled. When the time came to frame your wife for your murder, I'd thaw you out and dump your body where it would be discovered. Complete with a bullet from one of your guns and drugs in your pocket."

"You're not planning on killing Jamie?" CC was filled with a sense of relief.

"My client is still under the delusion that he and the good doctor are meant to be together. My job is to simply frame her. You should thank me for that. In the beginning, Fisher couldn't decide which one of you I should kill first. I convinced him that you were a much better candidate. He loved the idea of her being left on her own and vulnerable."

CC stood there for a moment, slack jawed, as she tried to digest everything Eunice eagerly confessed to.

"I don't get it. You are obviously a highly intelligent woman.

How did you end up in this line of work?"

"The pay is amazing, plus I get to travel and meet interesting people. How it began is simple. I discovered I had a knack for killing people."

"Just how does one discover that they have a knack for that?"

"Practice makes perfect. Like you, I had a less than amicable relationship with a stepparent. My father's wife was convinced she could take my mother's place. Quite arrogant if you ask me. She made a lame attempt to win me over by having clowns perform at my birthday parties. That is just sick, watching those creepy buggers with their floppy shoes and red noses trying to make balloon animals. Gave me nightmares. I looked forward to the day when I could be out on my own and not have to interact with my so-called parents. By the time I finished my first year in law school, I realized that neither of them would cut the apron strings, which left it up to me. To my credit, I didn't rush things. I waited and planned things very carefully. My father was attending an event in Canada. I knew her habits. My stepmother was one of those boring predictable types. I knew when she'd be out socializing and she would return home at no later than six. She would prepare for her evening meal while Daddy was away on business. Her meal would consist of a simple salad and a fifth of Makers Mark. The woman did enjoy her bourbon. Sadly, Father didn't approve of such things."

"So when your father was out of town, she'd get snockered."

"Yes. My timing was perfect. Everyone at my dorm was preparing for finals. I hung my Do Not Disturb sign up and made the drive from Georgetown to the house. I took the back roads, so no one would see me arrive. My stepmother was out socializing, so I hid in the attic and waited. Once the staff retired to their quarters located on the other side of the grounds, I waited for her to finish her liquid dinner and retire for the evening."

"You killed her?"

"Smothered her with a brand-new pillow. I bought it three weeks earlier. No sense leaving any clues behind. Then I stripped her, put her nightclothes in the laundry bin and carried her out of the house. Don't you just love those Rubbermaid trash bins? I do. They're very durable, and the handles lock."

"You stuffed her in the trash?" CC was stunned.

"No, silly. I stuffed her in a new trash barrel I had slipped into the garage earlier. Again, I had no intention of leaving any evidence behind. I wrapped a chain through the handles, locked it up tight, and rolled her down the street to where I had hidden my car. I drove to the marina where the family boat was docked. I was very careful as to where I parked and the route I took to board the boat. I didn't want my pretty face being caught on camera. The only hiccup in my plan was when we were out in the middle of the Potomac. I was a novice then and didn't know that when you strangle someone they will pass out before dying. The bitch wasn't dead. Imagine my surprise. No sense wasting the opportunity. I punctured the trash can. I wanted to make certain that it would sink. I couldn't resist having a little fun. I tossed a few lit matches inside, wheeled her off the side, and watched her sink in the water. The best part was listening to her screams."

"Then back to school, and no one ever knew." CC hoped Eunice would keep talking. *Okay, she wins the crazy bat-shit contest hands down.*

"According to law enforcement, she's a missing person."

"You do have a knack for this," CC conceded.

"Enough stalling. Time to wrap this up."

* * *

Ricky was exhausted by the time they landed in Boston, but Val was pumped up with excitement. It felt good to be on a chase. The Beaumont case had left a bad taste in her mouth. This case filled her with a sense of purpose. The moment they touched down and turned on their cell phones, the information poured in. They grabbed their belongings and set off to find a rental car.

"Idiot." Val's mood soured once she turned on her phone.

"Thank you?"

"Not you," Val said and groaned. "I'm getting a video stream from Calloway."

"Yeah?"

"Look, dark and blank. That phone is wasted on her. Let's head over to the three-three. If she's not there, we can start getting things together and make a game plan."

* * *

Leigh was busy retyping her report on the Fitzgibbons case. Her intention had been to go home, feed her cats, and get some rest. Something nagged at her. She couldn't shake the feeling that something was wrong. When her phone rang and she received a blank video from CC, she laughed.

"My God, Fred Flintstone is more technically savvy. Someone needs to teach her how to use that thing." She set it aside, not interested in watching a blank screen. She had been inspired to upgrade her phone after playing with Calloway's. "Maybe I can talk her into a trade," she said and snickered.

"I've got something." Wayne burst into the squad room. "Benjamin Augustus Dover has dual citizenship with the US and Canada."

"You can't do both."

"Actually you can. Our government just wants us to think that you can't. His passport is Canadian as is his driver's license. He's also dead."

"When and how?"

"Nineteen eighty-seven, when he was all of three months old. Crib death."

"Great, our hit man is using a dead baby's identity."

"Where the hell is Calloway?" Val asked as she and Ricky stormed into the squad room.

"I'm not certain." Mulligan ignored the deputy's brisk attitude. "I think she went to visit her wife at the hospital. How was the trip? Find anything useful?"

"Yes and no. We've got a person of interest."

"Who?" Mulligan practically jumped out of her chair.

"Eunice Cockburn."

"Wait. That's the name of the mother on Benjamin Dover's birth certificate," Wayne said.

"Ben Dover?" Val choked. "Really?"

"Cockburn. Isn't that Fisher's lawyer?" Mulligan tried to fit the pieces together.

"By day." Val said. "We think she moonlights as a hit man. Not a bad deal, since she can hide behind attorney-client privilege."

Rousseau joined the conversation. "The desk clerk at the motel never said it was a woman."

"That kid was so high he probably wouldn't have noticed if Angelina Jolie checked in." Mulligan reached for her cell phone. "I need to alert Cal—oh my God. Wayne, can you pull up the feed Calloway is sending me?"

"She did that to you, too?" Val asked while Wayne busied himself with Mulligan's laptop.

"We need to get a tactical unit in place." Mulligan shoved her phone at the captain.

"What the hell did you do?" Val gasped when she checked her phone.

CC's voice could be heard loud and clear. "Keep stalling," Leigh muttered while her partner began to explain how she figured out everything. "Wayne, I need a GPS on her phone. Now!" she added when he failed to move.

"We don't have a warrant." Wayne said.

"We don't need one," Val bluntly informed them.

* * *

Val and Ricky were already calling in every favor they could muster. "Mills, I don't care that your team is in trouble for not waiting for a warrant. Calloway gave my department permission to access her phone records after Beaumont died. Just tell your idiot boss that at this very moment a cop is being held at gunpoint. I don't know about you, but I'm not in the mood to wait for some jackwagon to fill out the necessary forms."

"I want a Medivac chopper," Ricky said into his phone. "No, I'm not certain we'll need it. Do you want to wait?"

"Location?" Leigh asked while the captain tried to organize the squad room.

"Pine Banks Park," Wayne finally told the frazzled group.

"Where is that?" Val was pleased when Wayne explained by turning the laptop around. "Captain, we'll take Leigh once she's ready. The rest of your people need to stand down."

"No fucking way."

"We have the Fugitive Task Force, the FBI, and the Marshal Service gearing up. Quite frankly, your people will be in the way."

Ricky quickly stepped in. "You can't leave your precinct empty. A little diplomacy, Brownie," he added grabbing her by the arm.

"Not my strong point."

"Screw the diplomacy." Leigh shrugged into a Kevlar vest. "My partner is in trouble. Mills' team is already heading towards Malden. Agent Brown, do we have a team and helicopter?"

"Yes."

"Good. Wayne, feed everything to tactical. I'm climbing on the bus now. If you're planning on joining me, get moving."

* * *

Mulligan watched as CC tried to stall. She wished there was a way to let her partner know they were coming.

"The problem with Fisher is," Cockburn said, "not only do I

have to do what I do best, make their deaths look like an unfortunate event, I have to add the element of shame."

"The drugs you planted on Max. The DVD of kiddy porn you placed in Brooks' bedroom and leaving Bitsy Marsden out in the open, half naked. And I'll disappear under a cloud of suspicion."

"I put a great deal of thought into my artistry. How did you figure out I offed Simon's daddy?"

"That took time for me. I knew Bert was a distraction. I just couldn't resist falling for it. Good job with that."

"Thank you."

"When we caught up with Bert and saw the text messages, I knew Brooks had been right. If that was true, then it all started with Malcolm Fisher. One quick phone call to San Diego and a short chat with a very confused medical examiner confirmed my theory. I should have suspected that you were the one, simply because you were the only one smart enough to pull this off. I have to admire the logic. Anything you say or do is covered by attorney-client privilege."

* * *

CC tensed when her captor stood. She tried to calculate how hard she would have to throw the shovel in order for it to be effective. The lanky blonde carefully approached just as the rain started. The wild look in her eyes made CC's knees tremble.

"I'm glad you appreciate my efforts." Eunice aimed her gun directly at CC. "The weather has started to turn. Time to get this show on the road."

CC hurled the small shovel, aiming directly for the gun. It whizzed through the air. Eunice cackled and shifted slightly. The shovel missed her by mere inches.

CHECKMATE

"I'm going to need that shovel." Eunice wagged her finger at her. "Nice try, though. Pity that it has to end this way. I've enjoyed the game. But now's the time for my last move. Checkmate, Detective."

Chapter 43

The tactical vehicles plowed through the streets. Leigh continued to watch in horror as her partner tried to keep a crazy woman distracted. Ricky was busy working on the computer, barking orders into his headset.

"For the love of God, keep her talking," Leigh shouted as the van that sheltered Val's team raced towards Malden.

"How is she keeping her going?" Ricky seemed stunned that Calloway was still alive.

"The real question is can she keep her talking long enough for us to get there," Val said nervously.

Ricky looked up. "The chopper should be circling right about now. We have teams covering all four exits. Can you drive all the way into the park?"

"In theory, no," Mulligan said as she checked her gun. "Teenagers seem to manage it after dark without any trouble."

The black, government-issue SUVs plowed into the park and the teams quickly unloaded. Mills didn't hesitate; she ordered her team of snipers to follow them.

"Flank out," she said. "Remember, we want this bitch alive."

Why hasn't she seen the camera? Val trudged closer to the spot where she hoped they would find the detective. The last thing she wanted to do was to face Stevie if things went wrong. Her breath caught as she saw the hurled shovel miss its target. "Let's move, people. We just ran out of time."

"Checkmate, Detective," echoed from her phone.

The lawyer's cold words were quickly followed by a loud

pop. Val held her breath as she watched the video image spin out of control until it was showing nothing but the night sky. In the distance, Val could see the lights of the helicopter looming above.

* * *

"Hurts, doesn't it?" Eunice loomed over CC's prone body.

CC tried to fight against the pain as she lay in the makeshift grave. She had assumed she would never forget how painful taking a bullet was, yet this time seemed far worse. Somehow she managed to steady her breathing, an action that seemed to upset her captor. CC cried out when Eunice decided to poke her wound with a stick.

"Bet you're wondering why it hurts so much and why I haven't just killed you yet."

"Kind of," CC choked out wondering why she hadn't passed out like she had the first time she had been shot.

"I dipped the bullets in lemon juice then in a mixture of cayenne pepper and garlic salt."

"Because?" CC barely got the question out.

"I get a bonus if I make you suffer. Just like Elizabeth. Fisher doesn't really care if I embarrass you, he just wants you to suffer. For Ms. Pryce the hemlock and white oleander certainly did the trick. From what I understand, the pain is excruciating. Some say it feels as if your intestines are being twisted in a knot. Do you think that in the end she prayed for death? Do you think you will? Simon was certainly pleased when I explained in great detail the method I used. He viewed Elizabeth as the catalyst for all of his troubles."

"I doubt that she was the catalyst. I think Fisher would have gone around the bend without his girlfriend dumping his sorry ass."

Each word was a struggle she forced herself to keep talking. She hoped if Eunice was busy gloating she just might not shoot her again.

"I'm inclined to agree with you. We really need to wrap things up. Since you've been videotaping our evening together, I'll have the proof I need. I should thank you for that. Also, for not being smart enough to be able to broadcast. Seriously, didn't you think I'd notice that brightly lit camera on your belt? I'll be taking that with me. Of course I'll edit out the parts where I refer to my client as an idiot. Or maybe you do know how to work that impressive gadget," Eunice explained with a snarl.

* * *

Thirteen of them, all dressed in black, made their way through the woods. Val allowed Ricky to take the lead. Silently the team surrounded the opening. Val saw the wiry blonde standing by a mound of dirt with her gun carefully aimed.

"Eunice Cockburn, Federal agents! Lower your weapon!" Ricky's harsh tone left no room for debate.

Val aimed her Glock, the light rain, and darkness failed to hinder her view. Eunice turned slightly, the feral look in her eyes spoke volumes. Val clenched her jaw. She already knew how this was going to end. Eunice turned and aimed her gun down at the hole in the ground.

Val leveled her gun and chose a spot just behind Eunice's ear. She felt calm, silently reasoning that if Eunice didn't want to be taken alive, then so be it. Simultaneous shots rang out. Eunice managed to get off one shot that nicked CC's ear while Val delivered a perfect kill shot.

"I said alive," Mills snarled.

"She wasn't going to be taken alive."

CHECKMATE

"Now you're psychic?"

"Not my first rodeo. Ricky, bring the chopper down."

* * *

"Jamie." Stella beckoned her over to the nurses' station. "Melrose Wakefield is diverting calls. There's a pileup on Route 60. Triage is already prepared."

"Thank you." Jamie rolled her shoulders and wondered if she'd ever see her home again.

"We have a GSW being medivaced in from Malden," Stella called out.

"Great." Jamie yawned. "Assemble a team and have them meet me at the service elevators. I guess my team is getting their first trip to the helipad."

"Already done. They're waiting for you, and the elevators are ready to hold for transport."

"What would I do without you, Stella?" Jamie couldn't help smiling.

* * *

"Calloway, don't you dare die on me," Val threatened as she unclipped the cell phone and handed it to Mills.

"I wasn't planning on it." CC struggled to get the words out. "Damn, hurts a lot more this time. She said she got a bonus if she made it hurt."

"We caught the whole show. Good thing you finally figured out how to use your phone."

"Didn't," CC said with a gurgle. "Accident."

"The shooter laced the bullets with lemon juice, garlic salt, and cayenne pepper," Val told the EMTs who had pushed her aside.

"Why?" one of them asked.

"She's a bitch. Excuse me, she was a bitch." Val couldn't resist sneering down at Eunice's body.

"We're taking her straight to BGH," the sturdy young man told Leigh.

"Isn't Melrose closer?"

"Diverting calls."

"Crap." Leigh quickly dialed her cell phone. "This is Detective Mulligan. I need to speak to whoever is in charge." To the rescue team, she said, "I'm riding with you." Everyone stepped back to allow the team to load CC into the helicopter and safely take off. The second team, led by Ledger, finally arrived.

"Bit late to the party," Val said curtly, not caring that he was her superior.

"I need your statement," Ledger said wryly. She handed him her gun and took a moment before answering.

"You'll get it at the hospital. You have my weapon. I just need to make a stop."

"Deputy, you know this isn't how things work."

"I'll meet you at the hospital, Brownie," Ricky said. "I just need to get Stevie."

"The locals will handle that, Agent," Ledger said. "We need to document what happened here tonight. Before the press or anyone else gets wind of this fiasco."

"Mills, give him a copy of the video." Val fought to remain calm. "As for my statement, based on evidence we gathered, Agent Samaria and I confirmed that Eunice Cockburn, Esquire, was behind the recent string of killings. Two of her victims were cops. She confessed on tape while holding Detective Caitlin Calloway of the Boylston PD hostage. She shot and wounded Detective Calloway. We identified ourselves, and she chose to ignore our demands. So I shot her in order to save Detective Calloway's life. That work for you, sir?"

"For now, that should suffice. Go."

* * *

Jamie and her team were wrapped up in tacky yellow gowns. Jamie briefly wondered why it rained or snowed every time they had a flight coming in. She reviewed the patient's vitals that had been radioed in and conveyed them to her team. She carefully explained what she expected of them. Just as the helicopter was landing on the pad, Rudy Lorening burst through the access door.

"Dr. Jameson, I need to take over."

"What? Rudy what's going on?"

"Please, Jamie, you need to step away."

"Mind telling me why?" She didn't appreciate him doing whatever he was doing in front of her students.

"It's your wife."

"What?"

"The patient arriving is your wife." He shouted over the noise of the helicopter and pointed towards the person being unloaded. Jamie's knees buckled, but she found the strength to step away.

"I'm sorry, Jamie. We have the OR ready for her," Rudy said as he stepped into Jamie's spot.

Jamie almost keeled over as CC's unmoving body was wheeled past her. Horrified, she watched helplessly as she fought against the urge to take over.

"Her blood type is A positive. No allergies."

"I've got it, Jamie," Rudy said as they entered the elevator. "I promise."

She couldn't focus and failed to notice that Leigh was there. In her mind, she tried to process the medical information. It was futile; the knowledge she possessed was suddenly useless gibberish. Within a few moments, she found herself sitting in the waiting area just outside the surgical unit. Rudy had requested that she not step in or watch from the observation room, more commonly known as the theatre. She finally noticed that Leigh Mulligan was beside her, holding her hand.

* * *

"I hate to disturb you at this hour, ma'am," Val said in a surly tone after awakening the woman.

"What is it now, Deputy?"

"I thought you might be interested to know that your daughter was wounded in the line of duty this evening. She's in surgery now. I don't have an update on how—"

"Not again." Maria began to shake.

"I came here to offer you the chance to be there for her. I

can take you the hospital."

"I..."

Maria's hesitation irked the hell out of Val. Unable to control her anger, she cut the elderly woman off before she could make excuses.

"Look, I'm going to be honest with you. I don't like you. For all your claims of wanting to make amends with your girls, here you are hesitating after being told your daughter is at the hospital fighting for her life. I'm heading down to my car. You've got two minutes before I'm out of here. The choice is yours."

* * *

The small waiting area quickly filled up with a steady stream of cops and hospital workers, all eager to find out what was happening. Despite Leigh's constant vigil, Jamie felt alone. Stevie finally burst through the crowd with Emma and Ricky in tow.

"Any word?" Stevie breathlessly asked. She handed Emma off to Ricky.

"Nothing yet. It's too soon." Jamie accepted the hug Stevie offered. "What happened?" she finally brought herself to ask Mulligan.

"She was grabbed here, in the hospital parking lot." Mulligan cleared her throat. "It was, uh, she was right. Fisher was behind the whole thing."

"Check with security. Caitlin always parks near a camera just in case," Jamie heard herself saying in an overly calm voice.

"We've already done that," Mills said gently. "Don't worry

about the case. CC pretty much wrapped it up. You just..."

"Just what?" Jamie almost laughed.

"I don't know," Mills confessed. "Seems like I should say something, you know, like don't worry she's a fighter. Hearing it out loud sounds lame."

"No, it's the truth." Jamie graciously accepted the officer's words. She sat there for a moment trying to digest everything. Her wife had been abducted at the hospital probably not long after they had made love in her office. It didn't make any sense. Then again, at that moment, very few things in their lives made sense. "Who did this to her?" she finally asked. "And where can I find them?"

"Eunice Cockburn. You can find her at the morgue," Mulligan said.

"Who in the name of God is Eunice Cockburn?"

"She is, or was, Simon Fisher's lawyer."

"Leigh, did you..." Jamie choked up, afraid to ask the question.

"No, it was Val," Ricky said.

"Perfect kill shot." Leigh gave Jamie's arm a squeeze.

"The lawyer did it." Stevie shook her head, clearly at a loss. "What is this world coming to when you can't trust a lawyer?"

Mac C's voice bellowed around them. "Who, what, when, where, how, and let me have a shot at the slimy bastard!"

Jamie watched in disbelief as CC's uncle was wheeled in by Frank. He had an extra oxygen tank hooked up to his wheelchair.

"Lawyer. Already dead, Uncle Mac," Stevie said, her voice

devoid of emotion.

Jamie was concerned as she realized this was the second time Stevie sat vigil waiting to see if her beloved sister would live or die. *At least this time she isn't alone*, Jamie silently reasoned. She felt a pang of guilt for her absence all those years ago.

Palmucci suddenly appeared, wagging his finger at Mac. "Where have you been?"

"Frank, wheel this sucker over this rude bastard's foot."

"Boys." Stevie nodded towards her daughter, who had been sitting on Ricky's lap watching the bizarre scene unfold. "If you can't behave, take it outside."

"Why wasn't I called?" Palmucci's softened tone did nothing to hide his disdain.

"We were a little busy," Ricky said. "Not to worry, we cleared your case. Or I should say Calloway cleared all the cases. Got the whole story on tape."

"Wait, I'm confused." Stevie looked at him. "Where did this happen? Was it at the station?"

"No," Ricky said with a hard swallow. "Pine Banks Park."

"Malden?"

"Her phone," Mulligan said. "Somehow she managed to feed us a live stream of the whole thing while the lawyer confessed to everything, including whacking her own stepmother when she was in college."

"Sounds like a lovely woman," Stevie said. "Remind me to thank Val later."

"Her phone?" Jamie almost laughed that the expensive gadget CC fought tooth and nail not to own might have saved her life. "I can't believe she figured out how to work it. Thank God, she did."

Val suddenly appeared. "She said it was an accident." A timid older woman was hiding behind her.

"What are you doing here?" Stevie shouted as she jumped out of her seat.

"Mommy," Emma wailed, clearly frightened.

"Mommy?" Maria repeated with a shadow of a smile.

"You don't belong here." Stevie struggled to contain the anger that had been building from the moment she heard what had happened to her sister.

"You heard the girl, Maria," Mac said with a snarl.

"I brought her," Val timidly confessed. "I thought..." her words trailed off when Stevie's glare clearly screamed *I will kill you later*.

"Who are you?" Jamie asked.

"Ricky, will you take Emma downstairs for a cup of hot chocolate?"

Ricky, who looked as if he couldn't wait to flee the scene, complied.

"You have a child and a husband?" Maria asked in an excited tone.

"Half right. Ricky isn't my husband. In fact, he's dating Emma's father.

"I asked for that," Maria mumbled.

"Maria, why don't you do what you do best and ignore your kids?" Mac struggled to get out of his chair until Frank placed a calming hand on his shoulder.

"From what I've heard," Maria said, "you weren't here the last time either. Bit of legal trouble?"

"Stop, all of you," Jamie said. "Either you play nice, or you can get the hell out." She was weary of the bickering.

"It's not up to us, Uncle Mac. It's up to Jamie."

Jamie felt her bones ache when she stood to greet the stranger who she could only assume was CC's mother. "I'm Dr. Jamie Jameson." She offered her hand, half-tempted to smack this woman rather than greet her. The last thing she wanted at that moment was more drama.

"Are you treating Caitlin?"

"No, I'm her wife."

"See, one of us got married," Stevie said.

"Stevie." Jamie gave her head a little shake. "Maria, please have a seat. Val, if anyone causes a ruckus, shoot them."

"Okay," Val readily agreed.

Jamie sat there slumped down, feeling defeated. She was uncomfortable sitting next to the woman who, for lack of a better term, was her mother in-law.

"Jamie?" Maria timidly said.

"Yes?"

"Would you mind if I prayed?"

"Not at all. A little prayer right now would be more than welcome." Jamie was taken aback by the question. She was thankful when Maria pulled out a string of rosary beads and silently prayed.

There was an eerie feeling in the air as more and more people crowded the small waiting area with no one speaking above a whisper. Jamie flashed back to waiting by her mother's bedside. The hardest part for her was the knowledge that there was nothing she could do. Silently she joined Maria in prayer.

"Emma." Jamie cleared her throat when Ricky and Emma returned. Normally, after a hearty cup of hot chocolate, Emma would be skipping. Emma's somber shuffle spoke volumes. She climbed onto her mother's lap and hugged Stevie tightly. She crawled off of her mother's lap, apparently not caring who she was stepping on, and made her way into Jamie's arms.

Stevie sat there bouncing her knee. For almost twenty years, she lived in fear of reliving the worst moment in her life. Now it happened again, and this time things were far worse. She felt a need to comfort Jamie, all the while she needed someone to comfort her. Someone to remind her that Caitlin was a fighter. Having her mother sitting beside her only made her more anxious. Her body relaxed slightly, when Val sat down beside her.

"Stevie..." her mother cautiously began to say.

"Don't."

"I was just going to say that your daughter is beautiful."

"Thank you." Stevie was still unable to look at her mother.

"No husband?" Maria sounded mystified.

"Oh for the love of—" Val's hand caressed her thigh and

effectively cut off the harsh comment that was forthcoming.

Stevie glared at her mother, who wisely chose to look down at her rosary beads. Every time a door opened or someone new appeared, Stevie jumped, anxious to hear something. She knew it could be hours before they knew anything. Jamie cast a weary look at her, and Stevie tried to smile in an effort to comfort her worried sister in-law.

Time clicked by slowly. Emma went from comforting to whiny. Hours had passed since CC had been wheeled into surgery. Jamie yearned to go up to the theatre and watch. Rudy had made it clear that his team would feel uneasy with her observing. All she could do was sit and wait.

Finally the doors swooshed open and Rudy emerged, covered with blood and looking as if he had aged ten years. Jamie bolted out of the hard plastic chair before he was noticed by the others.

"She's going to be okay, Jamie."

Jamie wanted to thank him. Instead, she burst into tears, not caring who was watching as she hugged him.

"Jameson, people will talk," he teased, hugging her tighter. "Take a few moments and catch your breath, and I'll take you down to recovery."

"No complications?"

"None. It was pretty routine. I'll go over the grisly details later."

"Thank you," she whispered. When she turned, Stevie, Leigh, and a half-dozen other people were hovering around her. "She's fine. I'm going down to recovery. It will be a few more hours before they settle her into a room and she's ready for visitors. Good God, Max. Put a robe on."

"Do you know how hard it was for me to break out of that penthouse you locked me up in? So excuse my attire."

"It isn't your attire that disturbs me," Jamie choked out, shielding her eyes. "It's your flag flapping in the wind."

"Sorry." He blushed and tugged his hospital gown tighter around his rotund body. Ricky took pity on him and found him a blanket to wrap around his waist. "Thanks. How's the kid?"

"She's going to be fine. I'm on my way to see her. Stevie, she should be zonked out for a while. Why don't you take Emma home and get some rest? I'll call you when Caitlin is settled into a room." Stevie blew out a heavy sigh. She thanked Jamie, gave her a quick kiss, and gathered up Emma and Ricky. Jamie endured everyone wishing her well before they left her with only Max, Maria, and Val. Jamie sensed that neither Maria nor Val had anywhere else to go.

"I'll go in first when she's responsive. You'll have to go in one at a time."

"I appreciate that, James," Max said. "I don't want to cut in on your time with her. I just want to see her to make sure she really is okay."

"No worries, Max."

* * *

CC was running. Distorted clowns were chasing her through a misty maze. Someone was singing *Ring around the Rosy.* The song eerily echoed from loud speakers. She had to get back and find her way home. Jamie needed her. She screamed Jamie's name over and over again. Her screams were drowned out by a maniacal cackle and sadistic nursery rhymes. The mist swirled around her and made her legs feel heavy. Unseen hands clawed at her ankles. She fought to keep moving to find Jamie.

"Caitlin, I'm right here."

"Where? Where?" Her search turned desperate as fun house mirrors appeared in the mist. The mirrors faded, and the mist turned to a calming fog. The sun came out. Somewhere in the distance she could hear the Beatles singing *Long and Winding Road*.

"Shall we skip the light fantastic?"

CC was more than a little surprised to see Helen Mirren standing before her in a simple, black, ball gown with the mist growing heavier.

"Okay." She stepped into Helen's open arms.

"I'm right here," Helen promised as they danced around the low-lying fog. "Caitlin? Caitlin?" she repeated, her voice not sounding the same. It sounded husky, a hint of a southern accent. It sounded the way Jamie sounded when she was tired or stressed.

"Where's Jamie?"

"Right here, baby."

CC struggled to open her eyes. When they finally gave way, a misty-eyed Jamie was staring back at her. "Jamie?"

"I'm right here. I won't leave you." Jamie placed a gentle kiss on her cheek. "How are you feeling?"

"I'm fine. I can skip the light fantastic if the clowns don't get me."

"Okay, you're stoned."

"Thirsty."

"Here." Jamie fed her some ice chips. "The surgery went well."

"Surgery?" CC still felt adrift. "The crazy lawyer shot me."

"Yes." Jamie sighed, sounding relieved.

"Where am I?" CC fought not to go back to sleep.

"Hospital."

"I feel like Monday morning in hell," she choked out. Her throat felt raw.

"Do you remember?"

"Yeah, kind of. Cock..."

"Excuse me?" Jamie squealed with a wide-eyed expression.

"Eunice Cockburn." CC struggled to speak. She fidgeted a bit and realized her left arm was restrained. "She..."

"Simon's lawyer."

"Did they..." CC felt lost. "They got her, right?"

"It worries me that was a question. Yes, they got her."

"Brown, right?"

"Yes." Jamie smiled briefly, and tears filled her eyes. "Don't ever do this to me again."

"I'll try not to. Why can't I move my arm?"

"It is in a sling. Hopefully, that will keep you from ripping your stitches out."

"I love you, James."

"I love you, Caitlin."

"Have you slept? How long have I been out of it?" Panic suddenly seized CC. The last time something like this happened, she was in a coma for weeks. The thought of losing that much time and having her loved ones suffer through it terrified her.

"It happened last night." Jamie's voice was soft and reassuring. Her hand caressing CC's thigh put the normally stoic policewoman at ease. "I have never been so frightened in my life."

"Sorry, baby. It wasn't planned."

"I hope not."

"She got me from behind."

"I know. Caitlin, I don't want to hear the gory details. I just want to look into your baby blues."

"Hey, can I come in? They're trying to drag me back up to the penthouse." Max barged in, completely disrupting the moment.

"Why are you wearing a toga? He is, isn't he?" CC wasn't certain that the drugs weren't still messing with her mind.

"It's a blanket," Max grumbled. "Apparently your wife isn't fond of seeing my stunning masculine form."

"Uh-huh."

"He came down to the waiting area in one of those skimpy johnnies."

"Eww. My wife doesn't need to be seeing that."

"How are you?" Max's jovial tone dropped. "You gonna be okay, kid?"

"So they tell me. Right, honey?"

"She's going to be just fine after some time off."

"What?" CC tried to sit up in order to protest, only to have her movements halted by Jamie's gentle touch.

"Oh, did I forget to tell you that you, my lovely wife, are grounded?"

CC gaped at her, fully ready to protest, until Jamie held up her hand. CC understood by the cold gleam in Jamie's eyes that she needed to tread carefully.

"Need I remind you," Jamie said before CC had the chance to voice her objections, "that you were shot by a crazed lunatic?"

"Which means I have work to do," CC said.

"It means you are going to rest and relax until I say otherwise."

Max laughed. "I can see that things are back to normal. I'll just give you some peace and quiet."

"Don't go yet." There was something CC needed to know. "Is our ever-friendly deputy wandering around?"

"I'll get her," Max left the room.

"You can thank her later," Jamie said.

"I'm not going to thank her," CC wearily explained. "I need to ask her some questions."

"Did you miss the part where I said you are grounded?"

"James?"

"No arguments. Two seconds ago, you were afraid that the clowns were going to get you. All I'm asking is that you put your feet up for a couple of days or weeks."

"Weeks?"

"Caitlin, I'm not going to waste my breath arguing with you. The department isn't going to clear you for active duty. Just suck it up and learn how to relax."

"How about some coffee?"

"Good heavens, woman, you just got out of surgery."

* * *

Val paced nervously. She had to get out of this town. Nothing about Boston made any sense to her. The roads, the plethora of Dunkin Donuts stores, and the women. She was convinced there was something hinky in the water. Nothing short of germ warfare could explain the drivers in this city or the way they move the letter *R* around willy-nilly. Standing there listening to Maria ramble on and on about nothing was the icing on the cake. The crazy old bat couldn't decide if she should love her children unconditionally or pray for their salvation.

Val was ready to bolt, fully prepared to leave Maria on her own to face the uncertainty of public transportation. Her heart skipped a beat when she turned and faced the real reason she wanted to get out of Boston. Emma skipped merrily down the hallway while holding her mother's hand. The shy smile Stevie offered melted her heart. *This is ridiculous. I should be out hunting down some scumbag who thinks eighteen months behind bars is an inconvenience*, her mind shouted in an effort to drown out the rapid beating of her heart.

"Stevie?" Maria sniffed.

"Great." Stevie rolled her dark brown eyes and offered Val a wistful smile. "Val, can I talk to you for a moment?"

Val just nodded her head, fearful her voice would betray her. Reluctantly, Stevie instructed Emma to sit with Maria.

"Good Lord, I hope she doesn't try to brainwash her," Stevie said once they had made their way around the corner. "I just wanted to thank you. From what I've heard, you saved my sister's life."

"Just doing my job."

"Thank you for doing it extremely well. I also wanted to say that I'm sorry. I wish things could be different."

"They could."

"Val," Stevie said quickly. "I get it. I truly do get it. I just can't handle knowing that the chances of sitting outside an operating room again are high. Every morning, I get up thankful that I didn't get a call in the middle of the night. My biggest fear is that someday I'll have to sit my daughter down and tell her that Auntie Caitlin isn't ever coming home because she died a hero."

"You don't think that she is?"

"Val, when you and your team bust down some door, not knowing what dangers are on the other side, are you the first one through the door?"

"Usually." Val frowned, completely mystified by the turn in the conversation.

"Just like my big sister. You lead the way because it's the right thing to do. You will do anything to protect the people behind you. And you'll do anything to protect the world from the evil waiting on the other side of that door. Caitlin is the same way. Both of you seem to have a blind spot. You forget that the people who love you are sitting up, pacing the floor, terrified that they will never see you again. I would never ask my sister, or any woman, to change who they are. Especially when who they are is a remarkable person who has the strength to put others' lives ahead of their own. Yes, I think my sister is a hero. As proud as I am of her, I do not want that to be her epitaph."

"I get it." Val accepted Stevie's words despite feeling her heart was being ripped out of her chest.

"You hate me?"

"Never. Come on. You should get back before your mother corrupts your daughter."

"Deputy?" she heard Max Sampson call out to her. "Calloway wants to talk to you."

* * *

CC knew that Jamie was beyond angry when Max and Val entered the room. She wished she could just heed her wife's advice, but there was something bothering her that went beyond dancing with a movie star and psycho clowns chasing her.

"How are you holding up?" Val asked.

"I've been better. I have to make this quick before my wife strangles me. First, thanks for saving my life."

"Just doing my job."

"I know." CC respected Val's humility. "Look, there's something bugging me. Maybe it's nothing more than the drugs screwing with me, but there's something I need to ask you and I need to do it with Max here."

"Because you trust him." Val scowled.

"CC?" Jamie gasped. "The woman saved your life."

"She's just doing her job," Val said. "What do you want to know?"

"How?" CC managed to utter, still struggling with her voice.

"How, what?" Val asked.

"How did she know where to find me?"

Based on the stunned look on everyone's face, CC could only guess that she had asked the right question. "I'm still fuzzy on the details and can't quite remember who I told I was coming here."

"Okay, that's enough." Jamie ushered the others out of the room. "I said no work." Her voice trembled as she spoke.

"James," CC said wearily. "Okay, fine. I'll behave. It's not like I can focus."

"Good. You just get comfortable. One more thing..." Jamie hesitated. "Your mother's waiting to see you."

"What?" CC wailed, setting off the monitors she was hooked up to.

* * *

"I need to talk to her," Val said while Max blocked her way. "I have to know who she talked to."

"You heard her. She's still a little out of it.

CHECKMATE

"But still clear enough to know someone sandbagged her," Val said tersely. "Sampson, with everything going on, her schedule is erratic to say the least. I want to know who was following her."

"So do I. Come up to my penthouse and we'll talk."

Chapter 44

"Are you satisfied?" Max smirked, much to Val's annoyance.

"You were right, she's not clearheaded," she said. "She was talking about clowns chasing her." Despite Max's objections, Val had gone back into Calloway's room and the glassy-eyed look she received had been a deterrent.

"Nice digs," she added after she glanced at the swanky hospital room Max had been staying in. Ricky looked up from the sofa and nodded.

"This had better be good." Ricky tried to stifle a yawn while he dug out his tablet. "I keep trying to leave, and you keep dragging me back. I do have a life you know."

"You didn't, up until you met the dancing queen," Val said before she could stop herself. "Look, I'm sorry to interrupt your fun, but Calloway asked Sampson and me a very important question."

"You just said she's hopped up on drugs from her surgery."

"True, but she still brought up a very important point," Max said. "It's a question I would like an answer to, also. How did the bitch that shot my partner find her? On a normal day, CC isn't the easiest person to track down. Yesterday, with all hell breaking loose, she would have been all over the place. Why don't we start with the basics. How did you find her?"

"She's a techno idiot." Val sounded defeated as she paced around the room. "She accidentally sent almost everyone she knew a videotape of her abduction."

"That sounds like my partner."

"So far, the bureau is sorting through Cockburn's office and home. The lady was very detail oriented. But they haven't dug up anything that would explain how she knew where Calloway was." Ricky was studying the screen of his tablet. "Once the judge signed the warrant, we stormed the place. She was very resourceful and had a long list of clients with mob connections. On an interesting note, the male alias she was using was her kid. She had him when she was a teenager. She claimed the father was Austin Dover, the son of a Canadian diplomat. "

"What happened to the kid?" Max asked.

"Crib death, I hope," Ricky answered. "Just wish they found out how she was tracking Calloway."

Max gave a snarl. "This sucks. All I know is, last night Calloway dropped by to see me and ran out claiming that I solved the case. Next thing I know, my boss showed up and told me that CC had been shot."

"Right before she gave you credit for solving the case, what exactly did you tell her?" Val asked.

"That the scumbag that popped me was humming *Humpty Dumpty*."

"On the tape, Cockburn was humming nursery rhymes," Val muttered. "Maybe that's what led her to figure it out. It still doesn't answer the million dollar question of how Cockburn knew to be waiting in the parking garage armed and ready."

"And without a car," Ricky said.

"Excuse me?" Max was clearly stunned.

"She jacked Calloway in her own car."

"Her car?" Max bellowed, his face ashen. "So she was

waiting with everything she needed in the parking garage? We need to find the son of a bitch who tipped her off. How in the hell are we going to do that? You only found her because of the video."

"Yes and no," Val said. "The video alerted us to the situation, but since it was dark out, we didn't have a clue as to exactly where she was. We used the GPS on her phone."

"I'll have to thank the judge who expedited that," Max said and clenched his jaw.

"We didn't have time for that." Val scoffed at the notion. "Fortunately we already had—"

"What?" Max demanded, his nerves clearly frayed.

"We had permission from Calloway." Val's voice drifted off as things suddenly made sense. "Damn, now I know how Calloway clears her cases. You just say shit, and she figures it out."

"So what brilliant thing did I say this time?"

"The federal government had permission to track information on your partner's phone. It helped us save her, but it also—"

"Put her in danger," Max said. "Anyone in your office could have tracked her, anytime they wanted to."

* * *

Val strode towards Ledger's office with a queasy feeling gnawing at her. She hated what she was about to do. His assistant smiled as she escorted Val inside. Ledger looked completely at ease; a freshly brewed cup of coffee sat on his desk.

"My reports." She handed him one of two files she held.

"I can't thank you enough for everything you've done,

Deputy. Despite your misgivings regarding our city, I do admire your dedication."

"I'm pleased to hear that," she said with a slight hesitation. "It will make what I'm about to show you easier." She handed him the second folder. "When I entered Annapolis, it filled me with a sense of honor. I felt the same when I joined the Marshal Service. What I learned today makes me sick."

Ledger's face turned ashen as he read the file. "Oh, my God." His hands trembled as he turned each page. "I'll take care of the bench warrant. Would you like to be present when we do the interview?"

"If I can. I need to be on a plane to the West Coast tonight. The FBI raided Cockburn's office, and the home office. They would like me to be there when they lower the hammer on Fisher. Cockburn kept meticulous records. Her phone logs confirm what you've just read."

Three hours later, the clock was ticking and Val needed to get to the airport. If not for the burning desire to know why, she would have already departed. Ledger looked miserable as they waited. He grumbled when Finn made his entrance.

"Hey, boss." Finn's smile faded when he spied Val. "You're still here. I thought you'd be gone by now."

"So did I."

"Have a seat," Ledger said, his face grim. "I need to inform you that if you desire legal representation that is your right."

"W-wait," Finn stammered, clearly stunned. "What the hell is going on? Are you explaining the Miranda to me?"

"Yes," Ledger said angrily. "Deputy, you have some explaining to do."

"For what?" Finn glared at Val, who just returned his anger with a cool look of indifference. "I don't know what this bitch is up to."

"That's Deputy Bitch to you," Val said calmly. "Deputy, can you explain why you accessed Detective Calloway's GPS coordinates not once, not twice, but seventeen times? The last time was the night she was shot. How do you explain tapping into her phone? Before you answer, remember you have the right to a lawyer and to remain silent."

"Calloway got me thrown off the Beaumont case," he said, looking flummoxed by the questions. "I know she did it, because she was clearly involved. I was following a lead."

"What lead?" Ledger demanded. "And why after the case was over? Beaumont was already dead the first time you accessed her Intel. Oh, and for the record, Calloway had nothing to do with you being bounced off the case. I did that because you weren't doing your job."

"I would have been doing my job if someone wasn't stirring things up." He jerked his thumb at Val.

"Still doesn't answer the question as to why you were tracking Calloway after the case was over." Val kept her composure. "Or why you were chatting with Eunice Cockburn. The FBI found your cell number listed in the logs of one of her burner phones. No call lasted less than twelve minutes. I don't get you. I'm proud to wear my silver star, and you use it to settle a personal vendetta. First you were lazy, sloppy, and generally didn't give a crap about finding a child molester, all because your ex-wife went on a date with the guy's stepdaughter. Then you stalk her and almost get her killed. Why?"

CHECKMATE

"Calloway was connected to Beaumont," Finn desperately tried to explain. "I was convinced she had something to do with his murder. She ruined my marriage. I wasn't about to let her ruin my career. Cockburn called and told me she was a PI working for a guy whose wife Calloway was screwing with."

"Okay, that's it." Val threw up her hands with disgust. "I got the answer I stuck around for. You know, Finn, let's be honest here about a few things, like in this little city of yours there are no secrets. Since I got here, everyone seems to think there's a big secret, and just so you know, everyone knows about your wife leaving you and the scuffle you had when you caught her with Calloway. You know what else everyone in this city knows? CC Calloway is a happily married woman. No way you thought she was stepping out with another woman. You did this because you're a sniveling, pathetic loser."

"I'm inclined to agree," Ledger said. "The state police are outside my office. They'll finish reading you your rights and informing you of the charges you're facing, which include attempted murder. All I want from you is your badge and your gun. Now."

Val braced herself, ready in case Finn decided to resist his situation. Thankfully, he truly was the pathetic man she assessed him to be and he surrendered.

* * *

It took several phone calls and two planes to get Val and Ricky to where they needed to be. When they arrived, Dr. Richards was waiting for them sporting a mischievous smirk.

"I think you're going to enjoy this just a little too much."

"Is that your professional opinion, Doc?"

Dr. Richards simply shook her head and checked her watch.

"Like you aren't going to enjoy wiping that smug look off his face," Val said. "Where the hell is this guy?"

"Lawyers." Dr. Richards scowled.

"I heard that," a gravelly voice boomed. "You must be Deputy Brown and Agent Samaria. I'm Daniel Ross with the attorney general's office. This is quite a load of crap you dumped on my desk."

"Happy to be of service," Val couldn't refrain from saying. "I don't know what you're worried about. This should be a slam dunk."

"Hah! Right! With attorney-client privilege and the prickly matter of legal insanity, yeah this should be a walk in the park. It might help our cause if you hadn't shot the accomplice."

"Yeah, you're right. I should have stood there and let her kill a cop."

"Give it a rest, Dan," Dr. Richards said. "This is a career maker, and you know it. If you can get this yo-yo strapped to a gurney, you'll be a God in the legal cesspool. That, and you get to publicly trash a defense attorney. The press is going to love you."

Dan grimaced. "You are such a suck-up. Okay, just so we're clear, today is about relaying legal information."

"And anything that might shake this cuckoo bird's tree is just a bonus. Make sure the tape is running," Val said to the cocky lawyer.

"I'll be watching with video running."

Val steadied herself. A small part of her wished she had her sidearm. Shooting the snotty like puke would please her immensely.

The three of them entered the sterile room. Val growled under her breath when she saw Fisher sitting there looking as confident as ever. Ricky and the shrink sat down in the uncomfortable plastic chairs lined up in front of the Formica table Fisher was comfortably resting his elbows on. Val opted to linger in the far corner of the room. Her arms were folded tightly against her chest. Her posture seemed to amuse Fisher.

"No coffee this time?" Simon confidently beamed.

"No," Val said dryly.

"Oh, I see. No more good cop, bad cop, but you did bring Dr. Richards. This must be a very auspicious occasion."

"Simon," Dr. Richards said slowly. Val couldn't help noticing the way the psychiatrist stared him down. "We are here to inform you…"

Simon eagerly leaned forward, apparently in expectation of good news. Val maintained her stoic appearance. She didn't want to spoil the moment.

"Simon," Richards repeated, somehow managing to keep her tone on an even keel. "I have to inform you that you need to find a new lawyer. I suggest that you do this as quickly as possible. There have been some issues raised over the past few weeks that will require legal counsel. Due to the urgency of some of these matters, someone from Legal Aid is on their way."

"What?" Simon rattled the chains clamped to his wrists. "I have a very competent attorney." He obviously struggled to keep his cool facade in place. The beads of sweat suddenly forming on his brow gave him away.

"She's dead," Val said coldly.

"Excuse me?"

Val wanted to savor the moment for as long as possible. Fisher was slightly jangled, yet he seemed to be holding it together.

"That is sad news. How did it happen?" His calm demeanor irked Val.

"I shot her."

"Why would you do that?"

"You know why," Ricky said. "It didn't take much to figure out what you were up to."

"What is it you think you know?"

"She confessed to everything," Val told him.

"So you shot her? A bit extreme if you ask me. Not that it matters. She was my lawyer, which puts me in the clear."

Val's jaw clenched as she fought the urge to slam his head into the table.

"Unless she was complicit in your crimes."

"Well, I'm not an expert, Agent Samaria, but it sounds like Ms. Cockburn might have been unstable. What do you think, Dr. Richards?"

Before Dr. Richards could formulate an answer, a haggard little man burst into the room and demanded that everyone stop talking. Based on his pale complexion and cheap suit, Val deduced he was from Legal Aid.

"Mister..." He hesitated while he fumbled with a stack of folders. "Fisher. Mr. Fisher, I recommend that you stop talking."

"It's Dr. Fisher, and who the hell are you?"

CHECKMATE

"I'm Andrew McFarlane, your new attorney."

"You?"

"Yes, I think that this interview is over."

"You?" Simon looked the disheveled man up and down.

"Yes." McFarlane seemed surprised by Fisher's reaction. "I've been appointed by the court. It seems that your attorney of record is unavailable." He flipped through his files.

"That's because I shot her," Val said.

"Huh?"

"She shot her," Simon explained. "Do you know anything about my case?"

"Not yet. I'm just getting up to speed. As I said, this interview is over. My client and I need a chance to confer."

"Good luck, Doc." Val couldn't refrain from taunting Fisher before she and the others made their departure. She was filled with a sense of relief. Her work was done, and she could finally put the entire experience behind her after she did one last thing.

Epilogue

CC's time in the hospital was slow torture, and coming home proved equally torturous. Being told to sit around and do nothing while Fisher may or may not be preparing his next surprise drove her crazy. Once she felt certain that her family was finally safe and Jamie returned to work, she found herself lost in endless hours of boredom. The tedium was only broken by Emma's antics, Stevie's moping, and her mother's renewed interest in her life. Maria seemed determined to make up for lost time. If not for her revisionist history of CC and Stevie's childhood, the reunion might have been bearable.

At her wit's end, CC sheepishly looked around to assure herself that she was alone. She had no intention of getting busted not only for climbing up the ladder to change a lightbulb but also for using bad language. After weeks of being held captive due to her injury, she had dropped a week's pay in the cuss jar.

She tried to hurry and finish before Jamie returned. Her loving wife made it clear every day what CC was, and was not, allowed to do while she was out. Balancing on a ladder while trying to change a lightbulb with one hand was not the snap CC had thought it would be. Her heart lurched when the front door slammed and alerted her that she was busted.

"My God, what are you doing, you idiot?" Jamie scolded her.

"I'm changing the lightbulb," she said innocently.

"Get down before you hurt yourself," Jamie said with a growl.

CC didn't hesitate. She scurried down the ladder as quickly as possible. The horrified look Jamie sported led her to choose her next words carefully.

"Look, James. I know what you're going to say, but I was careful. I wrapped my arm so I wouldn't move it and hurt my shoulder."

"What did you use?" Much to CC's disappointment, Jamie seemed annoyed instead of being impressed by her ingenuity.

"Duct tape."

"Let me get my scissors."

"James," CC called after her, "the bulb was out, you were at work, Stevie's out, and Emma's at school. There's only so much television one woman can watch," she explained while Jamie jerked her bag open and extracted her scissors.

"I don't know what I'm going to do with you."

"I have a few suggestions," CC said eagerly. The smile she brandished disappeared when Jamie ripped the duct tape from her body. "Ouch! That was not on the list. Seriously, after I dug myself out of the hole Emma trapped me in with the chess game, I didn't know what to do with myself."

"She trapped you?"

"I know," CC said reluctantly. "I can't believe a seven-year-old has me chasing my tail. At least she still thinks thunderstorms happen when the angels go bowling. And she still believes in Santa Claus."

"So do you. I just started back at work and this is what you get yourself into." Jamie wagged her finger while she scolded her.

"Normally, I like it when you get bossy. Speaking of bosses, how is your new boss working out?"

"Stella was always the boss. The difference now is she's getting paid for it." Jamie smiled. "Some of the doctors aren't thrilled with her promotion."

"I don't get it," CC said. "Given all of her qualifications, why hadn't anyone considered her until you suggested it to Bradford?"

"Because she's a nurse, and most doctors still won't admit how much we rely on the talent of our nursing staff."

A knock on the door cut off CC's next comment. "I wonder who that can be."

"It's getting close to dinner. My guess would be your mother," Jamie said. "It's amazing how she gets herself invited to dinner at least three nights a week."

"She's trying. I just wish she'd stop by less or refrain from trying to teach Emma her revisionist version of our family history."

"Not your mother," Jamie said as she checked the monitor. "It's Val."

"Val?"

"Sit. I'll get it."

"Deputy Brown, what brings you by?" CC asked the weary looking woman while she struggled with the remaining duct tape.

"Just wrapping things up." Val shook her head and looked slightly amused. "What the hell did you do?"

"She was trying to be helpful," Jamie said. "Coffee?"

"No, thank you. I just stopped by to let you know what's been happening while you were tied up," Val said and snickered. "That was too easy. Nice shirt. Isn't it a sacrilege for you to be wearing a Ravens jersey?

CHECKMATE

"It belongs to Jamie." CC tugged on the Michael Oher jersey "I hope you dropped by to do more than give me crap."

"I found the leak. It was Finn."

"Seriously? I knew the guy hated me, but setting me up with that whack job was over the top."

"He tracked you by the GPS on your phone. Max will fill you in on the details." Val sounded frustrated. "I hate it when it's one of our own."

"I hear you," CC said while Jamie began to snip at the tape. "I appreciate everything you've done and put up with. Not my idea of a vacation, but I'm glad you don't know how to relax."

"Maybe next time I'll just go to Vegas and get loaded," Val tried to joke. "There's more. I wanted you to hear this from me,"

Val slowly began to say. "Sometime, depending on how quickly or slowly the wheels of justice spin, Simon Fisher will be released."

"What?" Jamie screeched.

"And will there be a Texas Ranger waiting for him?" CC asked before Jamie went ballistic.

"And a Florida State Trooper, along with Ricky, who is eager to get his hands on him. Between the two old cases and the federal case, I predict that Fisher will spend the rest of his miserable life sitting in a jail cell while he's on trial or waiting for his appeals to be heard. In the end, someone will put a needle in the little bastard's arm. Until then, his idealistic public defender is going to be very busy."

"Idealistic or ambitious?" CC winced as Jamie tore off the last of the tape. "I heard he fancies himself as the next F. Lee Bailey."

"He does, sorry bastard," Val answered, thoroughly amused. "Seriously, why were you wrapped up?"

"I needed to change a lightbulb," CC said innocently as Emma darted in.

"Hey, Deputy Val!" Emma let out a squeal. CC didn't miss the way Val's posture tightened before she squeaked out a polite greeting.

"Emma, take off your snow boots," CC calmly told the little imp. "Auntie Jamie has some cookies on the counter and the chessboard is waiting for you."

"W-well," Val stammered. "I guess that's my cue."

"Right. Heaven forbid you stick around and say hello to my sister."

"Calloway, with all the holiday shoppers out there, the traffic up here is worse than usual. I'll keep you updated. Happy holidays."

In a blink of an eye, Val was gone.

"No chocolate chip?" Emma asked.

"Aunty Jamie ate all the chocolate chip. What? You did," CC answered the nasty glare she received from her wife. "Emma, take your time with the chess game."

"I already made my move."

"Oh?"

"Checkmate," Emma said as CC sauntered over to the chessboard and reluctantly placed her queen down.

CHECKMATE

"Can we bake more chocolate chip cookies?"

"Yeah." CC couldn't help but smile. "It's official. Life is back to normal."

"When have our lives ever been normal?" Jamie asked with a wry grin.

"Never." CC offered a shy smile. "This is as close as we get. At least we know where the bad guys are, for now."

ABOUT THE AUTHOR

Boston native Mavis Applewater started writing at the request of a very wise woman; she claims that is why she married her. She is the author of four full length novels, *The Brass Ring, My Sisters Keeper, Tempus Fugit* and Goldie Winner *Whispering Pines.* She has also penned four collections of shorts stories including Goldie Finalist for best Erotica. She is looking forward to the release of two more romances, *Finding My Way* and *Remember When* and the first *Harper Winston* thriller.

Made in the USA
Charleston, SC
03 January 2015